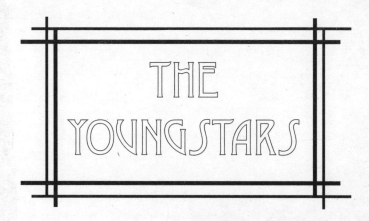

THE
YOUNGSTARS

For Puck

Published in Great Britain by
Inside Pocket Publishing Limited

First published in Great Britain 2012
Text copyright © Ursula Jones 2011

The right of Ursula Jones to be identified as
the author of this work has been asserted
by her in accordance with the
Copyright, Designs and Patents Act 1988

A CIP catalogue record for this book is available from
the British Library

ISBN 978 0956 7122 9 5

Inside Pocket Publishing Limited Reg. No. 06580097

Printed and bound in Great Britain by
CPI Group (UK) Ltd, Croydon, CR0 4YY

www.insidepocket.co.uk

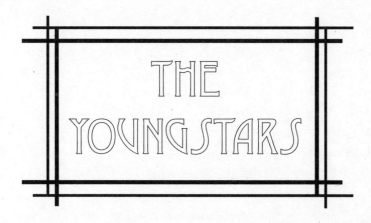

THE YOUNGSTARS

Ursula Jones

PROLOGUE

THE WHEEL OF DEATH

Frankfurt, Germany 1928

They were going away on a big ship tomorrow. That's why he had woken up – to see if it was tomorrow yet; but it wasn't. He was still lying under her coat on the cushions in the bright room where she'd put him to bed. His mother must still be at work then, and it must still be the night before they sailed away.

Usually when he woke up it was the next day and he'd find himself where she called 'at home'; but now it was night and exciting, and he lay and wondered what a big ship was. Ships sailed the sea, she'd said. What was the sea like? He would go and ask.

He got up and stood on tiptoe to reach the doorknob. He could just turn it. He knew he shouldn't, but he opened the door. He'd been told never, never to go out of the bright room alone, but he did and he walked down the corridor. He could hear happy music. He shouldn't, he knew, but he climbed up the iron steps towards the sound. The steps were big and tall. His feet caught in his nightshirt so he went up on all fours.

It was dark at the top. There were some people standing around looking at a twinkling, very light place ahead of them. A big voice said, 'Das Todesrad! Ladies and Gentlemen, The Wheel Of Death.' He looked through the people's legs at the light place.

A lady was tied to a huge wheel that was spinning round and she was going round with it. A drum was banging loud and fast. The man was throwing knives at the lady and they didn't hit her, even though she was going round so fast. The knives stuck into the wheel as it spun and each time a knife stuck there was a clashing noise. The knives stuck in close to her, all around her – zoink, zoink, zoink – and the drums banged.

And someone screamed; and then more people that he couldn't see screamed too, and he could hear chairs falling over and lots more screaming. And there was red, like long red ribbons flying out of the wheel: red stuff, but wet. Someone ran to the wheel and stopped it spinning, and the lady on the wheel was hanging with a knife stuck in her and red stuff coming out.

The lady looked up slowly and said his name. And then he screamed. He screamed for her and he ran to her and held on to her and screamed. Someone said, 'Es ist ihr Kind.' Many people were running to her now, and someone in the crowd said, 'Poor kid! He's only three.'

They laid the wheel flat and tried to untie her. Someone else said to get him away and they tugged his nightshirt, but he wouldn't let go of her because it was her, it was her, it was her.

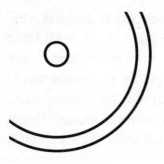

CHAPTER ONE

SECRET

The Grand Theatre, Bolton, England 1936

Schlerrk! The seat of Grinling's trousers split open with a noise like a whiplash. All six Youngstars were on stage performing their Pie Shop sketch: dancing and tumbling and slinging custard pies at each other.

The audience gasped. But before they could make up their minds that they really were looking at a bare bottom, Ollie, the youngest of the Youngstars, clapped a custard pie on it. The pie hit the mark with a squelch and Grinling sat down quickly in a big basket of fake pastries. And there he had to stay while the rest of the Youngstars finished the sketch with Ollie doing the work of two, filling in for him.

They were trying not to laugh at what had happened, or 'corpse', as it's called, though Ollie could never find out why; and they were praying that their manager was not out front, watching the act. Mr Pigott would not see the funny side.

Make the smallest mistake on stage, and Mr Pigott would shout, 'We're in Show Business, my Babies, and don't you forget it.' He would thrust his face, which was the colour of a wedge of cheese, close to theirs and say quietly, 'I manage a professional juvenile troupe, not a mob of one-legged hoofers. This is Variety and I don't mean the Heinz fifty-seven kind. You are Variety artists, you are...' Then he'd shout, very loudly, 'What are you?'

'The Youngstars,' they would mutter in response. That was how Mr Pigott billed them in the theatre programme: THE YOUNGSTARS – a troupe of stars in a star troupe! He never printed their names. 'What's it to the audience what you're called?' he'd say. 'It's what you do that matters.'

So there they were, six nameless stars. As well as Grinling, who was the comic, and Ollie, who was as solemn as Grinling was not, there was Jessie, the troupe's lead dancer. Jessie had just turned fifteen. She danced like a dream and talked like a mill girl. She talked sense too. For the most part, what Jessie said, the rest of the Youngstars fell in with.

Next in age was Heather, the lanky one. She was all skinny arms and legs, always at the back of the line-up, and so double-jointed she could have packed herself up in her own suitcase.

9

Then came Silver, who was fair and pretty – pretty enough to knock the breath out of you. At thirteen she was a talented singer and dancer and was definitely going places.

Finally, there was John. A few months younger than Silver, he was dark, tall and slim. John was born to dance. Everyone agreed that.

They also agreed that Mr Pigott did not like things to go wrong in front of the public; and anything Mr Pigott didn't like, you didn't do – unless you'd lost your mind. So, as the Youngstars aimed their pies and held down the laughter that was rising up inside them like gas in a lemonade bottle, they were also praying. They were praying that Mr Pigott was in his usual place early on a Saturday evening: the pub. And no one was praying harder than Ollie.

There wasn't a sign of their manager backstage after the act was over. Grinling disappeared into the boys' dressing room, clutching the seat of his pants, and Jessie went into the girls' room to clean up before the next show in an hour's time. The other four stood outside in the corridor laughing about the trousers.

'I heard a bang,' said Heather, 'and I thought Cripes! We must be off form. The audience is shooting at us.' The Youngstars rocked with laughter. They were smothered in the mixture of talc and Fuller's Earth that they used for flour in the Pie Shop sketch. As they laughed, it fell out of their chef's costumes in circles round their feet on the concrete floor. The cleaners wouldn't thank them!

They knew they'd been lucky. Bare bums on stage were forbidden. Indecency it was called. The police got involved. They'd got away with it this time, thanks to Ollie and his custard pie, but they'd had a scare and it made them laugh even more.

'But I saw it happen.' John's handsome face was screwed up like a squeezed sponge. 'Course I laughed and course I got a custard pie right in the tonsils.' This time the laughter was sympathetic.

It was one of Ollie's jobs before the show to prepare the custard for the pies. He spent ages beating together grated shaving soap and glycerine, turning the handle of a little egg whisk until his arm ached and he was satisfied that the wobbly froth was thick enough. Get a mixture like that in your mouth and you could blow bubbles for a week.

'They'll be saying I've got rabies,' John complained.

They only stopped laughing when Miss Bellamy, their matron, came out of the boys' dressing room. She was slowly shaking her frizzy, greying head over Grinling's ripped trousers. Miss Bellamy did everything for the Youngstars but, whatever it was, she did it slowly; even head shaking.

'They'll need...' she said, but her sentence died. When it came to speaking, Miss Bellamy went from Slow to Dead Slow as if she feared conversational rocks or sandbanks ahead.

'Mending.' Heather kindly inserted the missing word for her. But Miss Bellamy shook her head. That wasn't what she meant.

Silver had a guess. 'Stitching, then?' She took off her chef's hat and tossed her beautiful fair hair loose.

'Patching!' Miss Bellamy flung herself on the word like a drowning sailor on a lifebelt.

Ollie felt a stab of anxiety. It would take Miss Bellamy until curtain-up to patch those trousers. Who would go to the chippy instead of her for the take-away suppers they always ate before the last show on Saturday nights?

Not me, not me, please not me, he wished silently.

Ollie had a secret rendezvous to keep in a few minutes' time. The very thought of it made his heart thump like a steam-hammer with excitement. Fetching those six suppers could stop it happening at all.

He eased himself out of the group and into the boys' dressing room. Grinling was sitting at one of the scuffed wooden dressing tables that ran the length of the room on either side. He was almost hidden behind his evening paper. Ollie could only see his bare legs, swinging cheekily.

Ollie hung his chef's jacket and hat on the dress rail that was bulging with the Youngstars' costumes, then he sat down at his own place. If he could stay unnoticed for the next ten minutes, no one would pick on him and he'd make that rendezvous. It was hard to be unnoticeable, though; the room was so narrow that he and Grinling were practically touching backs on their upright wooden chairs.

Act normal, he thought, and began re-doing his

12

makeup. One of the light bulbs surrounding his wall mirror was out. He gave it a flick and it came to life with an electrical fizz. The mirror lights weren't only useful to see by, they were the sole source of heating, too. So every bulb counted.

He pinned back his floppy brown hair. It was the one real bit of himself that was visible. The rest of his face was covered with greasepaint and powder – and flour, of course. It had even got into his ears.

He had a bad feeling deep down in his boots that however quiet he kept they'd make him fetch the suppers. He always ended up doing things like that. But he couldn't go wandering about the streets of wherever they were this week – Bolton, that was it – looking for chips. Not tonight. He had to get out of it. Because tonight was Pyramid night.

Ollie stared in the mirror. Pyramid night! He remembered the moment clearly when he'd first had his brilliant idea, though it was months ago now. He'd known at once that the idea was the solution to all his problems – if only he could make it work. He'd just come off stage, he remembered, at the end of the Youngstars' act. It was the pantomime season. Aladdin. The next act was waiting to go on. And suddenly, the idea came to him. Boom! Just like the genie coming out of the magic lamp.

He remembered, as if it were yesterday, exactly what had happened next...

* * * * *

With a roll of drums from the orchestra, and an oriental wail, the Wonder Brothers whirled past Ollie onto the stage. Their act was part of the entertainment at Aladdin's wedding.

It was huge, friendly Pablo that Ollie was watching when the idea struck. And when it did, he felt bright and light, as if a roller blind had whirred up and let the sunshine into a dark room.

He raced upstairs to change. If he were quick he could have a word with Pablo at the end of the Wonder Brothers' act. Pablo wouldn't mind. Some of the grown-up artists were snobby about talking to a kid, but not Pablo. Cheery Pablo was as Spanish as an onion, and he had time for everyone.

Ollie selected his Guardian of the Lamp costume. He loved panto. The Youngstars played dozens of different roles, many more than they did in their usual act. He was constantly running up and down to the dressing room to change and so there was no time to think the usual questions that plagued him, like 'Where's my mother? What's she doing? What's she like?' Useless questions to ask because he didn't know the answers and, he imagined, he never would.

He changed hurriedly. The Guardian of the Lamp costume was right cruel to wear: all cut-glass beads that scoured your armpits like sandpaper. The treacherous blighters kept dropping off as you danced, too. Tread on a bead and you'd come a cropper – like John had during last night's show. Talk about corpse! Except for John. John hadn't seen the funny side. Face like a Monday morning. Wizard dancer though, John was – when he weren't gliding across the stage on his nose.

Ollie raced back to the stage and the dark, dusty wings. He inched his way round a pack of twenty chorus girls crowded together in the gloom, waiting to go on stage. It was like walking round a big bunch of flowers. Twenty different perfumes! They towered above him on legs as tall as factory chimneys. One of them gave a muffled squeak and slapped the top of his head. His blinking costume had only gone and grazed her bare midriff. Cripes! Don't let me have drawn blood, he prayed. She'll have me guts for garters. He edged past the last girl carefully and was just in time to catch the Wonder Brothers coming off stage.

'Pablo,' he whispered. You always had to whisper in the wings, particularly if you were a juvenile, like Ollie. 'Will you teach me acrobatics?'

'You too *leetle*,' came the hoarse reply.

Now that was a setback for his new idea. Ollie knew he was short for his age. His size was part of his problem: he was far too short to carry on being a dancer when he grew up. He got called Tiny, and Titch, and really witty names like that. But he fought back. 'I'm t-t-t-twelve,' he said, indignantly.

He couldn't wait to be thirteen either. He managed 'th's' without stammering but with 't's' all he could do was start off and hope to hear himself shut up in due course. It was as bad with 'd's'. Come thirteen, though, he'd be able to say his age for a whole seven

years without a worry in the world. As for twenty –
well, Jessie, who was his best friend, said you could
grow out of stammering same as you could grow
out of fits and spots. Who was to say you couldn't
grow deeper in, though?

The stammer was another big part of his
problem. There was no future in entertainment for
a stammerer; not in the theatre, nor on radio, nor
even in films now they were making talkies. It was
all talk, talk, talk. Acrobatics were the answer. That
way he'd be able to stay working on stage. And Ollie
was only happy when he was on stage. Other lads
might be happy as engine drivers or fishmongers or
miners or some such; but not him. On stage was the
only place he was free.

So how to get over this height obstacle? How do
you get an instant growth spurt? He looked round for
inspiration. The wings were as dark as a coal-hole
compared with the glare of the stage lights. It wasn't
easy for someone who had just come off stage, like
Pablo, to see that well. Ollie rose smoothly onto his
toes. He grew two inches. 'I'm big enough, Pablo.
Be a pal.'

'Is not law 'til you sixteen,' gasped Pablo,
accepting a towel from one of the Wonder Brothers
to wipe his streaming face. The 'Brothers' weren't
related at all. They came from all corners of the
world: Mexico, Poland, Italy, Austria – and then
there was their latest recruit, nicknamed 'Shtum'
because he hardly ever spoke and so no one knew
where he was from.

They were all blowing and puffing and sweating buckets. Their tight silver waistcoats would have to be wrung out later. And the heat coming off them! Ollie reckoned you could have fried an egg on them. All eight Brothers were hunched over with their hands on their knees, pulling in air and counting the length of time the audience applauded their act.

Funny-looking blokes they were, with wide shoulders, and small handsome heads, and muscly buttocks big enough for a carthorse. Ollie knew he had to be one of them. He didn't care what shape he turned out – even if his head looked like a processed pea and he had to buy outsize in trousers for evermore. He hadn't bargained for it being illegal for boys to train, though. That was a terrible complication. The solution to his problem was disappearing as fast as he'd thought of it. It was much more than an ordinary, everyday solution, too – it was an escape route. An escape route from his dad.

'Take a second call,' said the stage manager. Stage managers never whispered. The Brothers dropped their towels and pell-melled back on stage for their second bow. The stage manager clicked the switches on his control desk, where he was sitting tucked into the corner of the wings. Each switch warned the stage crew to get ready for a cue. 'Tell him you support the Republicans,' he snapped.

'Republicans? What team are they?' asked Ollie. But he kept his distance. If you distracted a stage manager in the middle of a cue, it could cause chaos on stage. He would be entitled to knock you into the middle of next week. Ollie decided to clear off. There was no sense in standing here on his points, begging for a clobbering.

'You juveniles!' the stage manager rapped out before Ollie could move. 'Don't you ever read the newspapers?' He clicked a second set of switches. Green lights came up on the panel and the cue was set in motion. 'Just tell Pablo you're a Republican.'

The band swung into the latest hit tune. The lighting on stage faded through deep lavender to a split second of darkness. The Brothers bounded into the wings. A spotlight picked out a glittering singer centre stage. The twenty chorus girls – dressed as the Sultan's belly dancers (one of them with a grazed one) – swayed on either side of her like twenty beauty queens. And she sang. The next act was on without a hitch.

'I'm a Republican,' Ollie hissed warily at Pablo. Stage managers could be terrible practical jokers.

'Okay. I teach,' said Pablo. 'Now climb off toes or they break.' The stage manager winked. Ollie wasn't sure if it was at him or the singer.

And that was the start of Ollie's secret training. He kept it secret from everyone because Mr Pigott would go up in flames if he found out that he was breaking the law. The police would get involved. Ollie didn't want to lose his licence to perform. That way he'd be finished.

The training was tough, though. Dancing could be tough enough but, in Ollie's opinion, half an hour's solid tap dancing was a cinch compared with ten minutes of acrobatics. But he had to stick with it.

Then, one matinée day he got a scare. He was alone in the green-room with Jessie. He was making them both a pot of tea and Jess was reading a comic, twisting her dark hair round her finger, when she said to him, dead casual, without looking up, 'I've been watching you and Pablo.' Ollie thought his heart would stop from fear. Surely Jess of all people wasn't going to tell on him? 'You're getting better by the minute, Ollie.' She smiled at him as she said it and he breathed again.

'You really think so?'

'Yeah. Mind, you were right terrible to start off with, our Oll. Couldn't have got worse.'

'You been watching all this time?'

'Someone has to make sure you don't break your neck.' She looked stern. 'You pay Pablo, Ollie?'

'Aw, Jess, don't talk daft.'

'Thought not. Well, we should. He's taking a big risk for you. I'll think up some treats. Nothing fancy.' And she did. Jess took over in the way that Jess took over most things for Ollie. It would be her job to keep all the nosey parkers out of their training sessions so Ollie's secret was safe; and she'd organise their playtime, too. 'Ollie's halfway too melancholy already,' she explained to Pablo. 'He's got to have a playtime on his afternoons off. You too.'

She was as good as her word. Ollie's favourite playtime was the flicks, but Jessie set such store on

19

novelty that the cinema didn't come round often. Once, she even took them to a Tea Dance. Ollie was bored stiff, but Pablo and Jessie swooped around the dance floor. She was a cracking mover, Ollie had to admit. No wonder she was their lead dancer. She was good to watch.

One day she turned up with hired bicycles. 'It is forbidden for an artist to travel further than five miles from the theatre,' she quoted from their theatre contracts in her clear Lancashire voice. 'On yer marks, get set,' and away she belted. 'GO!' she called back over her shoulder with Pablo laughing along behind, 'Cheat, cheat.'

Life with Jess, Ollie reflected, as he fell off for the tenth time, could be suicidal but never boring.

When at last Ollie's thirteenth birthday came round, Pablo did it in style. He bought fabulous foreign food for a picnic and even hired a car. Ollie couldn't believe his eyes when he saw it parked outside Pablo's digs. He and Jess had never driven in a car. The occasional taxi was all they'd known. This was going to be his best birthday ever.

Ollie was running his hand over the car's shiny bonnet when suddenly, Pablo staggered and clutched his chest. Jess gave a cry of concern as he sank onto the pavement. Ollie thought he was having a heart attack.

'My God, Ollie!' Pablo squeaked. 'You smile! I never see that before, did I?' It made Ollie laugh. Another rarity.

They folded back the car's soft hood and sped onto

the Yorkshire moors to look at the purple flowering heather. Pablo said it was famous. Jessie's long hair blew straight up on end and Ollie sat behind her to hold it down. Otherwise she'd look a scarecrow for tonight's show, she said. Pablo sang loud songs in Spanish and Ollie said over and over, under cover of the noise, 'I'm thirteen.' Just to hear his age without a stammer.

Soon, they were well beyond the five-mile limit.

The heather wasn't in bloom and the car's radiator boiled and then cracked. Pablo made a dent in the bonnet hitting it.

'In Spain, this make car go,' he said confidently. But the treatment didn't work in Yorkshire. There was nothing for it but to walk back to town. The three of them tramped doggedly along the empty flint track while the time for curtain-up crept nearer and nearer. They still had miles to go.

Jessie could barely speak for panic. Pablo smiled and said not to worry, but Ollie saw him check his wristwatch every few seconds. Pablo was as frightened as Jess, which made Ollie even more frightened. He would rather die than miss a performance; they all would. It wrecks the show. On top of that, they had broken their contracts. That gets you the sack.

This was a right disaster of a thirteenth birthday. Unlucky thirteen! It was horrible the way life tricked you: made you believe this was your best ever birthday when it was really the very worst. Life never did you a favour. It never started off horrendous and turned out happy ever after.

'What that?' Pablo stopped with his hand up for quiet.

'I can't hear...'

'Shh!' Jessie gripped Ollie's shoulder. Then he heard it, too: the faintest sound of horse's hooves, far ahead of them.

They broke into a run to catch the rider, shouting and caterwauling at them to stop. Ollie's lungs were ready to burst open. Then a dark blob emerged from the dusk. It grew bigger as they gained on it. They could make out a pony and trap. At last the driver heard their shrieks and pulled up. He was an elderly priest, propped in the driving seat of the little round cart with a rug round his knees. He introduced himself as Father Anthony.

Pablo began to spit and burble in Spanish. He disliked priests; it was part of being a Spanish Republican. But Jessie gave Pablo a sharp kick in the calf and, between gasps for breath, asked if Father Anthony would give them a lift in time for the show. 'How long have we got?' he quavered as they pushed Pablo, still crackling like a big squib, into the trap.

'T-t-t-t-twenty minutes.'

'We can but try.' He shook the reins but the pony wouldn't budge. They sat packed into the sagging trap while he pleaded with it and time ticked by.

'We too heavy,' Pablo said, eyeing poor old Father Anthony. He was obviously considering ditching him.

'We could d-d-do with a cowboy.'

Jessie was really irritable for her. 'Don't be daft, our Ollie. A cowboy would make us even heavier.' But Father Anthony looked encouraging.

'Give it a try, young chap, if you would.'

Ollie stood up to demonstrate. 'In the films, a cowboy would go...' Ollie let out a wild, 'Yipppeeee'. The pony shot off and Pablo only just prevented him toppling out of the cart. They reached the theatre with five minutes to spare and gabbled their goodbyes.

'See you around,' Ollie called and wished it were true. Father Anthony was a nice old bloke.

Pablo was a brilliant bloke too. Never pried. Never asked questions, except once when they were having their usual pre-training cup of tea in a café.

'Why you no at school?

John and Silver had asked him the same question when they set out for lessons and Ollie did not. He had made what he did instead of school sound so boring that they'd lost interest. It might be more difficult to persuade Pablo that playing truant was okay.

'It's like this,' Ollie explained. 'Us Youngstars d-don't go to usual school that often. We work funny hours for that. Besides, Jessie and Heather left once they passed fourteen. There's only Silver and John who are thirteen, and then me. I'm last. So they pull a poor old codger of a t-teacher out of retirement for the week to give us lessons.'

'Why you not with the poor old codger?'

'I'm sorry for him. I'm t-too d-daft to t-teach. So I d-do him a favour and stay away.' Pablo didn't look convinced so Ollie quickly changed the subject. 'How's the war going?'

He drank his hot tea gratefully and listened while Pablo described how his side, the Republicans, were doing in the civil war being fought in Spain. Ollie never let on that he'd thought the Republicans were a football team. That way you could spoil a beautiful friendship. And this particular friend had paid for the tea, too.

*   *   *   *   *

'Watch out!'

Ollie jerked back into the present at John's warning.

CHAPTER TWO

FORTUNE

John slid into his place at the dressing table next to Ollie. 'Watch out,' he warned again, 'Miss Bullfrog is on the warpath!' Sure enough there was a quick knock and Heather came in. Ollie knew at once she'd come about fetching the suppers, but Heather took her time.

She was wearing her green silk kimono. She'd had it for so long the cuffs were frayed to her elbows. 'Bullfrog' was not a kind name but Ollie had to admit it sort of fitted her. Her best party trick was to jump her own height from a standstill. Amazing! And very frog-like, particularly in a green kimono.

It was John who'd first coined the name. He'd been on his favourite topic at the time: *Our Careers*. He was not optimistic about Heather's. 'She'll never make it,' he'd said to Ollie.

All the Youngstars wanted to 'make it' to Hollywood stardom, and the buckets of money that came with it, as soon as they'd grown out of being a Youngstar. It went without saying that Ollie would never see Hollywood, not with his stammer. Heather was as keen as the rest, but John had said dismissively, 'Nose like a war memorial. She'd break the camera.'

John's sister was a starlet, signed up with a big film studio. Every week she wrote to him with all the studio gossip. This inside knowledge made John the authority on who would and who wouldn't 'make it'.

Ollie liked Heth. Heth was all right. Not like Jess was all right, but okay, and so he'd tried to improve her future.

'What about radio?' he'd suggested.

'Radio!' croaked John. He'd a tendency to croak now, Ollie had noticed. 'With her voice! A bullfrog would stand more chance.' And 'Bullfrog' stuck.

Heather tightened the kimono round her drainpipe body and said in her deep, bullfroggy voice, 'Us girls next door have been thinking.' Ollie knew he was right. This was going to be about fetching the suppers. He didn't meet her eye.

Nobody answered. Grinling read on, while John studied his handsome face in the mirror in that especially friendly way he kept for his own reflection. It took more than a silence to put Heather off. 'And Silver thinks Grinling should volunteer to go and fetch the suppers for us all.' Ollie could have crowed with happiness. He was off the hook.

Grinling's newspaper quivered and Heather threw it an apprehensive glance. It didn't do to cross Grinling, but she persisted. 'As it's his trousers are keeping Miss Bellamy from going, that's only fair, us girls think.'

She drew up a chair and sat between Ollie and John in a flurry of silk. The embroidery on the back of her kimono was coming apart, Ollie noticed. Heather swore the embroidery was a golden dragon, but to Ollie it had more the look of a winged banana. The state it was in, it wouldn't be anything at all for much longer. Her auntie had bought it for her, Heather said. She could do with auntie coughing up again.

Heather crossed her pale, lanky legs and twiddled a lock of her much too flaxen hair. 'Don't get me wrong. If I wasn't curling my hair...'

The door behind them closed gently. They looked round. Grinling's chair was empty. They looked at each other.

'That dwarf!' said John, bitterly, 'is not just an ugly face. He's scarpered.'

Heather was already at the door, peering down the corridor after Grinling. She poked a stunned face back into the room. 'And without his trousers!'

And so fetching the blasted suppers had come back to Ollie again. But they were forgotten temporarily while John and Heather laid bets on whether Grinling would dare go down to the pub

27

for his bottles of stout without his trousers.

It was Ollie's perfect moment to make a run for it. If they stopped him he'd stick up for himself, like Jess was always telling him to. He'd snap his fingers – that's if they weren't too sweaty – and say 'So long, folks' just like the cowboys did in the films, and leave.

Before he could try it, Heather said, 'I know! We'll have a lottery.'

There was only one thing to do – get Jess to help him out. Jess knew all about his rendezvous. She'd been there at the end of this morning's lesson when Pablo had announced, 'Tonight is great night for you, Ollie. Tonight the Brothers show you Human Pyramid during break.'

'Thanks, Pablo,' Ollie had said. 'But I d-d-do watch it from the wings. Every night. Never miss.'

'No, no. We form, then you take Brother Raphael's part.

'Which one of you is Raphael?'

'Shtum.'

'Crikey Moses! Shtum!' Shtum was the Brothers' 'top-mounter'! Ollie felt a thump of nervous excitement shoot right through him.

'That's right,' Pablo had said. 'We form pyramid and you go lightning quick to the top of us.'

This was real progress! Pablo thought he was ready to train with first class acrobats! Maybe if he did well enough tonight, the Brothers would take him on straight away as a sort of apprentice mascot. That way, he'd be fully trained in half the time

28

They'd arranged to do the pyramid on stage in the break between the second and third show tonight – in a few minutes' time. This could be his last opportunity for months.

The Wonder Brothers and the Youngstars weren't always booked into the same theatre or city. Pablo had to write complicated letters saying where he would be the next week in the hope that they would coincide. He always addressed the letters to Jess so that no one would suspect the secret of the lessons. But Ollie could follow Pablo about the northern circuit, a tantalising fifty miles or so apart, for weeks and weeks. He had to get on with training by himself then, which was nothing like as good.

Heather grabbed John's chef's hat from the dressing-table and dropped four of Ollie's precious greasepaint sticks into it. 'Whoever picks out this number 2 ½,' she held up a bright pink stick of John's greasepaint, 'goes for the supper.' The 2½ went into the hat too. 'The youngest first.' She offered it to Ollie.

He had to get Jessie onside. If Jess heard about this lottery she'd tell Heather that if she was that starved for her supper, to climb on her broomstick and fetch it herself. Jess would look out for him.

'Ladies first,' he said. 'That's only polite.' To his relief, Heather whisked off to take the hat to the girls' dressing room.

'Twerp!' John said genially. 'Why did you say that? The more sticks to choose from, the more chances we'd have had of not getting that 2½.' He combed his glossy black hair into a wave that Ollie would have given his best tap shoes for.

'I know what I'm doing, John.'

But he didn't know. Heather was back in seconds. She held the hat out. 'It's between you two, now.'

Ollie couldn't believe it was happening. What was the matter? Why hadn't Jess got him out of this mess? John fished into the hat. 'Bad luck, Ollie,' he smiled and held up a terracotta coloured stick of Number 9.

A voice outside boomed distantly from down the corridor. As it grew nearer Ollie could hear the words, 'Food! Food! Food!' Mr Pigott swept in with his coat draped over his shoulders, his trilby hat pushed to the back of his head and his arms full of newspaper parcels. 'Supper, my Babies,' he said. 'We'll eat in the girls' room. It's bigger. Follow me all.' And he swirled out again. The Misery engulfed Ollie; he'd never get away now.

Not even Jessie knew about the Misery. Ollie had a dim sort of feeling that there had once been a time when it hadn't been there; but now it only went away when he was doing a show. Afterwards, sooner or later, the Misery would thread its way through him and settle in as though it had never gone away. It always took him by surprise; that was the worst part. On stage, he completely forgot it, the same way you can forget the ache of toothache once it has gone or what winter is like when you are in the middle of a hot summer. So when it came back, it hit him hard, as if he'd never felt it before. At the same time it was as familiar as an old ghost. Sometimes he thought the only way to escape it was to turn into someone else so that there was no Ollie left for it to creep back into. Impossible, of course.

He tramped after the others and, like a long lost enemy, the Misery seeped into him. He remembered to crack a smile. He did that when the Misery came, otherwise he could expect remarks like 'Cheer up or I'll give you something to cry about'. Stuff like that.

They were held up briefly by an errand boy blocking the corridor with an enormous basket of red roses. The boy knocked on the girls' door. Silver appeared and took charge of the basket with an amazed 'For me? Really and truly for me?'

Ollie could never figure out why she bothered to sound amazed. It would be more amazing if she didn't get a bouquet. Whichever theatre they played, Silver always received a bouquet – or twenty – and at the sight of each one Miss Bellamy would say, 'Little girls of thirteen should not have admirers.' There were so many bouquets that Miss Bellamy had put together a routine threat which she could deliver with staggering swiftness: 'I'll tell your...' – she'd search for the word – 'parents.'

Silver would look sorry and the other Youngstars would scramble to find a vase for her. It paid off. Her admirers sent her as many boxes of chocolates as bouquets and she always gave them away, but only because she was *always* on a slimming diet. Silver was mean; and she was also going to be a film star. Even John said so.

Ollie reckoned this particular bouquet was a right waste of flowers. The Youngstars were packing up and leaving the theatre tonight, and by tomorrow they'd have left Bolton, too – and the roses. He trailed after the others into the girls' room. Jess was in her corner asleep with her head on her dressing table, which was peculiar. No one could sleep in the racket Mr Pigott was making.

'Eat, my Babies,' Mr Pigott was booming as he distributed the newspaper packets. 'Eat.' The Youngstars ate happily. All except Jess. And that was peculiar, too.

'Miss Bellamy, make some tea, dear,' Mr Pigott rumbled. 'Make some tea, dear,' he repeated rapidly, three or four times to get through to her. Miss Bellamy put down her patching, smoothed her black dress and slowly left the room. A minute later she stuck her head round the door:

'Tea? Did you say...?'

'Yes, yes, yes.' Mr Pigott shambled towards her clapping his hands and calling 'Yes, yes, yes,' to speed her on her way.

'All right...I...heard...' Her voice faded to nothing as she went.

Ollie unwrapped his supper. It lay steaming damply in his lap. Maybe he could rush it down, make an excuse and run. Behind him, the water pipes glugged. Dollops of dirty water pulsed up through the plughole, half filled the basin beside him, then slowly glugged away again, leaving behind a thick rime of orange scum. 'Eugh!' they all said. Somewhere, in another dressing room, another artist was cleaning off their make-up.

'It'll be typhoid for us next,' roared Mr Pigott. 'Why don't they call a plumber? The penny-pinching purveyors of plagues and pus.' He paused for breath and to tear a flap of pastry from his pie. 'Now they're spooning dysentery up the drains.'

Mr Pigott dragged himself away from the sound of his own voice to notice that Jessie hadn't moved since he came in. 'Eat up, Jessie, dear,' he roared. When she didn't, he beat a jovial tattoo on her back with her packet of food and boomed, 'Show a leg!' It made her jump and Ollie saw her digging her fingernails into the dressing table.

'D-d-d-don't,' he said fiercely; and then he could have bitten his tongue off.

Mr Pigott didn't speak immediately. He just looked at Ollie with an expression of hurt surprise on his face. It was a large, yellowish face, flushed maroon around the nostrils and cheeks by a tracery of broken veins. The eyes were round and cold. They opened now until they were rounder and colder than ever. The room went dead quiet. Mr Piggott asked him, in a puzzled way, 'What did you say?' The threat in his voice lay in wait for Ollie.

He daren't answer. Besides, there was no point. He could no more stop what was coming than stop the sun going down. The flour that was still caught in his eyelashes made a hazy aura around Mr Pigott's head – like an angel's halo, an angel of death.

'I said,' Mr Pigott insisted, with frightening civility, 'what did you say?'

Suddenly, all the Youngstars started talking at once. Silver took Mr Pigott's arm and smilingly offered him a chocolate. Heather caressed the enamel mugs in the tea basket. Two sugars or three for Mr Pigott? John produced the latest glamour shot of his sister and begged Mr Pigott's opinion. Jessie sat up as though she was a hundred years old and took her supper with a winning smile.

They were rescuing him. As usual, they were doing their level best to keep him from harm. He felt a mixture of gratitude and misery as he watched Mr Pigott closely. Would it work?

Ollie kept up the smile and the cheery face. If Pigott got a clue you were worried, he was at his most dangerous; and Theodore Pigott was a big man. His neck spilled over his starched collar as if it were an escape valve for his flesh. Everyone knew there was a panel of fabric let into the back of his waistcoat. It eased the pressure on his belly, which jutted out, like a boiled pudding, before retracting into miraculously narrow hips. He had a sweet, red-lipped smile and his greying hair was glassy with Brylcreem. His manners were impeccable if he wanted to get something from you; and if he didn't, he'd as easy throw you in the dustcart. As the Youngstars' manager, he hired them, licensed them, signed contracts with their parents and disliked every one of them in varying degrees. Jessie was his favourite. He was almost civil to her.

But even Jess's magic hadn't worked this time. Mr Pigott was definitely getting ready to hit him. No point in ducking. Pigott always got you in the end. Ollie did duck, though, as Pigott's fist came at him.

'Grub's up, is it?' a sour voice interrupted. 'Any left for little me?' Grinling seemed to have materialised in the room. He was holding a brown paper bag full of bottles of stout and wearing some very colourful pants. Pigott said he'd die of laughing at them. He didn't, but at least he forgot about hitting Ollie.

Grinling was wrapped around in a Mexican shawl that he must have borrowed from one of the chorus. They all mothered Grinling. They'd folded the shawl like a nappy and safety-pinned him into it. He looked like a seedy toddler, swigging on his bottle of stout. He waggled his bottom sexily so that the shawl's crimson fringe swung round his short, bowed legs. Pigott laughed his head off and crouched down to Grinling's level to hand feed him bits of pie.

As Grinling opened his mouth to accept them, he looked at Ollie over Pigott's shoulder and jerked his head very slightly at the door. He was telling him – 'Get out before he remembers to bash you.'

Ollie didn't need to be told twice. The Wonder Brothers would be thinking he wasn't coming by now. They'd be pacing the stage in their striped towelling dressing gowns. They'd be thinking about leaving.

He made it to the door without Mr Pigott noticing. He reached for the handle, but the door opened and Miss Bellamy came in with the tea. 'Tea's...' she said, and everyone rushed towards her, holding out their mugs. 'Up,' said Miss Bellamy, completing her sentence, and Ollie wished her – well, not exactly in hell, but nearly.

There was a wallop on the dressing room door and Pablo burst in. He spread his arms out to Ollie, his eyes filled with tears. Everyone watched him in startled silence. He tried to speak but couldn't. He blew his nose like a trumpet blast and tried again. 'My brother is *kill*,' he said.

There was a murmur of shock and sympathy from the entire room. Everyone liked the Wonder Brothers.

'Which one?' It was John, bluntly voicing the question the rest of them were longing to ask but didn't like to.

'No, no! My *leetle* real brother is *kill* in war.' Pablo was weeping now. Ollie felt terrible for him but he daren't say so, daren't let it show they were particular friends.

'I go Spain, Madrid,' Pablo continued, brokenly, 'to my Mum. Sorry, Ollie. No more lessons.' Then he clapped his big paw of a hand over his mouth and cried more because he had let out Ollie's secret.

Mr Pigott smiled at Ollie greasily. There was a string of meat dangling from his fingers on its way to his mouth. Ollie was so frightened by the look of suspicion in Pigott's round, grey eyes that he said, as off-handedly as he could, 'So long then, Pablo old chap,' and pushed his way to the wash basin to rinse away the orange scum.

He could see Pablo's stricken face in the many mirrors. 'Ollie,' he pleaded. Ollie didn't dare answer. He wished Pablo would stop crying. Crying is catching, sometimes.

Jessie got to her feet and put her arm round as much of Pablo as she could. Talc from her costume settled on him. 'Come on love,' she said softly. 'We can't have this, can we? You've got a show to get through tonight, you know, before you set out home.' She smiled up at Pablo, ignoring the circle of inquisitive people round them, and drew him gently out of the dressing room like a tug pulling a liner out of dock.

Ollie heard the door close behind them. He was aware of everyone turning in his direction and of an expectant silence. Now he was for it. Pigott started all mild and friendly, but no one was taken in. 'Lessons?' Pigott mused. He popped the dangle of meat into his mouth and licked the last of his mushy off the paper. He licked and licked for long enough to allow all hope of escape to drain out of Ollie.

Ollie kept his back to them all, leaning over the basin. He didn't know how to get out of this. When Pigott found out he'd been playing truant he'd murder him. The other Youngstars didn't look like rescuing him this time. Too scared. Besides, weren't they as keen to hear his answer as Mr Pigott was pretending not to be?

'Lessons, Ollie?' Pigott asked, a harder voice now. He shifted onto Jessie's chair – within easier reach. Out of the corner of his eye, Ollie saw a flake of pastry fall out of Pigott's mouth onto his tautly trousered thigh, saw Pigott squash it into a little pancake on the end of his finger and suck it in again with the rest. The man scared him sick.

'I was t-t-t-t-t.' He stuck badly.

'We hang upon your lips, dear boy.' The Youngstars smirked dutifully at their manager's little joke. Ollie tried again. 'I was giving him English lessons,' he lied, then flinched as Pigott's fist came out at him again. But this time Pigott only grinned, snatched Ollie's untouched supper and started eating it before he said, 'Oh y-y-you w-were, w-were y-you?'

Pigott tilted his chair onto its back legs and looked round to make sure everyone was enjoying the scene as much as they should be. 'Case of the dumb leading the dumb, eh?' He laughed. So did everyone else. They'd have been fools not to. The drama ended. The Youngstars settled to their supper and Ollie stood there, smiling.

His idea was over. Finished. All his hopes, all his months of work, had been shot down somewhere in Spain along with Pablo's brother. He had tried so hard to earn his living independently of Mr Pigott. In another three years, when he was sixteen, he could have launched himself as a fully-fledged acrobat. But nobody hires a half-trained acrobat, and acrobatics were his only chance.

He thought about his future. It was like looking down an endless tunnel of years, working his heart out for Theodore Pigott, the man he could never get away from: his truly, truly horrible father.

Grinling rattled an evening paper. 'The new king's got himself a pretty girl.'

Pigott belched. 'Yankee bitch.' He tucked into his son's food while Miss Bellamy handed Ollie a mug of tea.

'Yanks are all right,' Silver said. 'They invented Hollywood.'

One sip of his tea told Ollie it was full of sugar. Miss Bellamy knew he hated sugar. So she'd got her knife into him too, had she? Grinling put down his bottle carefully: there was money back on returned empties. 'Says here we're playing Liverpool next week, Boss.'

Pigott swallowed a lump of his son's supper. 'True.'

'That'll do me,' Grinling reflected. 'Treble the size of this hole.' Grinling knew just about every variety theatre in the country. 'I'll not be sorry to get on that train tomorrow.'

The call-boy knocked on the door. 'Half-an-hour please, ladies and gentlemen!' There was a general move to get ready for the third house.

Ollie was about to pour his sugary tea down the plughole when Miss Bellamy called out, really quickly for her, 'Wait!' She took his mug and fished out a stick of tea-leaf that was floating on the surface. 'You've got a...stranger.'

The Youngstars stopped what they were doing. Even John dropped his debonair act and looked alert. If Miss Bellamy was going to tell a fortune, it was worth listening to, however long it took. Silver's pretty face emerged crossly from the froth of spangled tulle she was getting into. She crouched on the seat of her chair with her skirt hanging round her neck like a ruff and her hands gripping the back strut, listening enviously.

Other artists would travel miles to hear their fortune told by Miss Bellamy. She had a reputation for getting it right. The Chorus Line always wore a path to the Youngstars' dressing room. But to Silver's frustration, however much she implored her, Miss Bellamy would never put an actual date on her departure for Hollywood. All she would say was that Silver would be going soon. And now here was Ollie getting a fortune without even asking.

Miss Bellamy put the tea-leaf on the back of her left hand. 'Let's see when your stranger is coming.' You could have heard a pin drop. 'Today is...'

'Saturday,' Silver and Heather prompted her. Miss Bellamy clapped the backs of her hands together and started counting off the days of the week: 'Sunday...' But the tea-leaf had already transferred to the back of her right hand. 'Sunday,' she repeated. 'Your stranger is coming on Sunday.'

'T-t-t-t-t.' Ollie stuck.

'Tomorrow,' Pigott snarled.

CHAPTER THREE

THE DAY OF THE STRANGER

The 'Day of The Stranger', as John would keep calling it, started off drizzly. But by the time Ollie and John were waiting at the stop for the tram to take them to the railway station, the rain was bucketing down and Ollie was soaked. He tucked the parcel, with his best boots in it, inside his blazer and thought of hot, dry deserts to warm himself up.

Spain was warm, Pablo had said. Don't, Ollie warned himself, don't think about Pablo. He shivered. The red blazer he was wearing was useless in the rain. It sucked up the water as eagerly as a sponge until the whole of his top half was squishy and cooling rapidly.

All the Youngstars wore red blazers. Ollie and John had red caps too. Mr Pigott insisted on it:

'For smartness,' he said. The Public always noticed smartness, he told the troupe, and what the Public did and did not notice was very, very important to Mr Pigott.

The uniforms were passed down from one generation of Youngstars to the next. Pigott was too tight-fisted to replace them until they were threadbare, so the troupe was kitted out in a ragbag of textures and colours that ranged from the newest – a fluffy scarlet, in Ollie's case – to the oldest – a mulberry patchwork of darns, in Heather's. She'd just outgrown it, to her relief, and thanks to Pigott's meanness, was in for a long wait for a replacement.

Jess had once inherited one that was like a pink cobweb. 'We're noticed all right,' she'd said, 'but not for smartness.' And Pablo had laughed. He'd put on Jessie's blazer back to front and he'd got one of his huge arms stuck in the sleeve. Don't think about Pablo, Ollie told himself.

They'd had to unpick the seam of the sleeve with Pablo's penknife to release him but they'd put fish paste all over Jessie's blazer because they'd been using the penknife to spread their picnic bread rolls. Jessie stank for days. Miss Bellamy had squirted her with eau–de–Cologne but the mixture of fish and scent made an even worse stink. Jessie had hung round Mr Pigott until he'd shouted, 'Streuth! What's died in here?'

'It's me blazer,' she'd told him. 'It's got bad breath.'

'Clear off,' he'd yelled. 'You're turning my

stomach.'

'You're not the only one,' she'd said. 'I passed the queue for tickets at the box office yesterday and there was a stampede to get away from me. 'Blimey!' I heard a man say, 'That's one of Theo Pigott's troupe'.'

Next day, Jessie had a new blazer.

'I do you good turn,' Pablo had chuckled.

Ollie wriggled about inside his wet clothes to see if there was a dry bit left on the inside to press against. He must stop thinking about Pablo. He flicked the rain out of his eyes and watched John soft-shoeing up and down the pavement under his umbrella. He was working out a new dance routine. When was he not? He probably danced in his sleep. He certainly tap danced with his feet while he was sitting eating his dinner.

When they set out from the digs, John had invited Ollie to share his umbrella and, for a while, Ollie had tried it. But if he stood up straight, the spokes dug him in the scalp as the umbrella rose and fell with John's dance, so he'd jogged alongside in a half squat. Then two girls had come by all dressed up for church. They were arm-in-arm under their buff umbrella and they'd crossed to the other side of the road to avoid him and John. It had made Ollie feel foolish and embarrassed so he'd come out into the rain.

Sometimes Ollie wondered what it would be like to be ordinary, like those two girls. Sometimes he'd have a look at the audience through a gap in the curtains; he'd watch them taking their seats in the theatre and he'd wonder what it was like to be 'a real person,' as he called them. Fun?

Ollie nudged a little rhythm with the toe of his boot against his father's bright, new trunk. John had helped him carry the trunk from the digs until the dancing took over. There was no mistaking whose trunk it was: *Theodore Pigott* was stamped on the front in gold letters outlined with black.

I can run away. The idea came to Ollie suddenly and gave him a terrible shock. He sat down on the trunk in a stupefied sort of plonk. It was such a simple idea and yet horribly complicated. But it was a way out. He felt wonderful, as though someone had switched on an electric light inside his head. Then a lump of mud hit him on the back of the neck and knocked his cap into the gutter. 'What the heck?' he said as the privet hedge behind him shook like fury. Raindrops flew and some kids came slithering out of hiding. They were bigger than Ollie and they were looking for a fight.

* * * * *

Up until then, it had been the usual sort of Sunday morning. They'd had breakfast with Grinling. The girls weren't there; they were staying in digs on the other side of town with Miss Bellamy. Mr Pigott hadn't come down yet. His place at the table remained laid but unused. Ollie was already finishing a second cup of tea when he heard his father on the stairs. He cracked a smile at once as Pigott came into the dining room.

Pigott's face was buttery yellow with a hangover from Saturday night's drinking. The landlady followed him in. His father's face looked right bilious as she filled his plate from a sputtering frying pan of sausage, eggs, bacon, black pudding and tinned tomatoes. Pigott swallowed a belch and felt for the silver watch chain that swagged across his belly and disappeared into his waistcoat pocket. The watch hadn't worked for years but Pigott pulled it out, peered at it and rumbled at the landlady, 'A thousand pardons, dear lady, but I shall be late for church if I tarry a minute longer.'

He swanned off into the hall in a sickly way, dragged his gabardine raincoat from the stand and shoved his trilby hat on the back of his head. Calling to Ollie to bring his trunk to the station, he went out into the rain with a slam that rattled the front door's stained glass panels in their lead frames.

Ollie twiddled the fringing of the moquette table-cover between his fingers and shot a cautious look at the landlady. Church! His father had gone for his early morning 'eye opener': a tot of whisky wheedled out of the nearest publican rash enough to risk his licence by serving him out of hours. Would the landlady guess? If she did, it meant a wasted morning of stammering apologies for the leftover breakfast. The Youngstars always made him do it, and Ollie knew better than to argue. If he did, someone always came up with the crushing line

'Well, he's your father.'

It wasn't an easy job, calming a landlady. A rejected breakfast could turn her into a tigress. This one was already looking at her frying pan as though it were a discus she was about to send whirling through the front door and spinning down the road in pursuit of Mr Pigott.

There was silence. John stared into the middle distance and looked charming, and Grinling put up his Sunday Pictorial paper like a wall. Why, Ollie wondered, would his father never learn? Once, Pigott had got back from the pub to find an enraged landlady had called the police. The row!

'And he knocks that little one into Kingdom Come,' she'd shouted, pointing at Ollie. The policeman had knelt down so his face was level with Ollie's. 'Is that true, lad?' He'd seemed so concerned that Ollie had felt quite guilty when he'd lied without a moment's hesitation, 'No, sir. It's not...'

His father had interposed with something about babes and sucklings, though where babies came into it Ollie couldn't imagine. Later, he realised that his father had cut in to prevent him having a go at the word 'true'. A stammer was often taken to be a sign of terror by grown-ups. Perhaps they were right. Perhaps he'd had one heck of a fright when he was too small to remember it and hadn't stopped quaking since.

'Swill,' Jessie had replied when he put that theory to her. 'You'll grow out of it, our Ollie.' And she'd pushed his hair about with her comb to tidy him up.

Ollie's lie to the police paid off and Pigott wasn't charged with cruelty to children. If he had been, all six Youngstars would have been out of a job which, to Ollie's way of reckoning, really would be cruelty to kids.

Ollie twiddled the moss green fringing and tried to say to the landlady 'Don't mind him', but all he could manage was a volley of d-d-d-d-d's. The landlady shoved Pigott's full plate under Ollie's nose. Crikey Moses! he thought; she's going to dunk me face in it, like a custard pie act. 'Get that down thee,' she said to him. 'You others, see he does.' She brushed some crumbs off the breakfast cloth. 'Tha boots are mended. They're ont' hall table in a parcel. Don't forget them.'

That shook Ollie; and even Grinling's newspaper gave a worried twitch. How was he going to pay for boot repairs? The rest of the Youngstars were paid a wage, but not Ollie. 'Yours goes into the Post Office,' Pigott would say slickly as he handed out pay packets to the rest of the troupe on the weekly Treasury Day. 'I'm building you a little nest egg, Ollie. What will you spend it on? Elocution lessons?'

But miraculously, the landlady said, 'There's nothing to pay.' Adding, as she closed the door behind her, 'That's taken care of.'

'You get all the perks, don't you?' John was almost surly. 'Strangers in tea cups, boots repaired by a fairy godmother, second breakfasts.' Ollie's mouth was too full to answer.

Grinling folded his Sunday Pic. 'That father

47

of yours knows the only church in Bolton where they serve communion scotch instead of wine.' John topped up Grinling's cup from the teapot and said, 'You can talk.' Grinling was unscrewing his brandy flask, turning the cap gently with his lumpy, big-jointed fingers that were like an old man's in miniature. Nobody could say how old Grinling was. 'Not sixty,' John had said scornfully when Ollie had hazarded a guess. 'Dwarves kick the bucket young. Twerp!'

Grinling's glass flask had a brown Bakelite cover that had split and been mended so often by Grinling with Elastoplast that it looked like a road accident. Recently it had shattered so badly that a friendly theatre electrician had wrapped it from top to bottom in sticky tape to hold it together. 'We've mummified the little devil,' Grinling told his fellow Youngstars. By now, weeks of dirt were stuck to it. 'You'll catch something off that,' Jessie had predicted, 'something incurable.' But Grinling wouldn't give it up. It had sentimental value, he said, whatever that was.

Grinling measured a capful of brandy into his tea. 'You're as bad as Pigott,' John teased him.

'Ah! But I'm honest about it, Johnny boy, I'm honest.' He took a sip of tea and went on dreamily, 'I love Sundays: no work, no show to do. I can drink all day and night and nobody gives a tinker's. No gallivanting round the stage acting like a kid with you lot. No having to make people laugh.'

'People always laugh at dwarves,' said John. Grinling took another sip.

'But Sundays I needn't pretend I don't mind.'

A bit later, he winked at the boys, slid down from his chair, and announced he was going to see a man about a horse. Grinling couldn't resist a street bet and seemed not to care at all that it was illegal. He was off now to collect his winnings. Ollie pulled back the lace curtain at the window to watch him go. All you could see under his huge umbrella were his black patent shoes. Ollie crossed his fingers for him.

Grinling had been with the troupe for as long as Ollie could remember. It wouldn't be the same at all if he landed up in jail. He waddled down the front garden path, looking more like a black mushroom than a crook, and went out of the gate.

The front garden was like every other garden in this suburb of town: tiny, with a concrete path down the middle and two runners of muddy grass surrounding two oblong flowerbeds the size of graves and about as cheerful.

* * * * *

It was a lump of earth from a bed like that which hit Ollie on the back of the neck as he waited with John at the tram stop.

His cap floated off along the gutter and he chased after it. His father would give him hell if he lost it. Out of the corner of his eye he saw that John had stopped dancing and was wiping a cake of mud off his face. His umbrella lay upturned like a saucer on the pavement beside him. Two of their attackers were creeping up behind him. Ollie shouted a warning. John snapped the umbrella shut, turned, and slashed the air with it so the lads couldn't get near him. John wouldn't get into a fight. Ollie knew that. He'd run as soon as he could. 'My face is my wage packet,' he'd said often enough.

All the Youngstars dreaded injury. Injury could make every minute on stage agony. Local kids always took the mickey because no Youngstar would even get into an argument, let alone an out-and-out brawl.

Ollie caught up with his cap. He stuffed it into his pocket while he sized up their situation. There were three boys after them. Two of them were about John's height, but broader. They were poor kids: poorer than the Youngstars. One wore patched short trousers and a jumper with holes in the elbows; the other didn't have a jumper at all. His trousers were shorn off at the knee and held up with braces that he wore over his naked top. This kid tried to catch the end of John's umbrella, but John whacked it across his hands. Then, while the kid was recovering, he whacked the other boy behind the knees so he blundered into the kid with the braces. This gave John time to retreat several yards down the pavement.

Ollie thought about running, too. But there was his dad's trunk; he daren't leave that. Besides, the third boy was engrossed in smashing one of their suitcases against the curb to open up the locks. The boy was barefoot and his head was shaved to keep off the lice. A string of snot swung from one of his nostrils as he crouched on the pavement, beating up the case like a manic, little old man. Suddenly it broke open and the boy came dashing towards Ollie, holding the case by its gaping lid. Everything Ollie owned was in it. His other shirt, his other vest, his best trousers – all splashed into the gutter.

'Never, never you fight,' Pablo had lectured him. 'No acrobat trust partner with broken fingers. How you grip him? No acrobat with broken fingers trust himself.' But he wasn't going to be an acrobat. Not now, thanks to Pablo and his stupid dead brother.

The barefoot boy shook Ollie's cigarette card collection into the gutter along with his hairbrush and pyjamas. He had nearly reached him by now. Aiming for Ollie's head, he swung the suitcase and threw it. Ollie ducked. He was good at that. It sailed over his head and the barefoot boy ran straight onto Ollie's bunched fist. Ollie felt the sticky snot on his knuckles. He also felt a great deal of pleasure when he heard the boy scream.

Where the reinforcements came from, Ollie never knew, but within seconds he was lying on his back, covered in yet more kids. There were so many of them they were hard-pressed to find a free bit of him to hurt. He caught upside down glimpses, between punches, of their ear lobes and scabby knees and of the bald boy's toenails, like little black crescent moons.

One of the kids was banging his head on the drain

in the gutter. It hurt so much he thought they'd kill him. It was all so unexpected and unprovoked. Why had they picked on him and John? Perfect strangers!

Suddenly, it seemed as though he'd turned to rubber. The kids were bouncing off him, leaping away from him like fleas deserting a corpse. Through the clatter of water draining into the sewers, he heard a police whistle. The kids' shouts of 'Police, police. Scram!' receded as he lay in the gutter with water running into his ears and blood running out of his nose.

Grinling's big face loomed over him, the police whistle still gripped between his teeth. Ollie tried to smile his gratitude. Trust Grinling to come up with a trick like that.

Later, at the railway station, they set to work cleaning up Ollie in the Gents before Pigott arrived and saw the state of the troupe's newest blazer. 'Some stranger!' said John, scrubbing away at the blazer with a handful of lavatory paper. 'Old Bellamy forgot to tell you he was a hairless, homicidal maniac, too. You could have put him back in your teacup if she had.'

Ollie was too tired and disappointed to answer. He wondered wearily why he had been daft enough to presume the stranger would be lucky, or good, or kind, or in any way helpful. Life wasn't like that. But ever since Miss Bellamy had foretold the stranger's arrival, he'd been banking secretly on the stranger to free him from his life with Pigott, like some kind of god or ancient hero. He'd pictured it all. Bang!

Wallop! The stranger would appear like the Demon King in a pantomime and whisk Ollie off to a new and better life, possibly pausing to poke Mr Pigott in the eye before he did so.

Grinling said, 'Glory to Christ! You've a nose like an elephant's, Ollie.' He ran the handkerchief that Silver had lent them under the cold-water tap and gave it to Ollie. 'Put that on it. It might take the swelling down. Has your head stopped bleeding?'

Ollie felt the back of his head gingerly. It was throbbing like a drum beat. But it wasn't bleeding any more.

'What about the lump on the back, though?' said John. 'It looks like he's borrowed another head.'

'Put your cap on,' Grinling suggested, 'Then your dad won't see. No,' he said, changing his mind, 'your cap looks as though it's been through a natural disaster. Pull your hair over it. It's lucky you've more than the little devil that did this to you or he could have bashed your brains out.'

John said something uncomplimentary about the likelihood of Ollie having brains being questionable, and they marched him out onto the platform to be inspected by Silver and Heather.

Ollie hoped he'd pass muster this time. They'd already sent him back three times for further cleaning. He knew they were only trying to keep him out of trouble with Pigott, but his body was aching all over as his bruises came to life and he wanted nothing but to sit by the waiting room fire with Jessie and tell her the whole unpleasant story. It was funny that she hadn't come out to him.

The rain had stopped. The two girls were sitting on one of the big skips that contained the Youngstars' costumes and props and travelled in the luggage van. They were up at the far end of the platform where shallow puddles reflected their red uniforms and the muted Sunday suits of a group of Silver's Admirers. The Admirers were all looking very mournful, partly because they had come to see her off, but mostly because none of them had known of the others' existence until now. The discovery of a crowd of rivals had made them doubly mournful. By now Miss Bellamy was there too, wearing her Sunday hat with its single feather that made her look like Robin Hood's auntie. She really had been to church, but now here she was, slowly getting their luggage into a muddle with the help of an obedient porter.

Heather said Miss Bellamy was so slow because she was a War Maiden and her heart was broken. 'All the boys were killed in the Great War and so there weren't enough husbands to go round,' she explained kindly to Ollie. But when Ollie said he didn't see how having a husband would speed her up, Silver sniggered and nudged Heather, who did grown-up sniffy laughing down her nose. Then they both wound their lipsticks round their mouths, looked wise, caught each other's eye in the mirror and exploded with laughter. Silver was always doing things like that to irritate him. She was always giggling about him, always pretending he was thick and that he didn't even know things like the facts of life, when she knew he did. Hadn't she told them to him!

Miss Bellamy had just noticed there was something odd about Ollie's suitcase – they'd tied it together with his trouser belt – when, with a flap of trailing raincoat, Mr Pigott breezed up, all the better for his morning drink. He offered everyone a handful of dolly mixture from a glass jar he'd somehow acquired during his outing. Ollie cracked a precautionary smile. It hurt. He'd gouged a chunk out of his bottom lip with his front teeth when he'd been punched in the mouth.

They crowded round Pigott for their share of dolly mixture. Even the Admirers came out of their dismal reverie and said they hadn't tasted dolly mixture since they were kiddies. They all listened appreciatively while Pigott described how he'd won the jar of sweets at a pub darts match the night before. His opponent had overdone the beer and thrown his dart at the barmaid's... Here Pigott lowered his voice and there was a burst of laughter from his listeners.

His father could always make people laugh, Ollie thought. Well, he could if he wanted to. Pigott came charging through the group bellowing, 'Ollie, lad. Have a d-d-d-dolly mixture.' But his face was like poison. Ollie had known all along that if they'd scrubbed him until next Christmas, his father wouldn't have been deceived. 'You've been fighting,' Pigott accused him. 'Look at that blazer. Come here. I'll give you fighting.' Ollie hitched his sagging trousers and went up to his father.

One of the Admirers said, 'Boys will be boys.' Pigott turned a surprised glare on him and the Admirer quailed. Then, spurred on by a dazzling smile from Silver, he rattled the coins in his pocket to give himself courage and repeated weakly, 'Boys will be boys.' There was a fervent murmur of agreement from the other Admirers, all of them frantic for a similar favour from Silver, and the porter said proudly, 'My nipper's a fighter.' He looked at Ollie with great respect. 'But he's never come home with a conk like that.'

It dawned on Mr Pigott that hitting his son would be an unpopular move and he disliked being unpopular with his public. So he laughed. 'Fighting eh?' Everyone else laughed, too. Heartily. The Youngstars nearly laughed themselves sick – anything to get Pigott to take a softer line. As they paused for breath, Pigott, the picture of outraged piety, slipped in, 'But on a Sunday!'

Nobody could deny the day of the week or, at least, not fast enough. They all stood there feeling unholy, wrong-footed and guilty, while Pigott, with a glance heavenward and a saintly sigh, gave his son a wincingly sharp crack on the ear.

It nearly took Ollie's head off. He was surprised not to see it bowling along the platform, skimming the puddles and off into the distance down the empty railway track.

If his father could hit him that hard on a Sunday – God's Day of Rest, as Miss Bellamy called it –

how hard would he hit him tomorrow, an ordinary working day, when he found out that Ollie's best boots were missing? Last seen disappearing down the road tucked under the arm of the bald, barefoot stranger.

CHAPTER FOUR

STRANGER STILL

Ollie's head didn't begin to recover until they were all chugging through the Lancashire countryside, packed like sardines into a non-smoking carriage. Mr Pigott had made a dickens of a fandango about that. Held up the train while he argued with the guard that they should be allowed into second class where there were plenty of smoker carriages. But the guard wasn't having any of it. So there they all were, sitting face to face on the prickly upholstered bench seats with the narrowest of gangways between them. You had to watch your feet didn't knock the person opposite.

Ollie wished there was a corridor like there was on the bigger, long distance trains; then he could have left the carriage to nurse his wounds in private.

Besides, corridors were fun. You could lurch down the length of the train, getting a sideways look at the posh people in the first class carriages and at the less posh ones in second. These usually included the other acts travelling with them. But now there wasn't much to help him forget his thumping head.

There were the usual paintings to look at. They were of seaside resorts that you could travel to by train: four falsely sunny destinations set into the pale wooden panelling above the seat back – except that one of them wasn't of the seaside. It was a picture of a big, ocean-going liner in Southampton docks, wherever that was.

There was a mirror up there, too, and a handle for adjusting the heating. When it was on, it was supposed to blow warm air from the dusty grille under the seats. It didn't, though. There was the luggage rack with all their suitcases in it. And there was the short strip of thin chain tucked in a boxed recess. It was for stopping the train, 'In case of emergency' said a little notice. John and Ollie had often dared one another to pull it, but the little notice also said, 'Penalty for improper use £5.' A five pound fine was a fortune!

And that was all there was to look at – except for Jessie sitting opposite him in the corner seat. Her eyes were closed and her face was pale as pale. Like she'd been made up to look ill.

Nobody else seemed to notice Jessie. Heather was darning a tear in the ruff of her white Pierrot costume, Grinling was reading his Sunday Pictorial and trying to steal a Sharpe's toffee from a paper bag in John's lap; and John was reading a comic and defending the toffees. Ollie knew it would be stupid to draw attention to Jessie if she really were ill. Illness threw his father into a rage second-to-none.

At the moment, Pigott seemed oblivious of everyone except Silver. He was watching her trying out new hairstyles in the mirror, using the pair of tortoise-shell combs a doleful Admirer had pressed on her as they left Bolton station. The other Admirers' gifts were stuffed into her suitcase on the rack. Silver's Bounty, the Youngstars always called it.

Miss Bellamy was asleep with her hat tilted raffishly over her ear. Mr Pigott began filling his pipe with tobacco without a glance at the No Smoking sign on the window. There was sweat on Jessie's face now. Ollie could see it clearly. He put his foot out and touched hers gently. No response. Had she fainted? If only he didn't feel so rotten himself he might think of a way of helping.

Mr Pigott lit his pipe and blue smoke trailed across the carriage. When it reached Jessie it made her cough. Ollie could see that coughing really hurt her. But his father didn't. He just stared blearily at Silver and remarked, 'That's a nice one,' as she made a sort of roll thing on the top of her head. Jessie coughed more, and Ollie said, 'D-d-d-d,' which was as far as he got with his intended 'Do you mind if I open the window?'

'Pack it in, you,' Pigott said. So Ollie stood up

and pulled the broad leather strap off the brass stud that held the window in place, letting it down with a bang.

The steam engine pulling the train wailed a warning and, with a roar, they entered a tunnel. The noise of the wheels on the tracks bounced off the pitchy walls. It was ear splitting. Auxiliary lighting flickered on, but you couldn't see across the carriage for thick grey smoke. The smoke usually flew harmlessly behind the engine like a dirty streamer and gradually dispersed into the air long after the train had passed. But not in a tunnel! In a tunnel it was trapped with nowhere to go unless someone unwisely left a window open; and then – in it came.

It was pouring in now. Everyone except Jessie threw themselves at the window strap. There was a horrible cry. From whom? Miss Bellamy, probably; it was hard to tell. Over the rattling crashing of the wheels, Pigott could just be heard bawling, 'Shut that ruddy window!'

The train rushed out into the light. Somehow Ollie had been pushed to the other side of the carriage. Nearly everyone else was jammed in the open window. Miss Bellamy was lying prone in the gap between the seats, both hands gripping her hat against her chest, a hat that any fool could see would never be the same again. The carriage was still full of smoke and it was making Jess cough worse, so Ollie let down the opposite window to clear it away.

The wind tore through the carriage. Grinling's Sunday Pictorial separated and the pages swirled about madly, like seabirds in a storm. Silver's hairstyle stood on end and the tortoise-shell combs scattered; and the remains of Miss Bellamy's hat were snatched from her hands and whisked out of the window.

'Shut that ruddy window!' Pigott was puce with rage. Ollie shut it. The sheets of newspaper dropped to the floor and settled on Miss Bellamy like a shroud. She seemed to have gone into a coma of bereavement for her hat. Pigott sat down in his place, all of a lump, and wiped the soot from his face. The rest of the troupe were blackened and grim and in no mood to protect Ollie. Heather certainly wasn't making a secret of the fact that her snowy Pierrot costume now had a pattern of sooty spots. Only Grinling, chewing happily on what must surely be a Sharpe's toffee, seemed kindly disposed towards him. Ollie gave them a rueful little smile. 'Sorry,' he said.

'Fat-head!' Jessie could hardly get the word out for coughing. He wanted to explain to her that he'd acted for her sake. How, if it came to it, he'd do almost anything for her sake. No, not almost anything – anything. But Pigott had started as though he'd been wound up with a key, never to stop. He went through it all: the ruined blazer; the wrecked and now, according to him, priceless Pierrot costume; Miss Bellamy's best Sunday hat – gone with the wind; Jessie coughing like Ollie had given her TB. Pigott was ranting by now. 'The rest of my troupe look like the Ink Spots,' he screamed, 'and you are merely sorry! Ollie Pigott, I'm going to give you a belting you'll never forget.' And he jumped up to do just that.

But instead of hitting Ollie, Pigott swung round with a cry of 'What the blazes!' to look over his own shoulder. Then, to everyone's amazement, Mr Pigott began to dance. The train was rocketing along now and Pigott was no ballerina, but there he was, pirouetting in circles like a dog chasing its tail. Naturally enough, with Miss Bellamy laid out on the floor he trod on a bit of her. She rose up with a scream fit for a haunted house and everyone except Jessie jumped up on their seats to keep out of the way.

Ollie found himself face-to-face with Mr Pigott's trunk up on the rack. It was the best moment of his life: someone (and who was brave enough?) had taken a stick of white greasepaint to the gold and black lettering. They had blanked out the ODORE and the GOTT of his father's name, leaving the words, THE PIG. The perfect name for his father!

The Pig, still spinning and slapping himself on the back as though he were congratulating himself, was shouting now, too. Words like: 'Oh! Ouch! Oh!' and 'Help!'

Heather did her famous 'frog jump' off the place where Pigott had been sitting. It was a miracle she didn't brain herself on the ceiling. She pointed. 'Look!' They looked. Several nuggets of smouldering pipe tobacco lay there. As they watched, devilish little flames leapt out of the upholstery. At the same time, smoke began to roll from the seat of Mr Pigott's trousers. The Pig was on fire and, what is more, he had set himself on fire.

Life is full of surprises; the last thing on earth Ollie had expected to do that day was to laugh.

Silver tried to smother the flaming seat with a sheet of the Sunday Pictorial but it caught fire, too, and disintegrated. Now they were all dodging about, clapping the drifting flares between their hands to extinguish them until Ollie could scarcely see his friends through the swirl of black ash flakes.

The Pig roared and danced while Grinling, with great presence of mind, took off John's scarlet cap and beat Mr Pigott on the bum with it to put him out. He missed quite often because the Pig would keep on going round and round; so Grinling was forced to hit him any-old-where.

Miss Bellamy gurgled something and pointed slowly at the tea hamper on the rack. John heaved it down, and Heather and he wrestled with its buckles and straps. By now the Pig was shouting terribly, and Grinling was begging him to 'Hold still, Boss.' John flung back the hamper lid and Heather poured the thermos flask of hot tea over the seat. The flames went out with a steamy hiss.

'All right, all right. I'm extinguished,' Mr Pigott bellowed at Grinling, who was going at him as if he were a punch-ball. Grinling gave him a final slap and replaced the cap. The Pig rubbed his tender buttocks. 'Thank you, Grinling,' he managed to say; but only just.

'My pleasure, Boss.' Grinling's expression was an innocent blank.

The Pig looked round the charred and dripping chaos, and Ollie tried to go invisible. Up front, the engine gave a derisory wail. It sounded like 'No chance.'

When the train pulled into Wigan station, the Pig said he'd see if he could get the thermos re-filled. With his gabardine raincoat clasped coyly round his burnt backside, he smarmed up to a porter. Everyone else got out onto the platform and left Ollie in the carriage to give him a chance to cry if he wanted to. Only Jessie stayed where she was. Was she asleep? Ollie watched her expectantly. Surely she'd open her eyes and say something to cheer him up. She didn't, and after a minute he turned away and looked out of the carriage window across the empty rails to the opposite platform.

The raw, stinging weals where his father had beaten him were competing with the duller throb of the bruises he'd got in the fight. He thought if anybody hit him any more he'd scream the place down. But he knew he wouldn't. He would have liked to be able to disintegrate and break up into flakes, like Grinling's newspaper. Anything to get away from the hitting. He knew he couldn't.

There was a pile of mailbags on the opposite platform. A pigeon was sitting on them. Some porters were standing around with trolleys. They must be expecting a train. A second pigeon joined the first one. He could see now that they weren't perched on the mailbags but on a cage of racing pigeons waiting to be loaded along with the mail. Beautiful little birds being sent somewhere so they could be released to fly all the way back to Wigan. They made the two station pigeons look very scruffy – like they weren't wearing their corsets.

A young train-spotter at the far end of the platform opened up his cream and green tin lunch box and took out – what? Ollie squinted sideways, his sore nose flattened by the carriage window. Bread and dripping, it looked like. The Pig hadn't allowed Ollie any of the troupe's Sunday dinner picnic and the second breakfast seemed to have made him hungrier, if anything.

The train-spotter took a big bite. There was something funny about the kid. Oh yes, it was his specs. One of the lenses was covered over. Like the whitewashed windows in an empty house. The kid must have a wonky eye, so they'd covered his good one to make the wonky one work. That's how they cured a wonky eye. How do you cure a wonky tongue?

The two pigeons deserted their thoroughbred cousins for the bread and dripping. The sun turned the underside of their wings almost white as they flew up out of Ollie's sight for a second and then reappeared, hopping excitedly round the train-spotter's feet.

Perhaps, thought Ollie, I could run away to Spain and Pablo. Tears blurred his vision and he had to wipe them away with his damp blazer sleeve. Why did thoughts often make him want to cry far more than the beatings his father gave him? Where was Spain, anyway? Over the sea, Pablo had said. Jessie might know. A shame to wake her. Over the sea meant money, passports. He didn't have either.

I'm like this carriage, he thought. I get pulled along rails that I can't get off: every week, from one theatre to the next, from one digs to a different digs, one teacher to another, landlady to landlady and always, always, the Pig.

To get rid of that last thought, Ollie turned his attention back to the opposite platform: to the two pigeons waiting for crumbs, the porters waiting to load the mailbags, the small train-spotter waiting to fill in his notebook. Everybody was waiting. The racing birds waiting for release and the struggle home. Ollie found himself drawn into the mood. He felt as though he was waiting, too. As if something was going to happen.

With a crash that rocked Ollie's carriage, a massive steam engine thundered past his window. An express. Its brakes ground into the metal track and its carriages passed Ollie more and more slowly until at last he caught glimpses of the passengers inside.

Some of them were standing up to get out. A woman was smiling down at her baby; the baby was kicking its legs and blowing a milky bubble out of its mouth. Then came the dining car. People still eating their dinners. There was a man smoking a cigar and holding his glass steady on the table.

67

Brandy the colour of medicine swayed in its bowl. Ollie just had time to see that the man was wearing a ring with a red stone the size of a kneecap, and then the man was gone, succeeded by other passengers. It was like a peep show on the pier at the seaside: you put your penny in the slot and different pictures slid by you.

The train came to a stop and Ollie was looking into a first class carriage. He could tell it was first. They were the ones with white serviettes on the back of the seats to keep people's heads clean, and there was a pink glass shaded light over each person's place.

The carriage had four occupants: there was a right-looking chump of a man holding a skein of wool on his hands for a pretty woman, sitting opposite him, to wind into a ball. The chump was talking nineteen-to-the-dozen to her. In one of the corner seats nearest Ollie there was a girl. Her dark hair hid her face as she leant over the book she was reading. Heavy going. No pictures. The fourth person was a boy.

He had turned away so that his back was to Ollie and he was saying something to the chump and the woman. He was bouncing up and down a bit. Then he bounced harder and the chump left off talking to the woman and they both looked at the boy. How? Ollie couldn't quite make out that look. They were attentive, somehow, but not really friendly. The boy was exactly opposite Ollie, and Ollie felt oddly curious about him. He longed for him to turn round.

Stop talking to that chump, he thought; look this way. And the boy did.

There was a thud in Ollie's midriff, as though he had been shot. The boy stared at Ollie, open-mouthed with surprise. Ollie tried to call out to Jess for help but his mouth was too dry to speak. The boy looked frightened now, so that Ollie felt sorry for him; and suddenly the boy smiled at Ollie sympathetically.

Ollie knew that smile. He knew the boy's face. He'd seen it looking at him from countless dressing room mirrors. It was his own smile, his own face. The boy was his double.

CHAPTER FIVE

RALPH

'Who are you?' Ralph had meant to shout the question but it came out as a frightened grunt.

'What's that, Ralph?'

Without taking his eyes off the boy in the other train, Ralph managed to answer his tutor in a rapid, scared voice. 'Come here quickly, Mr Fanfield. There's a boy exactly like me looking in the window.'

'Well observed, young Ralph,' Mr Fanfield said. 'You will find that this is called a *reflection*.'

Ralph could imagine Fanfield smiling his flirty smile at Mary Ellen behind his back as they wound her wool. 'I know a goddamn reflection when I see one.'

'Don't swear, Master Ralph,' Mary Ellen reproached him.

We should each open our windows, Ralph realised. How did English train windows work, though? 'Swearing before ladies is un-gentlemanly,' Fanfield was saying. Ralph glared at his tutor and his nurse. 'Open,' he ordered them, 'this **** window!' Their protests were drowned out by a blast from a locomotive whistle and a string of clanks. Ralph threw himself at the window. 'Wait, wait!'

But the boy had vanished. His train was clacking past Ralph's window faster and faster and faster, then it had gone. There was nothing left to see but the opposite platform, which was deserted except for an angry-looking man waving a thermos flask and running in the direction of the departing train. There was time for Ralph to see him trip and fall over the raincoat he was clutching round his lower half before Ralph's train pulled out of Wigan station too.

If Mr Fanfield couldn't stop Ralph swearing, he could outpoint him in an argument, and the argument about the existence of the boy in the other train was no exception. It was nonsense, and Mr Fanfield constructed a barrage of reasonableness that demonstrated just what nonsense it was. Arguing with Mr Fanfield was like trying to drown water and left you feeling that the only way out was to strangle him.

Ralph looked longingly at Mr Fanfield's clean, pink neck, and at its jigging Adam's apple, as he expounded the principles of reflection and light. Mary Ellen smiled an admiring smile at Mr Fanfield while she wound her wool, and Mr Fanfield flung back his head with an arpeggio of self-satisfied laughter at his own smartness.

Ralph said no more. He slid open the door into the corridor. Just before he left, he turned back and took the ball of wool from Mary Ellen, who watched in surprise as he shoved it between Mr Fanfield's teeth.

Alone in the corridor, Ralph pressed his forehead against the cold glass of the window and thought, 'I have just had the most amazing thing happen to me that could possibly happen to anyone, ever, but nobody believes me and nobody is going to do anything about it'.

A voice said quietly, 'Suis-moi.' Ralph squeezed up against the glass to let whoever it was pass by, but they didn't. The voice repeated, slightly impatiently, 'Suis-moi.' It was the girl who had been sharing their compartment.

Ralph hadn't taken much notice of her before. She'd been sitting by herself when they boarded the train in London and when Mary Ellen had asked if she minded if they joined her, the girl hadn't replied. She'd shaken her black hair round her face, opened her book and read from that moment to this. But now she was standing next to him, holding a little attaché case, looking at him from deep brown eyes and apparently talking gobbledegook.

'Pardon me?' he said.

'You do not speak French?'

'Certainly not,' Ralph replied, haughtily. 'I'm American. Is that what you're doing? Speaking

French?'

The girl sighed. It was a very elaborate sigh. It started with her raising the deep brown eyes in supplication to the ceiling and finished with her looking beyond Ralph, as if she were asking an infinitely wise person, standing just behind his right shoulder, to commiserate with her over what she had to put up with. Then she said, 'Follow me, please, where we cannot be seen by your know-it-all companion, Fanfield.'

'Fanfield's not my companion, he's my teacher.' But he followed her along the corridor. Anyone who didn't care for Fanfield deserved a hearing.

'Your teacher?' She seemed surprised. 'Where is the rest of your class?'

'There's only me.'

'A teacher all to yourself? You must be a very extra stupid boy.'

'I'm not stupid. I'm...well, my father pays for me to have my own teacher.'

'You are rich?'

'I guess you could put it that way.'

She looked at him incredulously. 'Then you are certainly stupid. If I had riches, I should pay the teacher to stay away.'

'Go to hell,' Ralph said, indifferently.

A passenger who was easing past them gave a surprised 'Humph' at his words and then made his way to the WC. He was a dead–ordinary-looking man except for his shoes. They were white leather with broad black stripes down the sides; they didn't match up with his navy blue serge suit and the flashy ring he was wearing with its big red stone. He gave Ralph a disapproving frown before he closed the door and snapped the engaged sign up.

The girl laughed and Ralph couldn't help grinning back at her. 'Now, about your doppelganger,' she said, briskly.

'Beg pardon?'

'Your double.'

'You saw him!' said Ralph joyfully.

'Yes, your double. It is called a doppelganger. It is German.'

Ralph didn't care if it was Double Dutch. 'He wasn't a reflection was he?'

'You wear a grey suit, he sports a red coat. How is this a reflection? You have a thin nose. He has a fat nose.'

'Did he? Mostly I remember he looked kinda solemn.'

This didn't seem to interest the girl much. 'And now,' she proclaimed, 'you will discover who he is.'

Ralph felt deflated. What a pity! The girl was crazy. Just when he was getting to like her, too. He said, listlessly, 'How?' The French girl did another of her sighs at her invisible sympathiser over his shoulder. 'You return to Wigan and enquire, while the trail is hot, to which destination your double's train is travelling.'

'Oh yeah! How? When I'm stuck in a train headed the opposite way at eighty miles an hour?'

For an answer the girl stood on tiptoe and pulled

74

down the communication cord. The brakes jammed on, locked metal wheels dragged along metal rails in a long scream, and Ralph and the girl were sent in a quick shuffle down the corridor, to be brought up with a bang against the WC door. There was an answering thump from inside as the Shoes Man hit the deck and a muffled curse that ordinarily would have interested Ralph. But now the train had stopped with a great gasp of steam, and the French girl opened the door to the outside. 'Jump!' she commanded. And Ralph did.

It was a huge drop. The stone chippings between the sleepers hurt the soles of his feet right through his shoes when he landed. He looked up at the girl, miles above him. 'Hide, stupid,' she called down to him and he scuttled into the undergrowth at the side of the track as she slammed the door shut – just in time.

Mr Fanfield slid open his compartment door and came down the corridor, adjusting his tie and smoothing his hair. Mary Ellen had been thrown into his lap when the train had stopped so abruptly and he'd got all mussed up while they were disentangling themselves. Other passengers were looking enquiringly out of their compartments. Mr Fanfield was calling Ralph's name in that pleasant but showily firm way that was meant to let everyone know that he was a really nice guy and could handle any kid, however difficult.

The girl caught his sleeve when he drew level with her and nodded delicately towards the 'Engaged' sign on the WC door. Mr Fanfield straightened his already straight tie to cover his discomposure and said tightly, 'Oh! In the john. Okay.' But then to her annoyance, he started up a conversation.

It would be too bad, she thought, if the monsieur with the strange shoes chose this moment to come out. He didn't, though. The sudden stop had sent Monsieur Shoes bouncing off the door onto the floor, where he was now lying, crammed between the wall and the WC.

Mr Fanfield smiled down at her. 'We pulled up kind of fast, didn't we?'

'Mais, oui,' she replied, pointing at the communication cord. 'I ring the bell for the waiter and – boom-bam! – we halt.'

Mr Fanfield was shocked. 'Bell!' he exclaimed. 'That's an emergency brake, little girl. You've stopped the train.' The child's large brown eyes filled with tears, and Mr Fanfield's heart was filled with remorse for being too harsh. 'Now, now,' he soothed, 'you're French are you? You said 'Oui', so sure you're French. Well, you can't help that.'

He crouched in front of her and said loudly and slowly. 'Not a cloche, comprenez?' She nodded and a little sob escaped her. Mr Fanfield melted. He drew a handkerchief from his top pocket and handed it to her. 'Here honey, have a mouchoir.' Gratefully, she pressed it to her face. 'Now don't take on,' Mr Fanfield comforted her. 'I'll go tell the guard there's been a misunderstanding; so brighten up, little girl.' He smiled conspiratorially. 'We all make the mistake, ness pah?' And away he went. A few minutes later, so did the train.

It set out with a violent jerk that rattled the cutlery in the dining car onto the floor and sent Monsieur Shoes, who had just struggled to his knees, lurching backwards. His head hit the washbasin with a thwack and he crumpled in slow, pudgy folds onto the floor again.

It seemed to Ralph, lying flat in the undergrowth, that the train got under way again in an unflatteringly short time. No one had missed him at all. Off it set with no fuss. It hissed a little as it went and he thought he'd heard a door bang, but that was all. He lay quite still until the guard's van had disappeared from sight. Then he stood up and looked round the utterly empty English landscape. 'Jeeze!' he said shakily.

* * * * *

It was about twenty minutes later that Mr Fanfield and Mary Ellen quit pleading at the locked WC door for Ralph to 'Open up honey,' and sent for the guard. A further ten minutes passed before the guard turned up with a hatchet. In horror, the tutor and nursemaid gazed down through the splintered door, not at their charge Ralph, but at a bulky gentleman in black and white shoes sitting slumped against the other side of the door. He was nervously eyeing the hatchet blade sticking through the panelling next to his ear.

So Ralph had a good start on them.

CHAPTER SIX

THE HUNT

It was about two hours later that Ralph decided England was made of mud and most of it was hanging off the bottom of his shoes. His legs were aching like they needed surgery, and though he'd never walked for so long in his life, there was still no sign of this Wigwam station he was looking for.

He'd started his journey walking back along the track the way the train had come; but soon other trains had rushed past him and he figured he was either going to get noticed and whisked back to Mr Fanfield or just plain killed. Both fates would wreck his chances of finding his double and he was determined to do that now, or bust. He took to the fields, being careful to keep the railroad in sight on his left so as not to get lost.

The fields were real tired from each other
home and they were ...ls made of rocks. He
by quaintly primiti.. yet another of the walls,
clambered wearily ribbon of skin off his palm as
which took a sp..
he did so. H..wered himself inexpertly into the
field on the other side, and wondered what he'd give
now to see Dad's limousine parked right here on the
grass, with Sam the chauffeur smiling at the wheel.
But there was no Sam; there was only a solitary
sheep in the far corner, and so Ralph toiled, with
aching legs, towards the other side.

But the ram had other plans for him. Soft
drumming, like impatient fingers on a tabletop,
alerted Ralph to its intentions. It was coming at him
like a woolly tank – spiky little feet thrumming
along, cutting the distance between them faster than
was healthy. It lowered its head, hung with horns
like sharp whirly seashells, ready to butt him into
the next county. Ralph fled.

It was stunning what a fright could do for you.
He'd run like the dickens when, a minute before,
he could hardly put one foot in front of the other
– crossed two fields without feeling a thing. There
could be money in it, he thought, if you could
bottle fright, or put it in a can, or compress it into a
pill. 'Ralph's Remarkable Dual Action Fright Pill!
Anaesthetises and Galvanises. Scare and Scoot.'
Then he noticed the railroad had disappeared. He
was lost.

He was starving, too, so finding a tablet of

chewing gum in his pocket was a lucky break – except while he was blowing the pocket lint off it, he dropped it in the mud. Could he find it! While he was searching, he suddenly noticed, a few fields away to his right, that there were trucks, automobiles and carts moving along the top of a bank on what was obviously a highway. Then a motorbike with a sidecar slowed to a stop and a figure stood up in the sidecar, looking his way.

Ralph ducked, tripped, and fell through a mass of tall weeds into a ditch. He felt as though he'd been eaten alive. He crouched there with the water bubbling over his shoes, wondering if he'd disturbed a wasps' nest. His face was smarting and painful, and white bumps were popping up on the backs of his hands. There was no sign of a wasp, though, so he pulled himself up by the weeds to take another look at the motorbike. The weeds bit him viciously and he fell back into the ditch with a cry of pain. This was his first encounter with English stinging nettles.

He forgot the nettles when he finally poked his head out of the ditch and saw the now stationary bike. The driver was standing on the skyline. Another portly figure was slithering, with tiny steps and flailing arms, down the steep bank. And then – Whoops! – tipping head over heels into the ploughed field at the bottom.

Ralph floundered along in the ditch, bent low to stay out of sight. They could be stopping for a dozen reasons but he certainly wasn't going to stick around to find out if they were hunting for him. But if they were, who the hell could they be? They weren't Fanfield and Mary Ellen, and they weren't dressed right to be police. All English bobbies wore domed helmets. He knew that as well as he knew that the English drove crazy two-storey buses and had a king, like in a fairy story, instead of a proper president.

It was about then that he found the chewing gum he'd lost, stuck to the sole of his shoe. He'd trodden on it when he dropped it. The flattened grey tiddlywink of gum came away in long, sticky strands when he pulled it off. They waved about like feelers before attaching themselves to every bit of him. He considered eating it just to get it out of his life, but decided he wasn't that hungry and ran on with the stuff clinging to him. It seemed determined not to let him get away.

There was a smell in the air that reminded him of sulphur, or something like it. It would be just his luck to run into the devil today. Massive dollars to be made out of a meeting with Mr Big of Hades, though: 'Satan's Secrets – as brought to you by Ralph. Old Nick enflames his Fans.' The thought of flames made him notice he was quite cold now in his grey flannel suit, and he pictured his tweed overcoat chuffing northwards in the train.

Solid dark clouds were coming up over the horizon, and in the near distance there were peculiar black hillocks, with pointed summits, that looked kind of menacing. He must be nearly there, he comforted himself. He clambered over the umpteenth rock wall and rolled over and over to the bottom of a sunken lane on the other side. He lay there cursing. Not so much because of the fall but because of the stump of a milestone, like a midget tombstone, that he'd landed next to. 'Wigan 7 Miles,' it said. He felt the first flicks of rain on his face. Then he saw the dog.

It was a small dog, running slowly towards him. He could see the red ribbon of its tongue hanging so far out of its mouth it looked like it would trip over it. It didn't heed him on the ground. As it drew level, he heard its breath going in and out fast, like the sound of a saw going through wood. Each paw was weighed down with a ball of mud. It was done-in. The wet brown fur of its tail touched Ralph's hand as it passed him, scarcely running now, and he saw it wasn't a dog at all. It was a fox. It disappeared round a curve further down the lane.

He sat up quickly as a baying, hollering pack of hounds flooded into the lane. A frieze of brown and white dogs' legs scissored past him. Galloping behind came men in red jackets, riding high above him on tall horses. One of them was blowing a horn. The noise made Ralph's skin tingle with the thrill of it. He could see the man's bulging cheeks as he swept past, followed by a river of excited riders. They filled the lane with creaking leather and shouts. Hundreds of thudding hooves flicked up gobbets of wet earth that flew into the air like a mud storm and then slackened to nothing as a few little kids brought up the rear on plump ponies going flat out. It was like someone had smacked an old-fashioned Christmas card down in the lane for a second and then whipped it away again, as they all careered around the corner, and out of sight.

'Abroad' could sure throw some surprises at you. He'd never imagined they did this for real anymore. He'd thought it was an olden-days thing, not a modern, 1936 thing. Dad always said the English were keen on fair play – like they invented it. Maybe this was the exception that proved the rule. Skunky exception!

The rain pattered onto the lane, empty now except for – 'Oh Glory be!' as Mary Ellen would say – a riderless pony, trotting sedately in the hunt's wake. Not exactly Dad's limousine, but definitely free transport.

Ralph made encouraging clicking noises with his tongue and it stopped and looked at him warily. Very gently, he eased towards it. 'That's my baby,' he said quietly, and just as gently he stretched out, then grabbed the loose reins. The pony didn't object, and allowed itself to be led up to the milestone.

Ralph had never got up on a horse without a leg-up from one of Dad's ranch hands, so the milestone was a vital mounting block. Unhappily, the pony didn't see eye-to-eye with his proposal. As soon as Ralph had placed his toe through the stirrup, it moved off, with Ralph hopping backwards alongside it on his free foot. 'Bitch horse,' he said, and the heavens opened.

Then, someone took the reins and a boy's voice said, 'I say! Thanks most awfully. You've caught my pony for me.'

'You're welcome,' Ralph white-lied and, without explaining why it was there, removed his foot from the stirrup.

Ralph sized up the boy, brushing the rain out of his eyes and turning up the collar of his jacket, while the boy went on. 'I came off just back there, by Peghams's barn. You know? Poor old Pegs, who's gone bust? Like a lot round here. Place is deserted.' The boy was older than Ralph. He seemed nice enough.

'Would you sell it? The pony?'

The boy looked distinctly unfriendly. 'Not local are you?'

'The pony, though? Dad will pay more than he's worth. Like treble.' The boy shook his head. 'It's a she, actually. Who's this dad of yours who's so flush with money?' Ralph told him. The boy laughed. 'I didn't catch which loony bin you said you'd escaped from, old chap? Now help me up on her like a good man. My leg's taken a bit of a knock.'

'Use the **** milestone like I was going to.'

The boy was taken aback, but he didn't argue and he tried to do what Ralph had told him, while Ralph folded his arms and watched. The leg obviously hurt; and by the look of it, one of his hands hurt even more. The teeming rain didn't help, either. The boy got worse and worse at it under Ralph's silent scrutiny. Serve him right, thought Ralph, remembering the exhausted fox. But after a while he relented.

'Say, Hopalong Cassidy,' said Ralph, but the boy didn't look up. So, not only did this guy have no sense of humour, he never went to the movies, either. 'Do me a favour?' Ralph bargained. 'Call my dad? Tell him I'm okay. And I'll help you up.' The light was fading and the rain was blinding but Ralph thought he saw a slight nod and gave the boy a leg up. So masses of mud on the boy were transferred to Ralph. As soon as the boy was in the saddle, he set off. Ralph called after him sarcastically, 'Thanks most awfully,' and trudged in the direction of 'poor old Peg's' barn.

He heard it before he saw it. It was a stone building at the end of a short track that ran off the lane. The wind was banging the top half of a stable door open and shut. He sloshed up the track. The boy was right: there was no one around. A dunghill at one end of the building steamed slightly in the rain. There was another door wide enough to take a cart, but it was barred and padlocked. It wasn't exactly homey, but it was shelter. Deftly, he clipped the top of the door to the lower half and went in. It was dark once he'd closed the door. A horribly familiar voice said, 'You fix that loud door? Good.' A torch clicked on. It was the French girl.

* * * * *

It was about this time that Mr Fanfield got the

sack. The stationmaster where Ralph's train had made an unscheduled stop was shovelling more coals onto the fire in his waiting room, which the police had taken over as an enquiry office. He was reflecting that it would be a long time until he saw his tea, and his Mrs, that evening when he heard the police Inspector, who was questioning the Yankee fellow, read out the telegram from Ralph's father: 'Fire the tutor!' And Mr Fanfield had gentlemanly hysterics.

The stationmaster gave him an unsympathetic look and went off to calm the other passengers, now shunted into a siding on the stationary train. Meanwhile, Mr Fanfield flew through the story of Ralph's disappearance yet again.

'A little French girl, you say?' the Inspector asked. Mr Fanfield rolled up his tie between anxious fingers until it looked like a cocktail sausage resting against his Adam's apple. Then, he let it unroll again. His eyes were glazed with injured innocence. He licked dry lips. He nodded.

The Inspector shook his head. The nursemaid, Mary Ellen, when questioned, had said, 'What little French girl? I don't know no French girl.' The Inspector passed Mr Fanfield a handkerchief.

'That's your monogram embroidered in the corner, you say. Am I right?'

'Yes'

'How do you explain your handkerchief's presence on the track where the train was halted?'

'I lent it to the French child. She stopped the

train.'

'I see.' said the Inspector, heavily.

His sergeant handed him a second telegram. It was from a *High Up* in the government. A *very High Up*.

'REQUEST AND REQUIRE COMPLETE NEWS BLACKOUT ON YOUR PRESENT ENQUIRY STOP'

CHAPTER SEVEN

HUNTED

Ralph couldn't believe his eyes. The French girl was sitting on a bale of straw – one of the hundreds stacked in the barn – and her ankle socks and shoes were laid out to dry on another bale. She had her attaché case open beside her, filled with delicious looking goodies, and she was calmly spreading pâté onto a round of bread by the light of a miniature torch.

She offered him the bread. 'Hungry?' It was a good guess.

'You gave me a scare,' he said, several bites later. She smiled and began spreading a second slice of bread.

He sat down on the bale next to hers. He couldn't work out what the girl was doing there. He looked into the gloom on the edge of her bright torch-light for clues. There seemed to be nothing else in there but oblong bales of dusty smelling straw. After a while he asked, 'Excuse me. Do you live here?'

'Here!' The girl looked round the barn contemptuously. 'Paris.' Ralph was even more puzzled.

'Then how come you're sitting here handing out sandwiches?' The girl nibbled her bread and pâté before she answered.

'I follow you.' He was so surprised he stopped eating.

'Whatever for?'

'I fear you are too stupid to succeed alone.'

Ralph saw red. He was annoyed enough that he hadn't spotted her following him and he hoped she hadn't watched his embarrassing flight from the ram. But it was the superior way she kept saying he was stupid that really got to him. 'Now see here,' he exploded, and then realised he didn't know her name. Asking her would take the wind out of his sails, so he pushed on regardless. 'Now see here, Whatever's-your-name.'

'Giselle.'

'Gis...' But it got the better of him. 'Gis...what?' He petered out.

'Elle. It is French. I am French.'

'And I'm not stupid,' he said emphatically. She smiled.

'Yet you travel without food.'

'I didn't even know I was getting off the train,' he

protested. She raised a supercilious eyebrow.

'Neither did I.'

Oh, she was smug! He wanted to sock her one. Instead, he said sarcastically, 'Well, you're so smart I guess you have your four-poster bed tucked away in that bag, too.' Giselle spread a third round of bread, then put her head on one side and considered him. 'I get off the train, too,' she explained, 'because I prefer your adventure to mine. It is more extraordinary.' He took the second piece of bread she was offering. She wasn't going to get round him that easily. 'Well, you can't come on my extraordinary adventure. Not unless you stop saying I'm stupid.'

'Very well, I'll stop saying it.'

He'd brought her to heel. It felt good.

'I will just think it.'

He almost choked with anger on her meat paste. He had to show this girl who was in charge. 'Well,' he said grandly, 'you can stay for as long as the food lasts or 'til we find my double. Whichever is the shorter.' Giselle held out her hand. After a second, he realised he was supposed to shake on the deal. She snatched her hand back. 'I point, not shake!'

She rubbed off the mud he'd left on her hand with her hanky. Boy! This girl could make you feel small. 'I point there.' She shone her torch on a hurricane lamp hanging on a hook by the stable door. It made encouraging swilling noises when he took it down; so there was fuel in it. 'But we don't have matches,' he groaned. 'What kind of person keeps a lamp here without matches?'

'A smoker, perhaps.' She felt in her neat coat pocket and handed him a book of matches with a non-committal little shrug.

He took them silently. He wasn't going to ask her if she smoked. Wild horses wouldn't drag the question out of him. Not that he wasn't curious, bursting to ask in fact, but he couldn't tell what it would do to his status if she said yes, she did smoke, and she wasn't ashamed of it; because then it would be bound to come out that he'd tried it once and puked. He couldn't have that. So he lit the lamp and hung it back on the hook and went on eating his bread and meat paste without a word.

The bales now had a pleasing golden glow that reminded him of a time in baby school when he'd acted in a Nativity play. The kid who was playing Mary had been a cute, cuddly little girl. Not like this French one. He remembered, with a spasm of irritation, that he'd been cast as the Ass back then as well.

She interrupted his thoughts. 'Once we have found your double, then I continue my voyage to the Scottish friends of my parents.' She rubbed her hanky over some more invisible mud on her finger. 'They have two loud boys. They play on Bad Pipes.'

'Bag,' Ralph corrected her. He was ridiculously pleased to be able to fault her.

'Comment?'

Now what in the hell did that mean? 'They're called *bag*-pipes,' was all he said, careful not to lose ground. Giselle shuddered. 'It make no difference how you call them, the noise is very rude. They wear also pleated skirts that show purple kneecaps and in the morning they consume hot glue.'

'You're kidding?'

Giselle shook her head vehemently. 'They call it porridge, which is Scottish for hot glue.' She'd made another mistake! Hot glue! He felt a disproportionate surge of joy.

'Talking of what folks eat,' he began, 'My dad...' He hesitated.

'Your rich dad,' she prompted him kindly.

'He says that in France...' He hesitated again. He wasn't sure how to put the question. It didn't bother him if he offended her, but on the other hand he didn't want to end up looking a fool. Foreigners were so darned superior. 'He's pulling my leg, I guess,' he said to cover himself. 'He says they...well, that you...' – it came out in a rush – 'eat snails!'

Giselle looked at him steadily. 'Not the shells.'

Ralph stared at the remains of his bread, spread so thickly with paste. But paste made of what? 'And frogs?' he queried. He was dead worried now about the meat paste. 'Dad was joking about the frogs, wasn't he?' Giselle went on eating placidly and Ralph laughed lightly to disguise his concern. But the laugh came out a bit crazed. 'Like, who eats frogs?' He looked questioningly at the paste. 'Do you?' he almost squealed.

Giselle said, 'The legs are the best bit.' She gathered up her shoes, socks and attaché case. While she was doing it, Ralph quietly placed his bread on the floor.

'I sleep upstairs,' she said to his surprise and took herself off to a ladder, pinned into the wall, that he hadn't noticed before. He supposed there must be some kind of a loft above them. There was a trapdoor at the top, propped open with a wooden stake. 'I mount,' she informed him unnecessarily. While she did, she advised him to turn in because they had to make an early start. 'Tomorrow, they will come seeking you,' she warned. But Ralph wasn't going to let her off lightly.

'Gis – er,' he began.

'Elle.' She looked down on him patiently.

'Yes. Well, eating frogs' legs is cruel.' She treated him to a supercilious stare. She was too much. 'And wrong,' he persisted. 'And disgusting.'

'You eat legs,' was all she said. He was outraged.

'I do not,' he yelled up at her. 'I do not eat legs.' Giselle resumed her climb.

'Lamb's legs,' she said. 'Chicken legs...'

'Smart arse!' he growled.

Giselle climbed through the trapdoor and called down to him, 'Tomorrow we find your doppelganger and then I wipe my hands of you.'

'Wash my hands,' he corrected her joyfully.

'You go outside for that, I hope,' she said sternly. 'Even Americans.' And she disappeared from sight.

She shone her torch into the loft. Rain was dripping through the roof slates and the wind moaned through a boarded-up window. 'How cosy!' she cried, falsely, and took away the stake prop. 'I am snug as a bug on the mat!' And she dropped the trap down.

'In a rug,' Ralph said through gritted teeth.

There was nothing to do and nowhere to go, but he was damned if he would obey her orders and bed down for the night. He paced up and down. She really was too much. He didn't know many kids; in truth, he didn't know any. A few got pulled in for things like his birthday party but he never met up with them again. Even so, even though he didn't have a stock of friends to compare her with, the girl in the loft had to be the most irritating kid in Europe. No. In the world. No. The Universe. This satisfying verdict arrived at, he calmed down. He took off his wet jacket and spread it out to dry on a straw bale. Then he sat next to it and thought about his solemn-faced doppelganger.

The effect his double had on him was strange: it filled him with a kind of excited compulsion, something he'd never felt previously. He remembered, when he was small, doing an experiment with a tutor he'd had before Mr Fanfield – several tutors before him, they never lasted long. The experiment was all about magnetic forces. They'd held a magnet over some paperclips and watched them leap to attach themselves to it. Then his tutor had given him two magnetic bars to hold and said one end of each magnet was south and the other north. When Ralph had placed the two north ends of both magnets together the magnetic bars had been pushed apart; but when he had turned one of them around so its south end was facing the other magnet's north end, he had felt the magnets pulling and pulling. Finally, he'd let his second magnet clamp itself to the first one as though it would never let go. And that's how he felt now. His double was the first magnet and he was the second – turned around suddenly. He was being drawn towards his double so compulsively that he knew he would cross continents to find him. He was wondering if his doppelganger was feeling the same way about him when he thought he heard the sound of an engine.

He turned out the hurricane lamp and listened hard. The rain splattering against the wooden door drowned out all other sounds. But then he heard it again, and it was getting louder. He opened the stable door a crack and took a look outside. It was pitch dark. He could see a single headlamp in the lane, lighting up the streaming rain. Then it swung in his direction. Jeeze! he thought. It's coming up the track. They'll find me.

He shut the door and groped his way, stumbling and tripping, to the ladder. It was hard to climb straight up the wall in the dark like a frigging monkey. The old ladder was full of splinters, too. He banged on the trapdoor. 'Open up,' he hissed. 'Someone's coming.' He heard her scratching about over his head. 'Open up,' he implored, but she whispered back, 'I cannot. There is no handle.'

Her torch was lighting the empty slot in the trap where there should have been a metal ring to pull it up by. 'You must push your side,' she whispered.

He held the top rung with one hand, found the trapdoor with the other and pushed hard. It wouldn't budge. 'Push, stupid boy,' Giselle whispered. He whispered back, furiously, 'What do you think I'm **** doing?'

'Push harder, then, stupid.'

He lent back, letting the top rung take most of his weight, and pushed harder. But the rung he was standing on snapped beneath his feet and, with a jolt, Ralph was left clinging to the ladder with one hand. Gymnastics were not his favourite thing. In fact, they were not his thing at all. He hung there like a sack of frightened potatoes. Then, his weight tore the entire ladder from the wall and he sailed backwards through the dark barn.

The door opened in a blazing rectangle as the headlamp of the vehicle outside cut a shaft of light right into the barn. A man in a heavy overcoat and trilby hat moved into the doorway. All Ralph saw of him against the glare was his broad silhouette, and his long shadow thrown across the floor, before the door crashed shut and there was darkness.

He blinked away the light image of the figure jumping in his eyes and peered out from behind the straw bales where he'd landed on his back. There was silence. Had they gone?

He ducked back as a torch flicked on and the beam wandered across the barn towards him. He froze as it passed him and went on its way, only to move onto his jacket spread out to dry. Ralph cursed inwardly for being such a fool as to leave it there. The owner of the torch stepped forward. Ralph saw the toes of his shoes enter the circle of light cast on the floor. They were strange black and white shoes that were somehow familiar. Then the beam wheeled back to his bale and the shoes started towards his hiding place. They were coming for him.

One of the shoes stepped heavily onto his rejected slice of bread and pâté. The shoe skidded, then both shoes disappeared from Ralph's sight as their owner's feet went from under him. Ralph heard him land with a heck of a thump on the floor, and the crunch of breaking glass as the torch went out.

The silence that followed was so intense Ralph could hear the beat of his own blood in his ears. It went on for so long, he wondered if the man had knocked himself out; but no such luck.

A highish, wheezy sort of voice said quietly, 'Hello there. Hello?' Ralph held his breath. You could have heard a feather fall. Not a peep from the French girl. 'Lend us a hand up, eh? Young feller, me lad.' The voice wheedled softly. Ralph sat like a stone. The girl in the hayloft was still as a stiff. After a while, he heard grunting and snorting, like a pig farm had moved in. Ralph strained his eyes to see what was happening. Then, the barn door swung open again and, in the light, he saw a bulky figure crawling out into the rain. On the threshold, the man coiled back like a slug to pull the door shut after him. Ralph caught a glimpse of his profile. It wasn't pretty.

An engine started up again outside, but he stayed

hidden. There might be more than one of them –
someone left behind to nab him as soon as he put
his head out of the door. And anyway, Ralph was
scared. He'd expected Fanfield or the police to come
after him, not a stranger in the dark. Who the heck
was he?

He waited until long after the engine had died
away and he could hear nothing but the rain lashing
against the door. He made his way over to it. Very,
very slowly, his hand found the latch. He raised it
soundlessly and inched open the door. Except it
didn't open. He forgot about being cautious and
gave it a real shove, but it still didn't move. The
Shoes Man had shot the bolts on the other side and
locked him in.

He leant against the door. A rumble of thunder
mingled with the sound of the rain falling outside
– outside, where he'd give anything to be right now.

Then he remembered the girl in the hayloft. 'Oh
boy!' Ralph said in her direction. 'We've sure got
problems, Gis...er...olé.'

CHAPTER EIGHT

NO STRANGER

Ollie opened his eyes. It was black as the ace of spades. Lightning flickered behind some thin curtains and lit up a bedroom. Of course, that's where he was – in bed in the new digs. Was it the lightning or the hunger that had woken him?

He remembered how the Pig had arrived at the digs by taxi, still nursing a burnt bum and a grievance, and in a foul temper. He was three-and-a-half hours behind everyone else, but just in time to ban Ollie the supper on offer. As soon as he had found a spare pair of trousers, he took himself off for the evening to 'a little place' he knew that was open on a Sunday night. Bedroom lamps had to be out by nine, he instructed them and walked off into the rain.

Jess had already gone upstairs and Grinling was lying, pickled out of his head, up in a small box room of his own. The landlady invited Miss Bellamy and the rest of them into the back parlour to listen to the wireless. As it turned out, there was so much interference that all it could do was make a noise like chips frying. The landlady said it was a sign of bad weather, so they gave up twiddling the tuning knob and played a game of draughts instead.

There was a good fire downstairs and it encouraged them all to stay up and enjoy themselves. The landlady's daughter sang songs at the piano. Everyone else tried to prevent the landlady from seeing Silver, who was doing mocking, silent warbling behind the girl's back. No one upstaged Silver.

Towards bedtime, the landlady sent her daughter to fetch a leather suitcase from the top of her wardrobe. She opened it up and lifted out sheets of yellowing tissue paper that smelt so strongly of moth balls it made your eyes water. Underneath was a wedding dress – a really old-fashioned one – and while Heather helped Silver to try on the veil, the landlady brought out a boy's grey pullover, woollen socks and a tie, and a grey flannel suit. They were hardly worn, and she offered them to Ollie because his own were in such a mess after the fight. He turned them down politely because he couldn't pay for them, but she said he was to get them on and no arguing. It wasn't the money she was looking for; just someone they'd fit.

Ollie heard John give a snort of disbelief as, yet again, Ollie was given something for nowt. Miss Bellamy said it would be okay to accept them; it would save her taking Ollie to the ragman in the market tomorrow for a second-hand coat. Well, she got through saying about a half of it. They guessed at the other half.

The clothes were the warmest Ollie had ever worn, but he reckoned feeling comfy in them would take him time. They were obviously a dead boy's clothes. The boy's feet had been bigger than his. Right whoppers! But the rest fitted a treat. He lay in bed and remembered what a surprise it had been to see himself in the mirror. He'd looked exactly like every other respectable schoolboy in town in his grey flannel suit. One of the crowd. Almost like a 'real' person.

He closed his eyes. But a scream made him open them again, fast. There was another scream, then another. Cripes! What sort of digs was this? The screams were gruesome. Is that what had woken him? He badly wanted to snap on a light, but like most of the places they stayed in, there was no electricity in the upstairs part of the house.

'It's coming from the girls,' he heard John say, sleepily, from his corner of the room. Ollie got out of bed, trying to remember where the girls' room was.

Heather woke so fast that she was sitting on the edge of her bed before she realised that it was the screaming that had woken her. She could just see

Silver by the light of the street lamp filtering through the curtains. She was sitting up in bed with her hair in curlers, so it had to be Jess who'd screamed. She'd stopped now, though, and was just moaning.

'Light the lamp, Silver,' Heather said, trying to sound calm and grown-up.

'God! She scared me,' Silver complained, feeling around on the bedside locker for the matches. 'Sh... ugar!' she said as she heard them hit the floor. She slid out of bed in her long white nightdress and crawled about, hunting for them.

'Just light the lamp.' Heather was making her way over to Jess's bed.

Lightning flashed across the washstand, with its pitcher of water and basin and the slop pail underneath. It lit up the crowd of bedsteads in the small room where the girls were sleeping. A clap of thunder followed the lightning, and Silver put her head under Heather's bedspread. 'Mother!' she exclaimed.

Heather bent over Jess anxiously, who murmured at her not to light the lamp. 'It'll land us in trouble.'

Jess could tell from Heather's comical face, looking down from under the tightest of hairnets, that she was almost as frightened as Silver was. She patted Heather's hand comfortingly. 'I had a nightmare.' But Heather could scarcely hear what she was saying. The pain in Jess's side came again and she gasped. 'I've got such a pain in me guts, Heth. A right corker.'

The bedroom door opened and Silver and Heather

leapt back into bed. 'Ollie Pigott,' Heather scolded when she saw him in his pyjamas in the doorway, holding a candle. 'We thought it was your dad back from the pub.'

Heather climbed out of bed again. Her floral nightdress was as worn out as the rest of her clothes, and it was so short that she must have owned it since she was half the height she was now. She gave it a precautionary, cover-up tug.

'Who's screaming?' asked Ollie.

'Jess is poorly,' she replied, and Ollie felt a spasm of fright in his stomach. Jess was never ill.

Jess wouldn't hear of it, though, when Heather said she'd fetch Miss Bellamy from downstairs, and Ollie backed her up. Miss Bellamy's understanding of illness was as minimal as her cures. She had two: one was Vic ointment – a single sneeze and she'd smear a pungent dollop of it round your nostrils so the smell snaked up your sinuses and blew the top off your skull. You could forget about having a nose, let alone a cold! For everything else that wasn't a cold, there was Ex-Lax. It was the Ex-Lax that had earned her the nickname of 'Nurse Toilet Trots'.

Heather said dolefully, 'She's got onto that TCP gargle now.'

'You'd be better off fire-eating,' Jess murmured.

'Now now, Jess. Charity. Judge not lest ye be judged. She means to do good.'

That was Heather all over, thought Ollie. Just as you'd got into your stride, grousing about someone, she'd go all Goddy on you and make you feel right guilty and mean. That was because Heather had found the Lord. Ollie once made the mistake of asking her where she had mislaid Him in the first place, and got an earful. 'God and jokes do not mix, Ollie Pigott.' Trouble was, he hadn't been joking.

Heather smoothed Jessie's bed cover. 'The TCP is in case it's catching.'

'Catching!' Silver backed away from Jess's bed at a rate of knots. 'Do you reckon she'll pass it on?' She returned Heather's reproachful look with an artless little simper. Ollie wondered why Heather couldn't ever get it through her head that if you were going to be a star, like Silver was, then you had to think about yourself, and nothing but yourself, every minute of the day and night. Naturally, with such a packed timetable, there was no time to fit in worrying about anyone else. But then Silver took Ollie by surprise. 'You're ever so sweaty,' she told Jess. 'You should have a doctor.'

There was another flurried dash for the beds as the bedroom door opened again. Ollie went under Jess's. But it was only a groggy-looking Grinling brandishing a chamber pot and demanding where the murder was, and John yawning behind him. They looked very grave, though, when Heather put them in the picture about Jess. The entire troupe stood round Jess's iron bedstead in the cold room staring at her helplessly, while the thunder grumbled in the distance.

Ollie adjusted the candle he'd put down on her bedside cupboard so it wouldn't singe the photo of her mum she had propped there.

Heather kept a prayer book on her locker, Ollie noticed. Silver just had her jewel box, which was a cigar box covered in gold paper. She never let it out of her sight.

Jess's face screwed up with pain and Silver said again, 'Can't we run for the doctor?' She nudged Grinling with his chamber pot. 'Do you mind, Grinling? You're tipping that at me.' Grinling promptly turned the chamber pot upside down over her head and Silver shrieked.

But the chamber pot was empty. 'It's me weapon against the murderer,' Grinling told her. 'You'd have been delighted to see me and me *po*, Silver, if you was being murdered.'

Jessie said faintly, 'I can't waste good money on a doctor, Silver.'

'Not even a cheap one?' Jess shook her head on the thin wedge of a pillow. 'There's nine of us back at our house.'

Ollie knew what she meant. Jess's mum was a widow, and her eldest brother had been out of work for months. Every payday, Jess went down to the post office and sent most of her wages to her mother in a registered envelope. Jess was the only breadwinner in her family.

The troupe hung about unhappily. Grinling felt Jess's pulse and asked if the pain was girl's trouble. Jess shook her head again. No one dared mention Pigott, except in a roundabout way. Even bringing up his name was like asking for some kind of vicious comeback from the fates.

'The landlady's nice,' said Ollie. 'Maybe she'll let you have a lie-in.' The Youngstars weren't due to rehearse with the new theatre's orchestra for Monday night's show until after John, Silver and Ollie got out of lessons. 'You could stay in bed 'til the band call. I could ask...' He stammered on the word 'Dad'.

Jess tried to sit up, gave a groan of pain, and everyone moved to help her lie down again. At last she said, 'Are you nuts, Ollie? If Pigott finds out I'm poorly, I'll be out of the troupe and on the street with me suitcase, faster than wink. Then where would me mam be?'

No one argued with her. Jess had told Ollie that things were so bad that her brother had walked all the way to London with hundreds of other men to show the blokes in the Houses of Parliament that there was no work and no money for food. A Hunger March, she'd said it was called. After the treatment the Pig had handed out to him, Ollie felt qualified to go with them. He was starving.

Another worried silence fell while the Youngstars stood about indecisively. Then Jess said, 'Now you lads, back to bed. Us girls need our night's beauty sleep.'

She sounded more like herself, so they all cheered up and trooped off obediently. John paused in the doorway and grinned at Heather. 'It would take more than a night's beauty sleep, Heth to get you up to scratch. More like a month of Sundays.' He dodged as Heather threw a shoe at him.

The shoe hit Ollie instead, but he didn't say anything because Jess was beckoning him to come back. She nodded at the drawer in her bedside locker and when he opened it, he found the sandwich she'd been given on the train. He couldn't wait to get his teeth into it. He tried to smile at her with a bulging mouth. She smiled back faintly. 'I thought you could do with it.' She closed her eyes.

He stood next to her, chewing. The lino floor felt cold to his bare feet. He knew he shouldn't disturb her, but he always discussed everything with Jess and he was longing to broach the subject of the boy in the train. But she murmured, with her eyes still closed, 'Don't start again about doubles, Ollie Pigott. I told you, you're seeing things.'

Silver sat up straight in bed. 'Seeing things! Not ghosts?' Her curlers stood on end. 'I don't want to hear about ghosts. Anyway, who believes in ghosts?'

Heather said quietly, 'Simmer down, Silver. If you don't believe in them, you can't be scared of them.'

Silver flounced down on her pillow. 'I shan't sleep,' she warned, as if it were a catastrophe that would blight not just her own but all of their lives.

Ollie lowered his voice in deference to Silver. 'I did see him, Jess. It were really weird.' Jessie sighed. It hurt to talk, but she was worried about Ollie. He could get very peculiar ideas in his head and it was hard to shift them once they were there. 'Look,' she said patiently, 'your dad half starves

108

you, so you see things. People do see things when they're starved. It's called hallucinating.' Ollie looked terribly disappointed, but then an idea struck him. 'Hallucinatin'! Do you reckon I could use it in the act?'

The front door slammed downstairs and Ollie was out of the room and into his bed in a flash. The Pig was back.

When Ollie had gone, Heather whispered, 'Did you hear what Grinling answered when Ollie asked him if he believed in doubles?'

Silver giggled, 'Only in a whisky glass.'

'Yes, but did you hear what else he said?'

'That's enough, Heth.' Jess's voice came sharp enough through the dark to shut her up. Heather turned on her side and prayed silently to God that Ollie would never, *never* meet his double because Grinling had said, 'If you meet your double, one of you has to die.'

Not long after that, his bedroom door opened and Ollie watched his father through half-closed eyes. The Pig was carrying a lamp and he held it over John's and then Ollie's face. Ollie shut his eyes. The lamplight made blood red patches of colour behind his eyelids. His father said tenderly, 'Sweet dreams, lads,' and went out. So Dad was in a good mood. He must have won at darts again tonight. He usually did win.

Ollie could tell by John's breathing that he really was asleep. He lay and thought about his double in the train who turned out now to be whatever Jess had called it. A mirage, was it? Whatever it was, it meant he was seeing things that didn't exist. So that was another nail in today's coffin; he needed specs now!

Then he wondered what he'd do if Jess wasn't better tomorrow. She will be, he comforted himself. It would be hard leaving her if she was poorly, though; and he was definitely leaving. Tomorrow night, after the show, he'd run away. He'd got it all planned.

CHAPTER NINE

NO EXIT?

'Attention!'

Ralph snapped awake. He was freezing. He felt half dead.

'He returns.'

Whose lips were pressed so close to his ear? Who was whispering? Yuk! The French girl!

He jerked his head away and sat up in the rustling straw. Her hand gripped his arm like a claw. 'Silence,' she ordered, and now he could hear why. There was the sound of an approaching engine. Narrow lines of daylight were showing in the cracks at the top and bottom of the stable door and he swore silently. They'd been caught on the hop. Goddammit! He was aching to pee, too.

He glanced at the massive staircase of straw bales

he'd built the night before to rescue her, dimly lit now by the bluish morning light. It was the shape of half a side of a pyramid and by the time he'd finished hauling and dragging and lifting the bales, it felt like he'd built a pyramid, too. His arms hurt with stiffness. He'd never worked like that for anyone. And for no money too!

When at last he'd reached her and pushed the trapdoor open, she'd climbed down without a word of thanks, let alone praise, and they'd sat and wrangled about what they were going to do next until the lamp burnt out of fuel and they must have gone to sleep. And now here they both were without a plan in place.

Something blotted out the lines of light slicing through the door cracks. It had to be a person. Sure enough, the bolts outside were shot back. As one, they rolled behind a bale. The door swung open. There was no one on the threshold. After an interminable pause a corpulent figure slid into the barn and stood, just inside, in the gloom.

Ralph was almost sure it was the same man as the night before. He looked the same wide shape. Then he saw the black and white shoes. Definitely the same guy. He was big, but was he too big for the pair of them to bring him down? Ralph cursed again that they hadn't made a plan. Too bad if he started something and the French girl turned out not to be the fighting type. He didn't stand a chance on his own. If only he didn't want to pee so much.

But now the Shoes Man closed and bolted the

bottom half of the door and began pulling bales of straw across it. He did it so darned easily compared with the hours of heaving it had taken Ralph. But why in hell was he doing it? Then the answer dawned. He was blocking their way out but leaving enough light for himself to see by.

He lifted one bale after another, as if it had been a pack of thistle down, until there was a narrow gap left at the top of the doorway. That done, he took a cursory look around the barn but his real attention was on the stairway Ralph had made. It was five bales high, but it had taken Ralph fifteen of the things to build it.

The Shoes Man hoisted himself up onto the first bale and shone his torch up at the open trapdoor. Then he went up another massive step. If he turned round now, Ralph thought, he would look straight down on the French girl and himself, where they were hiding. A bird's eye view of his quarry. But he didn't. He climbed on up the whispering, rustling giant steps and then, with a lot of puffing, wormed his way up through the trapdoor. They saw his black and white shoes vanish into the loft.

Ralph shot up the steps like a terrier after a rat. He got a glimpse of the man's back as he examined a boarded-up window. Ralph leant across, found the far edge of the trap and pulled it up over his head so that it crashed shut, trapping the Shoes Man in the loft.

As he tumbled down the bales again, he could see Giselle hadn't wasted her time, nor had she attempted to unblock the doorway, but simply clambered up and posted herself through the gap at the top. Ralph saw a flash of legs and white socks as she disappeared. In seconds he'd followed and was spread-eagled in the mud next to her in the shining daylight.

But there was no time to celebrate. They could hear the Shoes Man tearing at the boards across the blocked window and then, unmistakably and horrifyingly, the sound of a pistol shot. Giselle grabbed Ralph and dragged him to the other side of the Shoes Man's Standard car parked a few paces away.

'Out of firing.' She could hardly speak and Ralph was so scared he'd stopped wanting to pee. They clutched each other as another crack of a bullet rang out. Ralph eased himself up just high enough to see straight through the car's windows. As he did, the man's hand appeared through the boards that were blocking the window above them, prising them apart. He'd shot his way out. Any second he'd pick them off too.

Then something went their way. 'The keys are in the ignition,' he hissed. Giselle's query came back. 'You motor?' Ralph shook his head.

'Then I do.' Still crouching on the ground she reached up and opened the passenger door. 'Zut!' She exclaimed. 'There is no steering wheel.'

'It's over on the far side.' He was as surprised as she was.

She slid over into the driver's seat and Ralph

whisked in beside her. As he did, they heard Shoes rend another board away. The little car was really basic, nothing like Dad's limousine. He shook the trivial thought away. It was a car, for skunk's sake. And this was a crisis.

Giselle turned the key. The starting motor whirred funereally and fell silent. A couple of boards from the window crashed down beside them. The man's face was at the window. Giselle turned the key again, she was panting with fright. The engine started. Her right hand scrabbled at space. 'Nothing is right,' she moaned to Ralph. 'All is like a mirror.'

It was the kind of thing a preacher said, not a kid making a getaway. Then he saw what she meant. It wasn't just the steering wheel; all the other controls were the opposite to where they should be, too. 'Well you're the genius, French,' he shouted. 'Drive through the ******* looking glass.'

She took the long, walking stick of a gear lever with her left hand and pushed it into first gear. Ralph had the presence of mind to release the hand brake in between them – it took both hands – and the little car bounded forward in a series of bunny hops so that Ralph's teeth crashed together. A bullet smacked up splatters of mud on Giselle's window as she pushed the car into second gear and they rolled away down the track.

Ralph looked back, craning to see through the slit of a rear window. The Shoes Man was out, sitting on the sill with his legs hanging in the air. Ralph saw him launch himself at the ground and land up to his neck in the dung heap below. Ralph chuckled and Giselle shot him a surprised, concentrated look as she turned a wild right off the track and rumbled along the lane. 'He's in deep shit,' Ralph explained.

*   *   *   *   *

A couple of hours later, Jill and Pamela, out hacking in the glorious half term freedom, came upon a tramp squatting by the brook in his underpants and vest. His trousers were spread on the grass and his coat and clownish little hat hung from the branch of a willow.

'Put your trousers on at once, you dirty thing,' Jill scolded him from the commanding height of her pony. They'd cantered off home and told Mummy, and Mummy had telephoned the police, speaking into the daffodil head mouthpiece in a hushed voice. But when the police constable had laboured up the drive on his bicycle an hour later to interview them, all they could really remember about the 'dirty man' was that he had been wearing black and white shoes and a big ruby red ring.

The constable noted it down with a sigh. It had been a trying morning. Yesterday had been bad enough, with the entire force called out looking for a little lad snatched from a train and he wasn't allowed to breathe a word about it, not even to his sympathetic wife, who had dosed him with cocoa when he'd turned in at last. The lad must be a 'someone' all right to merit a news blackout. But this morning was worse. There had been three independent reports of a Standard car being driven in the direction of Wigan in a very erratic manner. The driver must be mad or drunk.

*　*　*　*　*

'These English,' Giselle gasped as she swung the little Standard from under the wheels of an oncoming lorry. 'They drive like they wish to die.' And Ralph couldn't agree more.

'Why,' he asked after their fourth near miss, 'don't they stick to their side of the road?' But they were already zigzagging into their fifth bout of slow, evasive action before she could reply.

The driver of the approaching car was white-faced and pop-eyed with disbelief as the Standard, still grinding along in second gear (Giselle couldn't locate a higher one) drove steadily towards him on his side of the road. Thinking of his wife and children, he squealed around the Standard and left it out of sight round a bend where it trickled over the verge and finished up, tip-tilted with one wheel in the ditch.

'Bon!' Giselle said, calmly switching off the engine and looking down at Ralph who was on the side, hanging in the ditch, 'We are stationary.'

'Stationary!' Ralph was boiling with anger at the motorist. 'We're stuck, French, thanks to that maniac, and we're still miles from Wigan!'

'Cheer upwards,' she advised.

'Up,' he muttered.

'Without the help of your maniac, we would drive straight past Wigan. I have no knowledge of how to halt.'

She got out of the car and Ralph followed, clambering over the leather bucket seats and onto the verge. 'So merci, Monsieur Road Dog.'

'Hog,' Ralph corrected her.

'Fly!' She replied. Before he could tell her that there was no such thing as a Road Fly, Giselle was hustling him down into the ditch, through the hedge, and dragging him at speed into a field of cows, who all cavorted playfully after them. She threw a clod of earth at them and they frolicked away.

'What the heck?' Ralph asked, but she didn't need to answer. He could hear for himself the regular trilling of a police car's bell and saw, back on the road, a bunch of policemen pile out of a patrol car to examine the ditched Standard. 'Beat it,' he said and they ran like rabbits to the shelter of some woods.

Once in the safety of the trees, Giselle selected a mighty oak.

'I go to the cabinets,' she announced.

'Do you?' He was mystified. She frowned and waved her hands at him. Now what did that mean? Wave back? She treated him to one of her sighs. So no – she definitely had not meant him to wave back. She walked behind the oak. And light dawned.

He backed off and selected his own tree. 'Going to the cabinets,' he repeated. 'Now that's a new one.' He sighed with the wonderful relief.

CHAPTER TEN

WIGAN

Ralph eased a potato from the small of his back and watched the countryside rumble by. If anyone had told him yesterday that he'd be riding along in a horse and cart, piled high with muddy potatoes, he would have laughed in their face.

Gis-*whatever-her-name-was* hadn't taken too kindly to his running up out of the fields and begging a ride. She was all for not drawing attention to themselves. But the boy driving the cart hadn't seemed at all surprised to see them both. He'd touched his cap and said something about a half term, which Ralph thought was probably an English measurement of the distance to Wigan.

Giselle explained later that it was a school holiday. 'It comes between the main holidays,' she said. 'It is for rich kids. I think they get tired quickly, these rich kids like you.' He wished she wouldn't go on about him being rich. As if it made him some kind of weakling. In fact he wished she wouldn't go on about most of the things she went on about. He gritted his teeth. He was stuck with her until he found his double, but when he did find him – Oh boy! she wouldn't see him for dust.

As the cart got under way, they'd exchanged nervous looks and Ralph had called out to the boy, 'Say, Buddy.' 'Buddy' was what the men on his dad's ranch called one another. 'Buddy, are you happy with this side of the road?' And the boy called back that he was completely happy and if Ralph wasn't, all he had to do was jump off. 'Don't mind me,' Ralph had replied hastily.

'I won't,' the boy had answered. Then a car had driven by, going the opposite way, without a toot of protest. 'Do you know what?' Ralph had whispered. 'I think these English folk drive on the wrong side of the road, Gis.'

'Elle,' she said. 'Barbaric!'

'It sure feels kind of murderous,' Ralph agreed.

'In Scotland, it is worse. They drive pony carts in the middle.'

It had begun to drizzle and the boy had pulled up and come round to the back and given them each a split potato sack. He'd shown them how to put the corner over their heads and hug the rest round them like a hessian cape. They sat and discussed the Shoes Man as the cart trundled towards Wigan. The

120

boy pointed it out to them as the patch of grey mist in the distance.

They had both seen Shoes on the train. They were united on that, but not on how or why he had followed them and tried to shoot them. 'It is my belief,' Giselle said emphatically, 'that this Shoes is a bad man who would like to kidnap you because your father is rich and will pay big, big money to retrieve you.'

'A ransom?' Ralph wasn't so sure.

They stopped arguing for a minute to take in the changing landscape. The fields were giving way to slate coloured hills with such smooth sides and pointed tops that they looked like vast, abandoned witch's hats. There were railway lines running this way and that between them. They could see black bucket-shaped containers crawling up the hills' sides and disgorging more slate grey stuff on the summit. Some of them seemed to be on fire and there was that smell of sulphur again, Ralph noticed. The sky was as grey as the hills. A train, running parallel with the road, puffed grey smoke out of its funnel as it drew a clinking line of trucks, heaped with coal, through the scrubby, grey land. The driver told them the hills were slag heaps, which meant nothing to either of them.

Ralph resumed the argument. 'If Shoes is after a ransom for me, why did he try and shoot me? I'm his hostage.'

'Maybe he just shoot our tyres? To halt you?' By now the horse was clopping through the outskirts of Wigan. They passed what, to Ralph, looked like a huge spinning wheel stuck up on pylons. It dominated a mess of large grimy sheds, railway lines and conveyor belts. He could see dirty young women pushing iron tubs about on tracks. There was a sign on one of the sheds: a name painted in dusty letters, which was the only clue to what the place was. When they asked him, the boy driver replied that surely they knew a colliery when they saw one. Even the air was gritty with coal.

A gang of men came out of the colliery gates. Their clothes and faces were black with coal dust; by contrast their teeth flashed brilliant white as they spoke to each other. Ralph thought that if they hadn't looked so tired, he could have taken them for a minstrel show. Their wooden clogs made a rhythmic noise like tap dancers as they walked towards the town.

'Maybe it's you Shoes wants to kidnap?' Ralph suggested optimistically, through the din of the miners' clogs. He wriggled around on his pile of potatoes to face her under his sack. 'I mean, who in the hell are you?'

'Garçon!' Giselle called to their driver. 'Halt.' And she climbed down and ran across the road to a red telephone kiosk.

Ralph jumped down too and walked around on the pavement to chat to the boy. Fortunately, it took him out of sight of the four policemen driving by in the opposite direction. 'Police everywhere today,' the boy said. 'There's been a murder up on the railway, I heard.'

'That's shocking,' Ralph said absently. He was wondering whom the French girl could be talking to so hard on the phone.

*   *   *   *   *

It was at this point that Fergus, aged ten, took a phone call, though he was under strict instructions from his parents not to. It was for the servants to answer the telephone. But he happened to be passing through the great hall and picked up the receiver before anyone so much as heard it ring. Fergus listened intently, promised he would do as he was asked, and replaced the receiver.

With a quick yank of a knee sock, he set off in search of his mother, the pleats of his kilt swinging. From far above, a Scottish lament groaned. It was his father, playing his pipes as he stalked the battlements in a force eight gale.

Fergus located his mother in the morning room where she and his elder brother were sharing a thin fire. When he said, 'Giselle's just phoned,' she dropped her sewing and Alasdair laid down his newspaper, The Scotsman, which was boring anyway.

'And?' his mother prompted her son, quite overlooking his flagrant breaking of the telephone rule in her anxiety. 'The railway company have lost her luggage,' Fergus informed them cheerily. 'She thinks they might even have left it in Paris, but she's staying with some friends of her parents in Belgravia in London while she buys some more clothes. We're not to worry.'

'When will she be here?' his mother asked.

'She didn't say.' His mother put her sewing aside.

'The poor, poor little mite! Thank heavens she's safe.' She rushed away to convey the good news to her husband.

Alasdair looked out of the window at the endless snow and asked, 'Do you think that prayers can be answered?' He seemed uneasy.

'If they weren't, why would people pray?' Fergus replied. 'If it didn't get results, it would go out of fashion.'

'But answered this quickly!' Alasdair shook his head in sheer wonder. He grinned at Fergus. 'Phew!'

The lamenting bagpipes ceased. Their father was evidently receiving the glad news from their mother.

Fergus said, 'I'll tell you one thing for sure: she wasn't phoning from friends. She was in a public phone box and she wasn't in Belgravia either. She reversed the charges and the operator asked if I would accept the call from a place called Wigan.'

'Wigan!' Alasdair looked distinctly guilty. 'She sounded cheerful though, did she?' he questioned his brother anxiously.

'Perfectly.'

'I wouldn't have wanted her harmed. But Wigan! God has maybe over-reacted a wee bit.'

'Where is Wigan?'

'Lancashire,' Alasdair said, as though it were the

outskirts of hell.

'Let's go and build a snowman,' was all Fergus said in reply.

'Let's,' agreed Alasdair.

'And then let's guillotine it.'

The bagpipes skirled into action again. A merrier tune: 'Scotland Forever'.

* * * * *

The potato cart dropped Ralph and Giselle outside Wigan railway station. They returned the sacks to the driver gratefully and went into the booking hall. And came straight out again. There were two policemen on duty at the barrier.

* * * * *

It was about then that a police cell door slammed behind Mr Fanfield. His legs were shaking so badly that he had to sit down on the narrow ledge of a bed attached to the cell's brick wall. He fingered the single grimy blanket – the only bedding provided – and wondered how this injustice had come about. Within hours he'd gone from chief witness in the drama of Ralph's abduction to prime suspect. Even Mary Ellen had betrayed him. He was innocent but no one would believe a single word he said. He, Fanfield, who could win any argument hands down, had lost this one. He was in jail. He was in a mess; he was in what Ralph would have called *'deep shit'*.

CHAPTER ELEVEN

LIVERPOOL

Old habits die hard. Ollie meant to go to school, he really did. The Pig had failed to find an old codger to teach the Youngstars privately, so they were booked into a local school for the week. School wasn't Ollie's idea of paradise but he set out willingly with Silver and John. Silver had reported that Jess was no better and so he didn't want to do anything that would put the Pig's back up before the afternoon work-through with the band.

But somehow Ollie lagged behind. Soon, he found himself alone in the city, staring up at two great stone birds on top of one of the tallest buildings he'd ever seen. It was an exciting place, too. There were ships of all sizes. Some of them were massive and others were right tiddlers. They were almost on top of you, almost on the pavement it felt like, and every one of them was busy. He could see cranes dipping up and down as they unloaded their cargo. The wind smelt of the sea and of oil and there were gulls pitching about in it, calling that funny weeping scream that they make.

He was in the docks; they stretched for miles to left and right of him. The noise was something chronic, too, coming from the mass of horses and carts and lorries struggling round each other, to and from the big warehouses.

A little railway line that was raised up in the air with the engine puffing along, pulling the coaches like a ride at a fairground, made the place right rowdy. He had to strain to hear the newspaper sellers who were running along with the local paper and shouting out the headlines: something about a film star opening a cinema. It grew even noisier when a taxi horn blared right in his ear and a boy with his arm in a sling and his hand bandaged up leaned out of the window.

'Thank goodness I found you,' he said, to Ollie's surprise. He could see a bloke sitting next to the boy who was looking disapproving in a servile sort of way. But who on earth was this boy beckoning him up close with his good hand? 'They are onto you, old man,' he confided in a low voice. 'So be careful. True to my word, I tried to phone your pa and the police answered instead. Extraordinary luck I caught sight of you here of all places. Our man Johnson here has just brought me into town to have one of those X-ray things.'

But Ollie was gone; a disappearing back view, racing for the school. The 'Truant Men' must be after him. He'd had a brush with them before. They could run like a greyhound. It was their job to collar any kid out and about during school hours and take him back to school. If they caught him, the Pig would be in trouble with the law, and he would half kill Ollie. But who the heck was the posh lad who'd warned him? A guardian angel? And were all angels posh? That didn't seem like a fair balance.

As he ran, he wondered if his mum was an angel. Surely not a posh one? There was no way of knowing what his mum was really. The Pig walked out of the room if Ollie so much as started on the subject.

'Someone needs to pin their ears back and listen,' was how a jaunty man, wearing a big red rosette in his lapel, greeted Ollie as he panted up to the school gate.

He patted Ollie on the head. 'School's closed today. Your teacher must have told you.' Another man, who was sitting on a campstool and ticking off names on a list, said tartly, 'School's a polling station today.'

He was wearing a rosette, too, but his was blue. 'Do you know what a municipal election is, boy?' Ollie could tell by the sneer on his face that he didn't expect Ollie to know the answer. Well, who was he to disappoint Mr Blue Rosette? He shook his head and as Blue Rosette drew breath to explain, Ollie ran off, dodging through the trickle of grown-ups going in and out of the gates to cast their votes.

So the posh lad wasn't a guardian angel. A hoaxer of an angel? A practical joker? Whatever the boy with the sling was, it was peculiar the way he'd seemed to know him. Perhaps the lad had mixed him up with someone else. An angel who needed specs, like he did himself, maybe?

He noticed John's red blazer on the crowded pavement and caught up with him. He was staring into one of the windows of what, to Ollie, seemed like the biggest department store ever built.

'Look at that,' said John. He sounded right low. Ollie looked. The window was full of ladies' hats. 'Bargain Basement Bombshell' a notice read. 'Hand made hats all 3/11d.' He wished he could buy one for Miss Bellamy to replace the hat he'd ruined. But he'd only got the dinner money she'd handed out that morning. Not nearly enough.

John obviously expected a reaction to the hats, so Ollie picked on one at random. 'The green one is – very green,' he ventured. John gave him a shove with his elbow. 'Not the hats. Me!' He pointed at his reflection. 'I'm so tall,' he said gloomily.

For Ollie, who had the converse problem, it didn't seem too terrible a doom to live with. John's reflection was an envy- making head and shoulders above his own.

John went on. 'One of the chorus girls last week actually said to me, "You're a big lad for a juvenile, aren't you?"' He gave the hats an anguished look. 'What if I get too big?'

129

'You've got to grow up sometime,' Ollie objected. John turned a patient, handsome gaze on him. 'I'm thirteen, Ollie. When you're a juvenile you've got to look like one. It's rule one.'

Ollie smiled. 'Better ask Grinling how he does it.' A piece of advice he later regretted giving his friend.

The two of them mooched on at a loose end. They wandered past some huge buildings hemmed in with monuments and statues. 'Now that's what I call t-too t-tall,' said Ollie. He looked more closely at the inscription on the towering column with the figure of a man on top. 'Would you credit it!' he exclaimed. 'They've put this fellow up there for inventing the wellington. That's laying on the gratitude a bit thick.'

'It's his name, twerp,' John corrected him, without any malice. 'If you bothered going to lessons, Ollie, you'd know Wellington won the battle of Waterloo.'

Ollie had heard of Waterloo. It was a railway station in London. He didn't enquire why anyone should have a battle over it. Ignorance, he'd learned, was best kept hidden. 'Who d-did he beat?' .

'Forget.' John smiled his dark, handsome smile. It's not a fair world, Ollie thought: even ignorance just made John more decorative.

They passed a couple of lads busking in the shadow of a statue of a pouchy-cheeked woman on a horse. One boy was playing the fiddle and the smaller one was dancing. At long last there was something really interesting to look at. They'd never seen an

Irish jig before. John's feet were already tapping as he tried to pick up the steps. It was difficult, really difficult, even for John.

The older boy's cap was lying on the pavement guarded by a dog which, Ollie thought, had to be the ugliest dog in the world. The dog was sitting up next to the cap and begging. He was no crowd puller: people were rushing by without a glance, and the noise from the clanging trams nearly drowned out the violin. The cap was empty. On impulse, Ollie chucked in the money that Miss Bellamy had doled out to buy his dinner.

* * * * *

'Attention.'

Ralph had his head down against the wind that was blowing hard, but he looked up hopefully at Giselle's warning, expecting to see the two policemen emerging at last from Wigan station. They'd been hanging around outside, willing them to come off duty. But instead of the policemen, there was a small kid coming out of the station exit, carrying a grubby notebook and wearing cranky glasses with one lens blocked out. As the kid walked past them, Giselle caught his arm. 'I recall you.'

'You can call me what you like,' he replied. 'I'm not stopping. School dinner hour's nearly over. Let us go.'

But Giselle tightened her grip on his arm. Ralph knew how that felt. 'You write the trains?'

'It's a free country, me dad says.'

Ralph could tell he was trying to scare Giselle off, bringing in his dad like that. But the threat of a clout from a meaty dad had no effect on Giselle. She gripped him harder and the boy's one visible eye screwed up with pain. Ralph felt sorry for him and said quickly, 'Maybe you can help us.'

'Not likely!'

'With trains.'

The boy looked at him slantwise from an eye that seemed more interested in the side of his own nose than looking at Ralph.

'We were on the express yesterday, headed for – I don't know – Scotland?' The swivelly eye lit up.

'Best day of me life. It were diverted. Came into Wigan due to rail works. Like a king it came.'

The small train-spotter proved a mine of information. They soon learned that the train Ralph's double had been travelling in was going to a place quite close by, called Liverpool. Only then did Giselle release the kid and he went off to afternoon school rubbing his forearm. And their luck held: the two policemen came out of the station. One of them consulted a watch as they moved out of the station yard. They'd obviously given up on their replacements. Ralph was elated. 'Liverpool here we come,' he crowed.

But Giselle was white and leaning against the station wall. 'My case! I leave it behind the tree. It contains all. We have no money!' Ralph went the colour of a sheet.

'And no food.'

'Behold,' she said, 'a useful alligator.'

'No way am I eating alligator.'

He followed the direction of her point. A nun was forging towards them, her habit and wimple flung this way and that by the buffeting wind. Behind her, tripping along in demure crocodile formation, was a score or so of girls in dark blue school mackintoshes and matching brimmed felt hats.

The girls halted at the entrance while the nun went into the booking hall. Giselle darted in amongst them, all smiles. 'Your uniform is so chic!' Ralph heard her lie. 'What is your destiny?' A minute later she was back, holding one of their hats. She pummelled Ralph in amongst the giggling girls, bunged the hat on his head and pulled down the brim.

When the nun returned with a fistful of tickets, they all moved off again in her wake and the ticket inspector at the barrier waved the group through, with Ralph and Giselle unobserved amongst them.

The girls, it transpired, were a convent school choir and they were off to take part in a singing competition in Liverpool. Eight giggling members happily concealed Ralph and Giselle in their carriage, shared their packed lunch with them and parted company at Lyme Street station in Liverpool.

Ralph hadn't liked coming into the station. The train had crawled in between high, glistening rock and dirty brick walls, like a worm burrowing into a grave.

'Jiminy Cricket!' Ralph was even more put off when he saw the size of the city outside the station. 'This place is gigantic. How in hell do we find him in a place this size?' He stepped off the sidewalk and a car skidded and pulled up with a screech just short of him. A rugged, auburn-haired young man in a smart suit, who had so many freckles on his face it looked as if it had been splattered with mud, wound down the driver's window and yelled at him.

No one, for as far back as Ralph could remember, had ever yelled at him. The stream of servants who looked after him, and who'd come and gone over his eleven years, certainly didn't. They kept him clean and fed, but they rarely spoke. Being yelled at disagreed with him. He walked up to the open window and yelled back at the rugged young man – '****, ******,' – and so on – until they were surrounded by a jam of stationary trams, horses and carts, bicycles, and a car with loudspeakers on top, bawling at everyone to vote for a candidate and then at Ralph to get off the road. Giselle dragged him away.

'You draw the eye,' she scolded, and hurried him between the traffic, over the thin metal tramlines, to the other side of the road. 'Jeeze,' he said, gazing at a vastly wide stone building that was so dirty it looked charred. 'Upend that and it would be a skyscraper!'

A couple of shabby boys were crouching beneath the stained statue of a fat queen, called Victoria, on a horse. She had to be a fantastic rider, Ralph thought admiringly, riding on the horse sideways like that. The boys were engrossed in counting out some coins, watched over by an ugly dog. Giselle shook Ralph's arm. 'Chin up. The city is big, but we do not look for a needle in a stack,'

'Hay.'

'Hey what?'

'Not *hey* hay. *Hay* hay.'

Giselle looked at him frostily for a minute, then ignored him. 'He wore a red blazer. We search for a school with the uniform of a red blazer. Simple.'

The smaller of the two boys smiled up at Ralph. 'Tell your friend it's a lot harder than it seems.' Ralph smiled back. He didn't know the kid from Adam, but anyone who implied a criticism of old Frenchie Gis was a friend of Ralph's. 'It's a rare old dance,' the boy added. 'It could take years.'

Giselle bristled, but before she could give the boy a piece of her mind, a gawky girl ran up to Ralph. 'Quick, your dad wants you, he's looking for you!' Giselle grabbed Ralph's hand and ran with him, leaving Heather staring after them in surprise.

Giselle concealed them both behind a column and peered round it to satisfy herself that the gawky girl wasn't following. Then she turned on Ralph angrily. 'Why did you not say your rich dad was here in Liverpool?'

'Because I didn't **** well know,' he raged back at her. 'All I knew was me and Fanfield and Mary Ellen were going on a vacation to Scotland to see a monster in a lake and there was a chance Dad would join us.'

She gave him one of her sighs. But when she reached the point where she appealed to the invisible sympathiser behind his shoulder, she gasped and took a step back. 'You okay, French?' He glanced behind him and saw a harmless column with a guy on top and an inscription. She seized his hand again. 'Come away. There is a very, very bad man here.'

'Shoes?' He asked nervously.

'Wellington,' she hissed.

* * * * *

John sighed and Ollie looked up guiltily from the wet Nelly he was scoffing in the workmen's café down by the docks. John had paid for their lunch. 'I'll pay you back, John, honest.' John didn't ask how. Ollie never had any money.

'When your ship comes in,' he agreed and refrained from pointing out that Ollie had given the two boy buskers all the money he had in the world.

Together they left the café and drifted along towards the theatre. People crowded the quayside, jabbering and shouting. There were people from different parts of the world, too. Mostly there were working blokes in cloth caps and rolled-up shirtsleeves, even though it was cold. And there was a right multitude flooding off a local ferry. Posh men and women mingled with the crowds as they disembarked, and a sprinkling of extra-smart posh ones, too: men that looked as if they'd been hanging in their own wardrobes all night with their hats on. But the rest of the folk milling about were so poor you didn't like to stare at them.

Some sailors rolled by them – they really did walk with a roll, Ollie noticed. They each had a pack hoisted on their shoulder. One man had a little monkey balanced on top of his pack. It bared its teeth at Ollie in a crackpot smile. Ollie wished he had something he could give it. John pulled his arm. 'Time for work.'

The two boys caught up with Heather, who was also on her way into work. She nudged Ollie. 'So, our Ollie, who's the new girlfriend?' Ollie looked at her blankly. Girlfriend? Was this Heather's irritating way of talking about him and Jess again? She was always insinuating things about them, always pulling tricks – like drawing a red heart on his dressing room mirror in greasepaint, with Jess's and his initials at either end of the arrow that pierced it. Making it look as if he'd drawn it himself.

John gave Ollie a cheerful thump on his back. 'Hello, hello. What's all this then, Ollie?'

Heather smirked, pleased to have got their attention. 'Holding hands they were, John. In broad daylight.'

Ollie sighed. 'Tell whoever is writing your script for you, Heth, their plot's up the spout. They're sacked.'

They turned in at the stage door and there was Silver, snuggled into the stage doorkeeper's little booth and drinking a mug of tea he'd brewed for her. It didn't surprise them. Silver could get blood out of a stage doorkeeper but she seemed very quiet for Silver. 'Crowd of girls got after the poor lass,' the stage doorkeeper explained. 'Six against one did you say?' Silver nodded.

Miss Bellamy appeared, looking unusually animated. 'The Boss wants you in the bar,' was all they could get out of her and she sent them through the pass door into the opulent, thickly carpeted public area. They walked softly to the front of the theatre.

'Six girls!' John gave Silver an appraising glance. 'Got off lightly didn't you? Not a scratch on you.'

Silver tossed her head. 'I saw them off.'

Ollie looked at Silver with new respect. 'Get away!' This was a side of Silver he had never seen – a prizefighter side. She smiled. 'I gave them my tortoiseshell combs and, while they were fighting over which one of them was going to have them, I took off.'

'Nasty lot, the kids up here.' John was looking very Southern and superior. 'You today, Silver. Ollie and me yesterday.'

Silver tossed her beautiful hair. 'It's not everyone can carry off tortoiseshell combs. The girl who got them – she looked a dog's dinner.'

They'd reached the doors to the bar. Ollie didn't dare think about why his dad wanted them there. He knew it would be to do with Jess.

CHAPTER TWELVE

JESS

But Jess was there, in the gloomy room, perching on a tall stool by the bar and looking the picture of health. A thin woman seated at an upright piano took no notice of them but went on knitting a baby's white matinée jacket for all she was worth.

They hung around, not talking. The smell of booze and tobacco was so strong it seemed almost solid. Ollie thought that the unlit bar had a spooky feel, too. All the beer pump handles were shrouded in white tea towels. They looked like a chorus line of little ghosts.

Eventually Grinling turned up and introduced the piano woman as Miss Reeve. She nodded at them, took a drag on her fag, returned it to the metal ashtray balanced on her black keys, and went on clicking her needles while the rest of them stood around staring at their feet. Something was up.

Grinling had a go at making conversation by telling them about some new fangled thing that was being launched that night. The Youngstars weren't that interested and even less so when it transpired you had to live within a forty-mile radius of London to benefit. Grinling was enthusiastic, though. 'Imagine it,' he invited them. 'Imagine the wireless with pictures.'

No one seemed inclined to imagine anything at all at that moment, particularly the unimaginable. Grinling was so plainly disappointed that Ollie asked politely if the new contraption had a name. Grinling pronounced the word carefully. 'Television.' Miss Reeve took another drag at her cigarette. 'It will never catch on,' she said.

The swing doors smashed open and the Pig sailed in with his raincoat slung over his shoulder and the brim of his hat pushed back. He threw on the lights and came straight to the point. 'There's another ruddy juvenile troupe in town,' he told them. 'Down at the Pavilion.'

Grinling sucked in his breath between his teeth. 'That's bad planning.' Pigott looked daggers at him.

'They're not much competition, Grinling. Mostly a batch of dwarves pretending to be kids.' As he said it, the Pig took off his hat and bopped Grinling on the top of his head with it. There wasn't a flicker of feeling on Grinling's long, old face as he replied, 'Don't do that, Boss, that's how I got this size.' And

140

everyone laughed.

Ollie couldn't work out how he'd done it but Grinling had somehow scored higher than the Pig with that exchange. Beaten him with a joke. Ollie was glad. Show Pigott pain and you made his day.

'What's worse, meine Kinder,' Pigott mowed on, 'they are doing a Pie Shop sketch the spitting image of our Pie Shop sketch. Don't ask me how,' he snapped when they all looked up startled. 'It's a fact. I've been watching the talentless little hoofers rehearse.' He crammed his hat on. 'Right, meine Kinder! Let's tango!' And the Youngstars looked alert. The Pig always said, 'let's tango,' before he set to work. And this time they were really going to work.

The Pig chucked a roll of music from his raincoat pocket at Miss Reeve. 'I'm reviving the School Room sketch,' he announced. 'In which,' he added with a friendly tap on her shoulder, 'I play a leading role. Jess and Heth,' he boomed, 'you've done it before.'

'And me, Boss,' Grinling said.

'And Ollie,' the Pig boomed on, 'you've watched it a hundred times from the side when you were a little lad.' This was a lie for the benefit of Miss Reeve. Ollie had been appearing in the sketch since he was seven years old, which was illegal because he was too young to be granted a performance licence. The Pig's left eyelid drooped briefly over his round, boiled sweet-like eye and Ollie winked back cooperatively. No point in crossing his dad on the last rehearsal he'd ever have to go through with him.

Pigott handed round cue sheets. 'They're busy on stage,' he explained so they are letting us work in here for a couple of hours. Then we'll rehearse the ending with the school cupboard down on the green. They're giving the old thing a lick of paint in the dock for us.' A props man came in with a skip full of the props they would need. 'After that we'll run it through with the band.'

They swung into rehearsal, putting John and Silver into their new roles with the Pig starring as a sorely tried schoolmaster tormented by a class of disobedient pupils. It was hard work. There were lots of gags and funny biz to learn but Ollie was enjoying himself, even though he didn't have much to do. Pigott had cast him as a dunce, so he spent a lot of the time standing in the corner in a dunce's conical white hat; but all the same, time flew.

It was when the Pig had called to Miss Reeve, 'Let's be hearing you, Phyllis!'; and she had swung into the accompaniment for the final mad chase for the third time; and Pigott was leaping elephantine jumps round the bar, plagued by his pack of delinquents; and Miss Reeve's fingers were skidaddling all over the notes; and Pigott was roaring and whipping them all into a frenzy... that Jess fell over. The music stopped and they crouched round her, their breath coming in noisy gasps.

'Jess?' Ollie touched her shoulder shyly and then looked up at his father, who was looking down at

Jessie with an irritated, interrupted look. 'Ruddy hell!' he panted, 'That was the nearest we'd got to getting it right. Up you get, Jess. We've no time for messing about.'

It was Grinling who had the courage to say, 'Don't think she can hear you, Boss. The girl's fainted.'

'Streuth!' Pigott said. 'What a time to pick.'

He sat Jess up and pushed her head forward over her outstretched legs. Jess moaned and opened her eyes. Pigott was triumphant. 'Dr Pigott does the trick.' He put his hands under her armpits and stood her upright, gave her a little shake, and with an 'All right, my love?' let her go and only just caught her again. 'Oh for Pete's sake, Jess,' Pigott said.

Now Ollie was close to her, he could see why Jessie looked so healthy. She was smothered in make-up to hide how ill she was. He said to his father, 'Call a...' He'd wanted to say doctor but the word stuck and a fusillade of d's came out instead. Pigott pushed him with the toe of his shoe to shut him up, but John said, 'She needs a doctor.'

Pigott sneered. 'It's girl's trouble. Can't expect you to know girl's trouble when you see it though, can we, dear?' John flushed and shut up and Pigott spoke to Jess in a low, confidential tone. 'That's right isn't it, my love? A girl's thing? Nothing that an aspirin won't fix.' And Jess nodded.

Pigott lowered her into a bar chair and wiped the sweat off his face. He sent Heather to Miss Bellamy for an aspirin and watched while Ollie defiantly laid his new flannel jacket over Jess. 'For crying out loud,' the Pig muttered. Then he slapped his thigh and called, 'Righto! On we go.' He smiled at Jess. 'You sit this out, Jess. We can't rehearse your tap number on this carpet and you know it backwards anyway. You'll be right as rain after your aspirin.' And Jess nodded again.

The afternoon continued to be frantic. Miss Bellamy and Heather were up at the top of the theatre in the Wardrobe machining a costume for Silver, whose dress had to be made of masses of pretty but extremely finicky flounces. John came off badly: he was forced into a striped blazer and some short trousers, picked out of the theatre's stock of old costumes. It made him really grumpy. He very nearly looked plain. Everyone else was learning their lines, and Silver was going over and over her new song. Jess went to sleep on the floor of the girls' dressing room.

* * * * *

It was about then that a jaunty man wearing a red rosette said to Ralph, 'Don't you ever listen to a word you're told, young cloth ears?

'All I asked was what time the kids get out of school.' Ralph was indignant.

'Now, now, lad. What did I say to you?' What the hell was the guy talking about? 'Say? To me?'

Now, it was the jovial man's turn to look put out. 'This morning.'

'This morning?'

A man wearing a blue rosette butted in. 'Oh give over bothering with him, Frank,' he said to the jaunty man. 'Can't you see the boy is mental?' He waved his clipboard at Ralph. 'Shoo!' he said. 'Or I'll call a policeman.'

'Hold on, hold on, guys.' Ralph was suddenly excited. 'Are you telling me you've spoken to me before?' The jaunty man felt in his pocket and brought out a threepenny bit. Automatically, Ralph took it. 'Get yourself a good hot tea, son.' But Ralph felt he was onto something – a faint glimmer of hope. It was the first time he'd felt hopeful all afternoon.

So far, Giselle had bossed him until he was out of his mind. Maybe he was mental. She'd forced him to lurk in doorways while she stood on the pavement and, much to his disgust, burst into tears. She'd sobbed until she'd attracted the attention of several passers-by. Ralph couldn't catch what went on between them, but she did it three times in three different places and, at the end of it, she was five shillings up and rushed him off to buy a map of Liverpool with some of the money.

'These English have such tender brains,' she mused, pocketing her change.

'Hearts. What did you tell them?' he asked.

'That I was robbed by bad, bad, men.'

'But that's a lie!'

'I know. See what I do for you. I will go to hell.' She smiled heroically.

'Oh come on, French!' he objected. 'Are you saying it's my fault?'

She patted his hand kindly. 'Yes. But I forgive you.'

He put both hands behind his back so they could not possibly shoot out and smack her one. She was totally maddening. Was it surprising the rosette men thought he was crazy?

* * * * *

That night, when the curtain went up, the Youngstars were all nervous. Monday nights were usually rocky in a new theatre and a new sketch doubled the risk of things going wrong. But as Ollie ran out with the other Youngstars onto the bright stage and saw the dark oblong of the auditorium, filled with the barely visible faces of the audience in front of him, he felt the usual rush of controlled energy sweep over him. It was as if he'd come home.

They got off to a good start; the whole audience shook with laughter at the Pig's attempts to keep his class in order. Silver's sweetly subversive little song got a round of applause and Jess's high kicks round the classroom were cheered.

They were reaching the end. The Pig's final chase of his pupils was in full swing – a jumping, twirling, tumbling, brilliantly organised chaos of disobedience – when Jess fell over and didn't get up. Ollie could see she wasn't going to, either. Her eyes were open but they'd rolled back in her head so just the whites showed, like small birds eggs, in the sockets.

Not a Youngstar faltered. They all went on racing around the stage as if nothing had happened, but they were all thinking at top speed. They knew that the sketch ended with each Youngstar fooling the schoolmaster and hiding from him in the school cupboard.

In fact, the cupboard had a false back, painted to look as if it were stacked with school books, which could be opened to allow people to climb through to the back stage area and shut it behind them. When the schoolmaster finally realises what's going on and throws open the door, they all appear to have vanished. The schoolmaster slumps against the cupboard defeated. Blackout.

The lights go up on the downstage area for the next act to follow immediately – a couple of comedians. If Jess wasn't shifted, she'd be lying there throughout their act. The audience would cotton on that something had gone seriously wrong, which would kill the comedians' laughs stone dead. Unforgivable. It could get the Youngstars fired from the theatre.

The Pig reacted first. He picked up Jess, hung her over his arm and pretended to cane her. Then (a bit unimaginatively, Ollie thought) put her in the cupboard. A few bars of music later, when it was John's turn to open the cupboard and slip inside, Jess fell straight out again. Her head hit the stage with a terrible crack. The audience thought it was hilarious and all part of the fun. Grinling helped John up with Jess and all three crushed into the cupboard.

Meanwhile, Ollie, Heather and Silver were carrying on with the chase. Then Silver, unfamiliar with the sketch, mistook her cue – or so she said later – and took off into the cupboard too early, leaving them with what Ollie thought of as acres of notes of music to get through before he and Heather could follow suit; and besides, there was nothing rehearsed for the three of them alone.

He ran up to his father, who was filling in time galumphing about with his schoolmaster's cane, and snatched his mortarboard off his head. 'Chase me,' he instructed him and, still holding the mortarboard, did a back flip away from the Pig, followed by five more. Pigott did as he was told, clowning along behind Ollie, apparently unable to retrieve his hat.

Heather joined in, following Pigott with her special frog leaps and finishing with the splits. Frog leap, the splits, frog leap, the splits. Ollie cartwheeled past them both. 'Go, Heth,' he said, and she obeyed. She stuck one leg straight up over her head like a steeple, and jack-knifed herself into the cupboard.

Under the applause the audience gave her, Ollie told Pigott, 'On all fours, centre stage, act fuddled' and then did a triple forward roll across the front of the stage to put space between them. Pigott obeyed, executed a decent enough pratfall and landed on all fours, exactly where he'd been told. Ollie frog leapt him. 'Still as a rock,' he instructed his father and rammed the dunce hat on the Pig's head.

Then, using the routine Pablo had taught him, he jumped astride Pigott and straight up into a handstand on Pigott's back; he held it while the audience clapped, then went down into a back bend and off the Pig's back in a forward flip.

He kicked his father's bum once, twice, to howls of delight from the audience, and went into the cupboard on cue. Everyone was clapping, but the people high up in the cheap seats in the gallery, or 'the gods,' as it was called, stamped and cheered him as well. The Pig didn't have to act his collapse.

Ollie never stopped running until he reached the stage door. 'Call a d-d-d-d-doctor.'

'All done, lad,' the stage doorkeeper said, as a rugged, auburn-haired young man with a dense splattering of muddy freckles on his face came through the stage door. 'This is him now.'

Classy grey suit, Ollie noted. The rugged, young doctor gave Ollie a sharp look. 'All I have to say to you is 'Watch your tongue'.' Ollie nodded mutely. He was more than satisfied that Jess was getting the best. It had to be a right fantastic doctor who could diagnose his stammer just by looking at him.

He wondered how it was done. Maybe he gave off stutter signals that a doctor could pick up. He led the doctor up the flights of steps towards the girls' dressing room in silence, but then his curiosity got the better of him. 'How can you spot it?' he asked the doctor. 'That I stammer?' But the doctor wasn't giving away trade secrets. He said meaninglessly, 'Type of language you use, a speech impediment would be welcome.' Then really impressively he said, 'You certainly didn't stammer this afternoon.'

Which was nothing short of brilliant. The man even knew he didn't stammer in rehearsal because he had a silent role!

They hurried up more flights of steps, standing aside for a trick cyclist bounding downwards to make his entrance on stage. 'What's happened?' the doctor asked. 'One of your mates walked under a car's wheels too?' Ollie was stuck for a reply. He didn't know what the man was talking about.

In the dressing room, Miss Bellamy was holding smouldering brown paper under Jess's nose, which was Miss Bellamy's completely useless way of bringing someone round from a faint. The rest of the troupe huddled next to Jess, who was still unconscious on the floor. Grinling was trying to get a little brandy into her from his filthy flask.

The doctor didn't waste much time examining Jess. 'Hospital,' he said to Miss Bellamy and scooped Jess up in his arms. She lay with her head hanging back and her dark hair falling over the sleeve of his smart coat. 'We'll be quicker going in my car than calling an ambulance.'

Then Pigott barged in. He was all cleaned up after the act and smiling agreeably. He asked what the dickens was going on. No one dared tell him. The Youngstars fussed miserably round Jess. Ollie stroked Jess's hair and Heather straightened the skirt of her costume. 'Just where do you think you're taking that girl?' the Pig asked.

'Hospital. I'm the theatre doctor. She should have been taken there hours ago. '

The Youngstars glanced at each other guiltily. Ollie was confused. He'd covered up Jess's illness because she'd asked him to. But the doctor would say it was the worst thing he could have done for her, and that he'd acted like a stupid kid. And suddenly that's exactly what he felt like: a stupid kid.

But the Pig was blustering now and saying to all intents and purposes he was a father to Jess.

'Man to man,' he said, winking at the doctor. 'You know what kids are like. Anything for attention.' The doctor shook his head.

'I think she has a burst appendix.'

'Burst!' Pigott exclaimed. 'Jess hasn't burst anything. If she had, we'd have heard it go.' He appealed to the Youngstars. 'Anyone hear a bang from her? Course not. Anyway,' Pigott said, sliding seamlessly into a lie, 'her dad's a Christian Scientist. Doesn't believe in hospitals.'

Ollie said fiercely, 'He's d-d-d-d-'. But the Pig swept Ollie to one side.

'Doctor, the show must go on. Jess would be the first to say so. She's a great little trouper. I'll let her off the curtain call tonight and she'll be fit as a fiddle tomorrow.' He blocked the doctor's path. 'I'm responsible for this child. I say where she goes.'

It was then that Silver delivered her ultimatum. 'Mr Pigott,' she said in a high nervous voice, 'if you don't let Jess go to hospital this minute, you won't have a show at all because we,' she took a deep breath, 'will go on strike.'

The Youngstars looked at her as if she'd grown

three heads. Heather almost asked what a strike was. Ollie was ready to hug her. Silver addressed the other Youngstars. 'We will, won't we?' The Youngstars nodded hardly-at-all-nods but, none the less, nods.

Pigott opened his mouth to speak but not a word came out. Ollie was brimming with admiration for Silver but he couldn't help wondering if she would have been quite as ready to threaten Pigott if it hadn't been for the swap over to the School Room sketch. It had left Silver with a much smaller part to play than usual – smaller than Jess's, for example. He banished the thought. He was getting spiteful these days.

Silver was still facing Pigott down. 'What's more,' she said, 'we'll tell the newspapers why we're on strike.' That was enough for the Pig. He stepped aside and gestured the doctor to go. Miss Bellamy held the door open for the doctor and quietly followed as he left with Jessie.

Ollie was expecting a devil of an outburst from Pigott; they all were. But the Pig surprised them by laughing loudly. He ruffled Silver's hair and called her a little saucebox. Then he said he'd phone a few agencies for a substitute girl next morning. 'Get your skates on after the curtain call, Grinling,' he said, 'and we'll push off to the pub. I'll stand you a noggin.' As he left the dressing room, he called back, 'Silver, you take over Jessie's part.' The door slammed behind him and Ollie saw a hint of a smile of achievement cross Silver's pretty face.

Grinling took a gulp of brandy from the flask he was still holding. 'I've me own plans for tonight, thank you very much!' he told the closed door.

Ollie sat down at Jessie's place and straightened her already neat rows of make-up sticks on the dressing table. Now all the drama of her collapse was over, he felt frightened for her. What was hospital like? Jess would wake up in a strange place with no one she knew. Grinling touched him on the shoulder. 'Run down and ask stage door which hospital they took her to, Ollie. You'll be wanting to visit.'

After Ollie had left, Heather said, 'He was fantastic, our Ollie. Saved the act.'

* * * * *

It was about then that Ralph laid down his knife and fork with a contented sigh. Giselle had spent a good deal of their five shillings on a supper for them both in a café down by the docks. Ralph had never been in such squalor in his life. The place was hot and greasy and the tablecloths were nothing but layers of stained newspaper; but the pie and chips had been a feast. He looked out of the window at the reflection of the streetlights rumpling the dark water and felt happy, despite his surroundings. Tomorrow they would find his double. The need to find him, which had become so strong now that it almost hurt, was going to be satisfied. All they had to do was go back to the school where the jaunty man with the red rosette had sworn blind that Ralph had tried to go this morning. It just had to have been his double. By some miracle, in this huge crowded city, they'd hit on the one school his double attended. Everything was looking good for tomorrow. And the bonus was, he'd be rid of French.

An ugly thought came to him. 'Hey, French,' he asked. 'Where are we going to sleep?'

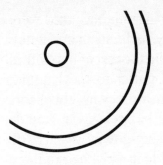

CHAPTER THIRTEEN

HIT AND MISS

Ollie hadn't expected it to be so cold out in the back yard where he was hiding in the washhouse. His candle lit up his breath so it looked as if he was smoking a fag. He wasn't sure if he was scared or excited but he was certainly breathing fast – he was puffing like a steamboat.

He had to take off the dead boy's shoes to get out of his pyjama trousers. The earth floor felt damp and slightly slimy to the soles of his feet; they'd been doing the Monday wash in here. There wasn't a smidgen of warmth, though, coming from the ashes of the fire they'd burned under the copper in the corner to heat up the water; it was well and truly out.

He hung the pyjamas over a hook on the back of

the door. They weren't really his pyjamas; they were the dead boy's. The landlady had lent them to him because Miss Bellamy had sent the rest of his clothes that had been tipped in the gutter to the laundry. The landlady had given him a dressing-gown too. He'd never had one of those before. Always made do with his mac. The dressing-gown was useful. He'd hidden his trousers inside it. Now he put them on. But he'd forgotten socks. Big mistake that; no socks makes you noticeable.

He put the dead boy's shoes on over his bare feet and thought how strange it was the way you keep to a plan despite a change in your circumstances. Here he was, still running away, even though Jess was ill in hospital. He must really want to go if he was prepared to leave her like that. He would write to her as soon as he got there. First thing he'd do when he arrived. Jess would understand. Then he had a good idea; Jess could join him when she was better.

Someone was outside in the yard. He blew out the candle and stood stock still in the dark. How many more unwanted meetings? He'd already met Heather on the stairs as she came up from the lavvy out here in the back yard. Then he'd run into his father reeling through the front door, average drunk. 'Lavvy,' he'd replied to the Pig's enquiring grunt and escaped into the yard with his candle. But now who was this?

He heard a crash as they opened the coalhouse door and a bang as they shut it; then another crash as they tried the lavvy door. Evidently it was what they were looking for. He heard the door close and the bolt rattle across. As soon as they'd flushed, he opened the washhouse door a crack to see who it was. Bad news! It was John, who'd been sound asleep when Ollie crept out of their bedroom; but now he must have noticed Ollie's bed was empty and be wondering where he was.

John still seemed half asleep, though. He was weaving about the back yard with his torch and nearly scalped himself on the landlady's clothes-line. The wooden dolly pegs she'd left pinned all along the rope jumped up and down like excited puppets. John steadied himself, muttered something about 'The Mother's Union,' and went indoors. Definitely half asleep.

Ollie wondered if he was going to have to wait for the entire troupe to spend a penny before he could make his getaway. Grinling was still out, though, and he hadn't seen Miss Bellamy since she left for the hospital. And Silver was occupied. Heather had told him she was sitting in bed and reading her collection of cuttings of newspaper reviews about herself that she'd pasted into an album. She kept a few loose ones about other girls in the back of the book to spit on. A rave for a fourteen year old called Nova Pillbeam in her first major film role was a big spit favourite. It was right mucky by now.

Eventually, he saw the light fade in the girls' bedroom window as they turned down the lamp. Every other window at the back of the house was in darkness, too, except for the landlady's parlour; but her curtains were drawn. He could hear her and his father laughing in there. So now for it!

He tried the high wooden back gate. It wasn't locked. Nothing to stop him going, then. He slipped out into an alleyway that cut between the rows of back yards on either side and set off, running towards the road at the end.

He took the long way round from Seymour Street to the station, the eightpence he'd wheedled out of John and Silver chinking in his pocket as he ran. He was definitely excited now because he was nearly free – racing down the lamp-lit street towards Lyme Street station.

*   *   *   *   *

It was at Lyme Street station that Ralph and Giselle were slumped on benches in the warm waiting room, trying to look like passengers about to board a train, though really they were going to spend the night there.

'It is very convenient for washing. Ladies and Gents. Parfait!' Giselle had consoled Ralph, who had imagined himself in a bed, however humble. He'd knocked confidently on the door of a lodging house and the landlady who'd opened it had pointed at a notice in the window and asked if they could read. 'No Irish' it said. 'I'm American,' Ralph had protested.

'Even worse,' the landlady replied, and slammed the door in his face. So after much bickering they settled for the station waiting room

And now Ollie was a matter of paces away from them at the station ticket office, holding his eightpence out to the clerk behind the grill. 'A half single please.'

'Where to?'

The question shook Ollie. He'd dreamt of this moment. He'd dreamt of putting as much distance as possible between himself and his father, but now that the dream had to be turned into a destination, he was stumped and bitterly disappointed with himself. What kind of a runaway is it that doesn't know where he's running to? He was so used to having where he was heading decided for him that he'd left this crucial factor out of his plan. A name shot into his head. 'Southampton.'

'There's no train to Southampton tonight.' He got a suspicious look from the ticket clerk – a pasty, gingery man with a little gravy coloured moustache and piercing eyes above wide nostrils. 'Where's your parents?'

'In the waiting room,' Ollie lied.

'Well, tell them there's no train to Southampton.'

'Where is there a t-t-t-train t-to?' The clerk's eyes became even more piercing and suspicious. 'Lots of places. Tell your parents to come out of the waiting room and tell me where they want you to go.' There was nothing for it. He was going to have to go into the waiting room and pretend to look for his parents.

A hand settled softly on his shoulder. Ollie looked down at it and saw an enormous red ring on one of its fingers. He twisted round to see the owner of the hand who was saying pleasantly to the clerk, 'I'll take over now.' It was a man wearing flashy shoes. Black and white. The Shoes Man was saying, 'He gets these ideas he'll hop on and off trains.' He held Ollie's shoulder harder and looked down at him. 'Time to go, kid,' he said.

'Cripes!' was all Ollie could think. He tried to twist away but the Shoes Man's hold tightened and now Ollie was really scared. If he didn't get away from this crackpot, he'd as likely end up murdered, not free as a bird in Southampton.

The ticket clerk was looking like he'd won an Oscar, he was that pleased with himself for guessing Ollie was lying. So there would be no convincing him that the Shoes Man was lying too. No help, then, from gravy gob. Ollie was scared right to the pit of his stomach.

Then, through his panic, he heard his father's voice saying, 'Just what do you think you're doing with my lad?' He'd never have thought he'd be happy to hear that voice. He felt the Pig take his arm and he looked up at him at the very moment when the Shoes Man reached over his head and hit the Pig in the eye – a right whopper.

The Pig fell over on his back. Splat! Onto the paved ground. A woman screamed. The ticket clerk screamed. The Pig screamed. Ollie tore himself free and helped his father lever himself up on one elbow. The Pig was bellowing at the Shoes Man now. 'It's you, isn't it? It's you sending the letters.' Ollie hadn't any idea what he meant.

By now, late travellers were gathering round: some to watch a fight, some to prevent one. The Shoes Man said to the Pig, 'You're drunk, man. Go home. Leave me and the boy alone.' And grabbed Ollie again.

*   *   *   *   *

It was about then that the gawky girl shook Ralph awake. He'd drifted off to sleep at last and wanted to stay that way.

His teeth felt as if each one of them had been individually wrapped in a coat of woolly scum, and now what in hell was this all-angles-and-thumbs girl saying? 'You're dad's looking for you. He says you've run away. Go back.'

Giselle was straightening her coat and tidying her hair and asking, 'Where is he?'

But the gawky girl snapped at her. 'You keep out of this, you floozy. I know your sort. It's you that's led him astray. Jezebel!' Which Ralph had to admit was a darn sight better shot at French's name than he'd ever made.

*   *   *   *   *

A few yards away outside, bystanders were helping the Pig to his feet, who unexpectedly launched a surprise attack on Shoes: using his head like a battering ram he drove it into the Shoes Man's stomach shouting, 'I'll see you damned before I pay.'

Ollie was pushed behind the Shoes Man and crushed up against one of the many pairs of steel pillars that supported the girders and the massive glass roof of the station. As the Pig pummelled Shoes, Ollie got the impact too; if he didn't take refuge he'd be squashed alive, so he did take it – upwards.

The pillars were coupled together with decorative metal roses and he used them as foot and handholds and shinned up like a cat burglar to the safety of one of the girders, thirty feet in the air. Not many people noticed him go; the fight was far too interesting. He swung himself along a girder. The steel was icy cold to his hands and he was glad to reach a narrow shelf that spanned the station and to snuggle into the shelter of the huge station clock. Its hands clunked onto midnight as he arrived.

He looked down on the tops of people's hats and heads and on the caps of the porters who had appeared and were trying to stop the fight. They were having some success, so he knew it was time to go. He eased his way across the face of the clock, steadying himself with the minute hand, and walked pigeon-toed along the shelf to the other side of the station where he climbed down another pair of pillars. As soon as he reached the ground he was surrounded by schoolgirls in navy blue hats.

They were laughing and saying, 'We won, we won.' One of them held up a silver cup. Another asked where his girlfriend was and kissed him on the cheek, then fell into her companions' arms giggling. Another serious one said, 'You're in deadly danger,' and Ollie wondered if she had second sight. How else did she know the man in the funny shoes had tried to kidnap him? 'So stop looking for your doppelganger,' the serious girl said.

Doppelganger! That was a new one! Sounded rude. He must remember to check it with Silver. 'It means one of you must die,' the serious girl said. So doppelganger wasn't rude, it was more of a death threat. He hadn't a clue why the girl was being so menacing but it sounded pretty much in line with the sort of thing that could happen tonight, so he did his best to get away from her, smiling gallantly. But they pressed round him eagerly and so he missed seeing his double emerge from the waiting room with a girl. They took one look at Shoes belting the Pig and bolted. And because they bolted, Ralph and Giselle missed seeing Ollie too.

'Girls, girls,' an exhausted looking nun called to the crowd round Ollie. 'Hurry, or we'll miss the *next* train as well.' And they all rushed after her, laughing. Ollie stood there rubbing his kissed cheek for a minute. More crazy angels. Liverpool was full of 'em. Then he took off.

* * * * *

It was about then that a tiny man, wearing a smart overcoat and hat, came bowling along Lyme Street towards Ralph and Giselle and greeted them warmly as they hurried away from the station. He raised his hat and smiled. 'It's a grand night for it,' he said and on he went. But they didn't notice its significance because they'd been too rattled by the sight of Monsieur Shoes, right there in Liverpool. Had he followed them? And why was he laying into someone else now with such terrifying efficiency?

'That guy sure was lucky Shoes didn't use his gun.' Ralph said, casting a longing glance at the Adelphi Hotel as they raced past. The very doors were bathed in luxury. 'Where to now, French?'

'Hurry,' was all she would say.

* * * * *

Ollie made for the digs. He had to. He couldn't think of anywhere else to go. Unwillingly, he retraced his footsteps. He passed The Hops, a big popular pub that had been bursting with life, when he'd gone by on his way to the station; it was closed now and the lights were all out. To his surprise, he ran into Shtum, the Wonder Brothers' 'top mounter', hanging about outside. He'd understood the Wonder Brothers had all stayed in Bolton while they found a replacement for Pablo.

'Where's your Dad?' Shtum asked him. Ollie was plain amazed. Shtum spoke! He'd never heard that before. Some people had even said Shtum was dumb.

'Station,' Ollie replied. 'There's a blighter beating him up.' Another surprise: Shtum looked interested.

'Help,' Shtum declared, and loped off in the direction of the station. A further surprise: Ollie had never even seen Shtum and his father so much as pass the time of day. The Pig could certainly claim some unlikely friends.

Ollie walked on even more slowly. He felt guilty. He should really go and help his father, too. The trouble was, he was too scared of him to go.

The landlady let him in through the front door and gave him a mug of delicious cocoa in her parlour. Her daughter brought him a biscuit. 'Your dad's in a right tantrum,' she warned him.

'Don't scare the lad, Hazel,' her mother said, and then added unhelpfully, 'He's wild is Mr Pigott.'

'Somebody tipped him off you'd done a bunk.'

'Who?' The girl shrugged. She didn't know.

It could only have been John, which was yet one more surprise; a depressing one, too. It wasn't like John to tell on another Youngstar. Ollie dunked his biscuit in his cocoa and waited for the wrath of his father to fall. He didn't have to wait long.

The Pig came in with a blood-stained handkerchief clamped to his nose and with eyes that looked like pin pricks in his swollen face. But he'd hardly pointed a trembling, accusing finger at Ollie before the landlady had the Pig lying out flat on the parlour floor and was putting a cold key down his back to stop the nose bleed and sending Hazel for a wet flannel to wipe his face. This silenced him temporarily, but before long he glared up at Ollie from behind the flannel, then snatched it away impatiently, catching the poor daughter a wet-fish flip with it. The Pig's outburst was delayed again while he begged her 'a thousand pardons, dear lady.'

But the storm couldn't be postponed forever. The Pig raged from his prone position. 'Look at me! Caught in a brawl on account of you. Battered because of you. My reputation in ribbons because of you. Wait 'til I get my hands on you.'

Grinling pushed open the door. 'Glory, Boss!' he exclaimed. 'You've a gory conk on you. What have you been up to?' The Pig drummed his heels on the floor with frustration. 'What have *I* been up to?'

The Pig tried to stand up but the landlady said he was to stay there or he'd have to pay for any blood on her carpet. The Pig lay still as a mouse at that and demanded, in a pent up fury, 'See what happens when you go roaming about after dark?' He swirled the wet, and now bloody, flannel like a propeller and everyone retreated. 'You could have been murdered by that madman.' The Pig mopped his nose. 'Fortunately, he left that job to me. Just wait, Ollie Pigott, 'til I'm on my feet. Just wait.'

Grinling said, 'He's growing up, Boss.'

'Not for much longer if I have anything to do with it. He'll be lucky if he sees the next five minutes.'

'Boss, Boss. He's a lad.' Ollie was grateful to Grinling for trying to rescue him but he couldn't see how stating the obvious would do the business. Not surprisingly, the Pig spluttered at Grinling, 'Of course he's a lad. Do you think I'm daft?'

'And what do lads get up to?' Grinling stepped

out of reach as the Pig lashed out with the flannel, and he gave him a playful look. The landlady began to laugh and nudged her daughter, who smiled broadly.

The Pig said, 'You mean he was meeting a girl?' His voice was packed with disbelief. Rightly, Ollie thought. But Grinling winked at Ollie and went on to describe the beautiful girl he'd seen him with – eyes like sloes, raven hair – until the Pig began to laugh, too, quietly at first, then uproariously. 'Trust you, Ollie.' His vast stomach convulsed on the carpet. 'Trust you to run into a nut-head on your first date!'

He lay there talking bewilderingly about wild oats. In the end, they were all laughing fit to bust, Grinling was offering brandy all round from his flask, and Ollie was off the hook. Puzzled, but definitely not in for the duffing-up of his life from his father.

*   *   *   *   *

It was about then, too, that Shtum, along with a crowd of bystanders at the station, watched a couple of firemen escort some *kisky cove* in black and white shoes down from a pillar that, for reasons best known to himself, he'd climbed up and then got stuck on.

CHAPTER FOURTEEN

A FRIEND IN NEED

It was cold now, really cold. Giselle had offered him the loan of one of her gloves but Ralph had declined. They were kind of lacy. He was sorry now, though. The street they were walking on was like all the others they'd been tramping: darkened little shop fronts, small terraced houses, hissing gas lamps and nobody around except policemen on the beat. They gave them a wide berth. Any place remotely sheltered was already occupied by sleeping humps of homeless people. They had no place to go.

They'd agreed to keep moving in case they froze to death but they were walking more and more slowly. The soles of Ralph's feet were aching with cold. He tried to cheer himself up with the thought that tomorrow morning, when they found his doppelganger, the boy would have some cosy little place he'd take them to – maybe not so little, a cosy mansion more likely – where they'd get fed, and rest up, and talk and discover – what? What would they discover about each other? He delved into his deepest thoughts. Did he have some information about his doppelganger there? But if he did, whatever it was, it remained elusive – or maybe just frozen solid.

A blast of hot air hit his legs as they walked past a basement grid. French must have felt it as well because they both stopped and stood over the grid, letting the warmth run into them. It was kind of relaxing. It softened his mind into an almost trance-like state of comfort and sleepiness until, with a jangle, the glazed shop door next to them opened and a small person popped out.

Ralph wasn't sure if it was a girl or a boy. A girl in trousers was a novelty. Ladies wore slacks sometimes, but surely girls were dress people, like French.

'You hungry?' The questioner was definitely a girl. They nodded. Her eyes slanted into creases under her coal black fringe as she smiled. She gave them each a cake, then folded her hands inside her short tunic's sleeves and watched them eat.

'My father horrible,' she announced. Ralph couldn't get a hold of the relevance of this remark until she went on in her odd flat accent. 'He call police to standing-on-hot-air vagrants. They put you in orphanage.' She turned to Giselle, 'You they take to convent to sleep.' Giselle could think of a lot worse fates than a stopover in a nunnery, but then the small girl added, 'In morning, the magistrate send you to place for bad ladies.' And Giselle thanked her for the warning and said they'd move on.

As she did, Ralph was aware of his cold aching feet. He licked his fingers, which were sticky from the cake, and saw one of them was white and bloodless at the tip. 'Jeeze! French.' His voice was shrill with alarm. 'I'm getting skunky frostbite here!'

The little girl smiled sympathetically. 'Maybe you like come inside?' And Ralph practically ran through the shop door after her. Giselle shrugged and followed them into a bare room with a simple shop counter. The floor to ceiling shelving behind it was filled with neatly packed brown paper parcels. Then the small girl led them through a door at the back into an inferno.

The room was swirling with steam. One huge man stood head and shoulders above four other equally foreign-looking folk circling a cauldron that was bubbling over a roasting coke fire. The cauldron was vast, about five feet across, and they were poking at something boiling inside it with long wooden pincers. Each time they did it, an angry rumble of seething bubbles broke on the surface and the sharp smell in the room increased as steam rolled over the rim.

It reminded Ralph of a cartoon, in a magazine back home, of a sedate looking missionary being boiled in a pot by hungry cannibals. Not so funny, now. What was in that pot? Or did he mean *who* was in it?

The big man came to meet them. He was sweaty – everyone was, but he was the most sweaty – his black hair was tied at the back of his head in a pigtail and his black eyebrows were drawn together in a bushy frown as he inspected the newcomers critically.

'They very small.' This comment, delivered in the same flat accent as the little girl's, did nothing to calm Ralph's fears.

'Best I could find,' the little girl argued. She explained to Ralph, 'We short of people.'

'Oh Jeeze!' he said faintly.

'You stay night. But...'

'What?'

'In return for work.'

Work! Ralph was outraged. Okay, he was delighted he wasn't going to be eaten; but he never worked – period! No way was he going to work in this hellhole – and certainly not for a bunch of savages with freaky hairstyles. He'd nearly killed himself with the straw bales the night before. All he wanted now was to go to sleep in some place warm.

But before he could say as much, French trod on his foot so hard he thought she'd flattened it. And then there she was, bowing to the big man, who bowed back, and she was saying stuff like, 'It would be an honour to be permitted to toil at his side' and if the big man 'out of the goodness of his generous heart could offer them hospitality in return, their gratitude would know no bounds'.

The big man replied, 'You on rinsing.' He pointed at Ralph. 'You. Starch.' Now what in the hell was starch? Before he could ask her, French was hustled away to a second, just as massive, vat of water.

The little girl said she would show Ralph how to starch collars and drew him through the steam, past a mound of coats and jackets on the floor. There was a red blazer amongst them. Probably a coincidence but Ralph pounced on it. 'Whose is this?' The little girl examined the Chinese writing on a label pinned to the blazer.

'Miss Bellamy.'

'Not a boy's name?' Ralph asked. 'It's a boy's blazer.' The little girl shook her head.

'What boy ever bring his own dry cleaning in? Lady always does it. Mostly mummy.'

Ralph was confused. Why was he suddenly mixed up with a stack of dry cleaning? 'What is this skunk den?'

'This is Chinese laundry,' she told him kindly. 'Clean, not skunk.'

'My name is Ralph.' It was as far as he'd go towards an apology. The little girl introduced herself as Wei and asked him to tell Giselle to ease up on the Chinese courtesies. 'She more Chinese than me,' she laughed.

Anyone who could find fault with French was a friend of Ralph's, so he made an effort to look alert when Wei positioned him at a slatted wooden bench with a washtub on it that was half full of what looked like water. A very small, wiry old lady dumped a basket with a higgledy-piggledy heap of washed and rinsed collars in it next to him.

While Wei demonstrated how to dunk a handful or so at a time in the water, and swirl them around and then lift them out onto a drainer, he learned how two of the laundry workers had been sent home sick and her father was tearing his pigtail off because they'd had so much work on hand.

She'd gone out to fetch some fill-ins for him. She shook her head regretfully. 'So many people without jobs, they easy to find.' But then she smiled at him. 'I not get far. I see Little French all cold and sad outside shop so I tell lies to you about police to get you inside.' She roared with laughter and left him to it, saying it would be supper in an hour.

He dunked listlessly. So it was, 'Little French', was it, not him, who'd got them in out of the cold? At home it was he, Ralph, who was the draw. What in hell had 'Little French' got that he hadn't?

At this point the very small, wiry old lady came back with a fresh basket of collars and directed a stream of vituperative bird noises at him. He didn't understand a word but it was easy to guess she meant:

*'Getamoveonwhatthehelldoyouthinkyouare
doingyounogoodsluggardlylayaboutyouare
creatingabottleneckinthesystem!'*

If he wanted to be Mr Popular, he was going to have to get dunking and swirling pronto.

The supper break came at last and he and Giselle crowded down to the end of the laundry, along

173

with the rest of the workforce, where Wei's mother dolloped delicious smelling food into each person's bowl. They all sat down at a table where she had put out plates of dumplings and spring rolls. Everyone set to; they were all hungry – Ralph was starving – but what was this? No fork, no knife, no spoon. He'd been given knitting needles to eat with. Was this a joke? Who could eat with knitting needles?

He glowered round the table, searching for the grinning practical joker, and saw that everyone else *could* eat with knitting needles and, wouldn't you know it, even French could. There she sat, across the table, daintily piling in the grub while he could only watch. It put him into a murderous fury. He folded his arms across his chest and sat staring at the enticing food. Soon, someone amongst these Chinks would notice he wasn't eating and give him some proper utensils. He sat on. Nobody even looked up. They were all engrossed in their bowls.

Then French skilfully scooped up a dumpling from the plate and, in so doing, caught his eye. He glared back. She looked surprised that he hadn't touched his food, then gave a little comprehending nod and extended the dumpling to him. No way was French going to baby-feed him! With a sour smile, he picked up his chopsticks.

By the time everyone else had finished, Ralph was about a quarter of the way through his bowl, and the food had gone cold. The starch had dried on his hands now, so it felt as if he were wearing a pair of stiff white mittens, which did nothing to improve his chopstick technique. He was miserable and feeling deprived. This was his adventure and yet French, who was talking animatedly to Wei, was getting all the food and the fun. He was hellish tired as well.

Wei's mother leant across the table and asked him how old he was. She shook her head at Wei when she heard he was eleven. Wei's huge father looked very grave and Wei bowed her head in contrition. Evidently it was a skunky crime to be eleven now, Ralph thought irritably. These people were getting on his wick. Next, Giselle was questioned about her age. She claimed she was fourteen – which was a lie – but the folks around the table were all smiles at the news.

Then a family row blew up. It was all in Chinese but it wasn't hard for Ralph to guess it was about him. Wei was doing some spirited talking but Big Dad (kind of ominously it seemed to Ralph) kept pointing at him and then at the door.

French edged over to him where he was still sitting at the table and whispered, 'Eleven is too young to work, stupid. Why did you not say you were fourteen like I?' Ralph blanched. 'You mean they're going to throw me out in the street?'

'Looks like it.'

Ralph had a mental picture of the dark, cold streets. Streets where Monsieur Shoes and his gun lay in wait. He could be killed out there, or frozen solid. He leant his elbows on the table and held his head in his hands. This was not the big adventure he'd envisaged.

But then a surprising ally waded into the argument. Ralph couldn't imagine where she stashed away the power to produce so many decibels of twittering chirrupings, but the very small, wiry old lady of the basket of collars, certainly topped the clamour – and some.

Everyone shut up and listened respectfully while she gave them an earful. It lasted for minutes and, at the end, it was Big Dad's turn to hang his head.

In the silence that followed, Wei ushered Ralph out of the kitchen and down some stairs into a warm-as-toast room, criss-crossed with wire clothes-lines where the laundry was hanging to dry. Curtains of damp sheets, vests, nurses' uniforms, shirts and blouses hung there; and on one line, all by themselves – collars – his collars. He felt a little surge of pride at the sight of them. He'd starched hundreds.

Wei plumped up some big cushions by a peculiar-looking coke stove. It had three tiers of shelves with flat irons perched on each tier so they would heat up on the fantastic heat it was radiating. She put him to lie down on the cushions and said goodnight. She smiled. 'My grandmother like you.'

And he liked Grandma, Ralph thought, as he snuggled down next to the stove. Liked her! He loved her. Good old small, wiry old lady had saved his bacon.

He was shattered, but he couldn't go to sleep. He lay and thought about the red blazer. His doppelganger's red blazer, was it? Liverpool was probably full of red blazers. But if it was the doppelganger's, then who was Miss Bellamy? The doppelganger's mom? Who was a Miss! Whoops! What the hell! Tomorrow he'd go back to that school where the rosette men had mistaken him for his double. He'd walk right in and he'd find him.

* * * * *

Not long after that, Ollie woke from a dream, or was he still asleep? It seemed to him someone was in the room. He couldn't see who it was because he was drifting back into the dream, though he didn't want to. He'd dreamed it so often. He knew how it ended.

He is lying face down on a soft, red carpet. He wants to stay lying there but something is trying to wrench him off it. He clings to the carpet, terrified of being pulled away. He is begging to be allowed to stay on the red carpet and whoever is prising him away cannot get any leverage because he is clinging so fast. Then suddenly he is flying in the air, looking down at the carpet, and weeping.

He woke again. There were tears on his face and right down his neck. There always were. Jess had said a red carpet is what you get to walk on when you're a star and that Ollie was only dreaming about how he wanted to make it to stardom. When he had made it, the dream would stop. Jess was usually right.

John was snoring, he noticed. Peculiar. John never snored. So that was the second unusual thing John had done tonight: he'd turned Ollie over to the Pig, and now he was snoring. Ollie stopped halfway through a yawn. The eightpence! Where was it? He needed that eightpence to run away again. Then he remembered his dad shouting, 'I'll see you damned before I pay'. What had he meant?

He propped his eyelids open with his forefingers so he'd stay awake. He was planning on leaving again that night when they were all asleep. No one would be expecting him to do that, so it was a good idea. Except – and the thought hit him like a funeral march – there was nowhere to run to, was there? And no one to welcome him when he got there. And the Pig had been frighteningly quick to come after him, considering the Pig disliked him so much. If he'd had a mum, he thought, he could have run to her. But to go to Southampton, wherever it was! What would a kid who needed specs do in Southampton? How would he live? He couldn't join another juvenile troupe without his dad's permission, even if they'd take him on. No, the trouble with being a kid was that the world is convinced you need looking after and so the world is organised in such a way that you have to be looked after, like it or not. So wherever he ran to, someone would notice he was on his own and send him back. He was trapped where he was. That thought kept him awake for a long time.

CHAPTER FIFTEEN

COVENTRY

No one discussed it – it just happened: John was sent to Coventry that morning for telling on Ollie. Not a Youngstar spoke to him. It affected John badly: he spilt a lake of milk over the breakfast table and spread marmalade on his fried bread. Silver ignored him during the walk to school. John had to tag along behind them while she chatted to Ollie about her future in film, a privilege usually bestowed on John.

Ollie knew he should grab this chance to bask in Silver's favour, because he'd never get another one, but he was too tired after the night before to bask at full throttle and anyway, he didn't deserve it. The Youngstars should be siding with John, not him. John had done the troupe a good turn by grassing on him; they would have been in a right terrible mess tonight with Ollie missing from the show as well as Jessie.

Ollie looked back at John and wondered if it had been easy for him to choose to do the right thing for the work and the wrong thing for their friendship. John gave him a really goofy wave and Ollie turned his back. They'd never be mates again, that was for sure, which was a horrible feeling.

Silver pinched him and said, 'Ollie Pigott, I am telling you something so unbelievable, so like my dreams come true, and you are gawking at John.'

'Sorry, sorry Silver, what were you t-t-t-telling me?

'I'm not now. Not if you're not interested'

'Please, Silver. T-t-t-tell.'

And so it went on, with him begging and Silver refusing to tell, until she considered he'd begged enough and he was stammering like a stuck record. She took him by the shoulders and turned him to face her. She said very slowly, 'Hal Havern is coming to town.'

It was spectacular news. Ollie's heart seemed to miss a beat. So it was Hal Havern, one of the biggest names in Hollywood, who was the star he'd heard the newspaper sellers down on the docks calling about yesterday. Silver was gazing at him like she'd just walked through the Pearly Gates. Eager to please, he threw in what the newsboys had been saying. 'He's coming to open a cinema.'

She looked furious. 'How did you know that?'

It didn't do to steal a march on Silver. That was

the end of the basking; she wouldn't speak for the rest of the walk. Disappointing, but it gave him time to concentrate on the small mystery of his morning. Who had brought his pyjama trousers and dressing-gown back from the washhouse and left them perfectly folded on the foot of his bed during the night? Perhaps he had a guardian angel. Liverpool bred angels.

The guardian angel was obviously on a tea break, though, when they arrived in the playground. Miss Bellamy had given Ollie his allowance to buy his dinner and the school bully took it off him. This particular thug was a beefy lad with a pointy nose and eyes too close to its bridge for glamour. He'd a gap between his front teeth that would bar him from Hollywood forever; but he'd muscles like a navvy.

The thug got Ollie up against the drinking fountain and gave him a thump in the chest that knocked everything out of him except the good sense to hand over the coins in his new coat pocket. But that wasn't the end of it. The thug's feet were bare and he was hell bent on getting Ollie's dead boy's shoes off him as well. He held Ollie in an agonizing headlock while one of his gang tugged at Ollie's feet.

The rest of the kids were terrified of the thug and kept out of the trouble, deliberately busying themselves with this week's playtime fashion: lashing a wooden top with a homemade whip to make it spin. Ollie was saved by the school bell summoning them inside, and the shoes stayed on.

But he'd lost his dinner. He seemed destined to be parted from food.

He saw Silver, drifting like a bright ruby in her Youngstar's blazer amongst the girls as they all marched through the door marked 'GIRLS'. He envied her. She never got beaten up at school. Perhaps he should just hand over the shoes and get it over with. The thug wasn't going to leave him alone until he did.

He looked up at the school as he trailed in after the other boys. It was the usual four-storey red brick building with thin, mean, arched windows. There was the usual school smell of disinfectant, too, once you got inside. He'd give a lot to get out of there and go somewhere nice, like the other end of the world.

The cloakrooms had a different pong – more like a wet dog – and the roller towel was already limp and sopping by the time Ollie got there because, as usual, most of the scrum of boys saved up washing themselves until they got to school, where soap was free and the water was hot. Not many of them had that at home. The wash basins were already grimy and spattered with grey droplets of water – as usual.

As usual, no talking was allowed. He went up flights of concrete stairs with the other seniors to the top hall, where everyone sat cross-legged on the parquet floor in silence. A tall man, with an exceptionally small head, almost goose-stepped into the room. He wore a brown pinstripe suit and held a cane very tightly against his pinstripe leg, as if, given half a chance, it would take off on its own on a punitive trip round his pupils.

'Hands together, eyes closed,' he instructed them and away he went on a prayer asking God to look after King Edward and to defend the British Empire and to make everyone present much, much better than they were now. The cane tapped against his calf while he prayed, as if impatient to be about its work. Then a teacher bashed out a hymn on an old joanna and they all roared tunelessly.

After that, John and Silver were allocated a teacher with a grey bun, while Ollie was given to Miss Mossop: a plump woman in an electric blue dress, whose powdered face was so pale it looked as if she'd used icing sugar for the job. Her smooth brown hair was curled above her ears in rigid rolls like brandy snaps that reminded Ollie he was going to miss his dinner.

Miss Mossop put Ollie to share a desk with a friendly boy in a torn pullover who unashamedly copied Ollie's answers to the mental arithmetic test Miss Mossop set them. The boy scored eight out of ten because the test was much easier for Ollie than the sums he always helped Miss Bellamy do when they were working out how much each Youngstar had to pay for their lodging. So Miss Mossop gave the boy a hiding because he usually got zero and she'd guessed he'd cheated. She sent him to stand, sore and sniffing, facing the wall in the corner of the room. Another child got slapped legs for writing with her left hand.

There were thirty-eight kids sitting at the rows of

desks in the class and before they were halfway into the morning, a good fifteen of them had had some kind of thrashing. The classroom was drizzling with tears and gulps. The usual sort of school, in fact.

'Oliver Pigott, you start.' Miss Mossop's voice brought Ollie jumping to attention. The friendly boy, released from the corner, was offering him the book that they were sharing. 'Read on, Oliver Pigott.' Miss Mossop patted one of her brandy snap rolls and Ollie stared at her, the blood wapp-wapping in his head. He could feel himself going red. Miss Mossop looked impatient. 'Read on, boy. Let's see if your reading is as good as your arithmetic.'

There was nothing for it. 'T...' he began, and the letter stuck with him and rattled out again and again like gunfire: 't-t-t-t-t-t-t.' The class began to titter. Miss Mossop's pale face stiffened. She rapped with her ruler on the lid of her big, high desk. Ollie fell silent – so did they all. No one wanted that ruler thwacking their knuckles.

'Oliver Pigott, come out.' Ollie slid off the bench seat of his desk and walked between the rows to Miss Mossop towering above him on her desk chair. He remembered Heather telling him that Jesus had said 'Come out' to a devil inside a person, just the way Miss Mossop had said it; and the devil had obeyed Jesus, and the person was cured of their illness. Ollie had asked Heather to try it on him for his stammer but Heather had said it was deadly wicked to copy Jesus and Ollie would go to hell which, by the look on Miss Mossop's icing sugar face, would be preferable to what she had in store for him with that ruler of hers.

But then a senior girl came into the classroom with a message from the Head. Oliver Pigott was wanted. Ollie was amazed that news of his offending stammer had reached the small-headed man in the brown suit so fast. He was in for it now. But then the classroom door banged open again and there stood John on the threshold. He spread his arms wide. 'Ta-raaah!'

He had a wild look to him. His usually well-combed hair was dishevelled and his face and clothes were covered in big blots of bright blue ink. He flapped an inky palm at Miss Mossop in her electric blue dress. 'Hello, sailor.'

Miss Mossop stared at him in total disbelief. Her ruler, still poised to strike, seemed frozen in mid-air. Her class was transfixed, terrified by this daring madness.

John sashayed into the room, swaying to his own crooning tune. 'Look Ollie,' he said. 'They made me ink monitor.' Ollie couldn't believe what he was seeing or hearing. John began to tap dance and sing. 'And now I'm all blue.' Tap-tap, tappity-tap, went his feet. He sank onto one knee in front of Miss Mossop. 'And so are *youooo*!' he sang.

Miss Mossop snapped out of her trance. Her ruler struck her desk with a crack like a breaking bone. She said in a huge voice, 'Silence!' Her class cringed.

'Silence!' John mimicked her, dancing up an aisle

of desks to the back of the class. 'Silence in court. Teacher wants to talk.' Miss Mossop pursued him crying, 'You wicked, wicked boy.'

John jumped up onto a desktop to dodge her and ran over the desk lids to the front of the class again with Miss Mossop slapping at his feet with her ruler. The class was in uproar: laughing, screaming, ducking out of the way.

The Headmaster appeared in the doorway. His small face went white with anger as John made a Fred Astaire leap that drew 'Oohs' of admiration from the class and landed on Miss Mossop's tall chair, from where he addressed the Head sorrowfully. 'Oh dear! Look who's here. Mr Dreary Brown Suit! You've failed your screen test, that's for sure, love.'

By now Ollie had a shrewd idea what was wrong with John and so had the Head.

'You, boy, are drunk.'

John jumped off the chair. 'As a punk in a bunk,' he agreed and planted a kiss on the Head's nose, who drew back with a snort of fury. 'Kiss me Hardy,' John cried, and charged Miss Mossop. And Miss Mossop, to the delight of her terrorised class, ran almost mewing with fright from the classroom.

John pounded on her desk. 'Repeat after me,' he told her class, 'all baboons have inky blue bums.' The class was convulsed, not by the terrible joke but by his sheer daring. 'Fetch the caretaker,' the Head said out of the side of his mouth to the senior girl who had been cowering behind the blackboard. 'And bring that fair child out of class, too.' The senior girl was flummoxed.

'Sir?'

'The other one of them,' the Headmaster snapped, 'with the ridiculous name. The other one of these performing scum.'

Up until then Ollie had been stunned by John's behaviour and then amused; and if he was honest, he was a bit ashamed of him, too. But now he closed ranks; no one called a Youngstar scum. He took John's elbow. 'Come on, John,' he said quietly. And John went with him, leaning on Ollie and breathing clouds of alcohol fumes.

As they passed him, the Headmaster handed Ollie an envelope. 'For your Manager.' He tried to go on but he could only manage to spit out another 'Scum.'

Ollie gave him a level look and said: 'The thing about scum, sir, is that it's always on the...'

'Top!' John cut in, drunkenly, but not so drunk that he couldn't rescue his friend from attempting that fatal 't'.

Silver was waiting for them outside the gates. She took John's other arm and they steered him away from the school. 'Whatever got into you?'

'Gin.' John answered. His voice was slurred now. 'Mother'sh ruin.' So that was what John had been muttering out in the back yard, Ollie realised; not Mothers' Union at all.

Silver shook the arm she was holding. All thoughts of Coventry had vanished with the crisis. 'How much have you had?

'A bottle nearly.'

'Cripes!' was all she could say. Ollie was puzzled.

'But you don't drink.'

'I do now,' John said proudly.

They manhandled him along the pavement while Silver diagnosed that John had taken to drink out of remorse. She shook his arm again. 'That's right isn't it?' she asked loudly, as though he were deaf as well as drunk. 'Drowning your sorrows, weren't you, because no one was talking to you?'

John frowned. 'What do you mean no one wazsh talking to me?' It was clear he'd been too drunk to notice he was in Coventry.

'For splitting on Ollie. Sneaking.'

John stopped and gave her a dignified look, which failed to come off because dignity was not part of his repertoire just at that moment. 'I don't know what you're talking about, Shilver. Ollie ish my friend.' He seemed to notice Ollie for the first time. 'Oh, hello Ollie. Talk of the devil.'

They lurched towards the digs and Ollie explained to Silver, between lurches, that John must have been drunk for hours. He'd been drunk last night in the back yard, which immediately threw doubt on whether he'd even been capable of telling on Ollie to Pigott.

'Dad would have noticed he was pickled,' Ollie said. 'Takes one to know one.' Which clinched John's innocence. But it left the question wide open again as to who had sneaked on Ollie. 'Not little John,' John avowed happily and began to dance again.

They were collecting a few looks from passers-by now, so Ollie pinned him up against some railings with his shoulder while Silver opened the letter from the Headmaster to Pigott.

The Head hadn't pulled his punches. He'd used words like 'rampaged' and 'riotous' to describe John's conduct, and 'insubordination, destruction and mayhem'.

'The Pig will kill him,' Silver said placidly. She read on silently. 'We're banned from the school.' Then her face changed. 'Sugar! He says the Pig must pay for the damage.' She replaced the letter in the envelope. 'We're dead.'

John began to cry. 'I only did it to make me little,' he sobbed. 'How do you stop growing? I asked Grinling.'

'Grinling!' Ollie was flabbergasted that John could have been so tactless. 'You asked Grinling that?' But John had his defence.

'You told me to ask him.'

'It were a joke, twerp.' Ollie was scathing. 'You upset him. No wonder he told you something idiotic.' John sat down on the pavement.

'Night-night.' He curled up against the railings and shut his eyes.

While they were hauling him home, Silver remembered a stage doorkeeper had once told her how they used to give child performers gin to stunt their growth. She'd thought he was joking but maybe Grinling had simply come up with an old fashioned remedy for John. You could be grown up, the stage doorkeeper had said, and still the height of a nine year old. 'Why would they want to d-do that, Silver?'

'It saved them having to train up new kids all the time.' Ollie shivered. It certainly wasn't all roses in Variety.

Fortunately, the digs had that silent deadened feeling that houses get when the owners are absent. Someone was vacuuming but it was miles away upstairs. Their idea was to sneak John to his bedroom to sleep it off. The only problem was, he wouldn't come. He sat on the bottom step crying that he was John the Giant and his career was over. 'My lovely, lovely career,' he cried.

They took him by the armpits and pulled him from behind, climbing upstairs backwards as they did. But even though Ollie and Silver reached the sixth stair, John's feet remained obstinately at the bottom in the hall. It was as if he'd turned into elastic. He just stretched. To make things worse, they began to giggle as they pulled, until they collapsed underneath him, shaking with laughter, their heads buried in the nape of John's neck, while John wept over the tomb of his career. And that's how Hazel, the landlady's daughter, found them as she descended with her vacuum cleaner.

Hazel took charge at once. She gave John a good shake and led him off to the scullery, warning they'd only twenty minutes to sober him up before her mother came back from the shops. There would be all hell let loose if she found John drunk.

'Why should I come with you?' John was weepily defiant. But Hazel was having no nonsense.

'Because I'm older than you and I'll slap you if you don't.'

Now someone else had taken over the drama, Ollie had time to feel apprehensive, or even downright frightened. If John hadn't sobered up by the time they were due to rehearse with Jess's substitute at two o'clock, the Pig would annihilate everyone in sight and Ollie would be the first down. He always was. He ought to go and help Hazel.

But Silver stopped him and beckoned him into the empty parlour. Without asking him, she threw the letter from the Head onto the fire where it curled into black coils and was gone. Ollie was shocked. 'Crumbs, Silver! What about paying for the damage?'

'What harm's a drop of ink?' Silver treated him to one of her radiant smiles. 'By the time they work out they're not going to get a reply, we will have moved on.'

Ollie thought uneasily of the Headmaster's description of them all. Wasn't this scummy behaviour? But there was no budging Silver. She swung her fair hair across her face. It was one of her tricks when she wanted her way. He knew that. It made her look extra pretty. And Silver was pretty – as pretty as John was handsome.

She sketched out her plan. They would pretend to leave for school each morning and take themselves off into town instead. 'Should be simple for you. It's what you do anyway.' She gave him an inquisitive, sideways look. 'Isn't it?'

But even though Pablo's lessons were over and done, Ollie wasn't telling and Silver didn't press him. What she did ask about was the girl he'd been meeting. The more Ollie denied there was one, the more convinced Silver became that he was lying. She only let up when Hazel brought John back, slightly less drunk and in clean clothes but still inky blue all over.

Hazel said the only cure for the ink was a right scrubbing and directed them to the public baths. It was a good walk but nobody had any money for a taxi. 'Ollie cleaned me out,' John said dismally. He made a face at Hazel. 'She made me sick,' he complained. 'Three times.' But no one took his side.

Then it came out that Ollie had lost the precious eightpence Silver and John had lent him, so it was Ollie's turn to be in the doghouse. There was no question of taking John on a tram in the state he was in, so it was agreed it was only fair Ollie should walk him there and supervise John's bath, since he'd used up all their cash.

'The bath's threepence,' Hazel said. 'Take your own towel to save money.'

Silver watched them from the top of the front steps as they meandered off down the street. The Titch and the Lamppost. She breathed a sigh of satisfaction and set off to her version of paradise – the department store – where they sold everything from hats to chocolate biscuits. But these were not what attracted Silver. She took the lift up to heaven.

On her way she ran into Miss Bellamy, which was problematic, but she smiled and told Miss Bellamy that the boys were using the lunch break to take a bath. Miss Bellamy seemed not to notice that it was nowhere near lunch-time yet, and Silver moved on, past hats, past lingerie, not even glancing at the hideous clothes for girls.

Like a shark after blood she knew where to find them – the evening gowns. Glimmering, slinky, clingy, sultry satins and silks. These were what she would be wearing when she was a film star. All day.

* * * * *

It was about then that Ralph and Giselle arrived at the school gates.

They'd had a trying few hours.

CHAPTER SIXTEEN

BATH

Ten o'clock! Big Dad was smiling down at Ralph and offering a thimble-size bowl of tea. The drying room was busy with people ironing laundry, the stove was rocking with heat and it was ten o'clock! French was asleep beside him. He gave her a shove. They had overslept. Disaster! School started at nine.

They gulped the tea, bowed and left messages of thanks for Wei, who'd already gone to school. Then they ran to the doppelganger's school. Nothing. An empty playground and the muffled chant of kids reciting their twelve times table.

But then children came pouring out of the school in droves. Playtime. Ralph couldn't see a red blazer so he plunged in among the boys, searching for his double. It would be easy. Like looking for himself.

'Hey, you.' A big boy, with a pointy nose and a gap between his front teeth that you could drive a wagon through, had him by the wrist. Other boys were hemming him in. 'Give us yer shoes.' Instinct told Ralph that mighty soon, right now in fact, Pointy Nose would twist one of his arms painfully behind his back. Ralph's trainer was always firm on this point. 'Be nice,' he instructed. 'Be sure the other guy wants a fight. But if you're out of time, be nasty.' Ralph reckoned he was out of time.

Pretty soon, the Thug's blood was splashing around the playground. The other kids had dropped their whips and tops; the entire school was encircling the fight and urging Ralph on, howling for more blood. The Thug had never been given such a drubbing in his life. Wherever he turned, there were twenty Ralphs with twenty pairs of fists and feet to meet him. Through the onslaught, the Thug wondered what the heck had happened to this wet Nelly of a kid in shoes. Had he eaten spinach like Popeye?

The Thug made a final savage attack – an all out, maximum strength, last effort attack – and the little pussyfoot he'd had up against the drinking fountain only that morning threw him bodily over his shoulder, to a mighty cheer from the watching school. As the Thug sailed through the air, the stolen dinner money flew out of his pocket. And the Thug moaned, as he crash-landed on the playground, ''ave it back.'

Never in his whole life had the Thug been so glad

to see a hated teacher pushing through the kids to his rescue, never been so glad to hear Miss Mossop shouting 'Not you again!' and running the lad off the premises. The Thug passed out. A roar of jeers was the last thing he heard.

Giselle said calmly, 'You did not get far with your search?' Ralph shook his head, brushing his clothes down. 'What in hell was all that about?'

Giselle said, 'I do not know. How did you anger the poor boy so?'

'French! I never even spoke to the kid.' But Giselle was not easily persuaded.

'You are very belligerent. Let us hope your double is not tarred with the same broom.'

'Brush.'

'Hush.'

'No, brush.'

'Be quiet. There is a boy in tatters who wishes to speak to us.'

A friendly looking boy with a hole in his pullover was waving at them through the bars of the school gate that Miss Mossop had shut on Ralph. He beckoned them over, smiling. So maybe the kid could help them. The boy said, 'Tommy took the train to Toxteth'. And so maybe he couldn't. The poor kid was a dope. 'Say it,' the kid commanded Ralph.

'Tommy took the train to Toxteth.' Ralph obeyed, just to humour him. The boy looked satisfied; his test had worked. 'It's not you.'

'Me?'

'Yes, you. Except it's not you. You can't do your t's when you're him. Well, you can, but you get stuck.' Giselle gripped the bars of the gate excitedly. She'd cottoned on long before Ralph

'Where is the teeless boy in the red blazer?'

'He don't have a blazer'

'No blazer?'

'No. He's same as you.'

'He is here?'

'Was. He's gone.'

'Where?'

'Don't know. Home? They chucked him out. His mate were drunk. It were right bloody wonderful.'

The school bell rang for Going In. 'I'm sorry you're not you. I liked yer.' The boy patted Ralph's shoulder through the bars. 'Mind you, you should have a medal for that knock-out. Cheer'o.' And he ran across the playground into school.

There was a very long, painful silence. At last, Giselle said brightly, 'Well, now we know he cannot say 't' as normal.' Ralph looked murder at her. They had the whole of Liverpool, miles and miles of it, to search now when an hour before his double had been right here, right on the very spot where they were standing.

Giselle said even more brightly, 'We have much information. He stutters, he wears no blazer and his comrades are alcoholics. Très promising,' she added dryly. Ralph rounded on her. Could she never quit sneering? Okay, she could sneer at him but not at his double. His double wasn't here to defend himself.

197

And that was her fault.

'Why did you have to go and oversleep?'

'Moi? It was you.'

They argued on, meandering back towards the city centre, not noticing where they were going they felt so angry and thwarted. Giselle was all for going back to the laundry and waiting for the mysterious 'Miss Bellamy', but Ralph said there could be a million red blazers in Liverpool. Why should the one at Big Dad's be the doppelganger's?

They were in a busy street of shops by now, with pedestrians packing the sidewalk and noisy traffic grinding by, when a dazed looking woman with frizzy greying hair waved a carrier bag at them from across the road. They could only just hear what she was saying. 'Back so soon? I thought you were at...' She paused, looking vague and sad.

Giselle just pulled Ralph back from running under a passing tram as he tried to cross to the woman. It frightened them both very much and they clung onto each other on the kerbside. Giselle said things like 'Merde!' which Ralph didn't understand, but he got the gist. His heart was pumping and the thought flashed through him like an electric shock that he could be dead now.

Giselle recovered first and screamed what seemed to Ralph to be gibberish across the traffic at the dazed looking woman; but surprisingly, the woman suddenly looked much less dazed and screamed gibberish back over the hubbub.

A tram drew up in front of the woman and when

it pulled away, she'd gone. Ralph was half frantic with frustration. 'What was all that gobbledygook?' Giselle looked at him thoughtfully. She was wondering what made the American boy so vexingly sure of his superiority. 'That 'gobbledygook' as you call it,' she said stiffly, 'was the diplomatic language of Europe and of the entire world.' She hammered home the point. 'She was talking French, my stupid friend.'

Ralph clenched his fists against his sides. She was so damn superior. He raised his eyes to the smoky sky, where Mary Ellen said the good Lord dwelt, and silently asked Him to relax His rules on murder, just this once. Sure, it would be ungrateful to slay French here on the sidewalk when a minute ago she'd saved him from ending up under a streetcar but, right now, all it would take was the green light from God.

But now French was hailing a cab and pushing him inside. 'The Public Baths. The nearest,' she told the driver and leant back in the seat next to Ralph. He was shocked. Here she was, landing him in more **** trouble. 'French? Where are you going to find the fare?'

'You have it. The boy with the charming gap in his teeth paid you to stop killing him. I saw you pick up the money.'

Ralph had been planning a lunch around that cash windfall. A solitary one.

'Alors!' She gave him a sweet smile that did nothing but deepen his disappointment. 'We are hot on the perfume again.'

'Scent.' It was almost a sob.

*   *   *   *   *

Ollie was fascinated by the swimming pool. It was wriggling with children – a whole class of them – all learning how to swim. The noise bouncing off the glass ceiling was deafening, like an amplified zoo. A sleepy looking teacher was watching from a gallery up above while an efficient lady, wearing divided skirts and plimsolls, was dashing up and down the edge. She was teaching some of the kids. She had them enclosed in strange floating trusses and was towing them along on the end of a rope, and she was calling instructions to other children, who were clutching bobbing cork floats and kicking and threshing like they were in the Olympics. No one was using the diving boards, though. He'd liked to have seen someone dive.

Ollie couldn't swim. He'd never been taught, but he loved the pool. He loved the colour of it; it was so bright and glamorous looking compared with blackened, old, filthy Liverpool. He stared at the squiggling kids in their rubber caps and their dark woollen bathing costumes, that made them look like so many tadpoles, and wondered what it felt like to be held up by water.

He'd left John up to his neck in the stuff in the public washing rooms. They'd managed to rent him a single bathroom, which was more expensive than a communal one, but sharing was out of the question. The four bathers in the adjoining baths would have had to be saints to put up with John in his present condition. If he wasn't crying he was singing, and if he wasn't doing either, he was apologising for everything he'd done that day, and everything he'd done wrong in the past from the moment he'd been born up until now. It was a bit wearing, so once Ollie had got the water to the right temperature, and set him scrubbing at his ink blots, he'd cleared off to explore the white-tiled passage outside the door and found the public swimming baths. He stood sniffing the strong whiffs of chlorine coming up from the choppy turquoise water and looked about him.

There were two entrances to the pool near each corner of the shallow end and the man with the black and white shoes was standing on the threshold of one of them. Fortunately, there was a row of individual changing cubicles on either side of the pool and Ollie backed into one of them fast.

He tripped over the duckboard on the floor and sat down with a bump on some belongings that had been left on the bench inside. The cubicles had wooden half doors, like a saloon door in a cowboy film, and a short canvas curtain hung above it for privacy. He drew the curtain across with a rattle.

All this activity alerted the sleepy teacher, watching from the gallery opposite, who wondered what the strange boy in the cubicle was doing. The teacher noticed he wasn't the only one who was curious. A man in black and white shoes, whom the teacher supposed was an attendant, was walking purposefully towards the cubicle.

Ollie watched the Shoes Man through a gap in the canvas curtain. He was right scared but there was nothing for it; he shot out of the cubicle. As he did, the efficient lady blew her whistle to get the kids out of the water and they all dog-paddled to the little flight of steps in the corner.

Ollie ran down the length of the pool towards the Shoes Man, pretending he hadn't noticed him. When the distance between them had closed to nearly nothing, Ollie turned round and sprinted in the other direction. He had much further to go that way to reach an exit and, just as he'd hoped, the Shoes Man realised and began to run back the other way to cut him off from the way out.

But the Shoes Man hadn't reckoned with the speed Ollie could put on, despite the fact he was running on slippery wet tiles. Nor had he reckoned with the gang of shivering children thronging the corner of the walkway as they climbed out of the pool. The Shoes Man was still wading through the tadpole kids as Ollie made it to the exit.

As Ollie left, Ralph came in through the other entrance. 'Jumping Jehoshaphat,' the watching teacher murmured as the same boy reappeared within a split second. That lad could be a credit to the nation. He moves at Olympian speed.

Ralph scanned the remaining kids in the water. They all looked so darned alike in the rubber bathing caps that gripped their little faces so tightly you'd think their brains would be squeezed out. Then he heard French give him a warning shout from the door. He looked up and there was Monsieur Shoes bearing down on him.

It was at that moment that Ollie burst into John's bathroom. 'Cripes, John! There's a bloke after me.' But John was fast asleep in a tepid bath. Ollie locked the door and shook him awake. 'Get us out of here, John.'

But John had a terrible headache and a limited capacity to understand anything that was said to him, least of all that Ollie needed an escape route. He was extremely surprised to find himself in a bath, even, and wondered how he'd got there.

He was still more surprised to find himself, wet and stark naked, giving Ollie a leg-up through a little frosted glass window that Ollie seemed to think gave off to the back of the building. Why couldn't he leave by the door?

John shook his aching head. He felt as though a dozen rotten eggs had been planted in his stomach while he wasn't looking. He began to dry himself. It was one of the hardest things he'd ever done.

*　*　*　*　*

The teacher in the gallery watched with interest, and so did his class, as the boy sped round the pool with the attendant in the shoes running after him and an exquisite dark child close behind them both. The dark girl hurled one of the efficient lady's weird

203

trusses at the Shoes Man. It hit him in the back. The Shoes Man buckled, then turned to hit back, but the dark girl had skipped out of sight into one of the changing cubicles. He turned back for Ralph. He'd gone too.

Then Shoes spotted him up on the top diving board and climbed up the ladder to the board. Climbing, the teacher observed, was not the attendant-in-the-shoes' strong point. When the boy peeled off his jacket and dropped it down over the attendant's head, he was even more disadvantaged. By the time Shoes had thrown off the jacket, Ralph had already reached the far end of the diving board. His heart was hammering with fright. There was nowhere left to go.

And now the teacher began to feel alarmed, too, as Shoes crawled along the board towards Ralph, causing the trapped boy to bounce perilously. For God's sake! The teacher sprang to his feet. The man had a gun. He ran to protect his class.

So the teacher missed Ralph's backward somersault that straightened out into a well-trained dive just before he hit the water. He missed him surfacing, far down the pool, and churning in a fast crawl to the steps at the other end. He also missed the downfall of Monsieur Shoes. As Ralph dived, the board bounced madly, and Shoes dropped his gun, tried to catch it, lost his balance, and swivelled underneath the diving board. There he clung – stout legs flailing over the water – until, inevitably, with a splash that rained water drops far and wide,

Monsieur Shoes fell in and sank straight to the aquamarine bottom.

*   *   *   *   *

Meanwhile, John was ready to leave – except that he'd mislaid his blazer. He stumbled round the bathtub searching for it in slow motion, forgetting that he'd hung his towel over it on the door peg. He knew he had something important to do. Rehearse, yes, that was it. The very thought brought evil juices into his mouth and his head hammered with pain. Maybe he'd left the blazer outside? He was unbolting his bathroom door with shaky fingers when it was thrust open from the other side and, to his surprise, Ollie ran back into the room. His clothes were soaking wet and his jacket was missing. What the dickens was outside that frosted glass window? The river Mersey?

'I gotta get out of here,' Ollie said in an American accent. John blinked his aching eyes.

'Why are you talking like the films?'

'Help me, feller. There's a guy out there who wants to kill me.'

John decided that one or other of them had taken leave of their senses and, judging by the way he felt, it was more likely to be him than Ollie. He said, 'We'll re-run the scene then. Through the window it is. Camera rolling. Sound running. Scene one. Take two.'

Ralph nodded in vehement agreement. If this

guy wanted to play at movie making, he'd go along with it. He'd do anything at this moment, anything at all to get away from Shoes. 'And ...Action!' Ralph roared.

*   *   *   *   *

It was about this time that the drowning Monsieur Shoes fought frantically with the efficient lady, who was efficiently saving his life. So, like all efficient lifesavers, she knocked him out. Giselle allowed herself the tiniest smile of pleasure before she went to look for Ralph.

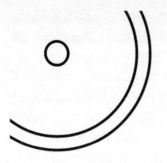

CHAPTER SEVENTEEN

BEGGARS CAN'T BE CHOOSERS

'We, meine Kinder, are up a gum tree.' It was a poor start to a rehearsal. It got worse when the Pig announced to the Youngstars that there wasn't a substitute for Jess to be found in the whole of Lancashire. And then it got even worse, because John was sick into a wastepaper basket.

'Out!' the Pig shouted at him. 'You're making me heave.' And he chased John out of the bar, swatting him with his trilby hat. 'And don't you go down with that bursting illness, same as Jess, or you're on your own.' He delivered a final swat.

'No substitute!' Silver was worried.

'They're all hired, sweetheart,' Pigott boomed at her. 'All the girls in Liverpool are rehearsing a gala stunt they're throwing on for some star to open a local fleapit. Every theatrical agent in town is coining the shekels and taking their phone off the hook.'

'So who is going to replace me in my part?' The Pig patted her head and told her he had a very talented little lady up his sleeve. Silver looked relieved until he laughed and told her she was to play Jess's and her own part as well.

The Pig swirled round the bar in his raincoat, re-allocating roles and hunks of the sketch. He treated Ollie to a honeyed, fatherly smile for the benefit of Miss Reeve at the piano. 'Ollie, you stick with your dunce; Grinling, you pick up the bits Silver can't do.' Then he heaped on the discouragement. 'It will be a disaster though.' And he was right.

An hour later, Silver looked even less happy. Ollie could see why. Silver was okay: her dancing wasn't in the same league as Jess's but she could be funny and she sang Jessie's number well. The problem was, Silver had a pert jauntiness to her that was all about 'Look at Me, Silver the Star' and not-at-all about the schoolroom riot.

Silver was pro enough to know something was going wrong with the sketch, but she'd no idea what. Ollie was dying to advise her – if you're going to act a riot, Silver, then you have to act that you really want to riot and not that you want the audience to think you're the sweetest little thing since saccharine.

It crossed his mind to tell her, except that she might slap his face. What didn't cross his mind, but was crossing everyone else's, was that if the Pig would only let Ollie do the finale he'd improvised the night before, the act would come alive. No one dared say it, though – not even Grinling.

The band was plain mutinous about being called for extra rehearsal, but Pigott persuaded them to run through the sketch with the troupe on stage. Afterwards, the Pig said quietly, 'Tea break, all. And if we can't do better tonight, I'm the one who'll be on strike, bambinos. It will be the sack for everyone.' They could see he meant it.

After the break, Ollie hung around on his own. The rest of the Youngstars had been summoned for a photo call on stage, but not Ollie. The Pig always banned Ollie because, as he put it candidly, Ollie wasn't as good as the other Youngstars. Ollie usually spent the banned time with Miss Bellamy in the green-room, coaxing tales out of her. But Miss Bellamy seemed to have floated off the planet. He hadn't seen her for ages.

He went down to the stage door for a chat with the keeper. It was as good a way as any of filling in the gap between tea and 'the half', and it also meant you got to say hello to the other artists coming in to do the show. The old boy looked very snug in his booth with his kettle and tea things and his phones and notepad, more like he was sitting in his parlour than a theatre. He tore a leaf off the pad and gave it to Ollie. 'Hospital visiting hours. Your matron said to let you have them.' Ollie looked at the paper. They were hopeless. His spirits sank.

He was low enough anyway at the prospect of

the terrible show ahead of him. They were going to go down like a cup of cold sick without Jess. And anyway, the schoolroom sketch was out of touch, he thought, in a sudden rush of exasperation with his father. It was nothing like Miss Mossop's hellish classroom.

He thanked the stage doorkeeper, who'd spread out his evening newspaper at a picture of the film star, Hal Havern. 'He's come a long way.' He winked at Ollie. 'When I knew him he were plain Harry Harper.' The old man shook his head and said no more. Ollie was an experienced enough listener to know exactly what to do. 'You d-don't say!' And sure enough, the stage doorkeeper had a tale to tell.

'Started in Variety, did your Hal Havern,' he said. 'A Boy Wonder act with whips; then he added in knives. Could hit a rat's eye from ten yards, could your Hal Havern. It were a great act. Shook us all when he turned legit.'

'Legit? What, he went into posh theatre?'

'Ay. Became a small part actor in Manchester and then, without warning, off he went to America – under a bit of a cloud, I seem to remember.'

There was no likelihood of learning any more about Hal Havern because one of the phones rang and the old man had to answer it, and so Ollie went outside. It was good to think that an ex-Variety artist could rise to be one of the biggest stars in Hollywood. There was hope for everyone then – everyone who didn't have a stammer, that was.

It was dark now and the street lamps shone on

the crowd queuing for the cheap seats in 'the gods'. He stood and watched the buskers entertaining them while they waited. He was suddenly aware of Grinling standing next to him. 'Photos finished already?'

'John vomited. We were out of there like a dose of salts.' Ollie decided it was time to broach the subject of the gin, but Grinling gave him the gentlest of smiles and said, 'He'll thank me one day. That boy will never touch another drop.'

It was clever of Grinling, Ollie thought, to convert his poor advice into an act of kindness. 'He'll do the show fine,' Grinling said. 'Dr Greasepaint will get him through.' Grinling pointed at a busker. 'Isn't that the neatest little dancer you ever did see?'

It was the small, shabby boy Ollie had seen earlier. He was dancing to the older boy's violin. The tune was fast and the boy's feet were hitting the pavement like hailstones. Ollie and Grinling stood together enjoying his work, but then Grinling said, 'Those little vixens would have had me, Ollie, but for you.' Grinling was looking all stiff and serious so Ollie didn't like to ask him straight out what he meant. It might offend his old friend to admit he hadn't noticed this vixen thing he was talking about.

Vixens? Ollie's mind spun with candidates. Heather? Silver? Silver might fit the description. There had obviously been a row of some sort, but Ollie was jiggered if he could remember it. Then Grinling said, 'Thanks, son,' which was even more baffling. Ollie stared at the boy buskers and wracked his brains.

People were clapping in time to the violin now, and throwing farthings and halfpennies into the boys' hat, that was guarded by The-Ugliest-Dog-On-Earth. What was the incident Grinling was thanking him for? Had he sleep-walked his way through a good deed that he hadn't a clue had happened? Thankfully, Grinling didn't say any more about his vixens; instead he said, 'Look at those coins fill the hat!' His tone changed. 'Oxo doesn't like it.'

As Grinling spoke, a brawny one-man-band, who was performing up at the other end of the queue, stopped playing his mouth organ and came clomping down to the boys. Every step he took made an instrument play – very loudly. The cymbals that were attached by wires to his feet clashed, his drums boinged and his triangles trilled like a bicycle bell. He began arguing with the boys. Evidently this was Oxo and Oxo didn't want the boys there.

They were on his gaff, he shouted, and stealing his living. Soon the queue got involved and took sides – mostly the boys' side. 'Big bully,' someone called, as a scuffle broke out between Oxo and the boys, punctuated by bangs, bongs and jingles for every move Oxo made. The-Ugliest-Dog-On-Earth went on begging in the middle of it all, like an appeal for calm.

'Let's go,' Ollie said to Grinling as, out of nowhere, three bobbies appeared. He walked back to the stage door. The Pig had trained him well: never tangle with the police. But now Oxo was demanding the boys show the officers their licence to busk and Ollie heard him shouting that the smaller boy was far too young to be a street trader. 'He's not legal!' he yelled, with a rattle of his snare drum.

The police took the older boy by the arms and the third policeman held the smaller lad by his coat collar. The older boy jerked his head at him. 'Run you little *idjeet*!'

The boy shrugged off his coat and ran, and the policeman was left holding an empty jacket. Two or three of the crowd gave the boy a start by somehow happening to get in the way of the police as they tried to give chase – Ollie couldn't tell if they did it on purpose or not – but Ollie completed the escape by holding open the stage door for the boy as he rushed by. A fellow performer deserved a chance.

The boy darted in. Ollie followed and shut the door, only to have it pushed open in his face. He thought it was going to be Grinling, but it wasn't; it was the Pig. 'And who is this little lass?' Ollie heard his father ask over the top of his head. When Ollie turned round, there was the young boy, now a young girl, his cap pulled off and a mass of curls the colour of tinned apricots tumbling round her shoulders. She had skin like vanilla ice cream – she was all the colours of Ollie's favourite pudding, in fact – and her navy blue eyes sparkled as she smiled gratefully at Ollie.

'She's the substitute d-d-dancer,' Ollie told his father. 'The agency just phoned through saying they had one after all.' He appealed to the stage doorkeeper. 'D-didn't they?'

'Oh ay,' the old man answered, promptly falling in with Ollie, and before Pigott could ask any more questions, he picked up one of the phones in his booth and suggested he should ring down to the stage to see if it was clear. 'You'll be needing a spot of rehearsal, won't you, Mr Pigott, sir?'

But at the rehearsal it was discovered that Trixie O'Hara, as the girl turned out to be called, could only dance Irish jigs. Trixie clocked Silver's spiteful little snigger at the news and said, 'But if what she does is anything to go by, I'll be picking it up in no time at all.'

Pigott hummed and hawed and roared with rage, and blew hot and cold about keeping Trixie on. He said beggars couldn't be choosers and sent someone flying off to find Miss Bellamy to fit Trixie into a costume. He flapped about the stage re-arranging the sketch until, at last, he came to the decision everyone longed for him to arrive at: Ollie was told grudgingly to come up with the same 'box of crackers' as he did last night. 'And you, girl,' the Pig roared at Trixie, 'you stand in the dunce's corner and jig your feet off 'til someone pushes you in the cupboard.'

'What cupboard?'

'Never mind what cupboard. Just do it.' She nodded her apricot head and everything would have been fine, just fine – but for The-Ugliest-Dog-On-Earth.

* * * * *

It was about then that Ralph closed his eyes on his situation.

Once the tall drunk boy at the municipal baths had squeezed him through the window, he'd landed on his hands and knees in a back alley that smelt like a piss place. He'd picked himself up and run as fast and as far away as he could. He'd been running up a street called Scotland Road, and for a second he'd thought he'd run so far he'd changed countries – he was that scared of Monsieur Shoes and his gun. Getting shot hurt unimaginably until you died. He'd once seen an accident at the ranch that he didn't like to remember, and he knew being shot was agony. But then he saw the trams were still marked Liverpool Corporation, which meant he was still in the city, and it felt more as if he was running on the spot. He slowed down.

The people on the street were the poorest looking he'd ever seen. Groups of ragged kids were playing in the rough, dirty side streets on either side of him. Down at the end of an alley, he saw some scruffy girls giving a thrashing to something on the ground. He thought it was a dog and moved in. Hell! No one should do that to a dog. Then he saw it was another kid.

He pushed his way in among the girls at the very moment the kid's hat was knocked off his head. Ralph saw greying hair and a long face, and he recognised him. It was the small friendly man

215

who'd greeted him and French the night before.

Ralph felt no compunction about laying into girls, not even the shortest one, who whimpered, 'We needed the money. We only did it 'cos we was paid to.' It was no excuse. By the time he'd finished, the alley was empty, except for a piece of torn skirt and a tortoiseshell comb.

By then, Grinling had picked himself up. 'See you at work,' he said. 'Scarper!' And he ran for it. So did Ralph. The girls were a bunch of vixens but even vixens could have friends to call out for a return match.

Back on the street, Ralph took a right and ran into a big covered market, crowded with shoppers, where they were selling fruit and vegetables. He felt safer here, among the grown-ups. His pullover was soaked through and his pants were developing pale blotches where the chlorine in the pool had bleached them; even so, his clothes were a lot finer than the rest of the kids around here had on, and he didn't want to get into another fight about who was going to wear them. Three fights in one day would be pushing it.

He walked around the stalls while he thought what to do next, but soon the apples and oranges and bananas got to him. He was starving, but he hadn't a cent to buy anything. 'Steal some!' The thought was so loud in his head that he looked round guiltily in case anyone else had heard it, too. 'Stealing is wrong,' he told the thought. 'Vamoose.' And the thought obeyed. But here it was back again. 'Just one apple.'

'I'd rather starve,' his conscience replied. The thought was silent, conquered by his virtue. Or was it?

'Watch yerself,' a boy next to him said as Ralph's hand closed round a cold, firm apple. 'Market keeper over yonder is onto you.' Ralph withdrew his hand fast. The boy who'd warned him took his elbow in a friendly way. 'Hungry? Come with us, and I'll show you grub for free.'

The boy's feet were bare and his baggy short trousers ended just below the knees of his thin legs. He was so poor that Ralph was surprised he was willing to share his free grub. Why didn't he do the sensible thing and keep it all for himself? 'Been in trouble have you?' the boy asked now, looking at Ralph's wet clothes. Ralph nodded. He was too scared of Monsieur Shoes to talk about him, so he asked what a market keeper was and was told it was a sort of policeman who held all the keys to the market.

The boy led him to a walled-off corner where the stallholders threw out reject fruit and vegetables. Two high gates, about ten feet tall, held the mountain of rubbish in place. All you had to do, the boy told Ralph, was climb up a gate, reach over the top of the pile and grab yourself a free dinner. Some lads were already up there, astride the top of the gates and peeling blackened bananas.

It took Ralph a while to get up there, but he finally made it. The black bananas looked like something

217

you'd see lying in the bottom of the john, and probably tasted like it too. He leant far out for an orange, lost his balance and fell into the pile. At first it didn't seem that serious until he realised he was sinking into the mountain of garbage. None of the lads' helping outstretched hands could reach him. He tried to struggle towards them and sank further. He was already up to his throat in the muck. There was nothing solid to rest his feet on. No way to control the sinking. He screamed as first the top of the gate and then the boys' horrified faces disappeared, and tons of rotten fruit closed over his head.

He was drowning. Why hadn't he made do with a black banana, like the other kids? He was drowning in a pulpy, putrid soup because he was hungry. Or was it because he was greedy? He was going to die, whichever it was. He choked and his lungs filled. He fought and fought and fought to stay alive, but he was losing the battle.

And then, abruptly, he was expelled in a wave of skins and stalks and sludge that surged forward and threw him out onto the floor of the market as the keeper, whom the other boys had raced to fetch, unlocked the gates and released him in a tidal wave of rubbish.

Ralph crawled and then ran, coughing and stinking and slimy, to get away from the hunger and the horror and the poverty that had nearly killed him. He ran and he ran until he ran slap into someone who exclaimed with disgust at the filth on him, then held him fast. He heard them say, 'Why

Master Ralph! If it isn't my sugar baby come back.' It was Mary Ellen, his nursemaid. She would look after him. He was safe again. And that was when he closed his eyes on his situation. He closed them so she wouldn't see he was crying.

*　*　*　*　*

It was not long after this that Mr Fanfield left the police station, where he had been held, and stepped out into the cold English evening. Without explanation, he'd been told he could leave. And he couldn't wait. 'America, here I come,' he whispered and then stood nonplussed, wondering exactly where he was.

*　*　*　*　*

It was about then, too, that the show was cracking along. The queue for the gods had stampeded up the steps to the top of the theatre, jockeying for the best seats. The 'Shover Up,' hired by the theatre management to do just that, had positioned his large self on the end of a full bench of spectators and shoved until there was enough room for another bottom to sit down. The wealthier folk were in their upholstered seats down in the stalls and the dress circle. The theatre was packed out.

An impressionist act had just gone down a storm, and now a singer was reaching the end of his number:

'She'll sigh for you, cry for you,
Yes, even die for you.
And that's what God made mothers for.'

'Sentimental trash,' Trixie O'Hara whispered in Ollie's ear, which made him feel a bit of a twerp. He'd been wondering whether his mum sighed and cried.

The Youngstars were waiting in the wings to make their entrance. Everyone stood up-wind of the Pig, who tended to fart on these occasions. Everyone was also wondering how Trixie would work out. And here came their theme tune, and standby and they were on!

It was exactly then that PC Wyatt, out on his beat, recognised Tudoe (The-Ugliest-Dog-On-Earth) sitting outside the stage door with a boy's cap in his mouth. And in he went.

* * * * *

The Youngstars' act was going well. Ollie was coming up to his finale. Then, horrors! He caught sight of Tudoe in the wings with PC Wyatt holding him on the end of a length of rope. But by now, Trixie O'Hara had disappeared into the cupboard just as she'd been told to. The Pig dropped on all fours but before Ollie could start his acrobatics, the cupboard doors crashed open again and Trixie burst out, determined to stay on stage out of the policeman's reach. 'Did I tell you the one about my Uncle Seamus?' she improvised. Ollie sat down on his father's back and beckoned her to join him. If it was going to be a catastrophe, better try and make it look meant. 'No. What about your Uncle Seamus?'

The bewildered band faltered. The two comedians, due on next, went hopping mad in the wings; nobody but them told jokes and lived. The Pig was outraged and bucked his bum to unseat her. Ollie gave him a slap on the rump. 'The Law's here!' he whispered and the Pig froze.

By now the delighted audience was joining in the punch lines of Trixie's creaky old jokes. Ollie could see the theatre manager had arrived in the wings, too, and was beckoning them furiously to come off stage. Big trouble!

But then, bang! The cupboard doors behind them flew open again. There was a roar of sarcastic welcome from the audience as on bounded Tudoe, towing an embarrassed PC Wyatt behind him on the end of the rope.

With a joyful bark of recognition, Tudoe rushed towards Trixie. The Pig felt a muzzle up his rear, craned over his shoulder and saw a mad dog about to savage him; but, worse by far, he also saw his most feared object – a policeman!

The Pig went into express mode and crawled towards the wing with Ollie and Trixie still on his back. Tudoe barked and ran round him in happy circles and PC Wyatt, clutching the end of his rope, was twirled at breakneck speed around their perimeter. The audience had no idea what all this had to do with a schoolroom, but they thought it was worth a good cheer as everyone disappeared at speed into the wings.

The manager marched Pigott off to his office, the comics took over the vacant stage and PC Wyatt recovered enough to ask in a loud, breathless voice, 'Where's this dog's owner?'

'Shut up!' snarled the stage manager from his corner.

'I'm the owner,' Ollie whispered firmly. 'He's mine.'

Grinling sidled down the wing. 'We've been hunting for him all day, officer.' The policeman simply laughed at him. Grinling smiled back happily, as if he didn't mind.

Ollie felt Miss Bellamy drop a towel round his shoulders for him to dry off. Not unnaturally, PC Wyatt mistook her for a sensible adult and lectured her in whispers. She gazed at him vacantly while he told her to keep her children's dog under control. 'He's been out there collecting the money for some Irish lads. Illegal busking. We've just shipped one back home on the ferry.'

Trixie O'Hara gasped and PC Wyatt gave her a sharp look. 'Keep your eye open for the other lad; he may try and steal your dog again.' He gave them all an even sharper look and whispered, 'If he is your dog. I'll be keeping an eye.' And PC Wyatt left.

* * * * *

After the curtain call, the Pig still hadn't reappeared and the Youngstars got busy. If PC Wyatt was on the prowl outside, Trixie mustn't be recognizable as the boy busker he was looking for when she left the theatre.

They hid her boy's clothes in a skip and got to work inventing a get-up for her – well, everyone did but Silver. Silver made no secret of her feelings – when did she ever? She didn't care for Trixie, or for her apricot curls.

Ollie went up to the wardrobe to wangle a dress out of the wardrobe mistress, but she wasn't there. Miss Bellamy was, though, hunting uselessly for a reel of cotton and she helped him, equally uselessly, to select a dress. 'For your pretty new friend?' she asked slowly. Then, with an unexpected turn of speed, 'Where is she from? Paris?' Ollie looked at her in surprise. Where in heaven had she got the idea that Trixie O'Hara was French? Even Ollie knew that Paris was not in Ireland, but he hated upsetting Miss Bellamy so he said it was very likely she was Parisian. Miss Bellamy said wistfully that she'd guessed as much, and he rushed off with the dress. It was pink velvet and, as Silver was quick to point out, clashed with Trixie's hair and her boy's boots. It was a tight squeeze, too. Silver said comfortingly that Trixie would look less like a raspberry pudding once she'd been on a month's diet. Trixie didn't lose her temper; she just said she'd get back in her boy's clothes and be on her way.

That frightened Ollie. If the police deported
223

Trixie back to Ireland like they had the other lad, the show would be in a right mess again. 'The frock is gorgeous,' Ollie said valiantly. Silver jeered. 'You would say that, Ollie Pigott. You'd say she was the Queen of bleeding Sheba to make her stay.'

Grinling butted in, quite angrily for him. 'Silver, if she goes out of that stage door as the Irish boy with the dog, they'll run us all in for harbouring her. Picture yourself behind bars. Did you ever hear of a convict that turned film star?' Silver looked daggers, but Trixie was already halfway out of the dress.

Ollie suddenly felt sorry for her. She was only a kid and she'd done her best for them; but here she was, surrounded by a crowd of bitchy strangers who only cared about their show and not about her at all. He was reminded of how the Headmaster had called them scum.

'Shame about your mate,' he said. Trixie gave him a pinched little nod.

'Me big brother. I'll be on me way now.' And it served them right, Ollie thought. They'd done nothing but use her.

Then John said, in a faint, hung-over voice, 'You know Ollie threw his last penny in the world into your hat this morning, Trixie, for you and your brother?' And Grinling asked, 'Who was it held the stage door open for you to run through when the police were after you? Remember? Who covered up for you to Mr Pigott and said you were the substitute dancer? Who told the police he owned your dog?'

Trixie stared at the dressing room floor. They waited and watched. Tudoe sighed and leant against her. And then Trixie sighed too and said that Ollie was a real pal even if some other people definitely weren't, and she glowered at Silver. Then she got back into the raspberry pudding dress and agreed to stay on, and they all headed for the stage door.

Ollie smiled encouragingly at her. 'See you at the matinée t-t-tomorrow, then.' The Pig's voice boomed down the passage, 'Oh no, we won't be seeing her tomorrow.'

He was pale and sweaty, so the remains of his stage make-up stood out in marmalade islands on his face. The manager had given him a bad time. He'd fired the Pig, no less, and it had taken all the Pig's guile and charm to make him change his mind. But the manager had warned him that if there were any more alterations to his act, particularly unrehearsed ones, the Youngstars would be out on their ear: off the bill.

The disgrace of such a thing happening had made the Pig quite faint. As for the loss of hard cash – the mere thought was enough to put him on the danger list. He couldn't wait to take it out on someone else. 'I need a dancer in my troupe,' he boomed, 'not a stale-joke-spouting Irish clodhopper with a mad mongrel.' Trixie looked fierce. 'You leave my dog out of this. Anyway, I wouldn't work for the likes of you, not if you paid me.'

'Right,' the Pig roared. 'We're agreed on one thing, then.'

He singled out Silver, who'd remained aloof and bored. 'You'll go back to the original plan, Silver. You play both your own and Jess's role.' He turned on Trixie. 'As for you, don't think you're getting a penny out of me for tonight's fiasco. Now make yourself scarce.'

'My pleasure,' Trixie O'Hara said, and clicked her tongue at Tudoe.

'I'll teach her to dance.' It was Silver – all dazzling smiles and hair tossing. 'She'll pick it up in no time, Mr Pigott. She's very talented.'

There was amazement all round. Ollie guessed that Silver would rather have seen Trixie in a meat mincing machine than teach her anything at all, let alone dancing; but the Pig had landed Silver with those two roles to play again that she couldn't handle. And Silver wasn't having it. Oh, no.

The rest of the troupe were giving her full marks for generosity, though; they were grinning like Halloween pumpkins. The Pig looked doubtful. Silver did her pretty hair flick. 'Please Mr Pigott, sir. You said yourself we're up a gum tree. She's all we've bleeding got.'

Ollie had to admire her. Silver was winning the Pig round. His father was thoughtful now. She was winning them all round; they were all looking enthusiastic. The Pig suddenly belted him round the ear. 'Who died, Fiddle Face? Silver's had a good idea. Hasn't she?'

Ollie rubbed his stinging ear. Then realised his father was actually waiting for him to give his opinion. He stammered an agreement and his father nodded at Silver. 'I want her passable by tomorrow matinée and one of the team by Thursday night.'

But now Ollie was worried. The thought of Silver giving lessons in anything but How I Am Going To Become A Famous Film Star was scary. With Silver in charge, the poor kid would most likely break her own neck. He'd never have okayed the lessons if his father hadn't surprised him with that bash on the head.

He tried to get John to take on the lessons; at least John knew what he was doing. He nudged John, who was still the colour of candle wax, to get him to offer. But Trixie O'Hara took a hand. 'I want him, too.' She was pointing at Ollie. 'He's the best.'

It was a remark guaranteed to drive every other Youngstar into a white-hot fury because each of them knew, beyond a shadow of doubt, that they, and they only, were the best. Fortunately, Miss Bellamy chose that moment to launch into a slow speech that swamped them all in a sea of boredom, and it was forgotten. As for Ollie, hadn't the Pig said Ollie was the worst? Ollie knew his dad was right. He always was.

The Pig listened impatiently to Miss Bellamy, who was moaning on about missed buses home and Jess's bed being available for Trixie. Trixie looked grateful, which made Ollie wonder where exactly 'home' was for her and Tudoe. The street? His dad checked the clock in the stage doorkeeper's booth – nearly closing time – and flapped his hands at Miss

Bellamy. 'Do as you please. Do as you please.' And he roared off down the passageway to get changed.

As the Youngstars were all leaving, Silver turned to Trixie O'Hara and asked the question she'd been longing to ask all evening. 'Is your hair natural?'

'It's not a wig – if that's what you mean – like I'm thinking yours is.'

The Youngstars exchanged grimaces. Sparks were going to fly during the dancing classes and Ollie had a good idea who was going to get singed. Him!

They pushed open the stage door and there was a pop and a brilliant flash. Trixie gave a shout and pulled Ollie in front of her, but too late; the newspaper photographer had been tipped off and had got what he'd been waiting for – a picture of the pretty young girl with the dog who'd caused chaos in the Youngstar's act that evening.

'It's free publicity,' Grinling comforted her.

'The Pig will be thrilled,' John assured her. 'He might even pay you!'

But Ollie could see Trixie was afraid. Now why was that? Why didn't she want her photo in the paper when all the other Youngstars would jump at it? Silver would give blood for a chance like that. Preferably Trixie O'Hara's!

CHAPTER EIGHTEEN

HOME SWEET HOME?

The Head-Fixer closed Ralph's bedroom door softly behind him and beckoned Mary Ellen into the luxurious sitting room. 'Head-Fixer' was the name Mary Ellen had privately given the doctor she had called to attend Ralph in their suite in the Adelphi Hotel. He was the best doctor in Liverpool and the suite was the biggest and best suite the hotel could provide. It oozed comfort and extravagance from every curtain and cushion.

Mary Ellen asked the Head-Fixer, 'Is it serious?'

The Head-Fixer wore a hothouse rose in the buttonhole of his black jacket. Snowy white spats peeped from beneath the bottom of his pinstripe trouser legs and his patent leather shoes dazzled. Ralph thought the man was wearing fancy dress when he first came into his bedroom, but it turned out the guy was just kind of slow in the head. No matter how often Ralph answered his questions, he asked them again.

'And when did you first see your double, young man?'

'Like I told you. In the train window.'

'A reflection.'

'No. Like I said, he had a red blazer and a fat nose. Then he didn't, but it was still him.'

'I see. He can change?'

'How should I know? I never met him.'

'But you wanted to?'

'Sure. So French pulled the chain.'

'The lavatory chain?'

'No.' Ralph sighed patiently. 'To find him.'

'You found him in the lavatory?'

'The guy who tried to kill me was in there.'

'Your double came up the lavatory and tried to kill you.'

'Would I go looking for my double if he tried to kill me? And who the hell lives down the john? Are you stupid or something?'

'He thinks he has a double,' the Head-Fixer reported to Mary Ellen. She stared at him. She could have told him that. Was this all they were going to get for their thirty guinea fee? She straightened the white pinafore apron she wore over her dark blue nursemaid's dress and wished she were in a nice, normal post back in the States. The Head-Fixer continued.

'It's not uncommon for an imaginative or insecure child to invent a friend,' he explained. 'Though inventing a double is rarer and more extreme. They furnish the child with a safe, intimate companion or even with an alternative and totally make-believe life.' The Head-Fixer seemed to expect some comment from her.

'He eats good,' Mary Ellen ventured. 'Like a horse with two arses.' The Head-Fixer hurried on.

'But young Ralph has taken the fantasy very far. Too far, I'm afraid. He is ill; indeed, gravely disturbed and should be treated immediately. Mary Ellen's eyes widened. 'The loony bin?'

'No, no. He's not dangerous. A nursing home will suffice. I'll arrange it. His parents are due, you say?'

'There's just his father. No mom.'

'When is the father arriving precisely?' But Mary Ellen didn't know. The tutor had dealt with all that. 'Leave it all to me,' the Head-Fixer reassured her. 'I'll arrange for an ambulance to collect him.' He consulted his fob watch. 'It's a little late to deal with now. Let's say tomorrow morning. Immediately after breakfast.' Mary Ellen nodded.

As she showed him out to the lift the Head-Fixer said 'By the way, I've given young Ralph a strong sedative. He won't be any trouble.'

Ralph wriggled down in his soft bed once the simple guy had left and then wriggled up again to re-lick his lunch pudding spoon. He was comfortable, he was warm, he had eaten three square meals and slept a whole night and then half of the next day.

He felt great. The ragged boys and their gift of the rotten fruit seemed a lifetime away. The thought of his near death in the garbage made him shudder. It sure took a bit of know-how to be poor.

Then he took a bath. He lay in the hot tub and listened to the English accents on the wireless. Like they had a mouthful of marbles. Then he got dressed. Then he discovered that he was locked in. He rattled the handle and called for Mary Ellen who answered softly through the closed door that it was doctor's orders. Ralph called her a treacherous cow and fell asleep.

* * * * *

Wednesday was Silver's fourteenth birthday. Ollie had borrowed sixpence from John to buy her a bracelet from Woolworth's, but he was so busy with the dancing lesson that the bracelet had turned into the promise of one.

It had taken just ten minutes for Silver to get bored and drift out of the class. She had even less use for Trixie once she'd discovered that Trixie never went to the cinema. 'And if you talk to her about film stars,' Silver reported to Ollie, 'she looks really snooty. As if you've said 'knickers' or worse. Who does she think she is?'

But Trixie was anything but snooty with Ollie. She was very quick to learn and they made steady progress. Tudoe watched from the side of the bar, his dreadful tail swinging out of time to the piano music that Miss Reeve was thumping out.

Halfway through the morning, Miss Bellamy turned up with three cups of tea for them and waited silently for the empties while they took a tea break. Miss Reeve became almost chatty. A musician friend had squeezed her a place in the cinema to watch Hal Havern at the opening ceremony, she told them. Tickets were like gold. Trixie stretched and said in an amused voice, 'My nanny said...'

'Nanny?' Ollie interrupted. 'Is that your Gran?'

'No, my nanny.' Trixie stopped, flushed and rubbed the top of Tudoe's head, and then said, 'To be sure yes, that's right, my Gran. She says that long ago Hal Havern eloped with a beautiful dancer to America. It was in the Irish papers.' Miss Reeve made shocked, clucking noises, and Ollie thought the elopement must be the 'spot of bother' the stage doorkeeper had talked about.

'But the beautiful girl changed her mind,' Trixie went on, 'and she got off the ship and left him to sail away on his own.' Miss Reeve made even more shocked noises. 'The only girl ever to jilt Hal Havern, nanny says,' Trixie finished and then corrected herself quickly. 'Granny says, I mean.' She drained her cup and thanked Miss Bellamy, who trailed away with the empty cups like a wisp of vapour; and on they went.

When Ollie called a halt at the end of the morning, they were all exhausted except Tudoe. Miss Reeve banged the piano lid shut. 'I'm off to lunch.'

'Me too,' Trixie agreed. 'Me and the dog's

famished.'

Ollie was starving, too. He was calculating whether he could use a bit of Silver's bracelet sixpence to buy something to eat and still get Silver a half decent present when Miss Reeve delved into her knitting bag and handed him a penny. 'Mr Pigott said to get yourself some chips.' She looked as unfriendly as ever, but Ollie knew she was lying. His dad never parted with money for Ollie's lunch. It was her own money she was giving him. He smiled his thanks. He hadn't suspected that Miss Reeve was another of the Liverpool angels. Her disguise was too deep.

At the afternoon's matinée, poor Trixie O'Hara was stiff as a board from all the dancing practice. But to Ollie's relief, she got through it without actually treading on anyone. The Pig said she was 'Fair enough'. He patted Silver's head and said she was a born little dancing teacher.

The Pig was in a good mood. The photograph of Trixie and Tudoe in the local paper was pulling in the crowds, even though Tudoe managed to look even uglier than he really was. 'Isn't it funny,' Silver said as she examined the picture, 'how dogs look just like their owners!' She cut out the photo carefully, though. Ollie guessed it was going into her spit collection.

Between the shows, they all went back to the digs for Silver's birthday tea.

The landlady had done her proud. There was a white embroidered tablecloth spread on the table, and scones, biscuits, jellies, blancmange, and dripping sandwiches (Silver's favourite) to eat and Tizer to drink, which Ollie thought was like fizzy heaven.

Everyone was there: the troupe, Pigott, the landlady, Hazel. Silver was just going to cut the cake Miss Bellamy had bought her when John said, 'I'll give you one guess what she's going to wish.' There was a unison howl round the table of 'Hollywood!' and then laughter.

Silver shut her eyes. The knife was poised over the cake. The presents she'd been given were stacked close to her plate, as if she didn't trust them out on their own: talc, soap, some silk stockings from Mr Pigott. The knife cut into the cake. Silver opened her eyes.

A greyish sort of couple was standing at the end of the table smiling at her. 'Hello, Mum. Hello, Dad. Where did you spring from?' The greeting was as colourless as the parents. Ollie tried to imagine his own mum coming into the room. What would she look like? What would he say to her? Probably make a right 'nana' of himself.

The landlady fussed around getting cups of tea and cake to make the newcomers welcome. They'd been on the train for hours. Their present to Silver was a grey knitted scarf. She gave it to Heather later. They chatted dully. Time was getting on. The Youngstars had to be back at the theatre for six-thirty. Then Silver's dad leaned back in his chair and delivered their bombshell. 'We've good news for you Silver.'

'Now you're fourteen and leaving school,' Mum said.

'And can go out to work,' Dad said.

'Your dad's found you a job.'

Everyone stopped talking.

The Pig said, 'Dear lady, your daughter already has a job – with me.' But Silver's mother said the job they'd found for Silver was a proper job, nice and near home, in a factory putting wireless parts together. The Pig's boiled sweet eyes were round with alarm. 'But you've signed her contract with me.'

'Only 'til she's fourteen,' the grey father said obstinately.

And the mum said they didn't want their daughter getting into *actressy* ways and then blushed to the roots of her greying hair. Ollie thought how *actressy* ways were the only sort of ways Silver would ever have. The father was saying that the factory money wasn't bad and they were taking Silver back with them. 'We want her back home,' he said.

'And what about what I want?' The question was loud. Half screamed. Silver's father looked at her in surprise. 'You're too young to know what you want, love.' And then Silver started. How she'd been old enough to earn them good money until now, and they'd been happy to take it. How they didn't care about her. How they would ruin her future. On and on. No one else knew where to put themselves; it was so private and violent.

But the grey parents were immovable. In the end, Silver was weeping and begging her parents to change their minds, but they wouldn't. They said they were doing the right thing for her, and Silver screamed that she hated them and ran into the back yard. She locked herself in the lavvy, but they could still hear crying and crying as if she would cry forever.

And then the Pig started. Hearing him talk to the parents, Ollie could see the Pig wasn't interested in Silver at all; all he cared about was his show. Ollie wondered guiltily if he wasn't a bit the same himself. Did he take after his father? He hoped not because if a replacement for Silver had walked into the room that second, the Pig would have dumped Silver there and then. But at the moment he needed her and so he talked and flattered and buttered up the parents.

He told them what thoughtful, caring parents they were. He said how Silver wasn't really cut out for the theatrical business. How perceptive it was of them both, he said, to have noticed her true talent lay in assembling wirelesses! And the deal was done: if they let Silver stay until the end of the week, the Pig would pay for her train fare home and refund them what they'd spent on the ticket they'd already bought. He handed them the money there and then at the table, and Silver's future as a film star was over.

It was arranged that the grey mother should stay on to keep an eye on Silver. Her father was preparing

237

to leave for the station when John, as usual, came out with the question they all wanted to ask. 'Aren't you going to stay and watch her in the show? Silver's our lead dancer now.' But the grey father said it wasn't really his sort of thing. The mum dabbed her eyes with a hanky at the sound of her daughter weeping down the yard. 'She'll get over it,' the dad said and away he went.

No one could persuade Silver to come out of the lavvy. Ollie wished Jess had been there. She could have done it. It was awkward, too: everyone was cross-legged. The Pig bundled them off to the theatre but plucked Ollie out of the group. Now what, Ollie thought, and cracked a smile at once. 'What are you grinning at? Get down that yard and fetch her out.'

'How?' he asked and backed away from the Pig's fist. He said quickly, 'No one else can get her out, D-dad, not even Heth. So how can I?'

'Don't ask. Do. Or else.'

Ollie went and stood outside the bolted door. Silver was quiet now except for a sob or so. The bleak thought came to Ollie that he didn't really know Silver very well, for all that he saw her every day. He didn't know anything about her that he could use to talk her round. All he knew about her was the thing she was crying about: Silver wanted to be a star. It was what she lived for. What misery it all was.

'Silver? It's Ollie. Can you hear me? They've given you 'til Sunday morning.' No answer. He tried again. 'I know you're right miserable.'

'Miserable!!' her voice was clogged with tears. 'I'm suicidal.' That scared Ollie. 'Listen, Silver.'

He pressed his mouth to the door and told her what he'd never told anyone. He told her about the Misery and how it went away while he was doing the show. 'The show isn't a cure for the Misery,' he finished up, 'it's more like you've swallowed a two hour 'forget it' pill. And it's a right rest from crying, take my word.' And Silver came out.

Ollie didn't know whether it was because of what he'd said to her or because Silver would hang rather than miss a show. He did notice that she was especially good that night and not her usual 'Love me, love me' self; as though she were working from a secret sad place inside herself that was where the true Silver lived. He thought what an unfair, rotten shame it was that Silver had learned how to do it right just when it had all come to an end.

CHAPTER NINETEEN

LOVE ME, LOVE ME NOT

'Madrid About To Fall!' All the paper sellers were shouting Thursday's headlines.

Madrid was where Pablo had gone. Trixie told Ollie that if Madrid fell it would be the equivalent of London being conquered – and there was he thinking Madrid was just the little village where Pablo's mother lived! Trixie O'Hara was suspiciously 'educated', Ollie noticed. But poor old Pablo! Ollie tried to imagine shells and bombs falling on the street he and Trixie and Tudoe were walking along on their way to Lewis's, the big store. It would be right terrifying.

The dancing lesson was over for the morning and they were shopping. Ollie was going to buy Jess some chocolates and Trixie had a whole pound to spend – well, she had until Ollie borrowed sixpence of it to buy the chocolates. The Pig had actually advanced Trixie a pound of her wages. 'Streuth!' he'd shouted at the sight of the pink velvet dress. 'You look like a blushing bunny. Buy yourself a frock that fits; and you can chuck those seven league boots out, too. I want to see dainty, ladylike shoes.'

'Why do you never have any money, Ollie?' Trixie laughed as she doled out the sixpence. 'Are you a secret gambler?' It was big headed of him, he knew, but he wanted Trixie to go on believing he was good enough to teach her dancing. So he smiled and said he lived a wicked private life that used up all his funds. He didn't want her to know the Pig didn't think he was worth paying. And Trixie laughed more.

Tudoe strolled along, well behind them both. But if a passer-by stopped them to congratulate them on last night's show – and lots did – Tudoe caught up and sat grinning kindly at them. It made even the most enthusiastic fan edgy, and they would soon clear off.

Ollie was glad of the Tudoe effect. It meant people didn't get round to asking why there weren't any photos of him in the display cases outside the theatre; and it saved him having to mumble some rubbish to them instead of the real reason: his dad didn't think he was any good. It didn't stop Trixie O'Hara asking, though. Questions, questions! That was Trixie. But by now Ollie knew how to handle her. 'Trix. What else can your dog do apart from beg?'

'Do?'

'Yeah. Can he dance for instance?'

Trixie's blue eyes blazed. 'It's bad enough for him being a dog without being forced to dance on top of it.'

'That's exactly what I was thinking. Come on. This is Lewis's.' Tudoe grinned at Ollie and there were no more questions about Ollie's photo.

* * * * *

It was about then that Ralph looked out of his hotel bedroom window for want of something better to do. From his vantage point he could see right down to the docks. He stared through the grey strings of smoke rising up from the hundreds of chimneys on the grimy buildings below him and thought of nothing.

Breakfast was over. A waiter had wheeled it in on a trolley, the same way all his other meals had been wheeled in, and Mary Ellen had stood guarding the door like a wardress while the guy laid it out.

He noticed they both watched him in a wary sort of way, out of the corner of their eye, kind of nervously. Then they'd both scoot out the door in a real hurry, and Mary Ellen would lock him in while he ate. She'd come back again and watch him in the same leery way when the cleaning maid came to clear it away; and then she'd lock him in again.

It was so unexpected, the way she'd turned into

his jailer. Doctor's orders, she said. But he wasn't sick. Far below, he watched an ambulance pull up outside and two big men in white coats climb out and go into the hotel. Some other poor guest must be really and truly sick.

Rain hit the windowpanes as he watched, and he wondered how French was doing down in that big city. It was the first time he'd thought of her since he'd left the swimming pool. He was surprised he hadn't remembered her before. She'd be looking for him. Or more likely, knowing French, she'd given up on him and headed off to Scotland. She'd be eating 'hot glue' this very minute.

He missed French. How about that for a turnaround? He missed French! You had to be really lonely to miss French.

Then a memory surfaced that he'd never had before; but he was certain it was a genuine memory, and not his imagination, because of the way it snapped into place as if it had always been there. The memory was to do with missing someone. And it was to do with the docks. And he was almost sure it was to do with his double. But how? How could he have a memory about his double when he hadn't known of his existence until last Sunday? Or had he known? Ralph shook his head in defeat. Surely it was impossible. He wrestled with the new memory, trying to pin it into a time and a name.

The memory said he'd been waiting at some docks on a quayside. But how could he have been? The only docks he'd ever visited were here in Liverpool and at Southampton, the other day, when he'd sailed in from the States with Mr Fanfield and Mary Ellen. But the memory insisted that this wasn't the case, and then it added in an extra factor: a lie. Someone had lied to him. But no matter how he bombarded the memory with questions, it refused to fill in any more details.

The memory had given him a shock. It made him realise that he'd lost track of his double, almost forgotten him, under a thick wadding of hotel comfort and warmth and food and sleep. He felt as if part of his brain had been blanked out and now it was breaking into existence again because here was his solemn double knocking on his mind, demanding attention. And it brought about another realisation. Ralph wanted to get out.

It was like the magnets experiment again; as if he'd been suddenly turned around and was being pulled towards his double. Just as two magnets were tugged together by a law of nature, he was drawn towards his double, whoever he was. He wanted to find him so badly it was like a craving.

Ralph took the butter knife from the dish. How dare they lock him up all alone like this? He set to work to pick the lock of the bedroom door with the knife. He must have been mad, he thought, to hang around in this hotel room like a zombie when the double was out there on the loose. He could be anywhere by now. Then he heard Mary Ellen talking on the other side of the door and a vacuum cleaner start up, which meant that the cleaning maid had arrived.

The butter knife wouldn't even fit into the keyhole. Ralph stabbed it into the pat of butter and sat down on his bed. He had to think of some other way out. The trouble was, he couldn't. He felt stupid and ineffectual and very low.

His bedroom door opened and the cleaning maid stood on the threshold in a uniform that was too long for her and with the vacuum in her hand roaring away like a drunken sailor. 'Allez,' she hissed. 'Your nurse knits in her room.' It was French! All dressed up as the maid. He could have hugged her but for the fact she looked so darned pleased with herself.

He just had time to snatch up his grey flannel jacket before Giselle had whistled him out of the suite, leaving the vacuum still roaring on the spot. 'I have maid's pass key,' was all the explanation she whispered, in the plushly carpeted passageway. She arranged to meet him outside, at the back of the hotel, once she'd picked up her own clothes. 'But how in heck did you know where to find me?' he asked.

'I saw your nurse capture you and escort you here.' Ralph flushed and hoped she hadn't noticed what a willing prisoner he had been. 'You take the main stairs,' she instructed as the nearby lift doors opened. Two burly ambulance men emerged and looked about them for a room number. 'I descend by the service lift.' Ralph rushed down the wide staircase without a word.

He felt great. He was out. He was on the move.

The search for his double was on again. And if he'd known how narrowly he'd just escaped the Head-Fixer's ambulance men, he would have been happier still.

The main stairs came out into a room the size of a baseball pitch, except this was no baseball pitch. Three mighty twinkling chandeliers hung from the high, frosted glass ceiling. The apple green walls were divided into arches by black marbled columns. Some were filled in with panes of glass from top to bottom, and there was mirrored glass everywhere that reflected the room back on itself, making it feel even vaster than it already was. The tall mirror doors were particularly disquieting: you could see yourself approaching as you were going.

Elegant people were sitting at tables all around the room drinking pre-lunch cocktails or reading newspapers; and one of them was Monsieur Shoes. He had his back to Ralph, but the shoes were sticking out in front of him. And besides, Ralph would have known that silhouette anywhere.

Shoes' presence could be a coincidence, Ralph told his thumping heart. But his heart only thumped harder. 'Vamoose!' it said. 'This guy is lying in wait for you – with his gun.' Shoes never looked round as Ralph fled down the last few stairs, into the foyer and out through the revolving door into the driving rain. As he went, the small man he had rescued came in the other way and smiled at Ralph as they spun slowly round one another. His smart coat was open. Underneath it, he was wearing a blazer. It wasn't red, but you could see it had been once. Ralph came out of the hotel and stood in the rain in a torment of indecision. He remembered now exactly what the guy had said to him after the fight with the vixens. Why hadn't he realised at the time that it proved he knew his doppelganger? If he went back into the hotel though, to talk to the small man, Shoes might kill him. If he died, he'd never find his double. That clinched it. Ralph hurtled past the stationary ambulance with its doors clipped back in readiness to receive him, and hurried on his way.

Giselle was sheltering from the rain in the staff entrance when Ralph reached the rear of the hotel building. She took his arm in an impatient, claw-like grip. 'We go to buy an umbrella,' she said. 'You have money?'

'Not a cent.'

'I have twopence. That should smother it.' He resisted correcting her. What the hell! 'Smother' made about as much sense as 'cover'.

'How did you get to work in the hotel?'

'I befriend a waiter. He is from Paris also. *Et alors*, he smuggles me in and I spring you out.' Ralph left that one alone, too.

As they pushed through the doors into Lewis's, Ralph remembered the small man again. 'French!' he said. 'I just figured something out. Remember that little guy we passed in the street? Well, he knows my double. They work together!' And he told her how the small man had said 'See you at work. Scarper.'

'What is 'scarper'?' Normally he would have been delighted to find another chink in French's armour of superiority, but now he just answered her.

'Run away.'

Her eyes widened. 'There is danger?'

'No, no. Well, yes, there is, in fact. I saw Shoes at the hotel.'

She looked very doubtful. 'But he drowned...'

'Well now he's un-drowned, unless he's got a double, too. And believe me, he's as scary as ever. But French, my doppelganger goes to work. It's a clue. And you know what? This time I saw him, the small man was wearing a red blazer too. Well, it was more a kind of washed-up cranberry, but you could see it had been red once.'

But Giselle took a lot of convincing. The double was too young to work. 'Maybe he's short for his age.' Ralph could feel himself getting angry with her. They stood beside a big display of fireworks, got up for Guy Fawkes that night, and argued heatedly about what a dwarf and a boy could possibly both do that involved wearing a red blazer.

After five minutes they still hadn't agreed. Ralph maintained they were baseball team mascots and Giselle, after her usual appeal to the invisible wise person over his right shoulder, declared they were definitely both lift operators and sent him off, fuming, to take a look at the elevators in the store.

And he'd thought he'd missed French! How wrong can you get? It was disappointing, but French was just someone to quarrel with.

248

Giselle sat on a chair at a mahogany counter while a tireless assistant brought her every umbrella in stock to inspect. She rejected the lot on the grounds that they were not à la mode, but actually it was because even the cheapest was threepence, a penny more than she had. A discreet withdrawal was called for. She waved a hand at the firework display and remarked that it was a bizarre world. 'In my country we celebrate the success of a glorious revolution; but in yours,' she told the startled assistant, 'you celebrate nipping one in the bum.' And she strolled away.

It was about then that the lift doors opened but before Ralph could get in, the most beautiful girl he had ever seen in his life stepped out. She tossed her fair hair when she saw him goggling at her. 'Quick,' she said, handing him a golden casket. 'Take this. I'll explain later.' And she disappeared into the crowd of shoppers.

Once he was over the breathtaking impact of her, he took a look at the casket, which turned out to be a cigar box covered in gold paper; but somehow that made it even more glamorous. He slid off the rubber band that held it shut. It was packed with English bank notes. This was the quickest buck he had ever made. Jeeze! This was a record for anyone – even Rockefeller.

At exactly the same time, Ollie was selecting the chocolates for Jess, carefully pointing out to the assistant on the confectionary counter which ones she should take out of the glass display case with her silver tongs. The assistant nestled each chocolate into a little frilly paper cup in a box while agreeing with Ollie that a girl in hospital would want variety and nothing too hard to chew. But then, while the assistant was weighing them, a dark girl came up to the counter and stood unusually close to Ollie for a stranger.

'How can you buy chocolates?' she challenged him. 'You have no money.' Ollie could see the assistant was a bit jumpy about that bit of information. And how did the dark girl know he was penniless, anyway? Was she another one of the Liverpool angels? He winked at her. She looked extremely disconcerted. 'I borrowed it.'

'Then give me a penny.' A grasping angel? Or – and now here was a question – do angels pee? And did this particular angel need to spend a penny?

Giselle noticed Ralph was up to his mean tricks again. She could see he wasn't sure about giving her a penny; he looked sort of surprised and amused, too, at the idea. But after a moment's hesitation, he asked the assistant to make it five pennyworth of chocolates, not six, and handed Giselle a penny.

'Merci,' she said ironically. And he turned back to the assistant. 'Chocolate,' Giselle persisted. 'Yet you had breakfast.' Ollie smiled patiently. He knew patience was the way to deal with aggressive fans, so it probably worked with angels too. 'They're for a girl.' Giselle was overwhelmed. Ralph was going to give her chocolates.

She managed a gruff 'That is *charmant*,' and

Ralph gave her another heart-warming smile.

'French?' He asked. And for once she didn't want to spit with resentment that Ralph could never get around to calling her by her proper name, 'Giselle'. She smiled back.

'Yes,' she said.

Then he pulled another surprise. 'A friend of mine knows France.' This was the first Giselle had heard of Ralph having a friend. The two things seemed incompatible. 'My friend says they perform plays there without words. Silently.'

Ollie hadn't meant to get into conversation with her, but meeting a French girl (angel?) was the chance of a lifetime to check on Miss Bellamy's tales. He kept it brief, choosing the words he used carefully. No t's, no d's. He didn't want to stammer. It put people off. 'Is that right – about the silent plays?'

Well! The chocolates were parcelled and paid for by the time Giselle was drawing to the end of her lecture on the famous French Mime. 'And not only without words,' she concluded. 'They have no objects either, but the people who mime are so brilliant they make you think that this invisible door, or dog, or bouncing ball, or gale force wind is really there. *Incroyable!*'

'Like hallucinating,' he said

For the first time ever, they were on the same wavelength. Giselle could see Ralph's face was alive with interest and, strangely enough, with longing too. He smiled again. 'Bye.' And he took the gilt box of chocolates from the assistant and, to Giselle's everlasting disappointment, instead of handing them to her, walked off in the direction of the lifts.

The shop assistant asked, 'Mate of yours, is he? Shame about the poor lad's girlfriend.'

'Girlfriend?'

'In hospital.' The child looked as if she'd been struck by lightning. 'Are you all right, love?'

'Zut!' Giselle exclaimed and ran after Ralph's double, pushing her way through the crowds of shoppers. But she'd lost him. She ran all over the shop despairing of ever finding him but then, to her delight, she caught up with him by the lifts with his gilt box and took his arm excitedly. 'Stay calm,' she warned Ralph's double, 'but your doppelganger is here, in town. The double whom you saw n'est-ce pas? On the train?'

And Ralph's double replied, 'Have you gone nuts or something, French?'

She said flatly, 'Oh! It's you.' Then she struck her forehead with her fist so hard that Ralph winced. 'I met with your double,' she wailed, 'and I mistook him for you! How could I do that? He does not even talk like you.'

She looked so upset Ralph actually postponed killing her and said, as evenly as possible, 'It's because we're so alike.'

'But you are *not* alike; *he* is *nice*.'

* * * * *

The visiting hours were 2-3pm and Ollie was outside the infirmary promptly. The evening hours were impossible: a mean three-quarters-of-an-hour that fell just when he would be preparing for the show. The infirmary was a grand looking, deep red, brick building with short brownish mottled columns all over it. It put him in mind of a brawn tea. It had turrets, too, and twiddly bits that gave its dignified appearance a touch of playfulness. It was like Queen Mary, Ollie thought, the King's regal old mum, but Queen Mary dancing the Lindy Hop.

He went through a porch into the broad hallway and started up a staircase with fat, mustard coloured ceramic banisters. Jess was in a right posh place. He couldn't wait to see her. But he was soon called down again by the receptionist. Children were not allowed in the wards on their own. 'No adult, no entry,' she told him and started dealing with the next enquiry; so he had to step aside.

He sat on a seat in the porch with his box of chocolates. It would take until next Christmas to get Miss Bellamy up here, and as for his dad, well – that was a laugh. This adult rule meant he wasn't going to see Jess.

Not to see her was completely unbearable. And what if Jessie wasn't better in time to move to the next date on Sunday? What if she never caught up with the troupe again? What if Trixie O'Hara stayed on? The Pig had already given her Jess's blazer. He jumped to his feet to try and escape from his own thoughts and cannoned into an old man who was

253

leaving. Ollie began to stammer an apology, but the old man said, 'It's Ollie, isn't it?'

It was Father Anthony, the old priest who had given Jess and Pablo and him a lift in his pony trap when their hired car broke down. He was a right pal.

Father Anthony explained he'd come over to Liverpool to visit a colleague who was a patient there. 'But whatever brings a youngster like you here?' Ollie told his story in stuttering stops and rushes and in no time Father Anthony had led him back to the receptionist and found out which ward Jess was in. He walked Ollie along cream tiled passageways and into a ward as round as a gasometer. It was easy to locate which was Jess's in the big circle of beds. Her mum was sitting next to her. She looked exhausted, but Ollie still recognised her from the photo Jess kept of her. After a quick word, Father Anthony went away, almost before Ollie could thank him.

Jess looked terribly ill. That was a shock. Hospital was supposed to make you better, not worse, and when Jess spoke, her voice was so faint he could hardly hear her.

'You get a cup of tea now, Mam. Ollie will look after me.' Once her mum had gone, Jess smiled slightly at Ollie, but the skin stretched over her face as though it would tear and he wished she wouldn't. He was so appalled by the look of her that, for once, he couldn't think what to say and sat at her bedside, dumb as a post.

He put the chocolates down on her locker. After

a minute he asked, 'How are you?'

There was a long pause. She seemed about to say something to him but then she changed her mind and instead of replying directly, she asked, 'Will you do something for me?'

He nodded.

'There's letters, lots of them, in my drawer. No, not here,' she said as his hand went to her locker. 'At the digs.' Her voice was even fainter. 'Burn them.'

'What?'

'Burn them. And don't tell. Promise?' He promised.

After a bit she said, so quietly he had to lean his ear down to her, 'Be brave, Ollie. One day, you'll be grown up and you can walk out on your old man and there'll be nothing he can do about it.'

He smiled at her gratefully. Trust Jess. It should be him doing the cheering up, not her. He said, 'Then we'll have some fun, won't we?' But she didn't smile back and say yes they would. Instead she reminded him how, on Sundays, the Youngstars always met at the railway station under the station clock for a head count. 'And we will this Sunday,' he said sharply. He didn't want her worrying she was going to be left behind.

But she took him off guard by asking in her faint voice if he believed in heaven. He wasn't sure what she was getting at. They'd never touched on religion much in their talks – left it to Heather – but then he remembered that Jessie's father was dead. She mustn't go upsetting herself about her dad, so he said that yes, there was definitely a heaven. It came out a bit shifty, though. 'D-d-do you think there is?' he asked, to cover up.

'Hope so.' It was almost a whisper and her eyes were closed. 'Because if there is, let's all meet under the clock, eh?'

'Yes,' he whispered back uncertainly because he was frightened now without knowing why. She was talking so strangely, so unlike herself. She was in an ill place that he was cut off from, an unreachable land where the language meant something different from what was actually being said. But he couldn't translate it for the life of him, couldn't understand what she was getting at or what she was trying to tell him.

'Under the clock it is then,' she whispered. Then she opened her eyes wide to look at him and the words came out good and strong like the Jess he knew. 'And make sure you're bleeding old by the time you get there, our Ollie, to please me.' Her eyes shut again and her voice faded. 'Thanks for the sweets. Go now.'

* * * * *

He found the bundle of letters just where Jess had said. He pushed them inside his jacket as Heather came in. 'Ollie Pigott, what are you doing in our room?'

'Nothing.'

'What did you hide in your jacket then?'

'Nothing.'

'Liar.'

'Stop poking your nose into my business, then, and I wouldn't have to lie, would I?' It was the nastiest he'd ever been to her. He saw it upset her, but he pushed past her and went down to the parlour.

The fire was smouldering smokily, so he opened up the damper and crouched on the hearth waiting for a good blaze to get going. And while he waited, he did something he would regret for the rest of his life. He took one of the letters out of its envelope. It was difficult writing but he could see it began, 'My Darling.' He turned the letter over. It was from Pablo. He turned it back and read:

'My Darling,
Next week, we no meet. Tell Ollie, your little friend, I sorry. No lessons this week. I am in York, you are not. I miss you. How I love my beautiful Jess. Each time you write that you love me too it make me so happy. You are why I live. Soon you are sixteen and like you say, we ask your mother if we can marry. That will be the best day...'

By now the sour feeling in Ollie's guts had somehow got into his brain and bones, too. He was all sourness. He felt half killed by it. He was angry now, too. Jess loved Pablo! How could she? The fire in the hearth jumped into life and he pushed the letters into the flames.

He could feel tears at the back of his eyes because

secretly, so secretly he almost didn't know it himself, he had always expected that Jess would love him one day. Not now, but later, when he'd caught up with her. It was an expectation that framed everything he thought and did. But Jess was never going to love him. The letter showed that. He was just her 'little friend'. The knowledge pounded at his loneliness and his need for her until he nearly broke down. He understood now that he loved Jess. And he hated her for loving someone else.

Heather barged in. 'What are you doing?' He kept his back to her, still looking into the fire, and said quietly: 'Get lost, Heth.' He heard her hurt gasp. Then she said, 'I know you know it was me. Even though I came and warned you straight after.'

'What do I know?'

'That it was me told on you to yer dad when you ran off to the station to meet that girl.' Ollie couldn't be bothered to deny the girl's existence, or even deny Heather had come and warned him either. 'It's over and done, Heth.'

'Not unless you forgive me.'

If only she would go. 'I do, I do. Now get lost.'

But she stayed and burbled stuff about money, stuff that went past him; but he turned to look at her for the first time when she said, 'Your dad gives me money if I tell tales on you all.'

It figured, he thought, staring at her comic face with its nose like a tortured carrot. The Pig knew so much about them all. Always one jump ahead. That was why the Pig had caught him so quickly at the station. Heather had been paid to sneak on him.

Heather was on about her auntie now. 'The one that gave me my kimono. She got married and she won't have me in the house any more. Every break from touring we have, I stay in lodgings. I've no home to go to. It's expensive. I'm sorry. I'm sorry.' She burst into tears.

'It's all right, Heth,' he said. 'It's all right.'

CHAPTER TWENTY

THE BOX

The last thing Ralph meant to do was to tell French about his golden box of money, but he'd been really nettled by what she'd said about him and his double so he showed her the box just to prove he was as 'nice' as his angelic doppelganger. He'd been right to want to keep it to himself, though. Ralph could hardly watch as Giselle blithely shelled out *his* cash on the fare for the taxi she'd taken to the Women's Hospital.

He slouched after her into the building. Everyone else thought he was nice, didn't they? What was wrong with French that she couldn't see it? He would make a list, that's what he'd do; he'd make a list of all the people they'd met who'd thought he was nice. That would show her.

But the list was depressingly short. It started and ended with the extremely old, wiry granny in the laundry until he remembered the boy with the hole in his pullover and added him to it. But even the boy had preferred his double. How about the small man? He'd been grateful when he'd rescued him. Maybe they'd all just been grateful to him. Maybe that didn't make him this elusive 'nice'.

Normally he wouldn't have given a damn about it but French seemed to go for the 'nice' thing in a big way. 'Hey, French,' he remembered. 'You never gave me back my change.'

But the women's hospital proved disappointing. The patients were mostly ladies with new babies ranging from wrinkly to rosy. Not a sign of the double and his girlfriend.

It didn't bother French. She whirled him off to another hospital where they'd hardly got through the door before they came up against the visiting hour restrictions. Off they went again, and now here she was, paying for their fourth taxi with his money, outside the infirmary, a quaint looking kind of castle in deep red brick. French sure could spend her way through other people's cash!

Ralph sat down in a grand porch while she went inside to check the visiting hours. He was still wrestling with the problem of what made you 'nice' when a truly great thought came *smackeroo* into his head: wasn't he doing the nice guys a favour by being nasty? Yes, by golly, he was! Because if everyone was 'nice' then 'nice' would be the norm and so the nice guys' 'niceness' wouldn't show up as being anything out of the ordinary at all. Ralph figured that all those popular 'nice' folks out there shouldn't be so down on nasty people like him. On the contrary, they should be glad to have him around. Nice people positively needed nasty people scattered in amongst them – for contrast. So hold on! Didn't that make him a useful commodity? He was wondering if there was money to be made out of being nasty when he happened to glance out at the busy road. He shot into the hallway after Giselle. 'Run, French!' he commanded. 'Shoes!' And while the receptionist was still bleating 'No adult, no entry,' they raced down cream tiled corridors into the heart of the hospital.

But Shoes was after them. They kept catching sight of him dodging round tiled corners close behind them, but they shook him off at last when Giselle pulled Ralph through a heavy door and slammed it behind them. They found themselves in a beautiful, calm room. The short pillars supporting the ceiling were tiled in lovely aquamarine and green embossed ceramic and gave the room a ripply, quiet feel as if they were under water. Ralph reckoned it might be a kind of holy room. Gradually they got their breath back and relaxed a little.

'We get nowhere with this cat and mousse,' Giselle said. 'Only twenty minutes remain before they throw up the visitors. I will go alone and entice Shoes away. Then we continue our search. You hide here so he does not kill you.'

'But what if he kills you, French?'

She shrugged. 'Then you are on your own.'

That was certainly an attractive prospect (and would save him money, too) but much as he was tempted, it wasn't fair to accept, and he said so. The argument was settled by Shoes, who came into the chapel.

All three of them were so surprised to confront each other that no one moved for a second. Then Shoes pounced and picked up Ralph. He held him under one arm, kicking and shouting, with Giselle hanging onto Ralph's jacket. But Shoes elbowed her off and bashed her head against a tiled pillar, which gave him time to get to the door with Ralph.

At which point, Father Anthony entered Ralph's life. He appeared in the doorway pushing his friend, an even older and frailer cleric than himself, in a wheelchair. He took in the scene in an instant. With a quavery cry of 'Hold tight, Brother John!' he rammed the old man's chair into Shoes. He did it so hard that Shoes dropped Ralph, fell over, and Father Anthony sort of mowed Brother John in his chair over the top of him. And Ralph ran for his life. As he ran past a few late visitors hurrying with flowers and bags of fruit to visit patients, Father Anthony's stern lecture to Shoes faded behind him '...God's House... God's children.'

Flying footsteps behind him made him put on speed but an 'Arrête, Ralph,' slowed him down for French to catch up. As one, they turned into a ward. It was a big, round room. Several visitors looked up in disapproval as they rushed in, so they braked down to a casual saunter. Ralph went one way round the circle of beds and Giselle the other, surreptitiously checking over the visitors at the bedsides for a sight of the doppelganger. They'd almost met in the middle when a battered Shoes followed them in.

Giselle simply dropped to the floor and crawled under a bed, much to the surprise of its occupant, and Ralph sidestepped round a trolley of medical equipment and slipped between the curtains drawn round one of the beds.

There was a nurse in there, leaning over a girl in the bed who was staring at the ceiling. An exhausted looking woman sat on her other side, stroking the girl's hand. Ralph watched the nurse feel the girl's pulse and then close the girl's eyes. He felt at once that he'd barged in on something serious, something awful that was none of his business, and he mumbled an embarrassed excuse for being there. The woman looked up and saw him. 'She's gone, my love,' she said to him. The anguish in her voice was unbearable. 'Our Jess has gone.' Ralph nodded dumbly and backed out the way he'd come.

To his terror, Shoes was standing practically next to him with his back to Ralph, darting looks this way and that round the ward. It was perilous, but it was also a golden opportunity; Ralph took a hypodermic needle from the trolley and drove it hard into Monsieur Shoes' buttock.

While Shoes hopped and writhed and squalled and a fleet of white-aproned nurses, wearing starched white hats the size of swans on their heads, swooped on him from all sides, Ralph and Giselle made their escape.

The night sky was popping and banging with fireworks. They walked fast in the direction of the river. There were bonfires burning on some of the side streets, and kids letting off firecrackers. Giselle led Ralph to a wide, open, rough site with deep trenches dug into it. They were building a cathedral there, she said. All you had to do was get past the night-watchman and you could sleep there. She pointed out an old man sitting inside a flimsy canvas shelter with a brazier of hot coke burning in front of it to keep him warm. The previous night, Giselle had found a place to sleep there in the foundations, where they'd already built most of the crypt.

It was a dark, wet and kind of scary place. It was also freezing cold. Ralph put off the evil hour and said they should find a café and eat, so they went on down to the river. Neither of them discussed Shoes. He'd become the deadliest hazard of their hazardous search, though Giselle did agree with Ralph that the old guys with the wheelchair had saved his life, which was nice of them, considering the old fellows didn't even know him. He didn't mention the curtained-off bed, or what he'd seen.

Nothing much was open; a street market was doing a roaring trade but the sight of families contentedly shopping by the light of the bright paraffin lamps on each stall made Ralph feel lonelier than he was already. Unintentionally, he'd poked his nose into a part of his double's life and found people there who grieved for one another and called each other 'My love.' Stuff he'd never come across before.

*   *   *   *   *

Silver held Ollie back on stage after the curtain call. 'Keep a secret?'

The other artists were trooping back to their dressing rooms to get out of their costumes and their make-up, and the electrician had dimmed the lights behind the closed curtain to a shadowy working light. As the flymen brought in the iron, it gradually cut out the sound of the audience on the other side, shuffling out to the exits. Silver waited in the silence until the stage was empty, then whispered, 'I've got a job as a stewardess on the Delambre'. She smiled brilliantly. 'A stage door friend of mine fixed it for me. I'm sailing to New York, Ollie.'

He didn't mean to be a wet blanket but the stage door friend troubled him: she could only have known him (and it had to be a him) for four days. 'You've got to be grown up to be a stewardess. Eighteen.' But Silver whispered that her friend could fix that. She had a passport from the time she'd done a dancing job in Brussels, so that wasn't a problem. She was alight with excitement as she told him her plan to jump ship at New York and walk to Hollywood. 'I'm meeting my friend tonight,' she whispered, and Ollie grew more anxious. 'All he wants in return is...' She stopped abruptly and said, 'I need the box back now. Mum was getting too interested. That's why I palmed it off on you.'

'What box?'

She looked taken aback then laughed. 'My gold box. Don't be funny.'

But Ollie said he wasn't being funny and tried to find out more about the mystery man with the job offer. Silver interrupted him fiercely. 'Ollie Pigott, give me back my gold box now.'

'I haven't got it,' he said and was surprised to see that it frightened her.

'Where is it, then?'

'I don't know. You never gave me your box.'

She took him by the lapels of his costume and shook him and shook him, whispering all the time that she'd given him the box in Lewis's. His denials came out in jerks as she shook him harder. He thought she must have gone insane. He'd never been near Lewis's with her. She called him a liar again; he tried to tear himself away from her, and she said she'd kill him. He could see she meant it, too. He looked around for help but they were alone. 'I'm not a liar.'

'Swear then that you haven't got it. Swear on the bible.'

The frills on her costume were trembling with her raging. Her beautiful face was close to his but it was an eerie, milky colour in the dull light and he was scared of the ruthless look that came over it when she hit upon a new idea. 'No, not the bible. Swear on something really important to you. Swear on Jess's life that you haven't got the box.' She gave him a crooked little smile. 'I know you won't dare. Because you have got it, you rat. I gave it to you.'

He tried to appeal to her. 'Silver. You didn't give it to me.'

She slapped his face. 'Swear.'

He didn't want to do it. It felt unlucky; no box could be as valuable as a life. But did he really still value Jess now she loved Pablo? And besides, Silver had him cornered. If he didn't obey her, she'd say it proved he'd got her box. What if she called the police? He said, 'I swear on Jess's life I haven't got your box.'

Silver began to scream. That brought Tudoe up on stage, anxiously swaying his tail. He tried to lick her hands. Silver began to beat Ollie, which made Tudoe bark furiously. Ollie covered his head with his arms to protect himself and prayed someone would step in and stop her. By the time Trixie and John arrived, Silver had knocked him onto the floor.

John held Silver off Ollie while she told her story in angry sobs and Ollie sat on the stage shaking his head. He felt as though he was in a terrible dream. And then it got much, much worse because Trixie said gravely that she had been in Lewis's at the same time as Ollie and seen Silver give Ollie the box by the lifts. Silver gave a scream of triumph and John looked grim. Trixie said she'd seen Ollie open the box. This incensed Silver even more, and she threatened to tear Ollie's eyes out. She would have, too, but for John's tight grip.

It was so unreal that Ollie decided the whole episode was a cruel, crazy joke and tried a smile. 'Are you two girls rigging this up against me?' No one answered. The girls looked at him as if he was a bad smell.

Then Trixie said that the box was full of bank notes and Silver turned on her, raging at her to mind her own business. Of course there wasn't money in the box.

But Trixie said Ollie lived a secret private life, Ollie had told her as much, which was why he was always short of money. That's why he'd kept the notes in the box. And Silver screamed that his secret private life had to be the reason Ollie never came to lessons. 'He's got a double life! That girl Heth saw him with is part of it,' she howled. 'He's given my box to that girl he meets.' And she implored John to let her loose so she could kill Ollie.

John hung on to her and tried to pour oil on troubled waters. He said that Ollie had a bad memory these days. Ollie had run in on him in the public baths and climbed out of the window, and ten minutes later he'd forgotten all about it and done it all over again. That showed they should give Ollie time to remember what he'd done with the box.

Ollie appreciated that John was trying to help him but John obviously believed he had the box, too. Inventing silly stories about the baths and giving him time to remember was just a lifeline, just a way for Ollie to disentangle himself from a lie – but it was a lie he hadn't told, so he said there wasn't any point. He didn't have the box. He felt ready to cry.

Silver pulled free from John and stood over Ollie. 'I curse you Ollie Pigott.'

She said it with such quiet ferocity that it sent a shiver of fear through him. 'I curse you for ruining my chances, you greedy little pig. I curse you for the rest of your life.' Silver walked off stage and Trixie O'Farrell crossed herself, as though trying to ward off an evil presence.

After that, the Youngstars' disapproval clamped down on Ollie like a cloak of lead. No one spoke to him, no one walked back to the digs with him, no one even met his eye. Only Grinling had given him a perturbed 'Ollie?'

'I d-didn't do it, Grin.' And Grinling had looked worried and told him to get some sleep.

* * * * *

The all night café Ralph and Giselle found was crammed with men on shift work and with sailors and dockworkers. They were all eating pies or hot-pot or boiled beef and carrots and gravy. Cigarette smoke filled the room to the ceiling. It heaved about in the draught, when Ralph opened the door, and a hot, fatty smell of cooking surged out at them both. They'd found a table at the front of the cafe next to a wide shop window. Condensation trickled down the pane and was soaked up at the bottom by the greasy lace curtain strung across its lower half.

French said she'd fetch them some more coffee

from the counter. English coffee was the next-stop-but-one to Hell, but getting through another cup would put off bedding down in that crypt and so Ralph gave her the money from his golden box. He took her advice and kept his elbow on it where it sat on the oilskin cloth next to him. No need to hand out free chances to thieves. He became aware of a pair of angry blue eyes glaring at him through the window over the top of the curtain. He turned away. Some drunk.

Next thing, a furious fiery-haired girl in a red blazer was standing by his chair. 'Wasn't I right?' She glowered down at him. 'You did have it.'

'Have what?'

'The box, you lying little shite.' Her blue eyes filled with tears. 'And there was I thinking you were the best of the lot of them! I've a mind to turn Tudoe on you, you rat.'

Ralph said coldly he hadn't a clue what she was raving about. This made her even angrier. 'The box!' She was talking too loudly for comfort now. She pointed. 'That box, that's what, and you know it. You stole it.'

Other diners were turning to look at them now. 'Shut up,' Ralph whispered. 'I was given the box in Lewis's.'

'Ah! You admit that?'

'Why should I deny it?'

'Why indeed, you little English snake.'

Ralph lost his temper and jumped to his feet. 'I'm American!' he shouted at her. But now Giselle was back at the table with the coffees and telling him to sit down. The girl said contemptuously, 'So this is your secret girlfriend, is it? Your accomplice, you little crook.' Ralph jumped to his feet again, beside himself with anger, but Giselle motioned him to sit down and said calmly, 'Regard. A girl in a red blazer who thinks she knows you.'

'Thinks!' the girl interrupted. 'Of course I know him. Hasn't he taught me dancing all week?'

'Sit down,' Giselle commanded the girl. 'You are a stepping-stone in our quest.'

'Is that what you call it? I've heard it called a fair cop,' the girl said. Giselle drew out a chair for her. 'Kindly sit down. We have an extraordinary story.'

'I bet you have,' the girl replied sarcastically, but she sat down and Giselle told her the whole story of Ralph and his double.

Trixie O'Hara listened intently, watching Ralph carefully as Giselle talked. When she'd finished, Trixie was dismissive. 'All of you lot can put on an American accent. Tricks of the trade.' She looked hard at Ralph. 'But either you're his mirror image,' – she looked at Giselle – 'or you're the best liar east of the Blarney Stone.' She gave Ralph another long look. 'Will you not let me have the box to give back and we'll say no more?'

'Alas! We do not know you from Eve,' Giselle said sweetly. Trixie said she knew Giselle. 'I saw the both of you down by those statues.' Giselle said politely that she didn't recall the pleasure of their meeting and coolly pointed out that the girl could be a confidence trickster.

'You too,' Trixie retorted, and stood up. 'There's one way to find out. We'll go and find him.'

'Nice try,' Giselle said, pulling Ralph down in his seat again.

'Meaning?'

'We go with you. You and your bad friends bang us on the head and the box is yours!' The girl said angrily, 'Then I'll go and fetch him. If he's not here now, sitting in front of me, then he's in his bed in misery and wrongly accused.' She told them to wait there for her. 'If I bring him back and you're still here, we've got a happy ending. If you're not here, then I'm a fool to let you get away with it.' She glared at Ralph. 'And you deserve everything that was wished on you.' And she went. And they waited.

Ralph had never been so nervous and so excited at one and the same time. It was like a hundred Christmas Eves rolled together. While they waited, he invented opening speeches he'd say to his double, then discarded them as unsuitable and re-invented them. And they waited, and waited. And the girl never came back. This is why.

* * * * *

'That's the dog, sir,' PC Wyatt said quietly to Detective Constable Farrell. Farrell shuddered at the sight of Tudoe sitting placidly outside a café.

'No mistaking him.'

'And that's her, sir,' PC Wyatt whispered as Trixie came out of the café and snapped her fingers at Tudoe. 'That's the girl whose photo was in the paper.'

Farrell nodded and stepped out of the shadows. 'Miss Beatrice Harrison? No, don't run away Miss Harrison. There are quite a few of us here; we would easily catch you.' He showed her his police identity. 'Your mother and father are beside themselves with worry about you, Miss Harrison, and we've their permission to escort you back to Ireland on the ferry where the Garda will take over and return you to your home. Now let's go quietly, shall we?'

Trixie begged and entreated and explained she had a really important errand to run before she went home. But Detective Constable Farrell said he'd heard that one before and told her to move it. Then she asked him to deliver a note to Mr Pigott to say she wouldn't be coming back to work. 'What work would that be, Miss Harrison?'

'Dancing and things.' She said evasively and Farrell agreed.

'But it will get this Pigott character, whoever he is, into trouble. Hiring a twelve-year-old without the parents' permission is illegal.' So the note was never sent. Trixie and Tudoe were led away and only Tudoe looked pleased, because he didn't know any better.

'Why did you do it, Miss Harrison?' Farrell asked as they walk away. 'You've a grand house to live in, I hear, and a fine school to go to. Why did you run away?' But Trixie had stopped short. 'The Lord help me!' she exclaimed. 'Why didn't I notice? He never stammered once! It was the truth they were telling me!'

*   *   *   *   *

Two hours and several foul coffees later, Ralph and Giselle agreed that the fiery-haired girl wasn't coming back. 'And you know what, French? We never asked what work my double did or his name or nothing. It was all about the skunky box.'

'A dancing master!' They looked at each other doubtfully. Giselle raised her eyebrows. 'Con artiste?' Ralph sighed and nodded.

'She ran circles round us.' And they pushed back their chairs and left.

Once outside, Ralph took the money out of the box and gave a good half to French. 'You did a great job with that con girl,' he said. 'You deserve it, French.' He shoved the box into an overflowing dustbin outside the café and was glad to ditch the thing. 'My double must be very trustworthy,' he said pensively. 'The girl who gave it to me really trusted him, I could tell.' And he felt envious of his double. He'd never had a beautiful friend, let alone one that trusted him. He looked so downcast that Giselle said gently, 'We will find him. We are hot on his toes.'

But Ralph was remembering the girl in the hospital bed and the exhausted woman stroking her hand. 'I think my double has bad news coming, French,' he said. 'I think his girlfriend is dead.'

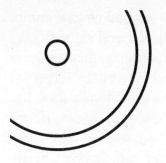

CHAPTER TWENTY-ONE

SHE'S GONE

She was just what Ollie was looking for: an ample mum with a brown paper bag of oranges and a batch of unruly children. She was waiting in the hospital foyer, like all the other people there, for the afternoon visiting hours to start. He stationed himself as close as possible to her. And then he waited, too.

He felt quite sleepy now. He'd been up since before dawn. The red carpet dream had woken him. He'd dressed quietly, let himself out of the silent house and walked through the city.

He'd walked in the dawn light thinking that his usual, everyday misery was nothing to the way he felt now. He could just about understand that Silver's parents had driven her crazy; but why had

Trixie turned against him – and taken the rest of the troupe with her? What had he ever done to her? But it wasn't the loss of all his friends that kept him walking; it was the oath he'd sworn to Silver on Jess's life. It felt wrong. He shouldn't have done it.

Silver had put a price ticket on Jess's life by inventing that oath and the price was all the money in Silver's box. Whatever Silver said, there obviously was blinking cash in it. But how could a life have a price? Why hadn't he had the guts to tell Silver that Jess's life couldn't be reckoned in money, and to stuff her box? Because he was a coward? Or another reason? He walked faster, as if he could outstrip the unwelcome answers to his own questions.

If he was forced to put a value on it, then Jess's, or anyone else's life for that matter, was worth however much that person wanted to be alive. And Jess wanted to be alive all right – for Pablo. The thought dropped into his mind like venom.

All the streets of Liverpool seemed to lead him to the docks. He didn't care. It took his mind off things to be among the people there: the teams of cleaning ladies, dockers arriving for work on their bikes or coming in on the overhead train. There were other boys on the quays, too, either working or nicking stuff under cover of the half-light. And right there, plonk in front of him, was Silver's liner, the Delambre.

A group of seamen were loafing around the bottom of the gang-plank, leaning on their packs and chatting to one another. Their breath hit the cold air in clouds. One of them was the sailor with the monkey on his shoulder. It bared its teeth at Ollie and Ollie attempted a smile back. It seemed an age since he'd last smiled.

The sailor glanced at Ollie indifferently, but then looked again, clapped him on the back and said that Ollie was a great little acrobat; he'd taken his girl to the show the previous night and seen him. They'd been in the gods. The sailor turned out his pocket and gave Ollie his last sixpence because he wouldn't need it when he went aboard. A couple of his shipmates did the same – the poor kid looked so solemn – and Ollie asked if the monkey enjoyed New York. He had a feeling it might prefer palm trees or whatever it was bananas grew on.

'New York!' The sailor scratched his monkey's head. 'We're bound for Brazil, my lad.' He laughed. 'Where the nuts come from. Time to board, mates.' They all groaned, hoisted up their packs and climbed the gang-plank. Ollie felt desolate now such friendly people had gone.

He didn't know where Brazil was but he had a fair idea that Silver was in for a terrible calamity. Nuts didn't sound like her style at all and they certainly didn't sound like Hollywood. Her stage door friend was pulling a fast one. He looked up at the rows of little blank portholes in the side of the liner, towering above him, and wondered if Silver was already up there, marooned behind one of them.

A cup of tea would cheer him up and he turned in to a caff doorway. But then he saw it: Silver's box, poking out of the dustbin outside. He picked it out gingerly from the rest of the rubbish. It was definitely hers. And it was empty. He couldn't imagine how it had got there, but his chief worry was what to do with it. If he took it back to the Youngstars they'd never believe he'd found it in a bin. He turned the box over and over in his hands. He could do with one of those Liverpool angels showing up now to advise him.

He soon reached his usual solution to any problem: to go and tell Jess. She'd sort it out. He'd play down the oath, though. Jess might not appreciate that.

But now Ollie came alert. The ample mum in the hospital foyer had risen to her feet, her eye fixed on the clock on the wall. At the start of visiting hours, she charged the corridor with her pack of kids at full stretch behind her. And Ollie went too, tearing along in her slipstream, and the hospital receptionist never noticed the ample mum had suddenly acquired an extra son.

As they rushed past Jess's ward, he peeled off from the rest of the party and went in to see her.

He crossed the ward to her bed. But there was an old lady in it. 'Where's Jess,' he asked her indignantly, but the old lady was asleep and so he went and stood in front of a nurse writing at a desk. She knew he was there all right, but she kept him waiting. 'Yes?' She said without looking up.

'Where's Jess?'

'Jess?'

'Jess Holingshead.' The nurse drew a list in front

of her and ran her pencil down it. The pencil stopped a third of the way down. 'Are you a relation?'

'No.' The nurse raised her head to him at last. Grim biddy. Definitely not a giggler. Her expression brightened, though, as she took him in. 'You were in the show last night! We were up in the gods. You were marvellous.'

He was used to it. Most punters were the same: one minute you were nothing – worse than a gob of phlegm in the street – but as soon as they recognised you, well, you could be an emperor. She was trilling on about him still and he cut her short. 'Thanks, nurse. About my best mate, Jess?'

The nurse took a furtive look up and down the ward then leant nearer. 'We're not supposed to inform non-relations.' The edge of her nurse's veil, so close to his cheek, was starched sharp as a shark's fin. She pulled a face like she was in church. 'She's gone,' she said quietly. 'You understand?'

He nodded. Jess had left hospital. Discharged. She was cured. He hurried back to the digs to find her. It was a slog of a walk. As he passed The Hops, there was Shtum again, leaning against the wall.

'Where's your dad?' Same question, Ollie noticed. He answered as patiently as he could, although he was longing to run up the last hill to Jess. 'I haven't a clue where he is, Shtum, mate. Inside, playing d-darts probably.' He tried to move on, but then something so outlandish happened that Ollie stayed where he was and stared: Shtum smiled. That was a new one! Shtum smiling.

'Only a kisky geezer plays darts against your dad,' Shtum said. He was still grinning. There were black holes where his canine teeth should be. 'Darts is baby-play for Dad.' Shtum coughed, a bubbling deep cough. 'Does Dad know your little man took a beating from some kids?'

Ollie frowned in surprise. Grinling had never mentioned being beaten up.

'You sure, Shtum?'

Shtum nodded through his cough. 'Sure I'm sure. And the pretty girl.' This certainly tied in with Silver's story of how she'd used her tortoiseshell combs to get away from a gang of girls.

'And you and Tall Boy.'

That was definitely true about him and John. But how did a grown-up – and Shtum of all grown-ups – know anything about something that was just between kids? And how could the attacks be connected? They'd even happened in different towns. And the idea that the Pig would be interested in hearing about it was a joke.

Shtum coughed again, then spat onto the pavement. The spit had a spreading blot of blood in it. They both saw it. Both stared at the spittle and blood lying between them.

An acrobat with tuberculosis hadn't much of a future. When Ollie looked up at Shtum he could see that Shtum knew it too. But all Shtum said was, 'Ask Dad, does he know about the kids?'

Ollie smiled weakly. Poor old Shtum wasn't making sense. He stepped carefully over the blood and left.

When he got to the digs, Silver was outside with her mother. They were standing together at the foot of the front steps. Silver was wearing a new grey coat and a grey headscarf over her hair and he noticed for the first time how alike she and her mother were.

He was so pleased she wasn't on her way to Brazil that he rushed up to them without thinking and held out the box triumphantly. 'Look what I found in a bin.' But she didn't take the box. She drew away from it with a little grimace. Her eyelids were pink as a pet rabbit's and her face was scrubbed bare. She said, 'You've really done it now, Ollie Pigott. That will teach you to lie.'

John came dashing down the steps carrying their two suitcases and Silver's mother took her daughter's arm. None of them gave Ollie any kind of explanation as to what they were doing, and all three set out together: a little raft of his friends who refused to let him on board. 'Where are you going?' he was forced to ask their retreating backs. Silver's mother wrapped a defensive arm round her daughter's waist. 'Home.'

Ollie was calling after them now. 'What about the show?'

'Pulled.' Silver shot the word over her grey shoulder like a bullet.

Ollie was stunned. He'd only been away for one morning and in that time Jess had come out of hospital, Silver had left the Youngstars and

283

the unheard of had happened: the act had been cancelled. He ran up the front steps two at a time.

The Pig's voice boomed from the parlour. 'I'll pay you four days of her wages and no more. God, woman! You'd try and get blood from a stone.' There was a murmur of protest, but the Pig ploughed on. 'She wrecked Monday's show. If it hadn't been for my son's extraordinary ingenuity...' Ollie stopped short of the door in confusion. So it wasn't his father talking in there, then – unless 'ingenuity' was a really bad word.

The door opened and Jess's mother came out into the hall with her handkerchief pressed into her face. No sign of Jess, though. Jess's mother didn't even notice Ollie was there, smiling at her, and the front door banged after her. This brought the total up to two mums in the space of five minutes to give him the cold shoulder. He stepped over the threshold.

The Pig was in his shirtsleeves, leaning forward aggressively out of an armchair and swilling a half bottle of whisky. He smacked his lips and remarked incomprehensibly, 'Funeral expenses, my eye!' When he noticed Ollie, he ran his hand over his glassy hair and said, 'Well, look what the cat's brought in. At least you're back.'

Ollie couldn't gauge his father's mood, but he knew he was quite drunk. The Pig said to the room, 'Pigott's luck, isn't it.' Then, for want of a better listener, settled on Ollie. 'Our first London booking, son.' He patted the arm of the chair invitingly and Ollie had to go and perch uncomfortably next to

284

him. He hadn't been so close to his father offstage for years. It made him squirm inside himself.

The Pig said, 'Our first London booking in the history of the Youngstars.' He sketched the name of the theatre in the air with his whisky bottle as he spoke it – 'The Holborn Empire!' He stared at the invisible writing for a moment; then he laughed – a quick bark of a laugh without a shred of a real laugh in it. 'And what happens? I lose Silver to that pair of prigs she sports as parents, and then Trixie O'Hara does a bunk. Never slept in her bed. Praise the Lord she took her hideous cur with her. I thought you'd scarpered too.'

Ollie interrupted him. 'We d-d-don't need Trixie. Not now Jess is back.'

'Catch up, Ollie,' his father said. 'Jess is dead.'

Ollie went ice cold, but at the same time sweat broke out on his face. He thought he was going to be sick. His father's figure and the armchair shivered out of focus. He grabbed at the back of the chair to stop himself toppling off the arm, so that the antimacassar hanging there slithered round his father's shoulders like a priest's cope. Ollie managed to argue faintly. 'The hospital said she'd left, though.' His father gulped down some whisky.

'In a box, you chump.'

The Pig glanced at Ollie and then wiped the mouth of his bottle on his shirtsleeve and offered it to him. He shrugged when Ollie didn't take it, but then he said kindly, 'Cheer up, Oll, old chap. It's not as if she didn't deserve it. Jess and that – what-was-his-name? – Pablo.' He nudged Ollie and grinned suggestively. 'Appendix indeed! Jess was a no-good girl.' The Pig proffered the bottle again and Ollie took it gratefully and smashed it over his father's skull. Then he ran out into the street and ran and ran.

He had killed Jess and he knew that if he ran for the rest of his life he'd never escape what he'd done. That's what Silver had meant about him lying. He'd sworn on Jess's life he hadn't got the box and so Jess had died. And he truly hadn't got it when he'd sworn. But just because he'd picked it out of the bin later, whoever was in charge up there had penetrated his most private, vile wishes and obligingly killed Jess for him. Because it was true, a bit of him had wanted her dead. As soon as he knew she loved Pablo and not him, an evil part of him had wanted her destroyed rather than let Pablo have her. But now that he'd made her die, the only thing in the whole wide world that he wanted was to have Jess back.

Let her love a hundred Pablos, if she had to, if only she would rumple his hair the way she did and say 'Come on, our Ollie. I'm here now. Don't cry...' Because he was crying. He was running and crying, the tears pouring down because Jess wasn't here and would never be here. She had gone and she wouldn't ever come back to him. She couldn't.

Someone stepped in front of him: a little Chinese girl. She said something about Miss Bellamy, but he brushed past, running and running away from himself and what he'd done. A car drew alongside and cruised next to him. The driver was leaning across the wheel and trying to open the passenger door. Ollie saw the great ruby ring on his finger. It was the Shoes Man. Ollie dodged him, cutting across a brewer's dray pulled by two shire horses. He skipped round cars and trams and round a rag-and-bone man's pony-cart to the other side of the road.

He ran down a slope and a uniformed man in a kiosk yelled something at him as he plunged under a white stone arch into a poorly lit tunnel full of traffic travelling busily in both directions. He'd never seen anything like it. The noise of their engines intensified to an echoing roar in the restricted space. There wasn't another pedestrian in sight. Horns blared as drivers practically clipped his shoulder while they pulled round him.

Ollie had the sense to hop up onto an emergency walkway at one side, and then went on running for all he was worth. His legs were heavy as sandbags now, and he'd hardly the breath left to keep going – and here was the car again with the Shoes Man squinting up at him sideways and leering.

'Let's all meet under the clock, Ollie,' Jess had said. So, of course, it was simple: all he had to do to see her again was to die too. Ollie stopped. The Shoes Man braked hard and the car behind smacked into his rear bumper.

Ollie turned and ran the other way. It would take the Shoes Man ages to extricate himself. He ran out of the tunnel into a weak November sun that sparkled on his tears and turned his vision into a zigzag of dazzling rainbow lights.

Horse hooves clattered and a man shouted a warning. Ollie saw one rolling eye and the dusty mane of the horse as it reared over him where he lay on the ground. He heard a scream and the smash of milk bottles and the clash of metal churns as they came off the milk cart he'd run under. He saw clearly the nails in the horse's shoe as it descended. Then, nothing.

TWENTY TWO

HAL HAVERN

He's flown in. The news spread like wildfire through the crowd on the quayside, where it was rumoured Hal Havern was going to dock, and so everyone streamed all the way out to Speke, the new airport, just in time to see him leave his plane and climb into the waiting Rolls parked out by the runway. They cheered. Some passed out. Some even noticed Hal Havern's face was strained; but he still had to be the best looking man on the globe.

Meanwhile, the rest of Liverpool waited patiently for him behind the police barriers set up outside his hotel – except the press photographers, who were allowed to stand in a privileged pack around the doors. Cheering broke out when a limousine glided to a stop, but the cheers quickly dissolved into hysterical laughter when a small man jumped out followed by an even smaller lady carrying a white bouquet that was practically as big as herself. The laughter increased as, one after another, more small men and women, with white carnations in their buttonholes, hopped out. The car must have been brimful of them.

The dwarves ignored the laughter and walked into the hotel, somehow encapsulating themselves in their own private dignity, until a few in the crowd grew ashamed and started shushing the rest. As the last dwarf reached the doors, Ralph broke though the line up of police and ran over to him. 'Excuse me, sir. Where do you guys work?'

'The Pavilion Theatre. Except Grin. He's the opposition. I'd move it now, son. There's a copper on your tail.'

The dwarf's warning came just in time and Ralph slipped out of reach of the angry policeman bearing down on him. The crowd manhandled him back over the barricade with a sardonic cheer at the policeman's expense, and Ralph disappeared amongst them.

Giselle sighed with exasperation. Ralph was always disappearing. She didn't try and follow. He'd turn up at the station eventually. Ralph had said he'd sooner sleep in a torture chamber than in the half built crypt, so they'd found a safe place to bed down under a bench in the waiting room. It was dusty but warm, and the station police never thought of looking under it.

She noticed Wei, who had found herself a good place, right at the front of the crowd of onlookers, and squeezed beneath elbows and past handbags and umbrellas to join her. Wei greeted her with, 'I got news about red blazer. I try tell Ralph, but Ralph run away.'

'Tell me,' Giselle said.

*　*　*　*　*

As Ralph worked his way through the fringes of the crowd and headed for the Pavilion, a sour looking man leaning against the wall of The Hops stopped him. 'Did you ask Dad?' It was hard to understand his English.

'What?'

'Did you ask Dad about his kids?' Ralph considered the question. It was possible his father had other kids, but Ralph had never heard him mention them. It was also possible that the sour man, who was coughing disgustingly now, had mistaken him for his double. 'Did you ask him like I told you to?' the man coughed out, and Ralph shook his head.

'I guess you were talking to a boy who looks exactly like me.'

The guy didn't take that too well. He went white as a ghost and seemed like he was going to throw a fit. Ralph touched his arm. 'You okay?' he asked helplessly. He hadn't an idea in hell how to call an English ambulance.

The man leant against the wall with his head back and his eyes closed. When he opened them again, they had a desperately sad look.

'There's two of you?'

Ralph nodded.

'If you're okay now, sir, I have to run.' The man seemed to shake himself; or it was more a violent kind of shudder. Then he grinned. Ralph stared into the holes where his teeth ought to have been and thought privately that, when it came to grinning, the man should be advised to pass on it. The man said, 'You going to be great acrobat.' It was not the kind of future Ralph had lined up for himself at all, but he smiled back politely. 'Thanks. I'll bear that in mind. So long, Mister.' But the man stopped him.

'Tell Dad, Shtum says forget the letters.' He was coughing horribly again, so it was hard for the man to speak. There was blood on his lips now, too. Ralph could hardly look. 'You take care now, Mister.' Ralph was going to give him some of the pound notes left from the gold box, but the man suddenly held Ralph's wrist tightly. He had a strong grip. 'Tell me. This other boy, this second one...?'

'You're hurting my wrist, sir,' Ralph interrupted, and the man let go at once.

'Sorry, sorry, child.' It was a hasty, pleading apology, which made Ralph feel mean. That surprised him. Normally Ralph might have staged a big scene about his wrist and forced the guy to beg before he'd tell him about his double; but what the hell was the point of throwing his weight around?

The man didn't deserve it. Ralph said, 'I'm going to find him. I was just on my way.'

'You find him,' the man agreed. The coughing stopped him speaking for a minute, and Ralph waited for him to recover. 'Tell him to come to me. You both come to me. I wait here.' The man reached into the breast pocket of his skimpy jacket and brought out a watch. It was a cheap looking thing. 'Sell this if you need money. Give him half. You both come to me.' Ralph took the watch. He didn't waste what little strength the man had arguing with him about whether he should agree to take it or not, because something important had cropped up: why did this guy accept without question that he had a double? No one else but French did, and that was only because she'd seen them both at the same time. 'What's all this to you, Mister? How do you come into it?'

'I know things I need to tell. Hurry back.' The man was bent over with another fit of coughing, but managed to hack out, 'You're nice boy. Both of you.' He waved Ralph on speechlessly. And Ralph went. 'So long, son,' the man said eventually.

*　*　*　*　*

Ralph did turn up at the station and, all things considered, he was unusually cheerful. The first thing he'd seen outside the Pavilion theatre was the tall boy who'd helped him escape from the swimming pool. The boy was coming away from the stage door, dancing and leaping along the pavement and kind of crowing happily, like he'd won a prize. Immediately he saw Ralph, he stopped doing it but he didn't speak.

Ralph bought a very expensive seat in the stalls of the Pavilion and sat through the rival juvenile troupe's act trying to single out his double. 'It was a really old fashioned show,' he told Giselle. 'Like a silent movie. And NO doppelganger, what's more.' He sat down beside her. 'They were mostly those dwarves we saw. And do you know what, French? It was like they were tipsy. They kept missing each other with their pies. One landed in amongst the audience.'

'It is not *like* they were tipsy,' she told him. 'They *were* tipsy. They had been to a wedding.' He looked at her uncritically.

'You know it all, don't you, French?'

'Yes,' she acknowledged.

As they settled down in their hiding place under the waiting room bench, he wondered how he was going to begin telling her about the other part of the afternoon.

The sick man had not been waiting outside The Hops like he'd said he'd be. Ralph had gone back to meet him hoping that, even though he hadn't brought his double with him, the man might be willing to tell what he'd hinted he knew about the boy. Ralph hung about on the pavement, undecided what to do next, until the door marked 'Public Bar' opened to let out a customer who walked off, a bit

294

over-carefully, along the crowded street. The door took its time to swing back and Ralph sidled inside without giving much thought to what he might find.

The smell of beer nearly knocked him flat, and the cigarette and pipe smoke made his eyes water. He was in a room that was stuffed with men and they were all drinking and smoking. It was darkish, even though the gas wall lamps were lit and their brilliant mantles reflected over and over in the engraved mirrors that hung on every wall. A continual rumble of talk rose from the men. They were standing in groups together, drinking and scuffling the sawdust strewn on the floor with their clogs, or sitting at tables set in wooden booths; or they were leaning at the long bar where the only women in the room drew seething brown beer from pumps into big glass mugs.

One group was watching a game, or maybe it was a match. They gave a concerted 'Ah!' of disappointment as a contestant aimed, threw a dart and missed his target. Then a big man stepped up to the line on the floor. Ralph knew him. It was the man he'd seen running along the platform at Wigan wearing his raincoat in an unusual way. And now he came to think of it, he was the guy whom Shoes had been beating up at the station. Strangely, the man was wearing his hat indoors. Silence fell. The man took aim.

There was a tense, showiness to the big man that drew Ralph into watching him as intently as the rest. The man gave off confidence, but it was a confidence mixed with a dash of uncertainty. It was as if he wanted everyone watching to fear, just as much as he himself feared, that infinitesimal error on his part that could tip the outcome the wrong way. He threw the dart and the watchers stirred with admiration as he hit fair and square and turned to shake his opponent's hand. The smile on his wedge of a face shrivelled to nothing when his round cold eyes met Ralph's across the room. Ralph stepped out of sight quickly behind some men arguing about an election.

So his double had enemies, too. The darts winner obviously hated him. The look on the man's face made Ralph really scared for his double. He pushed his way to the bar. It was so high he had to balance on the brass foot rail to get enough height to poke his head over the top of the wooden counter. Before he knew it, a section was raised and he was dragged behind it through the opening. A soft, pink, furious barmaid gave him a clip round the ear and said things in a low angry voice about losing their licence.

'I'm looking for a man,' Ralph kept repeating but she wouldn't listen. It was as if he didn't count at all in this grown-up man's world. She just kept on about lads not being allowed in there. She prodded him and pushed him with her long fingernails until he was out of the bar altogether and in a room full of beer casks where a down-trodden woman was stooping over a sink, washing up glasses. 'I'm trying to find the sick guy. He told me to meet him,' Ralph managed to insist.

The down-trodden woman hardly stopped her washing to open an outside door with a soapy hand; and the barmaid, who smelt of violets and sweat and face powder, gave him a final painful prod out into an alley where a crowd of poor folks – men and women and children – were gathered round a body lying on the ground. It was the sick man.

One of the women was kneeling beside him, wiping the man's mouth with the corner of her apron. He was in a bad way, Ralph saw at once, and hardly able to breathe. Ralph elbowed his way in to kneel next to her. 'Priest is on his way,' the woman said, 'if he lasts to benefit.'

A doctor would be more to the point, Ralph thought, but no one stirred when he asked them to send for one until he understood and slapped some of his money from the box down on the dirt. It was snatched up by another woman who flung her shawl round her head and ran.

'Mister?' The man didn't open his eyes, so Ralph pressed on, hoping the man could hear. 'I didn't find him, the other boy who looks like me, but I'll go on looking 'til I do. I promise. I know I'm close.' Blood and froth oozed from the man's mouth and was mopped up by the apron. 'Your mother,' the man whispered. The clogs and the boots surrounding Ralph stopped their shifting and stood stock still as everyone waited to catch what must surely be the man's last words. The man's eyes opened. 'Marina.' He could hardly get the name out.

'Don't fret now,' Ralph soothed him.

'The Wheel of Death,' the sick man whispered.

Ralph was frightened for him. 'They'll fix you up real good at the hospital, Mister. No worries.' He wriggled his way backwards out of the watchful, eavesdropping crowd and walked down the alley. Someone must be able to tell him how to get this man to hospital.

Unexpected tears stung his eyes. He didn't want the sick guy to die and he wished the man could speak to the right boy about his mom, Marina. What a life his double led! A life where terrible things happened, like his girl dying, and where people loved him and thought he was nice and he had a mom called Marina who Ralph guessed must love him too. His own life felt like a coat of varnish by comparison: thin and shiny and good to look at, but a kind of cover-up for a life – all surface.

He heard the back door of the pub bang. The darts winning man had come into the alley and was shoving his way through the people. Maybe he would sort out an ambulance. But then came a scream that sent the crowd heaving outwards as if it were exploding, blasted apart by the violence of it: 'Murderer! Murderer!' And the crowd was sucked in again and out again as Ralph heard the rising screams of 'Murderer!' until he covered his ears. But who? Who was screaming? And who was a murderer?

But now everyone was down on their knees and some were crossing themselves, and two little girls broke free and ran past Ralph whispering excitedly that they'd never seen a geezer die before.

*   *   *   *   *

Ralph squeezed a little further under the waiting room bench where he lay, lined up head to toe with French. He'd tell her about the awful screaming in the morning. It was bad enough that he couldn't stop thinking about it and hearing it in his head over and over. Why give French a bad time too? He couldn't keep from wondering who it was who'd screamed the terrible things, either. It had to be the darts winner man or the poor man with the cough. He wriggled about to try and get more comfortable, and his feet found a neat stack of carrier bags. 'What's all this shopping?'

'Just a few trifles.'

Ralph rolled round to stare at her suspiciously. Why would she stock up on dessert? 'You look a little like your dad,' she smiled, 'but not when you frown. Bonne nuit.'

He lay on his back and stared at the cobwebby underside of the bench. Quite a few people had told him he looked like Hal Havern. He couldn't see it himself. He'd always thought they just said it to suck up. But if French thought he looked like his dad, French who was the least un-sucking up person in the world, maybe there was a shred of truth in it – which meant he was probably a bit handsome. Ralph examined that possibility and found it pleasing. And then he remembered his double, who didn't look

299

anything at all like Hal Havern; so that meant he didn't either.

He sighed, a tad disappointed, but you can't have everything and hadn't he got the most unusual thing in the world – a mysterious solemn doppelganger who was nice? And wait a minute! Hadn't the man with the cough said that he, Ralph, was nice too? Yes, the man who was dead had said they were both nice. The man had put Ralph right up level with his double for niceness. And somehow, with the man being dead, it kind of made it truer, like a proclamation from heaven. 'Ralph Havern is NICE!'

Ralph smiled and withdrew the toes of his shoes so they were clear of French's trifles. 'Bun wee, French,' he said.

They hardly slept a wink. Apart from being a busy Friday night, all the world and its wife had come to see Hal Havern open the cinema and it felt as if most of them tramped past their hiding place. They both gave up trying in the small hours and when Giselle came back from the Ladies, she found Ralph reading a headline in the early edition of the newspaper.

'HAL HAVERN'S SON FOUND ALIVE'

Together they read on.

'Mr. Hal Havern's only son, eleven-year-old Ralph, who has been missing for some days, was involved in a traffic accident yesterday morning

in the entrance of the Mersey Tunnel Queensway. Mr Havern is at his son's hotel bedside waiting for him to regain consciousness when, it is to be hoped, further details surrounding his unexplained disappearance may emerge.

No one present at last night's Gala re-opening of the sumptuously refurbished Forum Cinema would have guessed what heartache Mr Havern...'

'****!' Ralph shoved the paper into his jacket pocket. 'That's terrible. My double's in a bad way. Let's go and see if he's okay.' And he ran the short distance to the Adelphi Hotel trying to picture his dad's face when he told him that he was nursing not Ralph but his double. He was so near now to coming face to face with the boy that he laughed as he ran. It was bad luck on his double to have been knocked down, but it meant Ralph's search was over at last. When his double came round – there was going to be one heck of a party.

He romped round the revolving doors up to a drowsy night porter on the reception desk and asked for Hal Havern's room. But the porter wouldn't let him go up. And when Ralph protested that he was Hal Havern's son the porter called him a heartless little fibber and pinged a round bell on the desk. Ralph tried to make a run for it up the stairs but two pageboys brought him down in a tackle and threw him out. Ralph saw himself in one of the many mirrors as they chucked him through the doors – a wild-haired, dirty-faced ragamuffin – no wonder they didn't believe him.

He raced back to the station to find French. They had to figure out what to do. Clean up for a start. While he was scrubbing himself in the Gents, he noticed the face that looked back from the mirror was sadder than usual. More solemn. More like his double in the train had looked. It made him a little scared; was he turning into his double? His double had certainly turned into him because there his double was, in the hotel and living his life for him; in which case, whose life was he, Ralph, leading? Could two people squeeze into one life? He didn't think so – not unless they were crazy or something. Was he crazy? He grinned into the mirror very deliberately to drive his melancholy double away, cracked a smile, and told himself to buck up. He went to find French.

French was not at the newspaper kiosk where Ralph had left her, so he hung about waiting for her. And that was where Theodore Pigott found him. He took him by the ear in silence and walked him away. It hurt so much that Ralph could only squeak for help, and so nobody took any notice.

They joined the remaining Youngstars waiting under the clock with Miss Bellamy. The Pig whacked Ralph to shut him up, and still leading him by the ear, which kept Ralph trotting alongside him for fear his ear would be torn off, he took him through the barrier and onto the platform where the slow train to London was waiting departure.

As the Pig shoved him into a third class carriage,

Ralph caught a sideways sight of Giselle, standing at the barrier, surrounded by her shopping bags and smiling at him. She didn't lift a finger to help him and she was smiling. She was goddam smiling!

* * * * *

It was a few hours after this that a telegram arrived. Fergus and Alasdair were seated at the breakfast table with their parents. The family was contentedly spooning up its hot porridge oats, served with butter and salt, when a frozen telegraph boy, on a bike, delivered the telegram through the snow. Telegrams tended to bring bad news. Would this one merit a lament on the bagpipes? Their father tore open the ochre envelope and read:

ALAS STOP CLOTHES REMAIN MISLAID STOP REGRET RETURNING TO PARIS STOP GISELLE

Fergus and Alasdair exchanged looks of pure joy and went on with their porridge. But their mother asked, 'Aren't her parents abroad on diplomatic work, though? That's why she was coming to us. Who will take care of the poor little thing, all alone in Paris?'

Their father flung down his spoon, strode across the great hall and began making a string of frantic, long distance telephone calls.

CHAPTER TWENTY-THREE

DANCE

Ralph hammered on the locked bedroom door until his fists hurt and the soiled, brown paintwork flaked off. But no one came. They had all gone out and left him. As soon as they'd arrived at the slum terraced house digs, in a place called Notting Hill Gate, those silent travellers, who'd shared the railway carriage with him as the train crawled down England, had turned into lively, jabbering 'party-people'. They'd changed into their glad-rags and hit London Town for a Saturday night out.

He knew them all: the small man, the all-angles gawky girl, the tall boy and the vague woman. And they all thought they knew him. Not that they spoke to him. They'd sat there ignoring him – from Liverpool to London – with their stern faces and their black mourning bands round the upper arms of their blazers. The vague woman had put a black band round the arm of his grey flannel jacket, too, with a whispered 'For Jess.'

The Pig man had locked him in the bedroom without supper and with the promise of no food until he came to his senses. The first time the Pig man had hit him, Ralph hit him back. It was an awful mistake. The Pig bashed him so hard he'd cut Ralph's eye, and the vague woman had made it hurt much more when she'd sopped up the blood with a bottle of fire water called TCP.

'Your name is Ollie Pigott,' the Pig told Ralph, as he locked him in. 'And you know it. And stop that terrible Yankee accent.' Ralph wondered what would happen if he dared reach up and rip off the broad strip of plaster that ran from the Pig's forehead to the nape of his neck. Its function seemed to be to strap the Pig's head together. If he dared do it, would the man's skull drop into two halves and his brain and scalding tongue come sluicing out so Ralph could run away and never come back? He knew he didn't dare try it.

Ralph gave up hammering and checked the window yet again. Still nailed shut. It was dark outside, but he'd looked so often now that he knew the drop down into the little, junk-crowded back yard was suicidal. But even if he did get out, he'd need some money. The Pig man had taken the last of the gold box money off him in the train when he'd made Ralph turn out his pockets. He'd found the sick man's watch, too. That was the only time the others had spoken to him. The gawky girl said derisively, 'Taking it up are you, Ollie? Thieving?' And the small man said, 'Glory Ollie! What's come over you? That's old Shtum's watch you've nicked. See his initials engraved on the back? R.L.'

'He gave it to me.'

'Shtum wouldn't part with that watch for the world. A wedding present from his old lady, he said. Always left it hidden in his boot in the dressing room while he was on stage.' The small man shook his head unhappily. 'Seems like I'm not the only one who knew that.'

The Pig had slipped the watch into his pocket and exclaimed sorrowfully, 'To think that a son of mine!'

The tall boy had muttered to Ralph, 'Now say you didn't steal Silver's box.'

'Silver?'

The boy gave him a scornful look and turned his back.

'If that's the name of the beautiful girl who gave me the box,' Ralph said wearily, 'she didn't know I was Ralph Havern.'

The small man had deliberately opened up his Daily Sketch newspaper then, like a wall between them, to show Ralph, right there, on the front page, a picture of Hal Havern and a headline: 'Son Ralph Safe And Sound' and a smaller caption, 'United Again'. His double was digging in all right. That cold, scared feeling came over Ralph even more strongly. If he did manage to contact his father, why should his dad believe he was Ralph when this Ollie character was making such a good job of it?

Ralph whipped round and ran to the door. Too late! The door had shut as quickly as it had just opened. And now there was a chipped white plate lying on the floor with a slice of dry bread on it. He tried the handle but the door was locked again. 'Hello?' he whispered through the keyhole. 'Hello?' But whoever it was had gone.

He was ravenous, but he knew enough about hunger now to save half the bread. He felt sure he'd need it even more later on. He left the electric light bulb hanging from the centre of the ceiling switched on and lay down in all his clothes on the hard bed. After a minute, he got up and pushed the chest of drawers against the door. That felt safer. Then he lay under the bed. That felt safer too. It also felt just a fraction less lonesome to know that someone – even if it was a pretty scared someone – was on his side.

*   *   *   *   *

Sunday Morning Rehearsal. Those were the last three words that meant anything to Ralph. The rest of the day was gruesome, humiliating gobbledygook. The Pig man had hired part of a church hall in a nearby back street to work in. Ralph could hear rollicking hymns coming from the upper floor, where a Sunday school was in full swing, while he sat below on the ground floor on one of the many folding chairs stacked round the walls. He was freezing cold and trying hard to understand what was going on.

The Pig man was instructing the two new girls he'd hired from a local dance school and was, what he called, 'putting them into it'. The Pig looked sick from drink and frantic to get his act ready for the next night. The vague woman picked out a tune on a piano that had got its soft pedal stuck down, and the Pig bawled how he was paying Sunday double time, whatever that meant. 'So let's tango, meine Kinder!' The Youngstars flung themselves into the sketch and Ralph stood on the edge, completely at sea, while people rushed past him and around him or tugged him or brushed his face.

The music petered out and the Pig asked quietly, 'Just what do you think you're doing, Ollie?' And though he was a million times more scared of him now, Ralph tried to get through to the Pig again. 'I'm not Ollie, I'm Ralph, sir.'

'Well whoever you are, ruddy well dance.' The music began again and stopped again as Ralph shouted, 'I can't dance, I don't know how to dance. I've never been taught to dance.' He saw surprised looks run between the small man Grinling, John, and Heather, the all-angles, gawky girl. He didn't know why.

The Pig man took him away and shut them both in a little office. He pushed an old typewriter aside to prop his big rear on the desk and took a long time filling his pipe and lighting it. Then he told Ralph not to get clever with him. Smoke wreathed the Pig's plastered head while he told him that, but for Miss Bellamy, he would have turned him over to the City Council and put him into a home for delinquent boys because he deserved no less for clumping the Pig over the head with a bottle.

It was some clump! Ralph's double went up in his estimation no end at that.

'But Miss Bellamy asked me to give you another chance,' the Pig told him. He took a menacingly long time to relight his pipe before going on, 'Now don't you stand there and tell me that you can't dance, boy, because you know, and I know, that for all your modest, namby-pamby, scaredy-cat ways, you take after your darned mother and are far and away the best dancer in this troupe. The best. Say it.' The Pig put his lemon-curd-coloured face close to Ralph's. His breath was bacon and beer and tobacco. 'What are you? Say it.'

'I'm Ralph sir. My mom died when I was born. Please send me back to my father.'

The Pig man roared back. 'I'm your frigging dad.' Then he marched Ralph back to the rehearsal and pushed and pulled him through the sketch, his fingers digging into Ralph's shoulders mercilessly.

As the day wore on, everyone else got better and better in the sketch. The new girls slotted in like cogs slipping into place, while Ralph hopped and shuffled and got progressively worse. He could feel the resentment streaming off everyone as, time and again, he wrecked their comedy business in the sketch that he was beginning to recognise as the Pie Shop routine he'd seen the dwarves perform.

Then, to his complete humiliation, the Pig made him do his bits all by himself while everyone else sat round the edge, watching. He was blushing with shame and falling over his own feet, and he saw the two new girls make secret faces about him to each other. 'Back flips!' The Pig raged at him. 'What's happened to those fabulous back flips you were supposed to have picked up by magic when we all know where you learned them?' Ralph didn't even know what a back flip was. 'Two, three! Give me a back flip NOW!' the Pig ranted and to his distress, Ralph began to cry.

'Tea break, everyone,' the Pig said. Ralph was left standing alone in the rehearsal space and hating himself for crying, while they all crowded into the far corner of the hall and put a match to a gas ring on the floor. They balanced a tin kettle on it, which took an age to come to the boil, and then poured hot water onto three spoonfuls of leaves in a stained teapot. They drank tea and chatted and laughed as if he were a hole in the air.

He began to cry less when he realised what he was doing wrong. He was trying to please the Pig and because he couldn't please him, and because he never would please the Pig, he was being turned into someone different – someone who was uncertain and miserable and stupid. Some of the old Ralph asserted itself then, and he wondered why he should please the man. I'm his prisoner, he thought, and he calls me his son. It was no wonder his double had escaped.

That night, back at the digs, the Pig got very drunk and threatened to beat Ralph with a poker; and the landlord, a black-haired man in pebble glasses and greasy overalls, squeezed up the stairs from the basement and asked the Pig if he was going to murder the boy. The Pig boomed back at him jovially, 'Spare the rod and spoil the child.'

'Never a truer word spoken,' the landlord agreed. 'But if it's murder you have in mind, take him off the premises to do it. Murder is bad for business, old man.'

While that was going on, Ralph scooted for his life up the stairs and into the first room he came to, which happened to be Heather's, and hid in her empty wardrobe. To his terror, the Pig came in looking for him and Ralph knew the girl would give him away. But all Heather said was, 'I'm doing my bible reading, Mr Pigott. It's Sunday. Saint Mark.'

Ralph heard the bed creak as the Pig sat down next to her. 'Give us the low down, Heather darling. What's up with Ollie? What's this dancing strike?'

'Have you noticed, Mr Pigott sir, he's lost his stammer too?' The Pig said he was jiggered if he had and then Heather said it was as if Ollie had been wiped clean.

'What? Off his rocker?'

There was rumbling talk then that Ralph couldn't hear properly. The next thing he heard was Heather reading a verse from the bible in her funny deep voice about a man with a speech impediment. The Pig got bored, creaked up from the bed, and left.

As soon as he'd gone, Heather opened the wardrobe. 'I don't know what's going on, Ollie Piggott, but we've got to get you through this or he's going to commit you.'

'What does that mean?'

'Send you to a mad house?'

Ralph felt sick with fear. 'You're kidding.'

'I'm not.' And Heather spent most of that night teaching Ralph to dance.

Ralph knew she was only helping him because she liked Ollie and because she thought he was Ollie, but did it matter? If his double, Ollie, could steal his life then why shouldn't Ralph steal his double's friends?

By dawn they were both exhausted. They'd worked, they'd had rows, they'd had one really terrible one about Jesus because Ralph kept saying 'Jeeze!' and Heather objected. They'd even laughed. But by the end of it, Ralph was a nearly competent dancer and knew every move of the Pie Shop routine. What's more, he genuinely liked Heather. She was such a comically serious girl; and because she liked him, too, it made a happy spot inside him that felt safe. Friends, he decided, were a great idea.

CHAPTER TWENTY-FOUR

IMPOSTER

Everyone was so kind to him. Not like Jess had been kind to him, though Ollie found it hard to put his finger on what the difference was. It was more as if they were all professionals at being kind. As if it were part of their job to be kind.

There was the nurse, for instance. Ollie thought she was an angel when he first woke up and found himself in a huge bed that was so soft he felt as if he hadn't got a body any more.

The nurse was sitting beside him in a room like a film set. There were glowing orbs of lamps on polished tables, and vases of flowers everywhere. There was a high, clean ceiling with a glinting chandelier and a white carpet that covered the entire floor. The dressing table and mirrors were fit for Marlene Dietrich, and the arm-chairs and sofas looked so comfortable they were just ordering you to 'sink into me'.

He'd asked the nurse where the clock was because he thought he'd made it to heaven and wanted to go and meet Jess. The nurse had put her cool palm on his cheek and said it was Sunday lunchtime.

The American lady was kind, too. She wore a blue uniform and was vaguely familiar. She called him 'Honey' and 'Sugar' and 'Baby' and held his hand when the nurse took the big bandage off his head and bathed the stitched-up gash over his eye. While they were doing this, the most handsome man in the world walked in and Ollie said, 'You're Hal Havern!'

And Hal Havern laughed and said, 'Who else?' And then Hal Havern was incredibly nice and attentive to him, too. He called him 'son', and helped him eat the best chicken soup he'd ever tasted with a special spoon called a *soup*-spoon. And not one of them referred to the oath Ollie had sworn and what he'd done to Jess. So if he wasn't in heaven, it was the next best thing.

A swanky doctor was just as kind as the others. The rose in his buttonhole smelt like beautiful Woolworth's talc when he leant over Ollie to take a look at him. He greeted him with 'Now then, young man,' and said there was nothing like a horse treading on your head to whip you into shape. 'You don't think you've got a double any more, do you young man?' And when Ollie shook his head, the doctor said he was cured. And they all looked so overjoyed that Ollie didn't say that he could have told them that he was cured himself and saved them the expense of a doctor. People who saw doubles only needed specs. Simple.

Everyone was so kind, in fact, that he didn't like to contradict them when they kept calling him by the wrong name. 'Ralph', they called him or even 'Master Ralph'. It might look impolite to correct them. And maybe you got renamed when you arrived at wherever this place was that he had arrived at.

So Ollie kept quiet because he didn't want to disappoint them – particularly Hal Havern, who was difficult to please. For example, when Ollie found out that he was lying in bed in the Adelphi Hotel, he fretted that he was too broke to pay the digs bill, which made Hal Havern laugh uneasily. And then, when Ollie asked why Hal Havern was being so good to him, Hal answered, really puzzlingly, 'You've picked up a swell English accent over the last few days, kid.'

Ollie was sure he'd always spoken like he did, but he slid ever so slightly into an American accent. Whatever he could do to please, he would do. And he noticed, too, that there was a touch of Silver about Hal Havern. It was the way Hal just couldn't help watching his own reflection in the mirror while he talked to you. But that was Stars for you.

Then came the shock. Hal Havern said, 'Of course I'm good to you. You're my son.' Well, it was more of a joke than a shock, really. Two jokes, in fact: first, the notion that a father could be good to his son was sort of hilarious; and the second, bigger joke was the idea that Hal Havern was his dad! Ollie chuckled and said, 'Pull the other one Hal, it's got bells on it.'

Hal Havern laughed and did up a button on Ollie's pyjama jacket for him. That was when Ollie noticed the pyjamas were silk and must have cost a dozen Youngstars' pay packets. Hal Havern, who was still laughing, said the horse had done Ralph's sense of humour a lot of good, too. It gave Ollie a sneaking feeling that, somehow or other, a very serious misunderstanding had happened between the time he ran into the milk cart on Friday morning and now.

'No offence,' he said, cautiously probing the situation. 'I'd prefer you for a father.' Hal Havern smiled even more uneasily and asked the nurse in a quiet voice if the boy was having a relapse. 'But unfortunately my father is the Pig,' Ollie explained. Hal Havern stopped smiling and said he'd never been called a pig before and Ollie said hastily that it wasn't what he had meant. He couldn't bear to offend him. He'd love Hal Havern for a father, he said. And it was true.

But then there was a quick knock on the door and in came the Shoes Man. Ollie screamed and scrambled out of bed to get away from him, but fell over with dizziness. There was uproar as everyone jumped up. The Shoes Man ran over to Ollie, and

Ollie screamed again as he picked him up in his arms and no one made a move to stop him. Ollie implored them to help him and screamed that the Shoes Man would kill him. 'Save me!' he begged them. 'Stop him taking me.'

Then, somehow, Ollie was in bed again and Hal Havern was saying Shoes was a private detective that he'd hired to keep an eye on him because stars' kids tended to get kidnapped these days. The Shoes Man had a wide smile on his face. 'The poor guy has been running around after you on your wild trip, trying to catch you,' Hal Havern said. 'Who put you up to it, son? Come on Ralph, open up.'

Ollie gazed up at their expectant faces and wondered if he could invent a story of Ralph, just to please them. And then he wondered if perhaps he really was Ralph after all and not Ollie Pigott. A voice inside him said it would be right ruddy marvellous to be this Ralph boy, and whether he was him or he wasn't him, did it matter? And why not go along with it? They'd all be happy.

Then a maid in an over-long uniform burst into the room and blew everything to pieces. 'Monsieur Havern,' she said. She pointed an accusing finger at Ollie and announced, 'This boy in the bed is not your son.' Hal Havern seemed transfixed – and Ollie saw, just for a fleeting second before Hal covered it up, that he was very, very scared by what she'd said. The maid seemed to see it too because she said, 'You have had a shock.' She turned to Mary Ellen. 'Pour him a cognac.' Mary Ellen obeyed meekly.

'And you may as well give me one, too,' the maid added. 'I am having a très strenuous week.'

Hal Havern recovered enough to ask, 'Are you completely crazy?'

'Not at all. I am in disguise.' And so saying, she whipped off her cap and pinafore to reveal brand new, clean clothes bought at Lewis's for the occasion. Ollie recognised her at once as the angel who had needed a penny.

She smiled brilliantly at Hal Havern. 'I can reveal where your son Ralph is, Monsieur Havern.' She downed the cognac Mary Ellen handed her as Hal asked, 'Are you suggesting this boy here is not my son Ralph?' There was a sense of relief coming off Hal, which Ollie found puzzling.

'That is precisely what I am suggesting,' the penny angel said.

So why was Hal Havern relieved? Ollie couldn't see much difference between the penny angel saying 'this boy is not your son' and 'this boy is not your son Ralph'. But Hal Havern obviously did,

The penny angel went on. 'And only I know where Ralph is. You wish to hear my terms?'

Shoes made a determined effort to take charge. 'This little kid has been bugging me for days, Mr Havern, sir. She was with Ralph.'

Giselle rounded on him. 'And a good thing too. Or you would have killed him.'

'Killed him!' Shoes was incensed. 'I was protecting my client from you.'

'Moi!' There was never a finer picture of

outraged innocence. 'I was helping him find his doppelganger.'

Shoes was stumped. 'His whattle hanger?'

'It's a double,' the nurse said, quietly straightening Ollie's bedclothes, and for some reason Hal Havern gave her such a black look that she knew she'd never dare ask him for his autograph now.

Ollie advised Shoes to think of it like a hallucination. 'I had one last Sunday. I thought I saw mine.'

Hal Havern came to his bedside and spoke to him kindly in the voice that had melted a million hearts. 'Let it go, old son. I know we don't always get along. Maybe we should see more of each other in future, but you're happy aren't you?'

'Oh yes!' Ollie said earnestly. 'I'm having a lovely...' He checked himself and changed the word to 'Sunday.'

'Well,' said Hal. 'I don't know why this French kid is backing you up. For cash, I guess; but for my sake, quit this fantasy.' Ollie wasn't sure what a fantasy was, but he'd have been delighted to quit most things for Hal Havern's sake. Before he could say as much, the penny angel pushed in next to Hal. Her eyes drilled into Ollie's.

'Tommy took the train to Toxteth.'

Everyone else in the room looked even more intimidated by her than they already were. 'Say it,' the penny angel commanded Ollie.

'No.' He was frantic. He didn't want this wonderful dream to be over. He didn't want to be

Ollie again: Ollie, son of the Pig and murderer of Jess.

'I insist! Try!'

Ollie prayed and prayed that he was really Ralph after all and that it would all be all right – and he tried. But the usual stammer rattled out of him on the first merciless 't' – the t's and the d's that he'd been avoiding the whole blasted afternoon. On and on and on it went, until the penny angel clapped her hands and he stopped with the shock of the sound. In the silence that followed, Hal Havern just about managed to whisper, 'Good Grief! He really isn't Ralph.'

'But he's his spitting image.' The words broke out of Mary Ellen in frightened gasps. At the same time, it crashed in on Ollie, like a wave breaking over his head, that for once Jess had been wrong; he *had* seen his double on the train. The double actually existed. Mary Ellen's voice rose. 'It's not natural. It's diabolical!'

This frightened Ollie, and he wished Heather was there. The devil was more her field than his. Did the American woman mean that his double was a devil who was tempting him? And tempting him to do what? He certainly had the most bewildering feeling about the double now that he knew he was real. It was an overpowering longing to see him again. The feeling was so strong that it wasn't just in Ollie's head; it was in his stomach, too – like first night nerves could be in your stomach. The feeling was as though he was starving hungry but at the same time as though he couldn't eat a thing.

But now the American lady was screaming like hell, so perhaps that was where they all were, really – in hell. The nurse gave her a slap on the cheek, which shut her up, thank goodness, and then, rather meanly, the American lady slapped the nurse back. Shoes took the American lady into a palatial corner and dosed her with cognac, and Hal Havern said he'd do anything to make it up to the nurse for the slap – and the nurse said his autograph would do the trick. And all the time, the penny angel stood there with a slight smile on her face.

Then Hal came and looked down on Ollie in bed, and Ollie noticed that, for once, Hal didn't even glance at a mirror. 'Where's your mother?' he asked Ollie.

'I d-don't know, sir. The Pig won't speak about her.'

'The pig?'

'Me father, sir.' Hal looked so aghast it made Ollie smile. 'It's a nickname,' he explained. 'A good 'un.'

'But he's married to your mom, Adolphus?'

'Pardon me?'

'That's your name, isn't it? Adolphus?' For a second Ollie thought he was having a laugh. 'Are you barmy or something, Mr Havern?' But the penny angel gave a snort of disbelief, too. 'Don't be ridiculous, Monsieur,' she reprimanded the biggest star in Hollywood. 'Absolutely no one is called Adolphus.' A shadow of a doubt crossed her

321

beautiful face. She turned to Ollie. 'Are you called Adolphus, chéri?'

'Cripes no!' Ollie said. 'I'm Oliver Pigott.'

Hal Havern shook his head and murmured that there was something so not right here. He decided on another line of questioning. 'Well, Oliver Pigott. Do you know where Ralph is?'

Ollie shook his head. 'It would be right grand to meet him, though. He's saved me the price of a pair of specs.'

It was Hal Havern's turn now to look at Ollie as if he had a screw loose.

The penny angel butted in again. 'I alone know where Ralph is.' Shoes said menacingly from his corner that she'd better get a move on and tell them where that was.

The penny angel smiled again and said they should hear her terms first. At which point Shoes almost somersaulted with anger, and Hal Havern looked as if he'd boil over. But he controlled himself sufficiently to ask if she was blackmailing him. 'You're only a child!' he exclaimed.

The penny angel looked at him severely. 'How much do you know about children, Monsieur Havern? About your own, for example? You fill your boy's head with joking, unkind jibes about my countrymen and about French cuisine; yet you are happy to drink our cognac, huh? You do not teach him 'Live and let live'. You send him, too, on a wild goose hunt for mythological monsters in Scottish lochs with false promises you will join him there.

Are you ever with him or are you always on a silver screen?'

Then she launched into a lecture about how neglectful he was, and ended up telling him he didn't deserve to know where Ralph was. She gave him a dressing down about leaving his son in the care of a gun-slinging, accident prone slob in clown's shoes, which made Shoes look very embarrassed. And she didn't let up. She went on then about the nursemaid and a tutor Hal had hired, who cared more about hanky-panky than about his son, at which point Mary Ellen tried hard to disappear into the wallpaper. Hal Havern slumped down on the end of Ollie's bed and gazed at the penny angel open-mouthed. Ollie felt much less envious of his double than he had. His life seemed so friendless.

The penny angel smiled round at them all. 'And now for my terms. I require exclusive, world press reporting rights on this whole story.' The entire roomful of people gaped back at her. Surely she was joking? Only Ollie had a shrewd idea she wasn't. This penny angel was a big player. Very big. It felt as if she was topping the bill, the star of this show.

'You can't be serious?'

'Deadly, Monsieur Shoes.' Nobody liked the use of that word 'deadly'. There was silence. The penny angel stood there, smiling a little, while the word lay between them all like a trump card she'd put down on the table.

Eventually, Hal broke the silence and said genially that he'd call his lawyer to sort out the technicalities. He made a move for the white phone by Ollie's bed, but he'd underestimated the penny angel. She picked up the phone ahead of him. 'Hold your hearses. You call the police instead, maybe? I would like a verbal yes or no to my terms now, before witnesses.'

Hal Havern treated her to the smile that had earned him a ton of dollars. Ollie could feel his charm flowing over the room like milk and honey. 'Look, little Miss, you're out of your league. I appreciate that one day, when you're a grown up lady, you'd like to be a reporter on a newspaper.'

'Not at all. I intend to own a newspaper – or two. Yes or no, monsieur?' Hal poured himself another cognac. Ollie couldn't read his expression, but he could tell Hal was talking to her on his own level now. No more dealing with a kid. 'This may backfire, blow up in your face, young lady.'

Ollie watched them both from his bed. Two tough people bargaining over a boy; a boy whom Ollie had begun to think of as his boy and yet here he was, sitting on the sidelines as usual, a small part player who just happened to look exactly like the lead. The only notice they would take of him was when they got around to turfing him out.

He wondered where the dickens he would land up now that the sumptuous life he'd been leading for the last couple of hours was coming to an end. Any minute now he'd be booted out of this bed. But where could he go? Where could someone who had murdered Jess go? Someone who couldn't even commit suicide properly and who'd nearly done himself in by mistake, under a milk cart?

Hal Havern put out his hand to the girl; they were going to shake on a deal. 'You'll take us to Ralph?'

'But of course, Monsieur Havern. We will go together.'

So, it's nearly over, thought Ollie, unhappily. But the penny angel withdrew her hand. The Shoes Man ground his teeth with frustration.

'One final point, Monsieur.'

Hal Havern was a good actor; Ollie had no hesitation in awarding him ten out of ten. You'd never have guessed he was ready to strangle her. He said lightly, 'Go ahead, little lady. What's your final point?'

'Oliver Pigott comes with us,' the penny angel said.

CHAPTER TWENTY-FIVE

LONDON

The fog started as a heavier hazing of the smoky air; then it thickened enough to veil the tops of Big Ben and St Paul's Cathedral. By the time Ollie, Giselle and Hal Havern touched down at Croydon in his aircraft, shreds of mist were whipping past the porthole windows and the grass on either side of the runway was white with dew. They climbed into Hal Havern's waiting motorcar and set out on a creeping, cautious journey to London, swaddled in thick mist.

Ollie was glad to be on the ground again. He'd been entranced when he looked down on England for the very first time and saw it was cut up into little squares of fields and cubes of buildings – nothing like it looked from a train – but riding the sky in the noisy little plane had felt like sitting inside a mad bluebottle. He wasn't keen.

Giselle, as he'd learned to call the penny angel, took it all in her stride, though. She'd been there before all right. He wondered if there was anything she hadn't done before. She smiled at him now from where she was sitting next to him on the leather upholstered back seat and he realised that he'd been staring at her. He knew it was rude and quickly looked out of the window – into fog.

Hal Havern was in the front of the car talking to Shoes, who was at the wheel with his nose practically pressed to the windscreen, trying to see the road. This was the first time Ollie had been more or less in private with the French girl, so he took the chance to ask her the question that had been puzzling him: why had she insisted he came to London too? 'I like you,' she replied. 'You are nice.' But something told him that this wasn't the real answer. It didn't seem worth asking her the next truly important question if she wasn't going to be straight with him, but he couldn't resist.

'My double, Ralph,' he said. 'What's he like?' Several indefinable expressions crossed her face before she said, 'He is nice too.' Ollie smiled. He'd guessed Ralph would be nice. He leaned back in the corner of the car and didn't see Giselle uncross her fingers.

By the time they reached the Savoy Hotel, the fog felt like a dense beige blindfold. Monstrous shapes quivered into being in front of Ollie, turned briefly into a person, and then shivered into nothing as they passed by. It was good to get inside the brightly lit hotel, where Giselle insisted they should have lunch before continuing the quest for Ralph – and everyone had to agree. She was the boss. The lunch, Giselle told Ollie, would be acceptable.

Acceptable! It were a right feast!

But Hal Havern had never arrived anywhere without twenty or so photographers waiting for him. This time, there weren't any because they didn't know he was coming. Giselle had seen to that. She, and no one else, had the rights on this story. Their absence caused a twinge of fear in Hal. It was as if the fog had blotted out his fame and he'd reverted to what he'd been in the past: an unknown, hungry actor. And there were things in that past which Hal Havern would prefer not to remember. He wished the fog would clear. But it didn't. It got worse.

It was a real 'pea-souper', in fact, and London began to close down. It prevented a third of the musicians getting to the Youngstars' band call on Monday afternoon. Worse than that, one of the new girls in the act lost the theatre. She kept ringing the stage door from telephone boxes in floods of tears but, as she didn't know where on earth she was, no one could give her directions.

The Pig waited for her at the stage door, re-lighting his pipe over-and-over and staring into the fog. It was made more impenetrable now by the blurred spheres of light from the street lamps. With quarter of an hour to curtain up, the Pig cursed and summoned his troupe. Ralph had high hopes that he'd cancel the act, but no – the Pig announced that he would take on the role himself. 'And you, Heth, you sing the songs,' he ordered. Heather looked a bit odd and asked if the Pig had ever heard her sing. 'Voice like a nightingale,' he assured her.

*   *   *   *   *

It was about then that Ollie reckoned he'd found out the real reason for Giselle bringing him along. They were all gathered in the hotel foyer: Shoes, Hal, Ollie and Giselle, ready to set out on the final stage of the journey to find Ralph.

Giselle had told Ollie all about the Chinese laundry during lunch: how Wei had tracked down Miss Bellamy through the red blazer, and how Giselle had discovered Miss Bellamy's connection with the Youngstars. Then, by a lucky accident, Giselle confided to Ollie, she'd just happened to see the Youngstars boarding the London train with Ralph.

But now in the foyer with the taxi waiting and Hal asking, 'Where to, Giselle?' she smiled and summoned the manager. He was some time coming. Shoes nearly blew a gasket with impatience. Eventually, the manager arrived and inclined his head to Giselle, who announced, 'I am expecting a telephone call from the French embassy.'

Clever move, thought Ollie. She's signalling to Hal: no foul play – there are important people who will want to know what's become of me. Giselle went on. 'Please tell them I am obliged to go to...' She clicked her fingers several times and seemed to be trying to remember something. She wrinkled her brow and asked Ollie, 'Remind me. Where is it the Youngstars are performing this week?'

'Holborn,'

'Yes, yes,' she replied impatiently, 'I know Holborn but it is the name of the theatre I mislay.'

By this time, Ollie didn't precisely like Giselle, but she'd certainly got under his skin. He hoped, for her sake, that he was the only person present who had spotted the old trick. She obviously hadn't a clue where Ralph actually was. All she knew was that he was in London. London was one of the biggest cities in the world, with dozens and dozens of theatres to choose from. That's why she'd brought him along: his role was to pinpoint Ralph's exact whereabouts, but only at the very last minute. That way, Hal Havern couldn't cut her out and organise a rescue party without her. Ollie was becoming increasingly suspicious, too, that Giselle was engineering what was happening to them all more than she was admitting. But whatever she was up to, why spoil her fun?

'You know,' he pretended to prompt her, 'The Empire.'

'Ah yes,' she said, 'I knew it was something so very British.' And away they all rushed. Even so, they were late getting there because the taxi lost its way in the fog on the short journey from the Savoy and the show had started by the time they arrived.

The others hurried into the Youngstars' dressing room, but although he was nervous and excited about meeting his double, Ollie was shy, too, and he hung back in the passage outside. Only Miss Bellamy was in there, though. The act was going on right now, she said slowly.

Hal and Shoes raced round to the front of the theatre and went in. Ollie followed them out of the stage door, limping slowly down the side of the building. The photographs of the Youngstars in the showcases outside were the old ones. None of him, of course, but there was Silver smiling as prettily as ever. And there was Jess. Beautiful Jess, dancing – like an angel. The guilt he felt was crushing.

*   *   *   *   *

Ralph slapped a custard pie in the Pig's face. He'd found the man's weakness at last: the Pig couldn't bear things to go wrong in front of the public. And boy! Had they gone wrong! No sooner had Heather started the charming song that Silver had always sung so well than the audience went up in a hurricane of laughter. Ralph had noticed Heather praying just before the show. He could understand why, now: she had a voice like a wire brush on a zinc bath. The audience crowed with laughter and the Pig scowled at her as if he'd kill her.

Poor old Heth blinked with hurt surprise at the effect she was having. Ralph, who really rated Heather because she'd got him through this dancing torment, tried to help out. After all, she was doing her best for the show and the song was old-fashioned crap anyway. He gave her a big wink of encouragement. But it had the reverse effect. Heather dropped an octave, so her voice boomed like a dinner gong, and added in some crazy jumps and splits, the craziest he'd ever seen. If he hadn't been busy with his own plan, he would have been flat on his back with laughter at her, like most of the audience.

He slapped a second pie on the Pig, who wasn't expecting it so it got in his eyes and mouth, and then Ralph tripped him up. Flump! Splat! Face down! And while the Pig was tilting like a seesaw on the jut of his own belly, Ralph tipped a sack of what was supposed to be flour all over him. He looked like an abominable snowman, kicking and writhing blindly on the stage.

The band kept going, despite this unexpected turn of affairs, until Ralph ran down to the footlights and said to the audience, 'Help me.' And the audience shrieked with laughter even more.

The Youngstars all stood still and gawped at him, their custard pies forgotten in their hands. 'This man has kidnapped me,' Ralph shouted. 'I'm not his son and he says I'm loopy.'

Someone shouted, 'He's right, too!'

And the audience went up again. So there was no help to be had from them. They'd never understand he was serious. He'd hoped they'd rise up and demand his release and have the Pig arrested, but they thought he was just part of the act. It was bitterly frustrating. He stared at the wall of laughing eyes and mouths in front of him and knew he was going to have to look after himself. So he broke every rule in the book of theatre. He crossed the boundary from the magical box of light into everyday life. He took a run and a leap off the stage and over the orchestra pit. There was an 'Ooooh!' from the audience as he didn't quite make it and the conductor caught him. Someone else called out, 'Hold on, kid. We're right here.'

But the Pig had managed to get to his knees and was crawling towards him, a terrifyingly angry sight. 'Help me. For God's sake help me,' Ralph gasped at the bandleader. But the man said, 'Get back on that ****ing stage,' as he held Ralph with one hand and conducted with the other. Ralph shook him off, snatched a trombone from its player and hurled it at the Pig, who by now had reached the edge of the stage. Smack! The Pig went down again. The audience was in a riot. Booing, whistling, screaming for more.

Ralph hurt his leg scrambling over the brass rail that separated the pit from the first row of seating. He ran, limping up the central aisle of the auditorium, crashed through the exit doors at the back into the foyer, and then out into the night and the fog.

He ran down the side of the building. As he ran, he stripped off his costume top and threw it away. It had been a tight fit over his jacket. His breath was giving out now and he was sobbing, but he was free!

He stopped under a street lamp to pull off the costume trousers and to rub the leg that was hurting. That's when he looked up and there was his double, shifting in and out of vision in the fog. Then the double came nearer, became solid. His double also had a bad eye now, and, like him, his double was limping. They were strangers and yet Ralph knew every detail of that face, that hair, that body – as if he'd known him all his life. But he hadn't. This was a reunion of strangers.

'Give me back my life,' Ralph said. 'And take your own back.'

And his double said hesitantly, 'Er... No, thanks.'

'Well you can't keep mine,' Ralph screamed at him. 'because I'm going to make sure there's only one of us. I'm going to kill you.' And he threw himself onto Ollie and knocked him down onto the pavement. He found his throat and pressed and pressed to throttle him and his double didn't resist. He just lay there.

Ralph sat back astride him. 'What's the matter? Are you dead already?'

'No. No. Not quite yet.'

'Then fight.'

'I want t-to d-d-die.'

With that, all the pleasure of the kill vanished, and Ralph stood up. 'Well, don't expect me to help you on your way.' His double looked up at him beseechingly from the pavement where he was still lying. 'But you offered.'

'That was when I thought you wanted to *skunky* live.'

'*Skunky*,' his double said reflectively. 'It's a right fantastic word.' Ralph sat down next to him. 'It's my own invention.'

'Like a swear word,' Ollie said, 'but not actually a swear word, so they can't have a go at you when you say it. Really clever.'

Ralph said rather formally, 'Feel free to use it.' A thought struck him. 'There's no t's or d's in it either. It's made for you. Why do you want to die?'

Ollie sat up on the kerb next to him and told Ralph about Jess and the oath and the guilt he felt that he'd made Jess die. 'Silver cornered me,' he explained.

'Silver? That's the name of the girl who gave me a gold box of money!'

'Ah!' was all Ollie said. 'So it *was* you.' It was so obvious now. He went on with his confession. 'Silver made me swear.' He looked and felt completely desolate now. 'It was after Thursday night's show.'

'Then you're in the clear, Oll.' Ralph blundered on without thinking. 'Your friend was already gone when you swore your oath.' Ollie was staring at him in such unhappy disbelief that Ralph gave him a friendly nudge. 'Hey! Lighten up, feller.' And he told Ollie how he'd been at the hospital earlier and seen Jess, who'd just died. 'Peacefully,' he lied firmly for his double's sake, trying to forget Jess's open, yearning eyes. 'Jeeze!' he said. 'Don't faint on me. Put your head between your knees.' And Ollie did.

He was dizzy with relief. He wasn't a murderer after all. The guilt had gone. It was as if his double had lifted a big heavy sack of coal off his back. The two boys sat together, as alike as two drops of water, and stayed like that in silence for a while. Then Ollie said, in a muffled voice, that he was feeling better. 'Thanks for telling me that about Jess,' he said with his head still between his knees, 'That was nice of you.'

'Most people think I'm nasty,' Ralph said to the top of Ollie's head. 'French, the girl I've been with, for instance.'

'Giselle you mean? She's not entirely sugar sweet herself, Ralph.' Ollie raised his head. 'I can't help liking her though. Who is she?'

'Search me, Ollie. She told me to jump the train and come after you and before I knew it, she'd tagged along too.'

Ollie nodded thoughtfully. 'So she's been kind of running this whole thing. What's the word I want for her?'

'Manipulative?'

'Maybe – if I knew what it meant.'

'Controlling it.'

'To get the press rights on the story.'

Ralph whistled. 'Pretty smart to make something happen and then earn big bucks out of it.' He sounded quite envious, Ollie noticed. 'Hey, that's why she was smiling like the Cheshire cat, Oll, when your dad collared me. Things were going to her plan.' They both gave a sage shake of their heads in unison, which made them grin – in unison.

'This 'nasty' thing, though,' Ralph persisted. 'I guess I gotta learn to live with it. I just can't keep up being nice the whole time, Oll. Nice comes and goes depending on what's happening to me.' Ralph had never spoken so openly to anyone else. He felt completely relaxed with his look-alike. He thought he could probably say anything to him and it would be okay.

'Everyone's got a nice and a nasty side.'

'Have you really got a nasty side, Oll? French doesn't think so. She goes all dreamy about you. When were you last nasty to someone?'

Ollie thought for a minute. 'Heather. I was right mean to her the other day.'

Ralph was surprised and just a little defensive too. 'Heather's great. What did you do to her?'

'Told her to get lost. I was upset about – something.'

Ralph said ironically, 'Evil! Take a black mark.' It made Ollie smile, which pleased Ralph. His double was so solemn; it was as if he were nursing a sorrow. Ralph didn't like that. It made him angry that something was hurting Ollie, and he wanted to take it away; but all he said was, 'Heather saved me from your dad.'

'And that's another one,' Ollie confessed. 'I bashed my dad on the head with a bottle.' But Ralph said that didn't count as nasty. That was a service to the nation. And Ralph was pleased that Ollie laughed delightedly at that. Then Ollie put the big question.

'Why do we look the same?'

Ralph said his theory was that they were actually the same person. 'Maybe we kind of split in half, by mistake, when we were born. I'm the bad side and you're the good side.' But Ollie said politely it was certainly a theory, but it should stay a theory. 'You're overdoing this nasty thing, Ralph. I think you're nice; and besides, I don't feel split.'

'I kind of do, though.' Ralph looked pensive. 'What I mean is, there was a part of me that knew you existed.'

'Can't say I knew you d-did. You gave me a right shock.'

This reminded Ralph of the sick man outside The Hops who'd been badly shocked to hear that there were two of them. Nonetheless, he'd accepted, without question, that there were. 'We'll never know why, now, or what it was he wanted to tell us. The poor guy died. He was asking about your dad when I first met him.'

Ollie knew at once that Ralph must be talking about Shtum. Another silence fell between them while they remembered the sick acrobat. Ralph was wondering if he should mention the scream of 'Murderer!' All he said eventually was, 'Only person ever called me nice was Shtum. Shtum said you and me were both nice'.

'There you are, then.' Ollie said, as if that drew a line under the debate. 'You're the same as me. Are we the same everything?' They stood up back to back. They were the same height. Ollie was astonished to hear Ralph was only eleven, though. 'You're bleeding big for your age.' But Ralph didn't comment when Ollie said that he was just thirteen. Ollie grinned. 'Go on. You can say it.'

'Say what?'

'Titch.' They both laughed again. Then they sat down again and talked about what it was like to be each other. Ralph assured Ollie that Heather was the best friend he could have, so long as you kept off God. The worst thing about the Pig was that you could never ever please him, no matter how hard you tried, because it suited the Pig not to be pleased; that was how he controlled you. And Ollie was really impressed that Ralph had worked that out, because he never had. 'Right clever,' he commented. Ralph said wryly that French wouldn't agree that there was anything at all about him that was clever.

Ollie thought Hal was difficult to please, too, but not for the same reason as the Pig was. Hal was difficult to please because he was so busy being pleased with himself. But Hal meant well. Definitely. Ralph didn't know that his father had once had a knife act, nor the story about Hal running away with a girl who jilted him. Ollie was tactful and said it was probably just gossip.

But then Ollie remembered why all this was happening and told Ralph that Hal was here, looking for him, and to go and find his dad. 'He's probably back-stage by now, shredding up mine.'

'Aren't you coming?'

'Think about it,' Ollie said. 'Would you, if you were me? And you have been me. Would you go back to my father?'

'Not if I was paid all the dollars in the world.' And Ralph really meant it. Even so, Ralph was taken completely off-guard when Ollie shook his hand and limped away into the fog. 'I'll find somewhere where I fit.'

Ralph wanted to shout: You fit here. Don't leave. We are us. What about me? This is the first time in my life I haven't felt lonely. Instead, he called into the fog after him, 'Imagine what your dad thought of me with my three left feet! At least he thinks you're the best dancer in his troupe.'

Ollie's figure came back into smudgy view. 'He said that?' He clearly didn't believe Ralph.

'Said you took after your mother.'

And Ollie yelled at him. 'My what?'

Ralph realised he'd overstepped some sort of mark. He backed off and said awkwardly, 'You know? Like, your mom, Marina?' But Ollie shook his head. He didn't know. He'd always wanted to know.

'What did he mean?'

'I don't know, Oll. Shtum talked about your mom, too. He was trying to tell me something, I guess. All he said was, your mother, Marina and the Wheel of Death...'

Ollie knew enough about Variety to know the Wheel of Death was part of a knife-throwing act. He didn't say so, though, nor anything more about

Hal's knife act. But Ralph looked at him curiously. 'What? What is it you know? You're holding out on me.'

'Like you did on me when we were talking about Shtum dying. You decided not to tell me something.'

'Jeeze! Can we read each other's minds?' He stopped there, because Ollie was sitting on the kerb again, holding his head in his hands and rocking back and forth.

'I sort of remember now. I was really little. I remember a Wheel of Death. A girl was spinning round on it. Ralph, do you think it was her? How could it have been if she was a dancer?'

'Maybe we should go ask your dad.'

CHAPTER TWENTY-SIX

SHOWDOWN

They heard the Pig before they tracked him down in the girls' dressing room. He was ranting at Heather, who was sitting hunched over her dressing table and crying. The new girl was doing her best to get out of the room before she got pulled into the row. Miss Bellamy was not daring to look up from the button she was sewing onto a costume.

No one saw the two boys come in. The Pig was still covered in Fuller's Earth and dried shaving soap. Ollie wasn't prepared for that. His dad looked like a gruesome carnival figure, with his ashy clothes and face and his painted red mouth that opened and shut – spouting insults.

'You gawk,' he screamed. Heather cringed inside her green kimono. 'You broom handle. Turn your songs into a freak show, would you?' And Heather sobbed that the audience had laughed at her, so she'd decided to make it funnier.

'I'll show you funnier, my lady,' the Pig bawled. 'You're sacked. How's that for funnier?' And Heather pleaded, 'I've got nowhere to go to, Mr Pigott.'

'You should have thought of that before.' As he said it, the Pig swung round and saw Ollie and Ralph standing side-by-side in the doorway. He jumped so violently that he cannoned into the dressing table, clutching his heart and scattering sticks of make-up over the floor. 'Streuth! It's true,' he said. Ollie saw his round, soap-caked eyes making fast calculations. He was wriggling out of trouble. 'Whichever one of you is the Havern kid,' he said, 'get out of here before I kill you for ruining my show. Get out now.'

'Not before you tell us about Ollie's mom, Marina.' Ollie didn't have time to blink before the Pig came at them and grabbed Ralph by the scruff of his neck. He lifted him off the floor so fast that Ralph's body swung into Ollie and knocked him down. The Pig headed for the door with Ralph, but Ollie hung on to his dad's foot and pulled with all his might, and the Pig crashed over. By now, the Pig looked as if he was trying to break Ralph's neck. All three of them were rolling on the floor while Ollie ripped and clawed at the Pig's fingers to rescue his double. Everyone was screaming with fear. The new girl ran for it, shouting for the police. Heather leapt to the open door. 'Murder, murder!' she yelled at the top of her voice. 'One of them is going die.'

John and Grinling hurried into the room, their faces glistening with make-up remover, their costumes half on and off. They pitched into the tangle of shouting, fighting bodies, while Miss Bellamy and Heather circled the pile, hitting whichever bit of the Pig they could see. At last, Mr Pigott lay, with Ralph and Ollie on either leg, and John and Grinling on each arm, subdued by his own troupe.

The expressions of amazement on Grinling and John's faces when they clocked there were two Ollies sitting on the Pig's legs was what Ollie described as 'worth a photo'.

'Now, where's Ollie's mom?' Ralph panted, but the Pig just glared out of his white face as if he wished him every evil in the world. Ollie thought they might all have to go on sitting on the Pig forever. At that point, a breathless Hal and Shoes appeared in the doorway with the theatre manager in tow, who was all of a jitter because he'd got a Hollywood star in his theatre – a star in a rage, moreover. When Grinling and John saw Hal Havern, Ollie reckoned they were worth another photo.

The men dragged the Pig up and sat him squarely in a chair. The Pig was blustering now about how the kid had wrecked his show. 'Thought he was my lad. That's why I was whacking him.' As usual, his father was on the dodge from trouble. But then Ollie noticed Ralph eying Shoes nervously and whispered to him that, unbelievable though it was, Shoes was

344

on their side.

Hal was terribly angry. Ollie was half expecting him to take a swing at the Pig like he did with the villains in his pictures. But then a complete stranger walked in. He looked like a bookie who'd come hot off a racecourse, with his cavalry twill cap and his camel hair coat, but he announced himself as Sidney Barnes, theatrical agent.

They all stared at him like roughly-awakened sleepwalkers. He treated them to a breezy smile, and then singled out Heather and handed her his card.

'Yours is the funniest act I've seen for years, Miss,' he said. 'Beats me why your name is not on the programme. Laugh! I nearly bust. You and I could do business. Give us a call if ever you feel like it.' And with a deferential touch of his cap to Hal Havern, he sauntered out again.

They all watched as, without a word, Heather collected up her day clothes. Ollie knew something was coming when she swished over to his father in her green kimono. But in his wildest dreams, Ollie would never have believed that Heather would blow a raspberry at the Pig and say, 'Up yours!' But she did.

Then she swished over to the door, where she paused and asked the two boys, 'Ollie?' Ollie half put up his hand. Heather pecked a surprising kiss on his cheek. 'Good luck, our Ollie, you'll need it.' She gave Ralph a peck on the cheek too. 'And you. God bless.' Then she left, for good.

Ralph shook himself, trying to get back on track,

and said again, 'So, Ollie's Mom, Marina?'

And Hal shouted, 'Marina! Marina was my girl!'

'The one that ran out on you? And you sailed away alone?' Ollie wanted to hear about Marina so badly that he blurted the question out. Hal looked hurt.

'She did no such thing.' Hal nodded at Shoes, who silently ushered the theatre manager out of the dressing room. This was not for his ears. The manager cast a frustrated look back as Shoes closed the door on him and leant against it. No one was going to come in and, by the look of it, Shoes was expecting someone to try and leave in a hurry too.

Hal said, 'Listen you two guys, I think you are twins. I think you are the twin babies Marina and I were on our way to Hollywood with.'

'How can we be?' Ollie wanted it to be true, but he knew it couldn't be. 'We're d-d-d...'

'Different ages and different nationalities,' Ralph cut in obligingly. And John said, 'Twins or doubles, I'm very sorry for not believing you.' Grinling nodded, 'Never sorrier. But pray Mr Havern is right, lads. For if you're doubles, the saints preserve us, they say that once you've met, one of you must pass away.'

Ralph and Ollie exchanged frightened looks. Ralph had tried to kill Ollie, and the Pig had tried to kill Ralph. Who would have a go at them next?

'Steady on,' Hal said to Grinling. He smiled at the two boys. 'I think you're twins. I can't prove it, but I think your mother is Marina Lepman.

She's a dancer and singer. She was from Ljubljana originally.' Hal took a photograph out of his wallet and the two boys pored over it. Everyone else in the room craned politely to see it. The old brown photo was criss-crossed with white creases, but Ollie could still make out the picture of the young, smiling woman. She was a bit like Ralph, which meant she must be a bit like him too. Surely she was their mother. Tears pricked Ollie's eyelids. One thing was certain: it was her, it was definitely her. It was the girl who had been tied to the Wheel of Death.

Hal asked gently, 'Recognise her?' Ollie didn't answer. There was a weird gap in his mind that wouldn't fill up with memory or information. He could remember bits of that horrible scene now, but not the face of the knife thrower. It was a man. But who was he?

'Marina and I were in love and poor as church mice,' Hal went on. 'We needed work, so we blew the last of our savings on tickets for the US. We were late boarding and Marina went straight up to see the ship's doctor with baby Adolphus. She was real worried about him – thought he was sick. I settled us in and fell asleep on the bunk. Ralph woke me, crying. By then, we were under way and well out to sea. Not a sign of Marina. The ship's doctors said she hadn't been near them. She'd jumped ship with Adolphus, back in port, and left me with the other baby.' Hal rumpled Ralph's hair. Ollie saw that it surprised Ralph; he obviously wasn't used to it.

Hal made a swift check on the multitude of his own perfect image in the dressing room mirrors before he went on. 'That was the day my heart broke.' There was a sympathetic rustle from the rest of the room. 'I was ready to kill myself over that girl.'

'But you went to Hollywood instead.' Ollie coaxed the story on. He was longing to hear about Marina, yet at the same time, he was dreading it.

Hal nodded. 'And three years later I got my big break in a Cecil B DeMille movie. That's when Marina wrote to me.' Ollie's stomach lurched as Marina came back into the story. 'Of course, she was desperate to know if her other little boy was okay.' He rumpled Ralph's hair again. Ralph shook him away.

'What is all this, Dad?' There was a nasty glint in his eye, now. 'You said my mom died when I was born.' Ollie thought that Hal looked 'right shifty' then, which was peculiar. Hal hurried on, ignoring his son.

'That was the first time Marina knew where to contact me. It turns out the ship's doctors lied to me. She did take the baby to them. They diagnosed scarlet fever, but they didn't tell Marina. They tricked her back on shore with some phoney story and set sail real fast.'

'Is this true, Dad? Why would they do that?'

'Money, Ralph. Scarlet fever is very contagious and dangerous. The whole shipload of passengers and crew should have been quarantined – hundreds of people. The shipping company stood to lose a mass of dollars, so they got rid of Marina. Told me she'd walked out on me to stop me making enquiries. In reality, they'd dumped her, penniless, on the quayside with a sick baby.'

'What d-did she d-do?'

'I don't know?' Hal spoke to the whole room. 'Anyone here who does?' No one answered. 'Let's see if we can prod someone's memory then. I replied to her letter at once. Sent tickets for her to sail to the States. Ralph and I went down to the docks to meet them. You'd be three then, Ralph. Like a fool, I'd told you they were coming. You were inconsolable when Marina did it again. She didn't show.'

Ralph said in a shaky voice, 'I remember now. I thought you'd lied about them coming.' Ollie felt sorry for him. Ralph wasn't all Mr Tough Guy. You could tell he missed their mother just as much as he did.

Hal said, 'I lied to you later, Ralph, to protect you. Better you thought her dead than that she'd forsaken you.'

'But why didn't she show?'

'I guess what really happened was your mom stuck with her husband.' Hal looked extremely uncomfortable. He nodded in the Pig's direction and added quickly, 'Your *real* dad.'

'You're not my dad?' Ralph sounded so bereft that everyone stirred in their places helplessly, not knowing how to comfort him. Ollie gripped the back of a chair and stared unhappily at the intricate lines of the wood in the seat. He'd believed for a few wonderful minutes that Hal might be his real father. But he wasn't. The disappointment was unbearable.

Parents had been whirling about as if they were being shaken into different patterns in a kaleidoscope. But now, here he was again, stuck with the terrible Pigott. The Pig was Marina's husband. Ralph and he were the Pig's sons. No one would have the right to take them away from their real father or to rescue them.

Ralph had gone white as cotton wool at the idea. Poor Ralph was in for a far worse time than he was. At least he was used to his dad.

Ralph asked miserably, 'But where is our mom then. Why did she forsake us?'

'She didn't,' Ollie said. 'She was dead.'

Suddenly, the knife thrower in his memory turned round and looked at him. And Ollie recognised him. 'Dad killed her,' he said.

'You diabolical little liar!' The Pig sprang up from his chair. Shoes and Hal just got to him before he reached Ollie. They held him back, but he went on raging at Ollie. 'You've always been a liar, you butter-wouldn't-melt-in-your-mouth bloody little liar.' Ollie could feel the Pig's spit hitting his face. He knew for sure that the Pig would kill him as soon as they were alone.

Hal said, 'It's a serious accusation, kid.' He clearly didn't believe him. 'You certain of what you're saying?'

'Course he's not.' The Pig had calmed down. 'The

boy's a stammering, nervous wreck. Half daft. I do my best by him. He's a born liar. He's lying now.'

'No, he's not.' Everyone looked at Miss Bellamy in amazement. 'I was there,' she said.

'You're not going to believe this old snail are you?' the Pig appealed to them all. But people were looking very uncertain. It was two against one, now, and so the Pig spoke up. Ollie could see he didn't want to, but he needed to get in his version ahead of Miss Bellamy's to wriggle out of trouble.

'All right,' he said. 'Marina and I were an act. It wasn't her kind of work, but times were hard. Marina wasn't easy; only happy when she was talking to the damn kid. Ruddy little millstone!' There was a murmur of disapproval in the room for what he'd said about his son. The Pig groped behind him for a chair and sat down heavily, staring at his fists clenched on his broad, floury knees. Everyone waited, but the Pig just sat there. Grinling prompted him softly, 'Boss?'

The Pig said at last, 'You see, I loved her. I loved her, but her heart was somewhere else.' He peered through crumbles of shaving soap at Hal's handsome profile, and Ollie guessed what the Pig was suffering. Pablo's letter to Jess had made him feel the same way.

The Pig swallowed hard, as if he were swallowing down his own jealousy, and went on. 'We were playing a German circuit. Clubs mostly. I had a knife act.'

'Oh Jeeze,' Ralph whispered and put his arm

351

round Ollie's shoulders.

'One night, the company came in to do the show and there was a letter from the States for her. It had been following us all over. It caught up with us there in Frankfurt. After she read it, she was transformed. She was always lovely, but that night she was like the blinking fairy queen. She said, "You must find yourself a new girl, I'm leaving". She was radiant. She said, "Tomorrow, me and my little Adolphus are sailing to the States to join the man I love". And then we went up on stage.

'It was a small club we were playing. An easy range. I couldn't possibly make a mistake. The last knife I threw, she moved. The silly cow moved. I swear she moved. It wasn't my fault. I loved her.' And the Pig began to weep.

'You killed her! With a knife?' Ralph could hardly form the question. Ollie sat down and cradled his head in his arms on the dressing table. He screwed up his eyes to stop the tears coming out. The Pig had taken his mother away from him, just as the Pig took everything away from him. She was as far from him as Jess.

Miss Bellamy said, 'Mademoiselle?'

Ollie had not noticed Giselle was there. She was sitting quietly, partially hidden by the costumes hanging on the rail. But now she rose and stood next to Miss Bellamy, who started talking French, very fast. Giselle translated for her, as rapidly as she could, and the rest of story came out in a jumble of their overlapping voices.

'The knife didn't kill her straight away. It was horrific. There was chaos on stage. I was there. I was the dresser for the artists. She knew it was the end. She was trying to speak – names I'd never heard 'til today – and then she made a big effort and said, 'Adolphus' and put my hand on her child, to give him to me. The little boy was clinging to his mother's body. Her costume was red with her blood. He was screaming and screaming for her to stay with him. I had to lift him off her.'

And Ollie knew, at last, where the red carpet dream came from. The dream was his three-year-old's memory of his mother's death. The red carpet wasn't a carpet – it was his mother's blood. But now he knew something very important, too: his mother had tried to look after him, even while she was dying. She'd loved him.

There was no stopping Miss Bellamy now. The story flowed out as if a dam had burst, and Giselle struggled to keep up with her.

'The Frankfurt police were asking questions. A lot of questions. This is the first I've heard of Monsieur Havern's letter. If I'd known about it, things would have turned out differently. As it was, Mr Pigott panicked. Thought he was going to be done for attempted murder. A lot of the company wanted him done. Done for murder. Oh yes. Said he'd meant to kill her. They wanted the guillotine for him. 'The knife for a knife', they said. The police ordered him to stay in Frankfurt while they made their enquiries. He was ready to run. I said,

'The least you can do for her is take her child'. He said, 'You take her child'. I said, 'On my wages? He'll starve'.'

Ollie interrupted. 'Her child? Just hers, Miss Bellamy? D-do you mean my d-dad, Mr Pigott, isn't our father?'

The Pig said violently through his tears: 'Of course I'm not your frigging dad.' And Ralph and Ollie hugged each other with relief.

Miss Bellamy hardly seemed to notice the interruption. '"Take us both", I said. And he said, "So long as you keep your mouth shut". And I always have, until now.' Giselle snatched a breath and hurried on after her.

'I've tried to see Ollie right. He'd been such a cheerful little boy, but after his mother, the change in him was total: he never smiled, the stammer came, he couldn't even say his own name he stammered so. "Ad-d-d-d," he'd say. So he cut off the beginning and the end and called himself 'Ollie'. Gradually we all did.

'I tried to see him fed. When things got very bad between him and Mr Pigott, I covered up for him when I could. I made arrangements too – privately – for him to get extra, you know, in the lodging houses.' Ollie thought gratefully how that explained the perks he got that John groused about. And Ralph guessed it was Miss Bellamy who had smuggled him that slice of bread on a plate.

Miss Bellamy went on, with Giselle a few words behind her. 'We moved all over Europe, always

354

running away. At last we came to England. Mr Pigott never threw another knife.' He may not have, Ollie thought, but it explained why the Pig could hit a dartboard wherever he wanted and set a bar-room in an uproar.

'He started his juvenile troupe,' Giselle translated. 'As soon as Ollie showed talent, the child was put to work to earn his keep. He upped Ollie's age by two years to get him a licence early. Ollie's eleven, really. And he kept him off the photos of the Youngstars – in case. He was frightened Ollie was too like his mother. Hated looking at him. Said it was like looking at a ghost. And in our business, too, someone always knows someone. He didn't want anyone jumping to the right conclusion.'

Although he'd never been so sad in his life, Ollie still felt a lift in his spirits to learn the real reason he was banned from the photos.

Giselle hurried on after Miss Bellamy. 'He changed his name to Pigott, changed the boy's too, but he was always scared. Always short of money.'

The Pig broke in with, 'Because somebody was onto me. Some devil has been after me for money. If I didn't pay, they said, they'd turn me over to the Frankfurt police. I tried stopping the payments but I always had another illiterate letter. The last one threatened to beat up my troupe to show me he meant business. When he didn't...'

But Ollie said, 'We were beaten up; by other kids.'

John butted in. He said that the Pig didn't hear
355

about the attacks because kids don't tell adults everything. And then John went very grown-up and said, 'Like some adults don't tell poor Ollie and Ralph who their real parents are. They pretend that they are their father just because it's convenient.' A mutter of agreement went round the room.

But Ollie wasn't interested in blame. He was wondering about the future. In the course of a few minutes, he and Ralph had lost their mother, and their so-called fathers. Who was going to look out for them now? The world didn't allow kids to walk around fending for themselves. He took a big breath and dared to ask for them both, 'Anyone know who our real d-dad is then? Where we find him?' But no one answered.

Then Miss Bellamy said slowly in English, 'Marina told me his name once. Raphael, I think she said it was.' Hal took his hands away from his face. He'd been crying.

'Raphael was your name too, Ralph. I shortened it down.'

'Shtum was a Raphael.' Ollie said.

Grinling slapped the dressing table top and exclaimed, 'Raphael Lepman! Lepman – that was his surname! Wasn't that Marina's surname? Shtum's your dad, surely?'

'We'll never know. He's dead too.' Ralph tried to give Ollie a smile but it was a very upset one. 'But when I told him I was one of two identical boys, Ollie, he nearly fainted; that must have been when he realised we were his long-lost twin sons. So he kind of cared about us, Oll. Fainting's a big deal.'

Ollie agreed. He was glad to know about this side of Shtum, because it was obviously Shtum who was the blackmailer. Why else did Shtum know that other kids were beating up the troupe? He was blackmailing the Pig for killing his wife, Marina.

Later, Ralph remembered how Shtum had said, "Tell Dad, Shtum says forget the letters". Shtum was referring to the letters that he'd been sending the Pig, threatening to expose him. Ralph said that Ollie took after the good half of their dad with his acrobatics, and that Ralph had got landed with the rotten half: the blackmailer. Ollie had given him a cheerful push in the chest and said Ralph was no blackmailer; and he'd given him another push and told him to 'stop his nonsense' when Ralph said regretfully, that no, he wouldn't use blackmail, but it sure was a money spinner.

But now Giselle flashed a charming smile at Hal across the dressing room. 'Monsieur Havern,' she said. 'This is a tasteless story, a scandal, and it will sell like hot buns. It will also ruin your career.' She produced a hand-written sheet of paper. 'Here is the agreement I have drawn up, in which you give me exclusive press rights on this story.'

It came like an electric shock; it was so cold-hearted. Shoes spluttered with outrage and Giselle treated him to one of her sighs. 'Be grateful,' she said. 'Without me, none of this would have happened.'

And that's when Ollie felt sure that he and Ralph had guessed right. Ever since she'd seen them in the two trains, Giselle had been pushing this story into being for her blasted press rights. And he was glad she had. It might have made him an orphan, but it had gained him a twin – a right tough one, too.

Giselle put away her piece of paper and went on briskly, 'But I do not intend to publish this story.' She stopped Hal trying to thank her with an imperious gesture. 'Not yet. Because it will hurt my friend Ollie too much.' It surprised Ollie to be promoted to Giselle's friend – he'd thought he was her stooge. So what was her game now? He soon found out.

Giselle went on. 'And now the fog is lifting. There is no more to be said. Ollie and I will leave immediately to catch the boat train to Paris, where he will study the great art of mime.' And then she extended a gracious invitation to Miss Bellamy to go too, to look after Ollie, and Miss Bellamy cried with joy.

Giselle's announcement nearly knocked him out. She'd outlined her plan for his future over their lunch at the Savoy, but he'd never credited her with being serious. He'd treated it as a tantalising but impossible dream. Crikey Moses! He hadn't been so far wrong when he'd called her the penny angel – she was certainly working a few miracles for him. He began to plan: he'd have to get down to learning the old '*parlez-vous*' right quick if he was to work in Paris.

And then came another massive surprise – the Misery was gone, the Misery that had dogged his every day. It had shrivelled up and left, without him noticing. He felt as light as if he'd taken off a pair of cement boots. Light as a puff of smoke. Was he his real self at last? He pictured the new Ollie – the mime artist – performing on stage without a thought for his stammer. And despite everything, he smiled. It was Ollie's version of total happiness.

Then Ralph said, 'No, I'm not losing Ollie a second time, not after all I've been through to find him.' He had that dangerous look to him again, as if he'd either cry or smash someone in the face. Ollie said quickly, 'Can't go without my twin.' Ralph grinned, but Giselle didn't.

'Hey, French?' Ralph appealed to her. You're my friend.' But Giselle's face was steely.

'Please, Giselle,' Ollie said. And it worked. Later he discovered why; unlike Ralph, he'd mastered saying her name properly.

Giselle put her arm round Ralph's neck. 'D'accord. And you will go to school in Paris, Ralph, and make many more friends, n'est-ce pas?'

'Yes,' Ralph said. 'Er...Wee.' And Giselle laughed, which pleased Ralph more than he thought possible.

Hal Havern brought them all down to earth. He asked what the hell the pair of them supposed they were going to live on in Paris. Ollie knew it was a good question.

'But Monsieur Havern,' Giselle replied sweetly, 'since you are so concerned, naturally you will fund the orphan twins yourself, and Madame Bellamy too, of course.' Then, with a look that was heavy with meaning, she finished, 'That way we keep our story hushed up and in the family, don't we?' Hal groaned and said that he wished Giselle was his agent, she was that good at getting deals out of people. 'I'll fund them on one condition,' he said.

'Name it, Monsieur.'

'That Ollie and Ralph come visit me in the US once a year, and I visit them in Paris – oh, I don't know – heaps!' Ralph smiled from ear to ear. 'Will you, Dad? That's a great idea.' And Hal beamed back at him until Giselle said, lightly, 'Is that all your condition is, Monsieur Havern? I thought you would out-smart me, and make your condition the return of our agreement.' She waved her piece of paper at him coquettishly. Hal looked so dumbfounded at the lost opportunity that everyone burst out laughing.

Then Grinling slid down from his chair and said he was on his way too. 'I've a wife to keep now, Boss,' he told the Pig. 'That's not a possibility on your wages.' He struck a quaint little pose. 'I'm a boss now. Me and the new missus, we've formed our own company. 'Tinymites'. That's us.' Everyone laughed again and congratulated him.

Then John said he was off as well. 'I've landed a dancing job in a Liverpool panto,' he explained. He gave both twins a farewell bear-hug because, as he said, he couldn't tell which one of them was his best mate Ollie, and anyway, what the hell!

At that moment, an immaculately elegant couple in evening dress rushed into the room. Giselle cried, 'Maman, Papa. So the hotel manager gave you my message. I've missed you both so, so, so very much.

Were you worried to distraction about me?' She had tears in her eyes. Genuine ones? Ollie couldn't tell. Her parents obviously couldn't either. All they could do was to look overjoyed that they'd found her.

'See. I am safe and sound,' she said, dragging Ollie and Ralph to face the couple. 'These are my little friends who have looked after me so tenderly while I was lost. They will be staying with us in the guest suite, at home, in Paris, for a while 'til they find their toes.'

'Feet, chérie,' her father corrected her helplessly. And her mother murmured 'Enchantée,' to the twins, just as helplessly. 'You are very welcome.'

There were goodbyes and more hugs until Giselle said '*Allons-y!* That is your first French lesson, boys. It means, 'Let's go'.' And everyone streamed out of the dressing room, talking and laughing and promising to keep in touch.

But Ollie lingered in front of the Pig, sitting as still as a rock in his chair, like a plaster statue with tear runnels in its cheeks.

'Mr Pigott, I know a bit what it feels like to have d-done what you d-did to my mother with that knife. I'm sorry. Thank you for taking me in when I was a little lad, when you d-didn't have to.' He offered the Pig his hand. 'Cheerio, then.'

For a long time, it seemed as if the Pig wasn't going to move, but, at last, he fumbled the watch that he'd taken from Ralph out of his pocket and gave it to Ollie. 'From your mum and dad.'

Then he shook Ollie's hand gently. 'Good luck,

Ollie. You've a great future ahead of you.'

THE END.

FIN.

Madame Giselle Lepman (newspaper proprietor).
Paris. France. 2010

Glossary

acre - About half a hectare.

biz - Short for 'business', which are actions or routines that are usually comic.

blackout - All the stage lights cut out together, leaving total darkness.

bobbies - Slang for policemen

brawn - A jellied meat loaf.

busking - Performing in the street for money.

call - Short for the 'curtain call' at the end of a show when the stage curtain rose and fell for the artists to line up and bow to the applauding audience. It can also mean a simple bow to mark the end of an Act without bringing in the curtain or the Tabs, as it is usually called.

call-boy - His job was to go to each dressing room and tell the artist how much time there was before curtain up. He started at 'the half,' (35 minutes before the show began) and finished with 'Overture and Beginners,' which called the artists who began the show down onto the stage. During the show, he would warn individual artists that they should go to the stage for their next entrance or for their act. Nowadays, the show is relayed on a sound system to the dressing rooms and the artists are called over the Tannoy. The 'half an hour please, ladies and gentlemen', the 'quarter', the 'five' and 'beginners' are still called by the stage management over the sound system.

Cecil B DeMille (1881-1959) - Famous film producer and director of Hollywood spectaculars such as The Ten Commandments.

Croydon - London's airport at the time.

cue sheets - Pages printed with the dialogue for a particular role with the 'cues', which are the previous speaker's last words inserted before each speech so that the artist knows when to come in with their part. Consequently, none of the players have any idea what the script is about until all the dialogue is fitted together.

damper - An adjustable part of a fire grate that controls the amount of air or draught admitted to the fire. The fire burns more strongly as the intake of air is increased.

divided skirt - Very long, slightly flared shorts.

dock - The scene dock. A large area where the scenery was often built and painted. It was usually situated behind the stage and had floor-to-ceiling 'dock doors' that opened onto the street so that scenery and large items could be delivered from vans, carts or lorries.

Dr Greasepaint - The adrenalin needed to do a show will often cure a sick artist temporarily while they perform – hence Dr Greasepaint. Nowadays referred to as Dr Theatre because artists no longer use greasepaint.

dunghill - A heap of horse/cattle/sheep/pig excrement or dung which was rotted down and used as manure or fertiliser.

farthing - A small copper-coloured coin worth a quarter of an old, pre-decimalised penny.

five feet - Approximately 1.5 metres.

fleapit - Slang for a local cinema

flicks - Slang for a cinema.

Fred Astaire (1899-1987) - An American film star. He was particularly famous for his brilliant dancing, as well as for his singing and acting.

gaff - A busker's performing place in the street. In this case, Oxo's pitch.

gags - Jokes.

greasepaint - Make-up that was made especially for use on stage. Stage lighting was not as strong as it is now. In order that artists' faces showed clearly, the make up was much heavier and brighter than street make-up, which was worn very sparingly in those days. Each greasepaint colour had a different number (though some had names such as carmine) and was sold in sticks wrapped in gold foil like fat, soft, greasy crayons. The most commonly used was made by a German firm – Leichner.

green-room - A room backstage where artists can sit comfortably (with luck) or meet up or wait for their entrance on stage and where, sometimes, they could make tea. Nowadays there's usually a microwave and fridge too.

guinea - A guinea was worth one pound and one shilling(21/-) of pre-decimalised money or £1.5p, though in 1936 it would purchase much more than the same amount today.

Guy Fawkes night - Now called Bonfire Night and still celebrated on November 5th. Children used to make a dummy figure of Guy Fawkes, who took part in a plot to blow up the king and the House of Lords during the opening of Parliament in 1605. Kids would prop up their guy effigy on the pavement, or wheel it around in an old pram or cart, and ask passers-by for 'a penny for the old Guy'. Eventually, the guy was burnt on a bonfire. There was guy rivalry: the better made your guy, the more money you were likely to collect to spend on fireworks. In 1936 children were allowed to buy and let off fireworks themselves.

halfpenny - A copper-coloured coin that was worth half an old, pre-decimalised penny.

Holborn Empire - A large London theatre destroyed by bombs during WWII.

Hopalong Cassidy - Cowboy hero of a popular series of American films. Cassidy was wounded in the leg and had a limp, which earned him his nickname: Hopalong.

Ink Spots - A celebrated all-male quartet of black singers.

laughs - The laughter responses from the audience.

legit - Short for 'legitimate theatre' to distinguish it from variety. Broadly, it means the presentation of plays by actresses and actors, rather than a variety act.

lines - The speeches or words that an artist has to say during their performance.

Lindy Hop - A dance that came into being in the 1920s and 30s in New York. It was not at all dignified. A version of it is still danced today. It was loosely based on the Charleston and was named after Charles Lindbergh's celebrated flight in a monoplane – the first solo, non-stop Atlantic crossing.

Liverpool Cathedral - Designed by the great architect, Sir Edward Landseer Lutyens, this Roman Catholic cathedral was never completed. After the interruption of World War Two, the cost of the project had soared and it was thought too expensive to proceed. Some say that it would have been the eighth wonder of the world. A large, scale model of it has recently been found and restored.

Marlene Dietrich (1901-1992) - A German actress and singer. A great beauty who began her career in German cinema and later moved to Hollywood where she became a famous star.

Nova Pilbeam (b1919) - A British child star of stage and screen. She began her notable career in 1934 at the age of fourteen. Her role as Lady Jane Grey in Tudor Rose (1936) would have particularly irritated Silver.

Olympics - The 1936 Olympics were held in Berlin, the capital of Germany.

pearly gates - The entrance to heaven.

photo call - Artists, wearing full costume and make-up, are photographed, in action, on stage. This is done either by the local press for use in the newspaper reviews or by freelance photographers for general publicity and for the display of pictures outside the theatre.

plimsolls - Old-fashioned trainers.

poker - A short, thin iron bar with an ornamental handle. It was used to poke the burning coals in the open fire grate and to clear the ash to make the fire burn better.

Popeye - An American sailor comic strip and cartoon character who can instantly amplify his strength by eating spinach. He still appears in comic strip form today.

pratfall - A comic trip over one's own feet, followed by a fall.

pro - Short for 'professional'.

props - Short for 'properties' i.e. any object, other than furniture, that is used on stage in the act.

record - 'Stammering like a stuck record' (see Chapter Fifteen). A gramophone record was an early version of a CD. It was a shiny black disc, about the size of a dinner plate, and was usually made of shellac. It had closely packed grooves cut into it. There was a small hole in the centre. A spindle in the middle of the gramophone's turntable fitted through the hole to keep the record in position while playing. A needle, or 'stylus', on the end of an arm was placed on the spinning record in order to play it. Sometimes the needle became stuck in a groove, which caused the music to repeat itself over and over.

skip - A large wickerwork trunk lined with canvas to keep out the dirt.

Rockefeller - John D Rockefeller Sr (1839-1937) an American multi-millionaire who was reputed to be the richest man in history. He was the founder of the Standard Oil Company.

slag heaps - Slag is a by-product or waste matter produced by the coal mining industry.

spats - A stiff fabric cover, shaped like a boot without a sole. It covered the top of the foot and shoe and extended up over the ankle. It was fastened by a row of buttons down the outside of the foot and ankle. An unseen strap under the sole of the foot helped hold the spats in place.

Speke Airport - Now Liverpool John Lennon Airport.

spend a penny - It cost one penny to use a ladies' public loo. 'To spend a penny' became a euphemism for, or a covered-up way of talking about, urinating.

starch - As used in laundries, starch was a white powder, usually derived from wheat. The powder was dissolved in hot water. Items like tablecloths and napkins and garments such as aprons, petticoats and collars were put through the starch which, when dry, stiffened the fabric. In 1936 men's shirt collars were usually detached from the shirt. They were very stiff and put on above the neck opening, then fastened with a collar stud so there was never a gap of neck showing between the two. Collars were washed and starched separately.

ten feet - Approximately 3 metres. 'Feet' (or a 'foot') were an old measurement of length, height, width or distance.

The Great War (1914-18) - Subsequently known as World War One.

the green - Slang for the stage.

the iron - A fire curtain (originally made of iron) that prevents any fire that may break out backstage from reaching the auditorium and any of the theatre's public areas.

threepenny bit - A small, gold coloured, twelve-sided coin with a value of three old, pre-decimalised pennies. Often pronounced thruppeny bit.

thirty feet - Just over 9 metres. Feet were an old measurement of length. 1 foot = 30.48 centimetres. 3 feet made one 'yard'.

third house - The third and final performance of the evening.

twelve times table - Pupils learned the tables by heart, from the two times table up to the twelve times table, because there weren't any calculators in school. The electronic calculator had yet to be invented. The class would chant in unison, 'once twelve is twelve, two twelves are twenty-four, three twelves are thirty-six...' and so on, all the way up to 'twelve twelves are one-hundred-and-forty-four.' Most kids agreed that the trickiest one to learn was the nine times table.

two inches - 5 centimetres – roughly.

Wet Nelly - A slice of bread, but sometimes a slice of cake or pastry that was soaked in syrup.

wings - The sides of the stage that the audience can't see into.

Woolworth's - A big chain of stores originally termed 'a penny and sixpence store'. It sold low priced small items from jewellery and spectacles to hardware.

yard - An old measurement of length or distance. Just under a metre.

Acknowledgements

My thanks to the actors Gabrielle Hamilton and Walter Sparrow for sharing their early memories with me of life in a juvenile troupe. Also to Tulah Tuke for the loan of memorabilia, and for her recollections of her work in variety theatre. Thanks too to Miriam Moran of Britannia Hotels at the Adelphi Hotel and to the Merseyside Maritime Museum for their help.

Grateful acknowledgement of J. Woods book, *Growing Up: One Scouser's Social History*, published by Palatine Books 2004.

Ursula Jones was born on the road to Wales.
She trained at RADA and works as an actress.
She has written TV scripts and plays for children,
and her picture books have won the gold Smartie
Award and the inaugural Roald Dahl Funny Prize.
She lives in London and on the edge of a forest.

Other books by Ursula Jones:

Dear Clare My Ex Best Friend

Kidnappers (Graffix)

The Witch's Children
The Witch's Children And The Queen
The Witch's Children Go To School
The Princess Who Had No Kingdom